INTO THAT FIRE

# INTO THAT

# FIRE

## MJ Cates

RANDOM HOUSE CANADA

PUBLISHED BY RANDOM HOUSE CANADA

Copyright © 2019 M. J. Cates

www.penguinrandomhouse.ca

Random House Canada and colophon are registered trademarks.

Library and Archives Canada Cataloguing in Publication

Cates, M. J., author
Into that fire / M.J. Cates.

Issued in print and electronic formats.
ISBN 978-0-7352-7376-4
eBook ISBN 978-0-7352-7374-0

I. Title.

PS8605.A87855I58 2019          C813'.6          C2018-902719-3
C2018-902720-7

Book design by Terri Nimmo

Cover image: © Kymberlie Dozois Photography / Getty Images

Printed and bound in Canada

2  4  6  8  9  7  5  3  1

Penguin
Random House
RANDOM HOUSE CANADA

*Light blue paper and retire to a safe distance.*

TRADITIONAL WARNING ON EXPLOSIVES

# 1

Does something always have to die in order for something else to be born? To Imogen, the idea seemed melodramatic. She considered herself a practical girl—woman—not the bluestocking, not the suffragette, not the pamphleteer her fellow medical students made her out to be. She just wanted to do some good, be some use in the world, and didn't see this ambition as unsuitable. Yet she knew that others—her father, Quentin—found it unusual because their reactions made it plain.

The church clock bonged the quarter hour. Only fifteen minutes before she was due to meet Quentin on the front steps of Rush College. She had been listening to the clock for hours, her German text open on the desk before her. She hadn't learned a single verb all morning. Consciousness of having soon to commit an unkindness had rendered her skull impenetrable.

She got up and checked herself in the mirror and started to fuss with her hair, then stopped. What was the point of trying to look pretty? Surely when you're about to tell someone that you don't love him it was best to be as ugly as possible.

Four hats sat on top of her rickety armoire. She took down the cream-coloured Java with the blue silk stripe. Quentin's favourite, true, but also her own, so why shouldn't she wear it? It was anticipating the summer a little, but the alternatives were all too formal.

Outside, the sun was bright, casting crisp shadows. She watched her own ripple ahead of her on the grass as she took a shortcut through a schoolyard, hat just so. Could you acquire a Bachelor of Science degree and membership in Phi Beta Kappa, and qualify for your MD in the top three of your class, and still care about hats? Apparently you could.

Her mood darkened as she got closer to Rush. In a few minutes she would have to tell Quentin that whatever it was they had shared could not continue, that it was over. Skinny, gawky Quentin with his bony hands and his pretty girl's mouth had been her ally, her refuge, in this strange adventure she had set for herself. She had never expected to make such a friend. She had come almost to believe that all men hated her.

The way the other students looked at her when she answered a question! Folding their arms and rolling their eyes or staring at the floor. How smug they were on those rare occasions when she got it wrong. Sometimes she bit her tongue, repressing the urge to answer, only to hate herself later for cowardice. The sexual insults—she had been completely unprepared for those. Anatomy class in particular. "How does this gentleman's penis compare to all the others you've seen, Miss Lang?"

She had not known, until then, that it was possible to blush all the way from sternum to occiput. Skin scorched, right across the shoulders, and rivulets of sweat travelling to unheard-of destinations beneath her smock and heavy clothes. It was not so much the sexual content of the remark that upset her, but the depth of hostility it revealed.

Another young woman might have run home to cry on her father's shoulder. Her own father, Josiah Lang—one of Chicago's top attorneys, a progressive, a friend of Clarence Darrow's no less—could have shut her classmates up with a single riposte. There had been a time when she would have run to him, when she valued his affection and good opinion above all others. What a joke that had turned out to be.

She had sought out the other four women in the class, thinking that together they might lighten each other's burdens. But two had dropped out in the first couple of months, and the other two were so competitive they would not so much as speak to her. They seemed to hate her even more than the men did.

And then there was Quentin.

Even if she had come to Rush in search of a man, which she most emphatically had not, the quality of her male classmates would have rapidly put her off her quest. Louts. Imogen had always imagined physicians to be a valiant example of the human male, rational and scientific, eager to be of service, even chivalrous. From what Avalon did such paragons arise? Certainly not from the Rush College class of 1916.

Except for Quentin. Quentin stood a good five inches taller than Imogen, who at five foot nine and a half was taller than most women. She loved the Euclidian angularity of him, the way he bent his neck forward to engage with his shorter colleagues, the loose-limbed way he would unfurl a long arm to point something out—a hawk riding a thermal over Lake Michigan, the sunlight blazing in the library windows. He had a disarming way of folding himself into or over a chair; he was incapable of sitting up straight anywhere except the dinner table, where he looked positively architectural. Everywhere else he slouched, he draped, he accordioned himself into, around, or over whatever support was available.

His physical being was a lovely contrast to his rationality. Professor Coughlin had posed him a question in cellular biology class once, something about mitosis, and Quentin had stood there mute, head bent, arms folded, still as a lamppost. Coughlin was sadistic enough to let dullards hang for ages before he would bail them out by posing the question to someone else. On this occasion he emitted an exasperated sputter. "Come, come, Mr. Goodchild, it's not a difficult question."

"It is for me, sir, because I'm thoughtful."

Everyone had laughed, including Imogen, because it was clear that Quentin's cranium was indeed humming all the time. And he did manage to retrieve the right answer before the laughter had quite faded from the hall.

Sometimes when they went for walks, around the campus or farther afield, he would be silent so long that Imogen would begin to get annoyed. "If you don't want to be here," she would begin.

"Sorry. I was just imagining the future when this is just a memory. Us walking down Harrison Street on a sunny day in 1916—how can that ever not be real? Not be present?"

"It'll be gone by tomorrow. Sooner, even."

"But this heat on my skin, those twin curls on your neck—they're just like parentheses—it's all so vivid, so real. How can it not be forever?"

Because nothing is forever, Imogen wanted to say but found herself silenced by his noticing her curls. In moments of absolute honesty, she could admit that she enjoyed the way he responded to her—the way he might tremble a little when helping her with a coat, a scarf, or even a book. Or when they sat side by side, how he would tilt a little away from her to avoid the most innocent touch.

Once, when they had both pointed to a page at the same time, their bare hands had collided and he'd reacted as if she were a red-hot poker, his cheeks turning scarlet. She was aware of possessing such power over him, and she did not like the part of herself that was gratified. All men were idiots when it came to lust, so she tried not to attribute any deeper meaning to Quentin's reactions. He was a man; she was a woman who was not ugly if not beautiful—of course he was attracted.

But Quentin was a wonderful person, someone she would want to know always. So why did she not react that way to him? She did not pine for him when they were apart, did not daydream about him, never wrote out his name just to see it in front of her. In short, she was not in love.

"I wish you were my brother," she had blurted out one hot afternoon when they had known each other for about a year. By then Quentin had dropped out of medical school to study at the University of Chicago. He had set his heart on a literary career, thus enraging his doctor father—an experience with which Imogen could sympathize.

They were in Lincoln Park, sharing a bench by the fountain, and a monarch butterfly had landed on Imogen's sleeve, brilliant wings opening and closing as it caught its breath after its long journey from Mexico or wherever. Imogen raised her arm so that the sunlight lit up the Tiffany wings.

"Hinge," Quentin said, and opened and closed his bony hand, four fingers in unison against his thumb. "Hinge," he repeated. "Excellent word." He turned on the bench and interposed a crooked forefinger between their two faces, curling it closed and open as if scratching the ear of an invisible cat. "Hinge," he said in a deeper voice, as if Imogen had just arrived from a foreign land and needed a lesson in English vocabulary.

Something about the way he said it—gravely, but with a touch of self-parody—threw her into a fit of giggles.

And Quentin became relentless. "Hinge," he said again, solemn as a judge. He got up and stood in front of her, held his arms out and crooked the elbows, first one then the other, a living marionette discovering his invisible strings. "Hinge."

"Stop," Imogen cried, laughing harder.

He lifted his knee, foot dangling and swinging, a pendulum of flesh and bone. "Hinge."

"No, really. I can't breathe," Imogen managed. "You'll kill me."

"All right. Sorry."

He plopped himself down beside her again, and folded his hands in his lap and looked out across the pond. The butterfly was gone. Imogen extricated a handkerchief from her bag and wiped her eyes and blew her nose.

When they had started walking back toward campus she touched Quentin's arm—she had never touched him before—and said, "I wish you were my brother."

"Oh," Quentin said. "Oh, I—well. Um, why?"

"Because you make me laugh. Because I love your company. And obviously because I have no brothers."

"But you don't have a husband, either."

Imogen stopped and looked down at her feet, at the grass, at a half-acorn with the twin grooves of a squirrel's teethmarks on it.

Quentin realized what he had said. "I'm sorry. It was just an observation. But why a brother? Why not some other male figure, I don't know, a piano instructor, or a priest or something? I didn't mean, you know . . ."

"No, of course not."

"I just meant—"

"No, why would you?"

"May we walk on? We're meeting Jack at three-fifteen."

Quentin veered away from the subject of husbands and on to John Dryden, how one could admire the poet's precision, his perception, his brilliance with verse, but *he* would never in his life want to write like Dryden, and he wasn't just talking about style. This was all so much persiflage to draw her attention away from what he had said. It was unlike Quentin to do this, and so all the more proof that he had blurted out his true feelings.

Imogen had never, not once, thought of Quentin as a possible husband; she didn't think of *any* man as a possible husband. But as they continued their walk toward the fine art museum it dawned on her that he was confusing friendship with courtship. That saddened her. To some degree it even annoyed her. He *shouldn't* raise the issue of marriage when they were obviously just colleagues. He had damaged this thing that was bringing her such joy, more joy than she had realized until that moment—right there, right then in Lincoln Park— when she faced its loss. In her eyes, marriage had no claim to superiority over friendship. Marriages were commonplace, even good marriages, not that Imogen had ever witnessed such a union. Fine friendships were rare—although Quentin certainly seemed to enjoy such a bond with Jack Wisdom, who waved to them from the museum steps as they approached.

Jack was a compact, lively man with jet-black hair and moustache, dark eyes of an almost Arabian cast, and an engaging grin that would surely be the envy of all con men.

"Are we ready to be cultured?" he said, as they came up the steps. "I have to say, the two of you already look quite refined."

"Imogen, maybe," Quentin said. "No one's ever accused me of looking refined."

Jack bounded ahead to open the door for them.

"Let me check your coats," he said, when they were inside. He was already reaching for Quentin's.

"We'll line up for tickets," Quentin said.

"Nope. Already got 'em."

"Well, let us pay you." Quentin reached into his jacket for his wallet.

"No, no—please. My treat. You two are still humble students, and here am I making a positive fortune at the *Trib*."

"It's very kind of you," Imogen said.

"Uh-huh," Quentin said. "And copy editing for a newspaper pays a fortune, does it?"

But Jack was already rushing off with their coats.

The special exhibit turned out to be a revelation for Imogen, who had never seen the works of the Pre-Raphaelites. Jack seemed well informed, chatting in a low voice to Quentin about Dante Gabriel Rossetti and his circle. Imogen lingered at each painting, preferring to take them in without commentary. She marvelled at the rich colours, the realistic detail, the slim, soulful figures.

"I feel as if I've had the most wonderful dream," she said, as they left the exhibit and headed to the cafeteria, "like I've visited a strange and beautiful world. It all seemed so real, and yet . . ."

"I knew you'd love them," Quentin said.

In the tea room, Jack pulled back Imogen's chair for her, and then did the same for Quentin.

"How are things going with Miss Gilbert?" Imogen asked.

"Oh, my." Jack put a melodramatic hand to his forehead. "Sometimes I think she'll be the death of me. Other times, I'm the happiest man in the world. But I promised myself I wouldn't whine about her today—I'm always bending Quentin's ear with my tale of woe."

"He's getting some good poems out of it," Quentin said.

Jack slapped the table smartly. "You know what I want to do—once I get a definitive answer out of that girl one way or the other?"

"No," Quentin said, "but I'm sure it's eminently sensible."

"I want to take the Grand Tour—you know—Paris, Vienna, Istanbul. You and me, Quentin, the Grand Tour."

"There is a war on, you know. Europe's a nightmare."

"My other thought was Texas—live on a ranch for a year. Wouldn't that be something? I feel the need to do something profound."

Quentin laughed. "We could write cowboy poems."

"I was thinking a rhyming novel—when was the last time anyone wrote a good rhyming novel?"

"You're perfectly insane, Jack. Just ask the psychiatrist here."

"Psychiatrist-to-be," Imogen said. "And no—my diagnosis would not be that he is insane, he's merely in love."

Now, here she was—what?—a year later, about to tell Quentin goodbye and wondering if she had not been as cruel as Jack Wisdom's beloved. If she had not been seeing Quentin with an eye to marriage, why was she so often alone with him? Women—respectable women—do not seek out men for friendship, they seek them out (discreetly, properly) for marriage. And respectable young ladies did not do the seeking at all; they waited to be sought.

My God, she thought, no wonder he has misunderstood everything. I have misunderstood everything. But Rush had only been admitting women for three or four years, and the university not much longer. Men and women of marriageable age in such proximity? There were bound to be misunderstandings. Of course, none of the women even lived on campus; they were in rooming houses that had sprung up on its fringes to meet this new need. Imogen lived in Miss Emma Sedgwick's Home for Young Ladies, run by a pleasant but firm spinster of sixty.

When Imogen had moved in, all had gone well for the first week. Her room was bright and comfortable, with a window that looked out on a luxuriant back garden. The bed could have been firmer and the armoire larger, but Imogen was not a complainer and adjusted her wardrobe accordingly. The desk was where she would be spending most of her time, in any case, and it was a massive rolltop that looked as if it had once furnished an office in a Dickens novel. Miss Sedgwick inquired several times if everything was to her liking, and encouraged her to speak up if she needed anything.

Then, on her first Saturday evening, Miss Sedgwick asked if Imogen did not require directions to a church for her Sunday worship.

"That won't be necessary," Imogen said. "I don't attend Sunday services."

"Oh. Are you a Hebrew, then? Lang is not a Jewish name, is it?"

"Not always, but it is in my case."

"Then we must find you a synagogue. I'm sure there's one in the area."

"There's no need. My family's not observant."

"But how do you tend to your spiritual life?"

"My spiritual life is not something I attend to in public."

"Then you are utterly without moral guidance?"

"No. I'm just without religion."

"Well, that's—I find this very surprising. Especially in the daughter of an attorney, a man who must deal daily in matters of right and wrong."

Oh, Imogen's father could be instructive in matters of right and wrong, all right. In public Josiah Lang was a liberal, a reformer, even a bit of a firebrand—thick with the union movement, representing several different organizations, the largest of which was the Chicago Teachers' Federation. He was often quoted in the papers, asked to give speeches, and urged to run for high office. Which he would never do—if his life became any more public the truth about him would emerge, he would be disgraced, and Imogen's family—her mother and her two younger sisters, anyway—would be destroyed.

Until she was twelve, Imogen had imagined her father to be as close to a perfect human being as human beings get. He read to his daughters, sang silly songs to them, took them to Chicago's wonderful beaches, gave them delightful gifts and, more than anything, enriched their lives with the gift of his attention. But that was before Imogen had seen him for what he really was, which rendered all her former happiness a lie.

So maybe Miss Sedgwick was right, she considered, as she crossed the street—maybe I have been brought up in such a manner as to be without a moral compass. She had realized that Quentin wanted more from her, but she could not cut him off. She had needed his friendship too much—their common intensity of purpose—even after their actual ambitions diverged. Imogen was determined to be a psychiatrist, Quentin a writer. One of the first common interests they had discovered was their reverence for authors of great novels. They both adored George Eliot—he for *Middlemarch*, she for *The Mill on the Floss*. Reading with Quentin, sharing the unique peace and contentment that comes from absorption in a book, became one of her greatest pleasures.

"Peace and contentment?" He looked a bit puzzled when she used those words to describe her experience of a good book. "I feel every good book is a challenge—one I'll never live up to—so I can't say it's all that peaceful for me. But I'm glad it is for you."

Quentin seemed to think he would be a novelist, but Imogen secretly thought he was more likely to be a poet. She thought the few verses he had shown her were very good indeed. And the way he lingered over individual words, tasting them, savouring them, spoke to her of a jeweller's precision, rather than the architectural scope of the novelist. It was true he could spin a lively anecdote, but that seemed to Imogen very different from inventing several hundred pages of human experience.

She had led him on—she knew that. There had been a jewel-like autumn day, rare in Chicago, low sun casting long shadows, and everywhere the smell of burning leaves. They had arranged to meet outside the university library. The grass of the main quadrangle was still brilliant green, and yet one could sense in the air a metallic fore-taste of winter. As she approached, she could see him sitting on the library steps, sunlight glinting off his spectacles. She was late; Dr. Gleason's lecture on endocrine secretions had gone overtime, and then the streetcar had tangled with a horse-drawn cab, the cab slamming over on its side, the horse breaking free and galloping away down the street. She began telling him about the incident while she was still a good ten yards away.

When she came to a stop at the foot of the steps, Quentin's expression was odd, one corner of his mouth lifted in a half smile, eyebrows closing in on each other and yet not what you would call knitted. An amused, assessing look.

"Why are you looking at me like that?"

"Sun's in my eyes. And I must say you look beautiful at this moment—now don't panic, it's just an observation of the sort one might make on seeing a fine painting. The sunlight, your hair, your story, and the way you were coming across the grass toward me. I've never seen anything so beautiful."

"Well, Mr. Goodchild, I'm sure I don't know what to make of such words."

"Construe them any way you like, Miss Lang, so long as it's positive."

Later they had a sunny little corner of the library to themselves, their books and papers spread between them. Imogen was memorizing the many bones of the hand, when Quentin said something under his breath and she looked up.

"What did you say?"

"*Imogen.*"

"What?"

"*Imogen,*" he whispered. "I was just saying your name."

"I see." She went back to the lunate, the scaphoid, the capitate. She had nearly had them all but now she couldn't concentrate. The rims of her ears were burning. She lowered her book again. "Why were you saying my name?"

Now it was Quentin's turn to look up, his pencil poised above the graph paper he preferred for composition. "Because it's beautiful," he said. "Beautiful and strange and evocative. Imogen—image, imago, magic, generation, imagination. Do you know what an imago is?"

"Yes. Now stop, please."

"It's the final phase in the development of a moth or butterfly."

"I said I know."

"Imogen."

"Desist, sir, or I shall quit your company this instant."

"Sorry. Yes, of course. Please don't be annoyed."

"Mr. Goodchild, you can be very wearing."

"You're not the first to remark on it. I wear on me too."

"Well. There you are."

At the time she had thought—she had chosen to think—that it was his writer's mind playing with words again.

Another time, just a few months ago, they had met at the cinema—they both loved Charlie Chaplin—and sat together and laughed together. When they came back out, the snow was four inches deeper and still falling in fat flakes that clung to their hats and coats. The Bijou was not far from Imogen's rooming house, and Quentin walked her home. Supper would still be on the stove.

When they reached her door, Imogen thought the proper thing to do would be to thank him, but he had neither suggested the evening nor paid for it. They were just friends who had been to the flickers together, so she turned to him and put out her hand for him to grasp and said, "That was a very amusing evening. I don't know exactly why I love Charlie Chaplin but I know that I do."

"I know why," Quentin said. "Because he's always defeated by objects but never by people."

Imogen smiled. "I think you may indeed be a writer."

"Let's hope you're right." He reached to wipe a snowflake from her eyebrow, ever so gently, with his thumb.

"Mr. Goodchild." She looked about to see if anyone had seen. "Really."

"Forgive me, Miss Lang. I forgot myself."

"Indeed you did," she replied, but as she spoke Quentin said something else. Breathed it really, it wasn't even quite a whisper. Three little words. Three words that once said cannot be unsaid.

"What did you say?"

"Nothing. I was just thinking to myself."

"No, you said something, Quentin."

He looked around to see if anyone had heard her use his first name.

"What did you say?"

"Nothing. Really. You know I'm always talking to myself."

"I thought I heard—"

"You didn't. It was nothing. Oh, look at the time. I must go. I've got so much work to do before tomorrow. Good night, Miss Lang." And he walked away, a thin, almost frail figure, who seemed to waver as the snow swirled around him.


That was the last week of February. They had not mentioned the evening or his words again and, although Imogen never forgot them, she had been almost successful in keeping them out of her mind.

But now it was the last day of May. Filthy patches of snow still steamed here and there but spring was definitely staking its claim. They had agreed to meet at Rush, even though Quentin was no longer a student there, because it was more or less halfway between their two locations. As she got closer to the college, she could smell the wet grass and soil, and then a trolley clanged by, replacing them with the odour of oil and steel.

It had been an eventful month. May second was her twenty-second birthday and she couldn't very well refuse her mother's invitation to come home for dinner to Emerald Avenue. That had been a dull, uncomfortable affair. Her father had stayed away—the Teachers' Federation contract was in play, and he was holed up in the Grace Hotel. Imogen knew that was not the real reason. The real reason was that she made him intensely uncomfortable, because she knew the truth about him and could not disguise her feelings about it.

And Alice, her older sister, had stayed away too. She had become a lawyer, just like their father, and now worked with him in his Monroe Street office. It would have been easy for the two sisters to get together for luncheon, as the law office was not far from Rush, but Alice had never suggested it and Imogen—the younger by nearly ten years—did not feel it was her place to do so.

Her mother had had Mrs. Bidwell, the housekeeper, bake a cake, and her two younger sisters, coltish adolescents, had dutifully been in attendance. They seemed to have no interests other than the fortunes of Mary Pickford and Mabel Normand, which made conversation impossible. Having raised his older daughters to be bookish, even scholarly, only to see Alice become a taciturn spinster and Imogen grow cold to him, their father had evidently decided to mould his younger daughters into marriageable young ladies—decorous and trivial.

"You know," Quentin had said to her once, "your father can't be as bad as you make out or you would never have turned out to be who you are."

"You're wrong," was all she had come up with for a reply.

Her mother had tried her best to perk up a little for this party. Perched at the head of the table, she smiled vacantly at her daughters, lines of pain radiating from the corners of her beautiful eyes. Rose Lang suffered from an ache so deep she gave no evidence of ever having lived without it. The most one could hope for was to distract her occasionally, come up with some way to entertain or charm her. Although Imogen had been good at this in her childhood, she'd grown tired of constantly struggling to appease her mother's unhappiness. Rose remained a kind of absence, a needy creature disguised as a mother, who spent most of her time in her bedroom with the curtains pulled and the lights turned low, a martyr to her "migraines."

Of course, the migraine was really her husband, and when she was twelve, Imogen had discovered why. Alice also knew why, but behaved as if she didn't. The two younger sisters had clearly been allowed to grow up in ignorance, which granted them, if not bliss, a good deal more happiness than either of their older siblings.

"Twenty-two," her mother had sighed, when the cake was brought in and the candles were lit. "Twenty-two and nearly a doctor. It's quite a thing." A thing, instead of an honour earned at tremendous cost. And nearly a doctor, because the actual graduation was still two weeks away.

Not one of her family members was coming to the graduation. No doubt her father had made sure of that. He had not contributed a cent toward Imogen's university education and, since he kept a tight grip on the household funds, her mother could not contribute either. Imogen had visited six banks, had sat across from six plump, mustachioed managers who had smiled indulgently and said no, they would not be lending money to a seventeen-year-old female who wanted to pursue a career in medicine.

In the end she had gone to Mason Kirschner, her mother's older brother, who, having no children of his own, had always lavished gifts and attention on the Lang girls. Upon receiving Imogen's formal letter requesting a meeting to discuss a certain "financial proposition," he responded as if she were an old and valued client. She sat across from him in his office high above the bustle of Clark Street and laid out her plans: science degree at the University of Chicago, followed by medicine at Rush—and then a career in psychiatry. She would start repaying the loan in full, with interest, at such time as she had an MD in one hand and a job in the other. He agreed to stake her the whole way.

Imogen had needed a moment or two to take this in. "You mean—you'll lend me the money?"

"I'll have my secretary draw up an agreement right away. I know a good investment when I see one. And just between you and me," he added, "your pappy is a damn fool."


Chicago's usual mass of cloud cover had separated into continents that were now breaking into archipelagos. A shaft of sunlight warmed

Imogen's face as she crossed Harrison Street. She could feel the tremor of streetcars in the pavement.

She stopped to check the time. Her watch told her she was two minutes late. *Perhaps I could write to him when I'm safely settled in Baltimore,* she thought—but no, that was the coward's way out. She could see Quentin now. He was leaning against a Romanesque arch, head bent, book in fist, a hatless, gloveless figure intent on his reading. Imogen raised a hand to wave but he didn't look up.

He didn't even look up when she was less than thirty feet away. You'd think the tap of her heels on the pavement would pique his interest, but very little came between Quentin and a book.

"Mr. Goodchild," she said, "you're looking very scholarly today." Despite her efforts to remain calm her heart had begun to race.

Quentin met her eyes and said, "I've brought you something." He reached into his satchel and pulled out a large book—a complete edition of Lewis Carroll, lavishly adorned with colour versions of Tenniel's original illustrations. "Remember? You said the other week you wished you had your old Alice books, that you still thought about them quite often. I was browsing through James and Powell—you know, the shop on Woodlawn—and I snapped it up."

"It's lovely," Imogen said, "but you mustn't give me presents."

"Hardly a present. It's something you should have."

"Thank you. It's kind of you. You're always ki—" The sudden lump in her throat choked her.

"What's wrong?"

She swallowed hard. She would not allow herself to cry.

"Listen," Quentin said, "let's take the streetcar to Jackson Park. It's essential to me that I see the lake today. I'm in the middle of writing a lakeside scene and—I don't know why my memory fails me so often—or not my memory but my vocabulary. Not vocabulary either, really, it's not a matter of the individual words. What fails me is the illustrative faculty, if there is such a thing in a person who can neither draw nor paint. A *rendering* faculty, I'd call it—although *rendering* rather smacks of Union Stock Yards, doesn't it. Rendering."

"It might be better if we just go for a walk around here. I've something to—"

"We can talk on the streetcar."

"No, I have something to tell you and I think it would be best to do so here. I don't want to go far afield and then—"

"But we see this old place all the time. Let's go to Jackson Park. I've got something to tell you, too."

A streetcar clanged, and he pointed. "Look, if we hurry we can catch it."

"Quentin, I don't want to catch it. Please."

At last, Quentin registered her mood. Excitement and good cheer vacated his features and were replaced by the first rough hints of dread. "You're giving me bad news, aren't you."

"Please," Imogen said. "Let's walk in the Kingsley garden."

Quentin followed her in silence around the east side of the building. As they stepped onto the little wooden bridge that led to the island garden, Quentin muttered, "Feels like the Bridge of Sighs . . ."

It took only a moment to see they were alone. Several benches looked out on the pond, but Imogen didn't want to sit. She took a deep breath, and turned to face him, clutching the book so she wouldn't reach out to take his hands in hers.

"Quentin," she began, "this is very difficult to say."

He raised a hand to cover his mouth, a gesture she'd never seen him make before. He knows, she thought. He already knows.

"It's time we went our separate ways."

He dropped his hand and looked away. She saw his Adam's apple rise and fall.

"Your friendship has meant a lot to me these last three years. I enjoy your company, I value your opinion, I admire your intellect. You are the perfect friend, Quentin. But I've come to see that you want something more than friendship."

"And you don't?" His voice quivered a little. "This has all been for nothing?"

"No, Quentin. Not for nothing. I shall always treasure the pleasant times we've had together."

"Pleasant?" He turned to face her again, and his expression shamed her.

"Much more than that," she said. "I don't think I would have been able to finish my degree without you. But I have to go to Baltimore to study psychiatry. I've been happy here—and I want *you* to be happy, but if we continue on this path— Well, will *you* be happy if, say, two years from now we are still discussing books and taking walks and nothing more?"

His eyes were filling. Imogen had only seen a man cry once and that was when Laura died. She felt a strong desire to touch Quentin, to comfort him.

"What does it matter what I want?" he said. "What I want is clearly of no relevance."

"That's not true," Imogen said. She wanted to say that, in fact, it was precisely because Quentin wanted something she did not that she was forced to do this. It was hurting him now, but would save him from far greater pain down the line.

Quentin was staring at the ground. "This—this hurts."

"That's the *last* thing I—" Her hand reached for his sleeve as if of its own volition. She was unaware of it until he tore away from her and strode back across the bridge.

"Quentin," she called. And then, "Your book!"

Stupid, *stupid*. He doesn't want the damn book.

The sun had retreated once more and a deep cold suffused her from head to toe. She looked around at the little island, the garden that was still in its winter ruin. She had sat here often. Sometimes alone, reading. But mostly with Quentin, talking. Laughing. It was quite true what she'd said—she had been happy.

# 2

At least the housekeeper is glad to see me, Imogen thought. Mrs. Bidwell had gone out of her way to prepare a meal of baked salmon with dill sauce, and had set the table with the special-occasion candles.

"You're home," her father said, as Imogen took her seat. "How good of you to grace our table."

"I've been looking forward to this," Imogen said. "Miss Sedgwick's cooking wasn't exactly haute cuisine."

"You require haute cuisine now, do you?"

He passed the salmon plate to her. Imogen served herself and passed it on to Caroline, the youngest, on her left. Her father busied himself with potatoes, beans, and sauce, and did not so much as glance at Imogen. Although she had closed her heart to him long ago, she experienced a contradictory yearning for his respect. He had the look of easy masculine authority—from his perfect moustache to his centurion's nose—that attracted women, dogs, and small children. People, not just daughters, naturally wanted to please him.

He inquired of Caroline about her French exam, and then of his second youngest, Victoria, about her history. Both girls were passing—barely—a circumstance that would have provoked a withering lecture when Imogen was in high school, but now he just gave each girl a nod that acknowledged their having met expectations.

And now he turned back to her. "Of course, if you'd stayed at home you could have enjoyed perfectly good meals without incurring extra expense."

"Yes, but I would have spent so much time on the streetcar I would've had little time to study."

"Oh, I know you had no shortage of justifications."

Imogen looked to her mother, but Rose made no effort to intervene, looking instead at Victoria, who had adopted the blank I'm-not-really-here face that Imogen herself used to use not so long ago. "Pass the sauce to your sister, Victoria."

"Rose," Lang said, "Alice had quite a triumph today. She's too modest to tell you herself, of course."

"Tell us, my dear," Rose said. "What is your triumph?"

Alice dabbed at her mouth with her napkin, and cleared her throat before speaking. She had her father's long nose, which seemed to lend a certain gravity to all her utterances.

"I won my appeal. Against Illinois Textile. They'll have to pay back wages after all."

"It's criminal what they pay those women," Lang said. "It's a tremendous victory."

"I'm so glad," Rose said, smiling faintly.

"I imagine you'll be itching to set up your practice," Lang said to Imogen. "Where will you go, I wonder. You won't want to tarry with the likes of us very long."

"I'll be staying here for the summer."

"And then what—Boston? New York? A shingle in Harley Street?"

"I'm not setting up anywhere, Father. In September, as you know, I'll be going to Baltimore."

"Baltimore. 'Home of Turks, Jews, and infidels.'"

"That's actually Rhode Island," Alice said. "People called it that, owing to their tolerance of Quakers."

Lang snapped his fingers and pointed an approving finger at his eldest. "Well done, Alice. I stand corrected."

He concentrated on his plate for a few moments, as Imogen's mother talked, to no one in particular, about her plans for the garden. The arbour was near collapse and needed replacing. And she'd had her heart set on American Beauties this year but the squirrels were merciless with rosebuds.

"Tell us about Baltimore, Imogen." Her father held his water glass up to the light and squinted at it, as if he suspected health violations. "What is the nature of your business there?"

"I've told you. I'll be doing my residency in psychiatry at the Phipps Clinic under Jonas Ganz."

"Ganz, no less." He raised his water glass again, as if in a toast. "Jonas Ganz, everyone."

"He *is* the most famous psychiatrist in the country," Imogen said.

"I grant you that," her father said. "But it's rather like being the most famous tap dancer. Impressive to the tiny circle of those who care. Who have psychiatrists ever cured?"

"Lots of people. Ten years ago half the beds in the asylums were taken up by paretics."

Alice paused with fork in midair. "Paretics?"

"Paresis . . ." Imogen began, but then had to search for an explanation that did not include the word *syphilis*. "Paresis is a permanent paralysis that occurs in the late stages of certain common psychoses. The discovery of Salvarsan has practically wiped it out. Tens of thousands of cases—so hardly a 'tiny circle.'"

"And did Dr. Ganz have anything to do with this miracle?"

"No, Father, but his clinic includes a laboratory that will be searching for similar cures. I can't wait to work in that lab. I want to learn everything I can about the human mind—both in its physical and mental aspects."

"And in the meantime, a summer of indolence."

"I have a job lined up. I'll be starting at a pharmacy in about two weeks."

"Exciting," her father said. "We'll have to stop by for a strawberry phosphate, won't we, Alice."

✻

It was only upon returning home from her boarding house each summer that Imogen realized that while she hadn't missed the unhappy members of her family, she had missed her room. The boarding house could not match the downy comfort of her bed with its fine linens. Nor could its windows compare with her bay window and reading nook, her shelves lined with the works of authors she loved: George Eliot, Lewis Carroll, and Thomas Hardy for fiction; Charles Darwin and Thomas Huxley for science.

At one time, she had shared this room with Laura, the twin sister she had lost when they were both five. There was a silver-framed photograph on her vanity of the two little girls in identical dresses, except for the white ribbon that dangled from Imogen's shoulders and the tiny notebook attached to it. At that time, Imogen could not speak owing to a severe tongue-tie—at least, could not speak without intolerable distortions of vowel and consonant. Surgery not being deemed advisable until the age of seven, Imogen often chose to communicate by printed note.

All that seemed a lifetime ago. For now, she had every intention of enjoying her two weeks of freedom. She vowed she would go for long walks, she would sit in the garden, and she would read anything but medical texts.

Unfortunately, Chicago's climate thwarted this plan with a series of bruise-coloured skies, unseasonably low temperatures, and almost constant drizzle. She resolved to remain cheerful despite her father's hostility, but found herself penned in and unable to stave off unhappy thoughts, harbingers of the dark mood that soon invaded her, robbing her days of all pleasure. Even her pretty room began to pall.

She forced herself to get up in the mornings and have breakfast with her mother. But afterwards she would go back and lie on the bed, curled up on her side. So an hour would pass—two—as the tide of depression flowed into her yet seemed never to ebb. She found herself counting all the reasons to be sad: she had broken her best friend's heart, her family thought her vain and selfish, her father clearly hated her and, worst of all, she found she could not blame them.

Sometimes she wrote in a notebook about her own state of mind, mostly questions. Was it depression, or was it a rational assessment of her situation? Was it driven by hormones? Certainly the onset of such moods had coincided with puberty. Had she inherited the tendency from her mother?

These were the kinds of questions that had initially sparked her interest in the human psyche. Of course, her mother had ample reason for unhappiness, having married a man who turned out to be far from the good, kind man she deserved, and that Josiah Lang had once been. Or seemed. And she had never fully recovered from the death of Laura. Despite her efforts to deal with them rationally, Imogen's feelings so oppressed her that it sometimes felt as if she were being smothered.

One day, catching her own reflection in the window, she thought how it could be Laura—grown-up Laura—arrayed in sunlight, the white muslin curtains billowing around her. She had always been a little bit bossy, in an affectionate kind of way. What would her twin say to her now, if she could see her?

"I'm not sure I recognize this Little Miss Gloom," Laura said gently. "The Imogen I recall was always chipper, eager for adventure."

"Yes," Imogen thought. "Because life was better when you were around—I was better."

"We were five years old, you goose. Life's more complicated now—for you, anyway—but it's going to get better, you'll see."

Imogen recognized the irony that her dead sister should be the one to reassure her. Scarlet fever killed many children, but it let many live; why had it not spared Laura?

She went to her desk and pulled out her notebook.

"No, I am not going mad," she wrote. "I know this ghostly Laura is just me—my better me. Which doesn't mean I should ignore her advice. This darkness will end," she added in heavy letters, and underlined it twice. "I must remember that life will be brighter again."

She was reminding herself of this again one day in early June when there was a light tapping at her door. She closed her notebook, picked up her copy of *The Lost Continent*, and sat in her reading nook.

"Come in."

"Who is writing you from Lake Placid, dear?"

Rose Lang's interest was not sparked by much but apparently the neat little envelope she held out to her daughter qualified.

"I don't know anyone in Lake Placid," Imogen said, taking it. And then she recognized the fine nib, the indigo ink, the machinelike cursive. Quentin had mentioned his family's summer place in upstate New York without being any more precise. Until now his letters had been coming from Rochester, and Imogen had managed to snatch them up before her mother noticed.

"Oh," she said. "It's a friend from UC."

"Eccentric handwriting." Her mother was standing over her, looking down at her with eyes slightly less melancholy than usual. "Oddly masculine."

Imogen tucked the envelope into her book. "I'll read it later."

When her mother was gone, Imogen went to her door and made sure it was latched. She opened the envelope and took out the letter—double-sided and closely written.

Dear Imogen,

I have a table to work on here that looks out on a veranda that in turn looks out on what surely must be one of the prettiest lakes in all of North America. Breathing the air here is like drinking from a spring that gushes pure oxygen. Woodpeckers, jays, flying squirrels, chipmunks, deer, groundhogs and who knows what else wander into view all day—the deer especially in the late evening light. Amid such beauty, it's hard to believe all of Europe is awash in the ugliness of war.

My father has not yet come down from Rochester. Jack came to visit for a week. As usual he was proposing mad ideas of travelling to exotic places together. We commiserated over our broken hearts—he is still brutally ignored by the famous Emma whom I've yet to meet. Even so, I'm afraid I annoyed him by being able to talk only of you. Even a midnight swim couldn't cheer us up.

Now that I have the place to myself I should be turning out poems, stories, novels, but my thoughts flee me. They see me coming and hide. And so I think of you.

I know you well enough, after three years, to know that the concord between us was not a figment of my imagination. I know that you felt it too, saw it in your shining eyes, heard it in your laughter, felt it in the intimacy of your confessions, treasured it in your honesty and your trust.

Oh, Imogen, I whispered your name because I had to; I whispered I love you because it is true.

I miss you beyond all telling.

Quentin

Imogen folded the letter and stuffed it back into the envelope. What could she do to stop this? Several letters ago she had told him she didn't think it was a good idea for her to reply. Perhaps she should have said she wouldn't even read them. The truth was she didn't want to think about Quentin anymore; she couldn't. That part of her life was over.

It was a Saturday morning, two days before she was to start her summer job, and for once it was not rainy or even overcast. Her equanimity had slowly reasserted itself, and Imogen had plans to devote the day to the simple pleasures of a walk in the park, a visit to the natural history museum, and a good browse in a bookstore or two. She was heading for the front door when her father called to her from his study, which was just off the front hall.

"Imogen? Would you come in here, please?"

She was startled to see him seated at his desk, looking at her as if he'd been waiting; she had assumed he was away on one of his "working weekends." She stepped into the office, clutching her bag and parasol.

"Sit down, please."

She did so without removing her hat, to let him know that she had no wish to linger.

Her father sat with his hands, framed by their starched white cuffs, clasped before him on the desk. "You're a medical person, now, and I'd appreciate your opinion on something. I'd like to know, in your *medical* opinion, what is wrong with your mother."

"Why, Father—is she ill?"

"You know she's ill. I think you're familiar with her symptoms. These constant migraines, for example. She's had them for years."

"I couldn't possibly diagnose her without examining her, and I doubt Mother would agree to that. Nor would it be proper to discuss any diagnosis with a third party."

"Your punctiliousness is bracing." Her father stared at her. "Then perhaps you would be so good as to speculate, based on your medical education, on a hypothetical. Suppose someone has been suffering constantly from headaches, has seen the doctors again and again over the years. Claims they can't help her. They find nothing."

"No one knows what causes migraines. It could be allergy, eye-strain, nervous distress—no one knows for sure."

"You must have studied the symptoms, in your training?"

"They vary. The main one is intense discomfort on one side of the cranium. It can be accompanied by hypersensitivity to light or sound—sometimes with nausea and vomiting. Sometimes with visual distortion or even partial blindness."

"And if the patient never shows those symptoms? No symptoms beyond headache and a desire to shut oneself away in a room?"

"Headache could be caused by many things."

"Yes, yes, headache . . ." He waved this idea away. "Suppose that's just a cover, an excuse. I'm talking about joylessness, a lack of emotion generally, in fact a kind of shrinking—from family, from life, from the world." He leaned forward and enunciated his next sentence heavily, emphasizing each syllable as if his daughter were hard of hearing. *"An inability to experience happiness or contentment."*

"Well, now you're describing depression."

"Your mother has everything a woman needs. I've made sure of that."

Imogen could think of several responses to this but made none.

"Suppose this hypothetical patient has every reason to be happy— a successful husband, four beautiful daughters, a beautiful house. Doesn't have to work, but has interests—gardening, the City Beautiful movement, books—and yet seems to find it impossible, physically impossible, to smile."

"Well, I'm not a psychiatrist yet, but I know that depression can be brought on by surrounding circumstances—overwhelming responsibilities, sudden reversals in romance or financial matters. Longer-term, it might be caused by an unaddressed grief. A death in the family . . ."

"People die, Imogen. Children die. You can't grieve for sixteen years. You survive, you go on, what choice is there?"

"Or perhaps a hidden anger."

"No." Lang shook his head. "No. You know your mother. Your mother is not an angry person. She's very even-tempered. Adults come to terms with things. Accept things."

"Yes, well." Imogen stood up, clutching bag and parasol. "Some things are harder to accept than others. Now really I must go."

He looked her up and down. "I can't help but observe that the benefits of a medical education seem few. Your mother is suffering, Imogen. We are all suffering. And you can't be of any assistance?"

"Because the problem you're describing, Father, is not medical. No one expects a doctor to cure heartbreak. Or loneliness. Or humiliation."

"You said yourself depression is at the heart of this case."

"What case is that?" Rose came in and set a tray down on the corner of the desk.

"A hypothetical, my dear."

She poured her husband a cup of coffee from a silver pot. "Ah, yes, your hypotheticals. Shall I bring a cup for you, Imogen?"

"No, thank you, Mother. I'm just on my way out."

"Shame. So nice to see you discussing case law with your father, though surely Alice is more qualified." She turned to her husband and picked up the tray, her pale features expressing nothing. "I believe I'll go and lie down for a while. These sudden changes in the weather always flatten one so."


Working at Willard's Sixty-Third Street Pharmacy four days a week proved to be demanding enough that Imogen could not think about her father, or her mother, or Quentin. It was hard on the back and the ankles to be standing behind a counter all day, but she needed the money, since her father was never going to support her psychiatric ambitions. When she had applied for the job, old Mr. Willard—a Victorian relic in apron and sleeve garters—asked her many questions about her scientific and medical education, so many she thought she might soon be compounding medicines at his side, a not unwelcome extension of her education.

But it was not to be. Willard's was a thriving enterprise, and its proprietor needed her help behind the counter, serving customers. At least he didn't expect her to man the soda fountain. That job belonged to a boy named Zach, who was probably the skinniest, and certainly the cheeriest, specimen of male adolescence Imogen had ever seen.

She sold two Owl Eye glass eyes one week, and a surprising number of Gold Pheasant condoms, not one of them to a man. She'd already had to put them on Mr. Willard's reorder list twice.

"Hah. Apparently we serve a troop of secret minxes," he said. "The good ladies are relieved to be buying their husbands' sheaths from a woman. Although at these numbers I sense a triumph of optimism over reality."

Physician or no, Imogen was not comfortable discussing condoms with her employer, and steered his attention to a recent run on Hoofland's German Tonic. "I don't understand it," she said. "It can't possibly do the things it claims."

"That's why they call it a tonic. General pick-me-up."

"I mean, at least the toothache drops work."

Mr. Willard regarded her, his face a collage of eyebrows and spectacles. "The field of medicine, my dear, is not a paradise of pure reason."

The shop's customers were mostly women, and they all expected a personal consultation with Mr. Willard, who had been prescribing for their colds, rashes, moods, and digestive issues for decades. He took great pride in having an MD on staff, and made sure all his customers knew it. When they began asking Imogen for advice, she was diffident about giving it and referred them to Mr. Willard. "No, no," he insisted, "by all means consult with Dr. Lang. She has my every confidence."

His view darkened, however, as the weeks went by and his customers began to tell him they would come back when the doctor was in. The only ladies who remained loyal to him were so aged that they found the idea of a female physician preposterous. He began to be grumpy with Imogen, even rude.

Some of the customers also began to chat with her on a personal level, encouraging her to forgo further education and remain in the pharmacy right there on Sixty-Third Street. She soon learned not to mention her plan to study psychiatry. Many did not know the term, and when she explained, they reacted with muted horror. Alienists, after all, worked in the state hospitals—asylums housing two or three thousand lost souls, most of them incurable.

One of her regulars was more sophisticated. "You should try for superintendent," Mrs. Ludlow told her. "They make the money, I'm telling you. Look at all the jobs they get to hand out. Plus you'd get a big fancy house for nothing. I don't believe there's ever been a woman in charge of a state hospital."

"No," Imogen said. "I'm sure not."

"The assistant psychiatrists have a bum time of it. I have a nephew who's an assistant at Worcester. Lives on the hospital grounds, never gets enough time off to go anywhere, and the pay is terrible."

"Well, their housing is paid for too."

"But it's a pokey little place. And it's not as if he ever cures anybody, is it? Teddy tells me the only people who get better are the maniacs."

"Manic-depressives, you mean."

"That's them. And they only get better because that's the nature of it. The spells come and go. Got nothing to do with the doctors. When it goes, they let 'em out."

"Well, I'm hoping to secure a position in a clinic. Some place much smaller than an asylum."

"You're not a follower of Herr Freud are you? Teddy told me about that man's theories. Disgusting."

"Yes, well, I don't imagine I'll be psychoanalyzing anyone anytime soon."

Detecting a certain cooling in Mrs. Ludlow's regard, Imogen placed her items—five-grain aspirin, Kelsey's Hair Restorer, and a bottle of Lloyd's Cocaine Drops for Toothache—in a paper sack and counted out her change.


Even though she had told Quentin she would no longer reply, his letters kept coming, sometimes consisting of no more than a single sentence, and not always a coherent one. *If only you were here*, he might write, *but you're not*. Another, more alarming, purported to be his own sardonic death notice; it was hard to tell from his tone how worried she should be. But when she received yet another letter that implied in various ways that his life was no longer worth living, Imogen felt she should notify someone.

She sat down one rainy afternoon on her day off to use the typewriter in her father's study.

Dear Dr. Goodchild,

In the course of my studies at Rush Medical College I had the good fortune to enjoy the friendship of your son, Quentin. Although our relationship was friendly, even affectionate, it was never romantic and I tried always to make clear the limits of my feelings. However, Quentin has been sending me letters this summer which would seem to indicate he has not accepted this, and that he wants a romantic involvement, which never existed, to extend into a limitless future.

That some woman will one day be made happy in marriage with your son, I have no doubt. Unfortunately, I am not she—not through any defect of Quentin's but owing to my own limitations and ambitions. One of Quentin's greatest qualities is his sensitivity, and please believe me that I grieve to be the one inflicting pain on him. He would be mortified and perhaps outraged to learn I have said even this much to you, but I feel I must because his letters have taken a darker turn and I fear he may harm himself in some way.

If you can somehow help him through this painful time without mentioning that I have written to you, that might be for the best. With every wish that we could have met under happier circumstances, I am,

Yours truly,
Imogen Lang

She pulled the sheet from the typewriter, signed it, and folded it in three. She typed the address on a plain envelope, put the letter inside, and sealed it. No return address. That would look peculiar—it might even alert Quentin—but using her own address was out of the question, and using a false one struck her as both dishonest and liable to backfire in some unforeseen manner.

She put a stamp on the envelope and left her father's study. The house was mostly quiet; her younger sisters were downtown, no doubt torturing the sales staff at Neiman Marcus and Marshall Field's. She could hear Mrs. Bidwell banging about the kitchen, preparing dinner.

Rose was upstairs in her bedroom, paralytic with migraine, she said. Her father and Alice would not be home for hours.

She collected the post and sorted through the bills and letters. Nothing for her father; most of his correspondence went to the office. Various letters in girlish handwriting for her sisters. Some official-looking envelopes from charitable foundations for her mother. Nothing, thankfully, from Quentin.

Imogen took her raincoat from the vestibule and put it on. She slipped the letter into her bag, selected a pearl-handled umbrella from the hall stand, and went out. If she hurried, she could make the three-fifteen post.

On a weekday afternoon toward the middle of August, Quentin himself turned up. Somehow he had discovered where she was employed, and figured out which streetcar she would have to take to get home. He was waiting at her stop like a figure in a dream. It must have taken him days, and more than one train, to travel from Lake Placid to this corner of Chicago.

"You're wrong, you know." That was the first thing he said to her.

Imogen did not know how to reply. The evening was cloudy, the light a smudged, dirty grey. People pushed by her as she stood there.

"You're wrong," he said again. Strain showed in the lines around his eyes, the tightness of his mouth.

"Quentin, you shouldn't have come."

"We're more than friends, Imogen. We always were, right from the start. We just didn't know what to call it. I didn't. I do now."

"Quentin, please."

She stepped into the lee of a newsstand to get out of the way of people heading home.

"Don't worry, I'm not here to make any more pleas. You needn't write to my father again."

"Oh, dear."

"He didn't come to the summer house this year. He's staying with friends in Canada."

"You open his mail?"

"You can hardly claim the moral high ground, contacting him behind my back."

"I was worried about you. You seemed so despairing. Your letter—"

"I know. I know. I don't want you to feel bad about me. But I just hate the idea of life without you."

"But you can't expect any one person to—"

"I know that—it's exactly what I told Jack, who told me not to come here, by the way. Doesn't matter. One thing I learned this summer, other than the fact that I can write even when I'm feeling desperate, is that I haven't the courage to kill myself. It would be easy enough— Lake Placid's full of shotguns, and there's no shortage of places to drown or cliffs to leap from, but I can't do it. So I'm going to let the Germans do it."

"The Germans! We're not even at war!"

"The U.S. isn't. But I've signed up with the Canadian Expeditionary Force—97th Battalion. They're calling us the American Legion. We ship out in a couple of weeks."

"Quentin, you'll get yourself killed."

"That's the idea. Some lucky Hun does me the favour, and I'm out of your way—and mine—forever."

"Quentin—please!" She clutched his arm but he pulled away. "I don't want you to die—I want you to live a long and happy life."

"Without you, that's not possible. You'll never know how much I, how much I—well, it doesn't matter now."

He turned and hurried away from her through the smoke and tumult of a Chicago evening. Imogen called his name until she could no longer see him, and then broke down in tears.

✁

That night she couldn't stop thinking of one of Quentin's poems, a ballad of many stanzas, each one ending with the phrase "into that fever, into that fire." Sometimes he seemed to be talking about love, sometimes about an inner struggle—the meaning changed with each repetition—but now there seemed no doubt at all about what he meant. She sought solace from her mother, something she had not done for several years. The two of them sat in the front parlour after dinner, on the blue velvet sofa that faced a mantelpiece covered with family photographs.

Imogen gave a condensed version of the situation. A friend, someone she'd known since her first year at Rush, was passionately in love with her but she was not in love with him. And now he had joined a foreign army in hopes of being killed.

"He sounds a very unstable fellow," her mother said.

"But he isn't. Not usually. I can't imagine anyone more honest, loyal, dependable."

"In that case, why don't you marry him—assuming he has an income."

"He's also eccentric and excitable."

"Obviously—if he's running off to join the Foreign Legion."

"The *American* Legion—it's part of a Canadian battalion. The Canadians are at war, Mother."

"Well, I don't know what you expect me to do about it—warn the border authorities? Broker a peace treaty?"

"No, I just—"

"Just what, dear? Surely you've noticed by now that men were put on this earth for the sole purpose of making life difficult."

"Never mind, Mother."

"Is that why you asked me in here? To make me feel useless?"

"Of course not. I just thought, you know, you might have had a similar experience at one time. That you—"

"That I what? That I had a kind and intelligent man fall in love with me? That I spurned him and lived to tell the tale?"

"I hoped you might be able to tell me how to deal with this."

"Your father was the only man who ever courted me. It never occurred to me to turn my back on him. If you have no wish to marry the man, I don't see what the loss is."

"Mother, he's my closest friend."

"Men and women can never be friends. Really, my dear, it's hard to see the point of medical school if you haven't learned that. Anyway, Miriam Landis is your best friend."

"I haven't seen Miriam in years. We have nothing in common anymore."

"I thought that's why you went to medical school—to be uncommon."

"To be useful. Not uncommon."

"And now you're going to study psychiatry. Hardly an endeavour designed to attract suitors. Quite the opposite I should say."

"Mother, I'm not talking about suitors. I'm talking about a friend."

"You didn't lose a friend. You lost a beau. He was right to declare his feelings—honest, as you say. He no longer chose to be deluded about what was going on—you, it seems, chose otherwise. In any case, the man has now seen the light. He is in love, you are not. Joining the army is quite traditional in such cases."

"But I feel so bereft!"

"You're not allowed to feel bereft after you send someone packing."

"I didn't send him packing. I just said I didn't want to marry him. I can't bear the thought of his being killed over there."

"Once he starts shooting at Germans, I don't see how you can be held responsible for the outcome." Her mother got up and went to the door, pausing for a moment with her hand on the knob. "I don't know why you're so keen on psychiatry, Imogen. You're an intelligent young woman, but you don't seem overly insightful."

"All the more reason to study it."

"A psychiatrist would require a deal of compassion, as well. Evidently not your strong suit."

"Thanks a million, Mother. Really. I feel so much better."

For the first time, Imogen wondered if her mother had always been like this. Could it be that her father's betrayal was as much a result of Rose Lang's blasted heart as a cause? She remembered overhearing the two of them talking once when she was very little, perhaps a year or two after Laura's death. "Are you resolved never to be happy again?" her father had asked. "Happy?" her mother responded. "No. I shall try to be cheerful at times, but I shall never be happy."

Now it was the last week of August and Imogen was seated on a bench in the first-class waiting room of Chicago's Union Station, watching the massive clock tick toward boarding time.

She had taken the Limited only once before, when she was a girl of six, with Alice and her mother. The younger girls were not yet born. Laura had died the year before, and the household was still enveloped in gloom. Perhaps as a welcome distraction, her father had planned an educational trip to Washington D.C. to show the girls the nation's centre of government. Her mother, not yet the near invalid she would become, was involved in the City Beautiful movement, and was gratified to learn from her travel brochure that the train tracks had at last been removed from the National Mall.

"They're planning to build a stupendous monument to Abraham Lincoln at the far end," she told the children, "so there will be a pure green vista from the White House to the memorial, whatever shape it may take. Oh, your father would've been so excited to see this."

"Then why didn't he come?" fifteen-year-old Alice inquired with a litigious edge.

"The poor man had to change plans at the last minute. You mustn't be upset, dears. Your father works tirelessly to support all of us. That is how he shows his love, and we must all be grateful for it."

Imogen remembered her mother's silhouette against the rushing green hills, the balled-up handkerchief she used to dab her eyes.

She had felt like crying too. Even with the excitement of the train trip, it was impossible to forget about Laura. Her own reflection in the window was a perfect, if transparent, reproduction of her dead sister's face. Despite her own ache for Laura, she tried to cheer her mother up. She didn't go anywhere without the miniature notepad and pencil that hung from the ribbon around her neck. She took the notepad now and printed one word in neat rounded letters and jabbed her finger against the windowpane, which was surprisingly cold.

"Don't, dear," her mother said, lightly clutching her wrist with two gloved fingers and holding it away. "You'll leave fingerprints."

"Shouldn't she be wearing gloves?" Alice said without looking up from her *Harper's Bazaar*. "Everyone else is."

"She's too young for gloves."

Imogen pointed again, without touching the glass.

"Yes, dear. Cows. Aren't they lovely."

Imogen printed a few more words and showed them to her mother.

"Happy? I'm not sure they look happy. Contented, perhaps."

Alice sat forward and glanced out the window. "They won't be happy when they find out what they're in for."

"Whatever can you mean, Alice? They're dairy cows. They're not going to the slaughterhouse."

"Well, not today."

Imogen printed *slotter* and a question mark in her notebook and showed it to her mother. You couldn't live in Chicago without smelling the slaughterhouses, but somehow her parents had managed to preserve her ignorance concerning the provenance of their Sunday roasts.

"Never mind, dear."

*What means slotter house?*

"You're too young for that word. Now take out your book, there's a good girl."

Imogen took a last lingering look at the picture of bovine meditation, the only movement the twirl of a leaf-shaped ear, the flick of a tail. All but one of the cattle were lying down, front legs neatly folded, back legs outstretched to one side. Dark liquid eyes contemplated the passing train.

An hour or two later, Imogen saw another patch of cows, curled up in similar positions under a similar tree, as if they had just been arranged there for the benefit of the approaching train. Even their expressions were the same.

Imogen printed urgently on her notepad, *Look, Mother. Same cows?*

Her mother glanced out the window.

"No, dear. Not the same cows. Those other cows must be eighty or ninety miles from here."

Imogen took the pad back. *Flying cows. They just landed.*

Her mother gave her a weak smile. "Flying cows. That must be it, dear."

"Cows don't fly," Alice said, "ignoramus."


"Dr. Lang? Dr. Lang?" A boy of about twelve, wearing the blue uniform of the Adams Express Company, was hurrying through the waiting room carrying two white buckets. Imogen looked around to see which of the moustached gentlemen might answer, before she realized he must be looking for her. He reached the end of the waiting room, pivoted on one heel like a mechanical toy, and started back. The buckets looked heavy for him.

Imogen rose from her seat and signalled him with a gloved hand.

"You have something for me?"

"Are you Dr. Lang?"

"Yes."

"Okey-doke." He put down the buckets, and took a receipt book from the leather pouch attached to his shoulder strap. "Just sign here, if you would, ma'am."

"What am I signing for—a telegram?"

"No, ma'am, but there's an envelope attached to one of these."

"Surely you can't mean the buckets."

"Why, yes, ma'am—Doctor, I should say—see here?" He pointed to the receipt. "Two sealed buckets. They're heavy. I'll fetch a porter for you."

"No, thank you. I'll manage."

"It's my instructions."

She signed his book and he tore off a yellow copy and handed it to her.

"Thank you."

"You're welcome, Doctor. Have a safe trip."

He lifted his cap, pivoted once more on his heel, and was gone.

Imogen sat down and pulled the buckets closer; they smelled of formalin. She detached the envelope and opened it. The note was from Dean Dodson—a nervous, rabbity, rushing sort of man who always reminded Imogen of the March Hare. But perhaps that was because the name Dodson was so like Dodgson.

Dear Dr. Lang,

   Please forgive my burdening you with these two brain specimens. One of the buckets, as you see, is for Professor William Welch, head of Hopkins' Pathology dep't, the other (clearly labelled) is for Dr. Ganz. I assure you they will be delighted to receive them, and it will be an excellent way for you to introduce yourself to men whose good opinion cannot be overvalued.

   Let me take this opportunity once again to congratulate you on your sterling achievement here at Rush, and wish you continued success in your sojourn at Hopkins and the Phipps. There simply could be no better place to learn the intricacies of modern psychiatry than at the feet of Jonas Ganz. You are a lucky young physician!

   With admiration and every good wish, I remain yours truly,

Prof. John W. Dodson, MD
Dean of Students
Rush Medical College

The clock struck four, and the double oak doors swung open. A man in the grey-and-blue livery of the B&O line walked swiftly through the waiting room announcing that Train No. 6 was now boarding. As the men in their bowlers and boaters rose around Imogen, a porter appeared and asked her if he could be of assistance.

"Oh, yes, please." She stood and pointed to the buckets.

"And the valise, miss?"

"I can manage that. The rest has been checked."

"Certainly. This way." She followed him as he plowed through the crowd, calling cheerfully, "Coming through, gentlemen. Lady coming through. Thank you, sir, thank you. Lady coming through."

The track shed, under its vast arched ceiling of iron and glass, was redolent of soot and smoke and hot metal. Imogen could feel coal dust filming her skin and wished she were wearing a hat with a veil like the more sensible women around her.

A conductor glanced at her ticket and helped her onto the step. "On your left, miss."

The porter followed.

"Miss, have you rode this train before today?"

"Only once. When I was a child."

"Oh, you'll find lots of changes then. I speck you'll be most comfortable. Next on your right, miss, that's it, let me get the do' for you."

He slid the door open and followed her in. He took her valise and set it on a fold-out rack in the miniature closet, and stowed the buckets under one of the seats.

Imogen tipped him and, after he was gone, stood for a while watching the passengers and porters hurrying by to their various cars. She picked up a folder tucked into the windowsill and read that dinner would be served between 5:30 and 7:00, breakfast from 5:45 to 8:30 a.m. Central Time.

She slid the folder back in place, removed her hat and gloves, and set them on the upper rack in the closet. Her seat was comfortable, its plush wings marked with the B&O trademark. She rested her head against one and closed her eyes, gathering herself. She had been keyed up for more than two weeks, what with all the planning and packing. She opened her eyes to check the platform for any member of her family but no one had come to see her off.

The train whistle shrieked and a jolt shuddered through the cars, the hitches adjusting like so many iron vertebrae. As the train rounded the first curve, Imogen looked back to watch the dome of Union Station receding. Warning bells clanged as the train crossed intersection after intersection, pedestrians covering their ears or averting their faces from the flying smoke and cinders.

Imogen had never been particularly fond of the city's skyscrapers, but in leaving them behind she felt as if she were venturing beyond the safe confines of a frontier fort. The thought caused a sudden ache in her throat. She got up and went into the tiny bathroom. The china fixtures had the miniature exquisiteness of dollhouse furniture and immediately cheered her. She washed her face, and held a cool facecloth to her eyes.

When the conductor came to punch her ticket, she asked what time they would reach Baltimore, although she knew the answer.

"Ten thirty-seven a.m.," he said, and slid the door shut again behind him.

Her compartment was meant for two passengers and Imogen soon found herself wishing for company, someone devastatingly interesting—perhaps one of those muckraking journalists one heard so much about. Or a New York psychiatrist, someone she could pepper with questions on Kraepelin's categories or Charcot's lectures on male hysterics.

It was at times like these Imogen found herself wishing for the one sister who could never be with her. She opened her bag and took out her wallet. From this she extracted a much-folded, much-weathered slip of newsprint not much bigger than a postage stamp, a death notice her parents had clipped from the *Tribune* some sixteen years past. *Laura Rose Lang, born May 3, 1894, died Friday, June 24, 1899, of a cruel illness which she endured with a Stoicism far beyond her years. Mourned by father Josiah, mother Rose, sisters Alice and Imogen. Private burial at Oak Park cemetery.*

Imogen fingered the slip of paper that was softened, almost moist, with age and handling. She pressed it between her palms for a few moments, then put it back in her wallet and put the wallet away.

She spoke to her reflection in the window, in a whisper, "And what do you have to say about all this?"

"Careful," Laura said. "You could end up in one of those buckets, if you keep talking to your dead sister."

Imogen pulled the buckets out from under the seat. According to the laboratory tags, one was an example of a degenerative disorder. The other was a female with dementia praecox. Imogen wondered how old she had been, how long she had been an asylum inmate. Dementia praecox cases could be admitted at age eighteen or twenty and spend the next forty years on a back ward. Nobody knew what caused it, and so far there was no cure.

"I just imagine you," she thought, looking back at her reflection. "It's not the same as hallucinating."

"Still," Laura said, "what would your two buckety friends make of it? Is there such a difference between you hearing the dead and a schizophrenic hearing voices?"

"There is a vast difference," Imogen thought, "because I know you're not really here."

She pulled the blind down and regarded the two buckets, imagining the brains still capable of thought, imprisoned in that darkness. She could not help them now and never could have. But maybe someday, if she worked hard.

She opened her satchel and took out Pierre Janet's *Histoire d'une idée fixe*, along with a *Petit Masson*, and tried to read a chapter. After half an hour of frustration, and to cheer herself up, she reached into the satchel again and took out the crisp envelope with the Johns Hopkins letterhead and once more read the letter that had thrilled her—and had changed her life—back in May.

Dear Dr. Lang,

I am most pleased to inform you that your application for a staff assignment here at the Phipps Psychiatric Clinic has been accepted. Your Bachelor of Science degree will set you in considerable measure above most of your colleagues, who will have MDs but lack your pure science background.

Most of your contemporaries, certainly those coming from within Johns Hopkins, will have had at minimum a semester of psychobiology, at least one rotation in an asylum, and some a good deal more. For your own benefit, I advise you to read Kraepelin's *Psychologie*, Charcot's *Leçons du mardi*, and Janet's *Histoire d'une idée fixe* before you arrive.

I note that you have only high school French and as far as I can tell no German. Acquiring both is simply essential if one is to keep up with the advances coming out of Zurich, Vienna, and Paris, as the journals are not available in English, and I warn you away from translated books as they are never current. Kraepelin in particular revises himself so thoroughly that each edition of his *Psychiatrie* is radically different from the previous one.

I have reserved a place for you beginning September 1, 1916. However, if there would be any prospect of your coming East before that I should be very glad to see you and to talk over the plans of work more specifically.

I look forward to our meeting with keen anticipation.

Yours truly,

Jonas Ganz, MD
Director, Henry Phipps Psychiatric Clinic
Johns Hopkins University
Baltimore Md.

At seven o'clock she went to the dining car, where a steward showed her to a table, and pointed out the menu. A highly efficient waiter brought her a basket of fragrant rolls and took her order. The elegance of her surroundings—the carved wood, the gently swinging lanterns, the sparkling glass and silver—was soothing. She enjoyed every bite of her cucumber salad and cutlet of capon, every sip of her chilled Chablis.

When she returned to her compartment the sleeping berth had been lowered. She sat on the seat opposite and pulled out her volume of Kraepelin but didn't open it. It was sad, really, having no one to share all this with: the beautiful service, the rippling hills that seemed like the landscape of another planet after the flatness of Chicago, not to mention her destination—a great university, where she would study under the man whom everybody called the dean of American psychiatry.

Night began to pool in the valleys of the Adirondacks. Patches of woods rushed up to the windows and as quickly receded. Fences whipped up and down. High on a hillside, in the last ounce of daylight, a herd of cows lay flicking their tails.

"Flying cows," she said softly.

She put Kraepelin aside and pulled the compartment blind as low as it would go. A small night lamp gave just enough glow that she could see to change into her nightdress and lay her clothes out for morning. She climbed into the berth and plumped two pillows, planning to read. She lay back, thinking of all she had to do and of her upcoming meeting with Professor Ganz. She thought of Laura, and how stupendous it would be if there really were two of them heading off to Johns Hopkins instead of just one.

She turned on her side and for a few moments indulged morbid thoughts about the contents of those buckets. Buckets of mad thoughts, mental storms, bolts of lightning in the cortex. For a few moments she pictured herself working with patients, calming those mental storms, making discoveries in the lab. And then she was asleep.

# 3

A few months after Vimy, a new lieutenant was brought in to replace his predecessor, who had been killed, not by Germans, but by the influenza virus. Lieutenant Pegram, like so many of the Canadian officers, had a crisp British manner and the wispy officer's moustache that had become *de rigueur*—the wispier the better. He had only been in place for a week when he summoned Quentin to his dugout.

"I'm told you're American."

"Yes, sir."

"What the hell are you doing fighting for George the Fifth?"

"I volunteered, sir."

"Says here you attested into the 97th in Windsor, Ontario, of your own free will."

"That's correct, sir."

"And then got shuffled into the 10th."

"Yes, sir."

"Got any special talents?"

"Talents, sir?"

"Skills. Useful abilities."

"I write pretty well, sir. And I'm an excellent typist."

"What sort of things do you write?"

"Stories, sir. And I'm working on a novel."

"Anything published?"

"Not yet, sir."

"I'm concerned about morale, Goodchild. The men need entertainment, humour, light moments. I'm dismayed to find this battalion has no newspaper."

"Newspaper, sir?"

"Lot of the battalions publish their own newspaper. Strictly unofficial, you understand, but a chance to whine and moan a bit—all in good fun. Why don't you write up a first issue and bring it to me? I've got a couple of samples you can look at."

"Is that an order, sir?"

"Does it have to be?"

"No, I—"

"Fine. Consider it an order. Forty-eight hours enough time? Make it Tuesday, just before lunch."

The sample sheets Pegram gave him were the kind of juvenile, jokey stuff Quentin would never pen himself. He tried a more literary approach, while including actual news such as the battalion honour roll, and entertainment plans for the upcoming training period.

"No, Goodchild, this will never do," Pegram told him. "You write a good sentence, but we can't have a serious discussion of the war. You have to make it funnier."

Quentin took another run at it, abandoning all literary ambition, and banged out several pages in a couple of hours. He took the new version to the lieutenant.

"That's it exactly, Goodchild," Pegram said. "You've hit the tone exactly. The men will love it."

Such was the birth of the 10th Battalion's *Dead Mule Gazette*.

The latest edition was to include an important interview.

BOCHES APOLOGIZE!

Yes, it's true. The moment we've all been waiting for has finally arrived. In an exclusive interview with the Mule, Gerhard Goetheimer extends a heartfelt apology to all the Allied Forces, but in particular to the 10th Battalion, 1st Canadian Division.

The interview took place at the *Mule* offices [location classified but easily locatable by the odour of expired mule]. Captain Goetheimer arrived looking tired but dapper in his customary whites, his knobby features softened by a rakish goatee. He declined the offer of tea but seemed to enjoy his evaporated milk. "It's been 18 months since I saw one of these in Germany," he said, taking a bite out of the tin. He proceeded to answer our questions with great good humour, in his accented English.

DM: You've been with us now six weeks, Captain Goetheimer.

GG: Please. Call me Gerhard. I'm not a captain anymore. I renounce all association with the German army.

DM: All right, Gerhard. Six weeks you've been with us. What would you say are the principal differences between Canadian troops and the Germans?

GG: Oh, your use of toilet paper. The Germans, as you know, refuse to use it on the grounds that it would be unmanly.

DM: Anything else?

GG: Your policy on the equitable treatment of goats. I wish more countries would adopt it but I don't see it happening anytime soon. I imagine women will get there first.

DM: All right, let's get down to brass tacks, shall we?

GG: By all means. I love tacks. Upholstery tacks, carpet tacks, really anything except gas attacks.

DM: Let's talk about those, Gerhard. What were you thinking?

GG: I suppose we thought it would be kinder than bullets and bayonets. No bloodshed. We thought you'd be grateful.

DM: Grateful for poison gas.

GG: You fellows use gas too, you know.

DM: Not mustard gas. Burning? Blistering? You think that's fair play?

GG: Well, it wouldn't have been my choice. I don't even like mustard on my bratwurst.

DM: Gerhard, you seem like a nice goat. Why did you start the war?

GG: I had a feeling you'd ask me that. I know it's been something
    of an inconvenience.

DM: Inconvenience!

GG: All right, a bother then.

DM: A bother! You do realize you've upset our hockey schedule
    for three years running?

GG: I know. It's regrettable.

DM: And more than a few of us have been forced to alter our
    vacation plans.

GG: You boys in the 10th?

DM: Of course us boys in the 10th!

GG: Well, I'm sorry. I—[pauses, apparently moved] I'm so sorry.
    Let me apologize right now—sincerely and without reserve—
    for interfering with your sports schedule. If we'd had any idea,
    honestly, we would never have started this little punch-up.
    Listen, may I ask you a question?

DM: Yes, of course.

GG: Who is this Arch-Duck Ferdinand?

Quentin tore the last page from the typewriter and headed outside.

The morning was uncharacteristically sunny for northern France. Men were kicking a soccer ball about. He stopped by the lieutenant's dugout and dropped off the typescript—the censors had to approve it before he could print it. The only question was whether there would be time to distribute it before the order came to attack.

For weeks now they had been arrayed nine miles behind the front lines for purposes of rehearsal. The objective was the French town of Lens, which the British (and thus the Canadians) needed for coal and the Germans needed for railways. The Germans had been holding it almost since they first set boot in France. Even from this distance, he could see the Canadian observation balloons tugging lazily at the ends of their wires, snouts toward the enemy.

The wrinkle in the plan was that in order to take Lens they had to first take Hill 70, which overlooked it. It was a ready-made redoubt, the area having been deeply mined for chalk. The Germans had added a warren of dugouts and trenches and barbed wire coiled yards deep and as high as a man. Concrete pillboxes protected a dozen or more machine gun units. Any attacking force risked drowning in its own blood; many would die, many would wish they had.

A group of volunteer scouts, working between the lines under cover of darkness, had confirmed the defensive details. One moonless night they had even managed to capture a fifty-man German patrol, an act of insane bravery for which they were berated by their captain before being decorated with Military Crosses.

The Canadian breakthrough at Vimy had been hailed as a miracle, but it had actually been the result of repeated, detailed, almost brutal rehearsal. Quentin and his platoon had been completely skeptical, resenting it bitterly at the time, but now found themselves glad to do it again at Lens. Of course it wasn't just the rehearsal. At Vimy they had learned the value of a relentless barrage. Quentin had actually felt sorry for the Germans as the heavier stuff pounded them for days and days. Surely nothing could live through that. When it came time to go over the top, his unit knew exactly where they were going and what to do when they got there.

This time the engineers had constructed a vast two-dimensional version of Hill 70, and marked out the three objectives: Blue Line was the Germans' firing trench, Red Line was their support trench, and Green Line their reserve trench at the top of the hill. They had been practising positions and advances for an entire month.

They'd drilled and attacked each other, covered head to toe in protective gear, including gas mask and respirator boxes in the murderous August heat. The visors of their masks steamed up in minutes, blinding them. Several men fainted and one died of heat prostration.

All this time they could hear the thud of Canadian and Royal artillery from the front lines, softening up the target. "Giving the bastards a taste of their own medicine," Lieutenant Pegram had said. "Nice thing about chlorine is, it's heavier than air. Sinks into those trenches and follows 'em right into those mines."

Quentin had always thought of Canadians, to the extent he'd thought of them at all, as rural, reasonable, polite. "It doesn't bother you, sir?" he said to Pegram.

"What, gas? I don't lose any sleep over it. The Hun is not your normal enemy. Different thing."

Different thing. Quentin had written the phrase in his notebook, and felt the first threads of a poem weaving around it. This war was definitely a "different thing."

At Vimy, the Germans had held a five-mile ridge that gave them a perfect vista over their enemy for years. By the time the Canadians had arrived, no man's land was a cratered, reeking graveyard littered with corpses, bones, teeth and even heads. Every so often a shell would hit and blast the buried once more into the murderous light. Quentin felt himself turning to stone, and knew it was either that or go mad.

If his joining up in Canada had been the first step in planned suicide, it soon became something else. He had had no understanding of how solitary his former life had been until the Canadian Expeditionary Force had ended that solitude. To be suddenly surrounded by crowds of other young men, mostly rough and untutored, had been a shock, and for the first couple of weeks of training he felt sick with regret.

It took several more weeks for him to admit that he was often enjoying himself. Of course, this happiness did not in any way resemble what he had imagined happiness to be. It involved no woman, it involved no literary success; it was a banishment of self. *The absence of all reflection is absolute opium*, he'd written in his notebook. *I inhale it and disappear and find myself, for the first time in my life, at peace.*

Even so, during basic training in Toronto he had pined for Imogen, and he was still yearning for her when he was shipped out of Montreal on the RMS *Metagama*. Through the weeks of drill and bayonet practice and exercises in trench-building he had managed to hold on to his suicidal ardour, his ambition to walk straight into the path of a German bullet. But then he found himself on the foredeck of the *Metagama* astounded, as so many poets before him, by the immensity of the sea—its power, its million shades of blue and black and green, its lace and froth of foam. He adored its noises, from sibilant whisper to thunderous crash, and wished for Imogen to turn to, his wonder demanding to be shared.

The *Metagama* was not huge, carrying only two hundred troops. They were not more than a few miles beyond Newfoundland when Reggie Bick, a Leamington farm boy who had attached himself to Quentin, had come running up the foredeck where Quentin was attempting to stave off seasickness by inhaling the wild wet breezes.

"You won't believe it," Bick said, taking hold of Quentin by both biceps and shaking him. "There's girls on board."

"There *are* girls on board."

"There *are* girls on board. There really are, boss. Supposed to be two dozen of 'em, and every one of 'em's a nurse. Ain't that a beautiful thing?"

"*Isn't* that a beautiful thing."

"Well, *isn't* it?"

"Indeed it is a beautiful thing," Quentin agreed, "if true."

"How can you speak proper English at a time like this?"

"You asked me to correct you."

"I know, but still. You should be more excited."

Quentin had intended to avoid friendship. To make a friend implied that you had a future. At night, turning in his narrow cot, the close air reeking with the smell of the vomit pails, he would curse himself for not being true to his aims. Perhaps he was too gregarious to be a good writer, or perhaps he was just vanquished by loneliness and hurt, but he found himself constantly drawn into conversations with the other men and even, sometimes, enjoying their rude company. The camaraderie of shared misfortune—bad food, overcrowding, stupid officers—was irresistible.

Private Bick had overheard Quentin describing to someone the clarity and calm of Lake Placid, and had edged closer as Quentin talked. Another time Bick was part of a card game after which a curious soldier had asked Quentin to name his favourite book. Quentin had ended up relating almost the entire plot of *Madame Bovary*, and Bick listened with a rapt expression.

The next day Quentin had been gripping the rail, having just ejected his breakfast into the St. Lawrence, when he had felt a tap on his shoulder.

"Sorry," Bick said. "I guess you're not feeling too well."

"You're a master of understatement, Bick."

"I just gotta ask you—quick, while there's no one else around. Promise you won't laugh at me?"

"At this moment, neither Fatty Arbuckle nor Charlie Chaplin could get a laugh out of me."

"Promise, though?"

"Solemn vow. Pain of death."

"I can't help but notice that you talk so good. I'm just wondering if I could learn to speak like that. You know—not fancy or nothing— just really getting the most out of it. I love listening to you, man! Would you do me a favour, just while we're crossing, of maybe correcting me when I speak wrong?"

Quentin had protested—it would be boring for both of them and would end up irritating Bick—but Bick would not be dissuaded. His eyes gleamed with terrible sincerity, and in the end Quentin said yes, fully expecting he wouldn't bump into Bick more than once or twice over the entire voyage—an expectation that proved unfounded as the little man sought him out time and again, wanting to chatter about anything at all so long as Quentin would correct him.

"If you was gonna recommend one author—just one author above all others—who taught you how to speak good English, who would you—"

"Charles Dickens."

"Dickens. Really? But I read that book—Tiny Tim and all that?—and I still talk pretty bad."

"Read some of the others. *David Copperfield, Great Expectations.* And it's speak badly, not talk bad."

"Speak badly. Why?"

"Because *speak* is a verb, and when you want to describe a verb you need an adverb, not an adjective. Stick an *-ly* on the end and you're all set."

"Magic. Thanks, Goodchild. See? You already got me speaking goodly. That's a joke. The *goodly*, I mean."

Bick was right about the nurses. There was a contingent of twenty-four on board the *Metagama*, and a dance was organized for Wednesday night. A list of rules for proper behaviour had been drawn up and much discussed; many wondered if the nursing sisters, too, had been similarly drilled. Quentin had felt somewhat uneasy before the dance, fearing that a few men might disgrace themselves in ways that would bring shame on them all. But perhaps it was the restricted amount of alcohol, perhaps it was being away from home for the first time, or simply that most of the men were so young—whatever the reason, they beheld these young women, most of them by no means beautiful, with something approaching awe.

Quentin was not exempt. Although he admired Imogen for being intrepid in her pursuit of a career in a distinctly male world, he had not previously associated women with the word *bravery*. All of these nurses were volunteers and, although they would not be placed right on the front lines, they would of necessity be located in extremely dangerous proximity. Already many nurses had been killed or wounded. *Sisters*: the British-Canadian term implied virginity and vocation, devotion, spirituality, humble if foolish self-sacrifice. The moment they entered the ship's recreation hall, in their blue-and-white uniforms and their chaste little caps, coming in two by two and smiling at everyone, the men let out a roar of approval, followed by more sedate applause.

There were not enough women to go round, but the nurses were well prepared for dealing with situations in which they were surrounded and outnumbered by men. No nurse would dance with any man twice in a row, nor would any nurse refuse to dance with any soldier.

Quentin was not an accomplished dancer but as this would be his last chance to enjoy this activity on Earth he decided to do so. He did the foxtrot with a woman from Kingston named Watson and, although he did not find her particularly attractive—features too coarse, too much brass in the voice—he could not help but admire her. The damp warmth of her hand on his shoulder aroused him and the instant the music stopped he found himself asking for another dance.

"Sorry, soldier. Orders are to keep moving."

"Right. I forgot. Well, thank you, Sister."

"Thank you, Private."

There was such a crush of men that he was unable to ask another woman to dance until four songs later. This was Nurse Morley, from Bracebridge originally, latterly a nurse at Toronto General. She was petite, making Quentin feel a lurching hulk by comparison, with an impish, witty look to her. She smelled wonderful.

It was pointless to get to know her, and yet he found himself firing questions at her over the music. He learned that her family was originally from Donegal (no surprise there; her shining black hair and wafer-pale skin were perfectly Irish) but she was born in Ontario. She came from a family of five brothers and two sisters, of which she was the youngest. She became a nurse because it was something an Irish Catholic girl might do other than teach or join a convent. Luckily, she told him, it turned out she loved nursing.

"It's a good feeling, helping people—maybe a selfish feeling, in the end."

"Selfish?"

She shrugged, the blue fabric of her uniform shifting at the shoulders. "I probably wouldn't do it if it didn't make me feel good, so I guess it must be counted as selfish. Are you a Yank?"

Quentin nodded. "From Rochester. And sometimes Lake Placid—upstate New York."

"You're not selfish then—to join up when you don't have to. Why did you?"

For some reason, this girl with her open Irish features compelled honesty. "It seemed a good way to get myself killed."

She searched his face. "Don't be silly. Death's for other people, haven't you heard?"

"I heard it was for everyone eventually."

"Exactly. No need to rush it, then. Do you have people you'll write to? Who'll write to you?"

"My father. I actually enjoy his letters—which is a bit surprising, considering he's usually annoyed with me. And my friend Jack, who sends me poems to criticize. I thought I was going to be a writer, but poetry's beyond me these days. I mostly send him lists of complaints."

"I imagine it's a bit hard, writing poems in the army."

"It is for me, anyway. But perhaps I'm not really a writer."

"Well, you'll just have to get through this war and find out, won't you."

The music stopped and several men were crossing the floor in their direction.

"I'd like to see you again," Quentin said. "On board, I mean. Just to talk. Would that be all right?"

"It would be fine with me," she said, "but I don't know how we could arrange it. They keep us pretty sequestered."

Quentin spoke in a rush: "I'll be on the foredeck every night at 9 p.m. sharp. Come, if you can. If you can't make it, well, have a safe journey—and a good life."

"You too, Private Goodchild," she said.

"Will you tell me your first name?"

"We're not supposed to."

"Mine's Quentin."

"Margaret," she said, and turned with a smile to a beefy lug named Higgins who spoke with a stutter and always lost at cards.

Quentin wandered out on the foredeck alone. The breeze was cold, the stars bright. He looked down at the furrowed sea, the white foam maps that formed and dissolved on its surface and formed again, and wondered why he had responded so easily to this young nurse. Was he prone to falling in love with any female who smiled at him? What would that say about his feelings for Imogen?

He returned to this spot at exactly nine o'clock the following night, when the moon was high. An iceberg gleamed a brilliant slippery white on the black of the sea and he wished that Margaret would come before it slid out of view but she did not. He returned each night thereafter and waited patiently and contemplatively, but still she did not come. Whether this was her choice or the result of a tyrannical matron he had no way of knowing. No other nurses appeared on deck either, in moonlight or daylight. They were kept as separate and apart as if they were sequestered in a convent somewhere amidships.


When the *Metagama* entered the harbour of Devonport, England, it was met by a pair of tugs that nudged it like twin sheepdogs toward shore. The soldiers and nurses disembarked separately and were herded toward their separate fates. Quentin endured a further round of training at West Sandling and by the time it was over he found that he could think of Imogen without pain. She was not "waiting" for him, as were the wives and fiancées of so many of his barracks mates. He had no one to go back to, but neither did he have anyone whose loyalty he had to fret over. Some of the lads struggled with the most corrosive jealousy. "None of that for me," he told himself.

And now on this sunny day in northern France a few miles south of Lens he stopped by the quartermaster's pens and untethered Gerhard the goat. A friend in supplies had fashioned him a leash from a destroyed bridle. He attached it to Gerhard's collar and led him out of the pen. There followed a twenty-minute walk during which it was impossible to go more than a dozen yards without a soldier stopping to pet the goat, or tug its ear. *How ya doing there, boy? Howzit going, eh?* Quentin would never have believed the power of a mascot had he not seen it first-hand. The men seemed genuinely heartened to see this scrawny, rickety creature still out and about. Gerhard's legend was well known among the troops but some of them liked to hear it again. *Is it true they found him in a blown-out dugout?* Yes, it was true. *Is it true he jumped a Fritzie and stopped him shooting one of our guys?* Could be, Quentin would say, but I didn't see that myself. I bet it's true, they'd say, wanting to hear only remarkable things about their pet.

On the way back from walking the goat Quentin bumped into Lieutenant Pegram.

"Can we go to press, sir?"

"We can. But best get it out on the double, Goodchild—big doings afoot."

"Yes, sir."

After he had printed up the paper and put it in the hands of the runners, Quentin rounded up Pratt and Stokely from his platoon and the three of them set out in search of a real meal. Pratt fancied himself a worldly sort, though until this war he'd never been out of Wawa, Ontario. He had suffered a chest wound at Ypres—Quentin had seen the hideous snaking scars—which had netted him a couple of months' recuperation in England before he got shipped back to France. Despite his injuries, Pratt walked with the stolid, unhurried gait of a Buddha, and insisted they take a small road into a village that wasn't even on their map.

They soon realized they were skirting the edge of an older battlefield. Stokely immediately had to step off the road and hunt for souvenirs.

"I would have thought you'd seen enough battlefields," Quentin said.

"Active ones, you bet. These I like."

Stokely, who had been at both Ypres and Vimy, had changed battalions so many times he'd lost count. He was a stocky, rough-edged little man—the sort you might expect to fix your furnace or mend the road—but he pocketed souvenirs with the avidity of an archaeologist.

He had an absolute passion for this, liked to send items back to some little town in Saskatchewan and could not be dissuaded.

"Look at that," Pratt said, pointing. "We got a *poilu*, I'd say."

A skeletonized body sprawled face up in the grassless waste that used to be a field. His uniform was the older French one of dark blue tunic and red trousers. His rifle lay at an angle a few feet away. Stokely bent with his trench knife and sawed off a couple of buttons and badges.

They walked on, the going easy in the current dry weather, where it must have been hellish in the heavy rains of spring. The locals claimed it had never rained like that in France, that the endless storms were the fault of all the shelling, the mines, the grenades. All these ungodly explosions had damaged the natural order of sky and cloud, and broke the rains loose.

Two or three kilometres later they came upon an abandoned trench. Stokely leapt in.

"Come on, ya slowpokes. Dry as a bone."

"German," Pratt noted. "They're always deeper than ours. Better made, too."

"They had the luxury of time," Quentin said, admiring the struts, the planking, the corrugated tin holding back the earth. Even the duckwalk and firing steps were intact.

The next bay, however, had suffered a direct hit and was impassable. As they turned back, Stokely said, "I think we've got a dugout here."

"Come on," Quentin said, "let's find our dinner."

"Just a quick peek." Stokely got down on his knees to clear away dirt and rubble from the opening.

They proceeded slowly down the steps, Stokely and Pratt holding cigarette lighters aloft. The dugout was deep enough to be shell-proof, with a wooden floor and straight wide planking for walls. There were shelves of provisions, tinned meat and fruit, loose tobacco, cigars, and a few books.

And it was occupied.

Two German soldiers, leathery mummies, sat across from one another over a box table, hands folded in front of them, heads lowered as if contemplating hands of cards that had long vanished. Three more soldiers leaned back against a wall, heads tipped back, mouths open as if they had been interrupted while singing a drinking song. They had been big men, all of them, not the kind of men you'd want to meet in hand-to-hand.

"Fuck me," Pratt said.

"Weird the way they're still sittin'," Stokely said. "You think it was gas?"

"You don't sit still when there's gas around. They'd be all twisted up, clutching their throats."

"Probably concussion," Quentin said. "From the shell next door."

"But how come they're sittin' there playing poker?"

Quentin shrugged. "Local kids? Probably sat 'em up for a joke."

The Germans were still as a museum tableau, but the flames from the lighters made their eye sockets seem to move.

"'At's not right," Stokely said. "Even if they are German."

"I'll see you up top," Quentin said, and turned to mount the stairs.

The others followed right behind. Back in the light, they climbed out of the trench and Quentin bent forward, clutching his knees and taking in deep lungfuls of air. Stokely knelt in the dirt and made the sign of the cross. Pratt walked off a little way and lit a cigarette.

"Well, that was something," he said, when Quentin joined him.

"Yeah."

Pratt called to Stokely. "You praying for Fritz, for Chrissake?"

Stokely stood up and slapped at his knees. "Not the live ones."

They walked for a long time without saying anything. Quentin had learned to slam shut the many entrances to his heart, and usually he was successful, but some things just caught you off guard. He knew he would long remember the scene, these strong young men brought to nothing.

There had also been that day in Mont Noir, a tiny house: in one
cramped room, lit only by a thin wash of light from a filthy window,
four women around ninety years old, refugees from some other village. They were cousins, two sets of sisters. A daughter appeared, no
youngster herself, and offered to take Quentin's picture. Every day
she walked the road with her camera, offering to take pictures for a
few coins—a way to help support the old women. Quentin knew the
battalion would be moving before she could develop the film, but he
posed for her anyway. He could not recall the daughter's face, but
those old women, with their pinched and ugly features from which all
hope had fled, would be with him always.

Also still with him, the Frenchwoman who had been selling pastries to the soldiers when they were bivouacked near her farm. In
her early thirties or thereabouts, she had loose brown curls and dark,
comma-shaped eyebrows, the kind of face you know is French without
being able to say precisely why. As the men were about to move out, a
few mortar shells came their way and a stray piece of shrapnel tore
one of her breasts almost clean off, the stretcher-bearers trying to hold
her together with field dressings until they could get her to a collection point up the line. Quentin had no philosophy into which such an
image could comfortably fit; he doubted any such philosophy existed.

Eventually the three soldiers came to a place called Lillers. Although
there was much evidence of shelling nearby, the village itself was
relatively undamaged. The streets were deserted, locals avoiding the
midday heat. A drowsy, sagging dog followed them for a short distance before curling up in a patch of shade. They found a small restaurant, also empty except for the *patronne*. There was no menu as such,
just one *plat* chalked on a blackboard: pork chop, green beans, and
*frites*, priced at two francs.

In one of those odd dislocations of war, the *patronne* turned out to
be English. She had moved to France with her husband, also English,
twenty years ago. He had purchased a brewery with the hope of pro-
ducing the first decent French beer, a project that turned out to be

fraught with peril. "He was naive, you see. Thought if you simply introduced proper English beer to the natives they'd lap it up. But the French simply do not love beer the way we British do."

"And us Canadians," Pratt said.

"And when they do want a beer they want a light, thin lager. So Roger had to rethink his principles and produce something suited to the French palate. And eventually he did."

"Where is he now?" Stokely asked.

"He was naive about that too. When the Germans took Mons he thought they'd be turned back after a month or two. Somehow it's impossible to conceive of Germans in France, they're such a different people. I mean, you wouldn't think they'd *want* to come. But they came and we had to flee to Paris. When we got back they'd dumped all the beer—might have been poisoned, mightn't it?—and even worse they'd dismantled all Roger's lovely new equipment and shipped it back to Germany."

"See," Pratt said to Stokely, "that's why Canada's in this bloody war. You can't go stealing a man's beer."

Stokely laughed.

"Anyway, that was it for Roger. He packed a bag and headed to the British lines and got himself into the army. He's somewhere near Avesnes at the moment."

"That's likely to heat up," Quentin said.

"He'll be all right. He's too old and nearsighted for the front line, so he's in the Quartermaster section. His knowledge of the region comes in helpful. Goodness, it's so good to talk English, I'm being a terrible *patronne*. Please—what can I bring you?"

They ordered the *plat*, and it turned out to be the best meal any of them had eaten in France or Flanders. Afterwards they drank many coffees, all three of them agreeing that, even though French beer was pure bat's piss, French coffee was the best in the world. They thanked the English lady and left extra francs on the table.

"Oh, no," she said. "You don't have to tip a *patronne*."

"Supporting the home front," Quentin said.

When they got back Quentin wrote a letter of farewell to his father—most of the troops did the same thing when facing a major action. Farewell letters would remain at the company's HQ and only those from men who actually perished would be sent on to their families.

"I know we have sometimes been at odds," Quentin wrote, "and I'm sorry for any disappointment I caused you over the years. Please remember that I've always loved and admired you, and feel a deep gratitude for the happy childhood and adolescence you and Mother gave me. I hope soon to see you again, but if fate decides otherwise, please know these words come from my heart."

He also wrote a separate letter to Jack, asking him, if he was killed in battle, to tell Imogen that she had always been his one true love and always would be.

Afterwards he stood outside with Stokely and watched half a dozen enemy aircraft go after four Royal Flying Corps machines. The Germans had always had the upper hand, with faster aircraft and longer pilot training, but this time the Brits chased them off, one of them spinning to earth, spewing smoke. The Germans got their own back two hours later by blasting away at a Canadian observation balloon. In an instant the fabric sausage turned into a flapping sheet of flame, the sole occupant parachuting to safety and Quentin hoped an extra shot of rum.

The order to move up the line came that evening.


Zero hour was 4:25 a.m. Assembly was three hours earlier along a straight line through the intersection of trenches with the homely names of "Yonge Street" and "Dundas." All through the night, the Royal Engineers had been hurling drums of burning oil that soaked the enemy lines in smoke and flame. To these they now added thousands upon thousands of gas shells, and the Germans responded with a gas attack of their own. The four companies were forced to assemble amid rolling lethal clouds of the stuff, stumbling in their goggles and hoods, respirators dangling on their chests. The extra ammunition they carried was heavy, not to mention the two grenades clipped to their belts. Quentin was glad he had set his rifle sight earlier, because you couldn't see through the goggles to do it.

Often before a battle, the men horsed around, play-fighting or hurling friendly insults at one another—anything to keep fear at bay. But the masks and respirators made this impossible. And the noise was shattering. The German whiz-bangs were bad enough, the whiz being just long enough to let you know it was coming, the bang a hammer blow to the eardrums. Then came the thin singing whine of shrapnel looking for limbs to maim, throats to slice. Heavier artillery roared over their heads, each shell loud as a locomotive. Through all of this, bullets thudded into sandbags, pinged off stone.

Nausea crept into Quentin's belly. He clutched his rifle and imagined his father getting his letter. He was angry at the gas, angry at his own trembling, angry at the Germans for forcing him into his own mind this way. You could not be in your own mind and go over the top.

At twenty minutes to zero hour the big guns opened up behind them and put a stop to the bullets. The ground shook, and if it got any louder Quentin knew he would shit himself. He had developed a deep fear of barbed wire, and both sides were protected with hedges of the stuff as much as fifteen feet deep. The engineers' job was to blast holes in it. Lack of success in this would mean catastrophe. Quentin had been out with work parties, struggling under the most murderous conditions, to clip gateways through their own barbed defences wide enough to allow hundreds of men to pour through. Despite the work gloves, his hands had been blistered from clipping. There had been ghastly instances in other battles where the job had not been complete. The troops jammed up and were machine-gunned into writhing mounds of dead and wounded.

Zero hour came and he tried to transmute fear into rage. There was an agonizing delay—one minute, two minutes—and then came the order to attack. They went over the top and immediately the enemy filled the sky with red flares. All along the lines the trenches jumped and shook in the flash of shellfire.

Quentin took cover in the nearest shell hole, five or six men piling in behind him. Their first objective was the Germans' firing line—the Blue Line. Two hundred yards of torn and cratered earth stood between them and it. Quentin peered over the lip and fired at what he thought was a German helmet, though it seemed impossible any enemy could be standing up under the barrage. The night was a smear of blacks and reds, intermittently blanched with silver. Sometimes the explosions were so close together that it was almost light as day. Two shell holes over he saw Lieutenant Pegram urging men on with the pitching motion of his forearm. He was yelling but there was no hearing him.

Quentin fired again and ran for the next shell hole. The earth shuddered. The engineers would stop any minute and set their guns for the next line. The idea was to get to the Blue Line before the enemy had a chance to gather his wits and point his rifle at you.

The soldier who landed next to him was named Fingal—a mousy little man who kept to himself and always walked with his head down as if he'd just been castigated for some misdeed. He took his gas mask off and yelled something Quentin couldn't hear. When Quentin shook his head, Fingal grabbed his sleeve and pointed off to the right and shrieked in his ear, "Good hole that way! Mine crater!"

Quentin took off his own mask. Through the stench of high explosives and burning oil ran the sweet smell of leftover gas. "All right," he said. "Let's run like hell." Quentin was first out. A bullet whizzed by his neck, but he made it to the crater and jumped in, Fingal right behind him. Quentin could tell by the feel under his boots that he had just landed on the back of a dead man. He looked down as a flash of shellfire lit up the pale features, which were almost unscathed, just one of the eyes obliterated. Presumably the dead man had thought this was a good crater too. It was at least thirty feet deep, a pool of water shining in the bottom.

Bullets fizzed and smacked into the earth around them.

They slid deeper into the hole, their backs to the objective.

"Coupla Huns in a listening post over that way." Fingal jerked his thumb in the direction of Lens. "We've gotta take 'em out."

"No. We have to stick to the objective."

"They've got a clean shot!"

"It's more important to reach the objective before they can regroup."

"We'll never make it with those bastards there. We gotta raid 'em."

"Fingal, no. You take a shot and run for the Blue Line. I'll take a shot and be right behind you."

"Fuck, man, they're gonna kill us."

"The barrage is about to stop. You want to face a whole line of Fritzes? Let's move it."

Fingal took his shot and was about to run when Quentin grabbed his belt and hauled him back.

"What the hell you doing, man? You told me to run!"

"Take a look. They've got some forward positions our spotters must've missed. I just saw a line of helmets heading for one straight ahead."

They waited for the next shell burst and peered over the rim of the hole. They could make out the bipod of a machine gun being set into place.

"No, sir," Fingal declared. "That is not going to happen."

Before Quentin could stop him Fingal was out of the hole and running straight for the emplacement, bellowing. Quentin charged after him. This would be it. He'd get one in the face, or right through the chest. It was the reason he had signed up, the fate he had sought, and now it had come. Which did nothing to calm the terror raging in his chest, or still the urge to curl himself into a ball, shrieking and weeping, until it was all over.

Off to his right, he could dimly make out the Germans who'd been potting at them from the direction of Lens. Were their rifles jammed? Were they dead? Why had they not shot him yet? And these helmets in the hole ahead, why had they not popped up like mechanical ducks in a midway gallery?

The Germans' machine gun was a belt-feed and the man feeding it was having trouble staying in position. The barrage had stopped. They had a minute, maybe two to get to the Blue Line. Well, it was irrelevant, now, Quentin considered, his boots pounding the ground. He wanted to cry out *Shoot me, for Christ sake, get it over with. I'm right here. Let's get it over with because I'm just too fucking terrified to live.*

And then Fingal was grabbing hold of the machine gun, tipping it back into the hole and screaming at the Germans. Quentin was there too, rifle pointing at the white face of an officer who held his hands up, yelling, "Peace! Peace! We like you! Canadians—please, we want to go with you!"

Quentin screamed at them to drop their weapons but they already had. There were eight of them, all with their hands up and smiling and yelling about how happy they were to be captured. "Please, we go with you! We like you!"

Quentin and Fingal were down in the hole with them now. Another three Canadians joined them.

"*Hände hoch!*" Quentin yelled. "Keep your hands up!"

"Look," the German officer said, "you can go this way." He indicated the communication trench. It was barely two feet wide but it was deep enough.

Quentin was just a private with no authority over the other Canadians in the hole. He turned to a corporal who seemed to be looking to him for direction. "We can send them back as soon as we take the Blue Line. You want to look after them until then, or shall I?"

The corporal seemed to collect himself. "We'll look after this bunch. You go ahead. Jesus, the barrage has stopped. I can hear myself."

"You only need two men for this," Quentin said. "The rest should come with me."

Nobody wanted to come. The Germans were handing out cigarettes and other tokens and grinning like fools.

"You believe these people?" the corporal said. "Kinda hard to stay mad at them."

"I think that's the idea."

Quentin and Fingal and a couple of others ran along the communication trench. After twenty yards, maybe thirty, it opened into a bay of the German firing line. It was empty except for two dead men and a soldier of about nineteen without a helmet, who was weeping and shaking uncontrollably. Quentin threw back the flap of a dugout and saw light below.

He yelled "*Hände hoch!*" once again but it was not necessary. Two of the Germans were in the same condition as the one upstairs, sheets of tears glistening on their faces. Another was huddled in a ball, weeping. Two others, sullen and fearful, stood in silence, hands raised.

Footsteps sounded on the stairs behind him and he turned to see Lieutenant Pegram.

"Well done, Goodchild, Fingal. We have our objective at"—he checked his field watch—"five twenty-one. Get the prisoners upstairs and keep an eye on them. I'm going to give this place a good going-over."

"Sir, you're wounded."

Pegram touched a hand to his neck and looked at the blood on his hand. "I didn't even realize."

Quentin and Fingal moved the six prisoners up the stairs, herding the shell-shocked ones off to one side. No one, friend or enemy, could bear such weeping for long.

One of the new prisoners spoke up. "It's not booby-trapped, you know. The dugout. This one is not booby-trapped. Others, yes."

Another prisoner took a wooden match from his pocket and lit it.

Quentin whirled on him and touched the tip of his bayonet to his chest. "Drop it."

The German did so.

"He doesn't have cigarettes," Fingal said. "I checked."

"Do that again," Quentin said to the German, "and you will regret it."

He turned back to the other prisoner. "Where are the communication trenches?"

"Communication?"

"Don't pretend you don't understand—your English is fine. The communication trenches to your reserve line. Where are they—how far?"

The prisoner pointed past Quentin's shoulder. "That way. Fifty metres or so." He pointed in the other direction. "This way, maybe hunnit metres, something."

Fingal cracked the other prisoner on the arm with his rifle. "Bastard did it again."

The lit match fell to the ground and went out.

"Get the lieutenant," Quentin said.

Fingal disappeared into the dugout.

"Are you trying to signal?" Quentin said. "Are you really that stupid?"

The German shifted his gaze as if to reply were beneath him.

The dugout flap opened and Lieutenant Pegram was there. "Is this the man?"

"Yes, sir."

"He lit a match and you warned him?"

"Yes, sir."

"And he did it again?"

"Yes, sir."

The lieutenant unsnapped his holster and raised his sidearm to the prisoner's forehead. He fired once, and reholstered his weapon.


Quentin and Fingal and several others stayed in the dugout, keeping their heads down as the heavy artillery whooshed over them to the Green Line, the Germans' support trench. Quentin did not envy the battalion whose job it would be to leapfrog the Blue Line and attack that machine gun–infested pit.

Daylight had come, but it was a daylight made evening by smoke and clouds of gas. They'd eaten their morning rations and now had to endure the waiting. Although they had not slept for thirty-six hours they were far too keyed up to even attempt it, despite their comfortable German quarters. The four bunks were all taken, Quentin being stretched out on a lower one. Fingal had drawn the short straw and was sitting near the steps with his back to the wall, resting his head against his rolled-up jersey. The usual dugout smells of burlap, earth, and candle wax were all but obliterated by the sinus-searing vestiges of their own chlorine gas.

Lieutenant Pegram, neck now swathed in a field dressing, was at the table, his face aglow between candles, scratching rapid notes on casualties, prisoners, and captured materiel.

"Fingal should be up for a medal," Quentin said, and told him about Fingal grabbing the machine gun and toppling it back onto the Germans.

"Naw, it just had to be done," Fingal said. "Lucky I didn't have time to think about it."

Until witnessing Fingal in action, Quentin had been skeptical of medals; they seemed to be given out too freely for too little. After Vimy, the list of awards and commendations had been endless. Well, perhaps it made sense. Just to survive the mud and the rain qualified as some kind of heroic feat. Hundreds of men had suffered horribly from trench foot. The skin, wet for days on end, eventually breaks down and bacteria seep into the flesh causing an infection so virulent that, if left untreated, it renders a man unable to walk in a matter of days.

Luckily Lens was dry, which also made rats less of a problem. The slaughter at Vimy had proved a feast for rodents in their thousands. Killing them took up more troop time than killing Germans. A plump brown rat tearing the lower lip from a dead man's face—that was another of those indelible sights lodged in Quentin's memory, now along with Lieutenant Pegram's putting a bullet between the eyes of a prisoner. The thought ran through Quentin's head, again and again: *How can I have seen such things and still be alive?*

A strange noise made them turn their heads toward the steps. The lieutenant looked up from his paperwork, pen in hand, as an unexploded shell, an eighteen-pounder, clattered down the steps and slithered onto Fingal's lap.

"Fuck me," he said, staring at the thing.

Pegram half-rose from the box he was sitting on.

"One of ours," someone said.

Nobody moved.

"Goodchild," the lieutenant said without taking his eyes off the shell, "remove that thing at once. Carefully."

Quentin got off his bunk and crossed the dugout to Fingal. He squatted and reached for the shell, then stood up, cradling it against his chest. It surprised him that it was not scorching hot, only warm. "I'm not actually much good at shot put," he said, but the joke fell flat.

"You don't throw it, Goodchild. You place it. Gently. Somewhere it will do the least harm."

Quentin carried it up the steps, treading in a stately fashion, as if he had been drawn into an unfamiliar but crucial ceremony. He was reminded of his youth as an altar boy, carrying book or candle at High Mass. He turned left in the trench and threaded his way to the nearest damaged area—a collapsed dugout thirty yards away. A soldier awaiting his turn on the firing step looked him up and down. "You don't have to deliver them to Fritz personally, you know."

He sat in the dirt where the top step of the dugout had been and hooched down through the debris until he could go no farther. He lodged the shell, with the utmost tenderness, into some loose soil, then covered it with sandbags. Some men, he reflected, fall in love with their trench. It's their cover, their mother, their saviour—the only thing between them and death or mutilation. But he knew, once this operation was over, his mission in life would be to extricate himself from the trenches and get himself assigned to other work.

The immediate project of the men on the Blue Line was consolidation. They reinforced strong points against the counterattacks that were sure to come. They humped sandbags, fixed firing slits, created tool and ammunition dumps. Quentin's section was already quite sound, and the men took great satisfaction in turning the Germans' own thoroughness against them.

When the next wave of Canadians came roaring across no man's land, file upon relentless file, men in the Blue Line cheered them from the trench as if they were observing a field day event. *Come on, boys! Show 'em how it's done! Give it to 'em good! Kill the bastards!* But Quentin could not bring himself to cheer.

In the event, it went quickly. Canadian scouts had secured crucial information on enemy emplacements and the artillery had neutralized most of them. Even so, the machine guns did their work, and the screams of the wounded soon put an end to all cheering.

The Red Line and in its turn the Green Line at the crest of the hill were taken and consolidated. Many prisoners and much materiel were funnelled back to the rear. Stretcher-bearers—to Quentin's mind the bravest people of the war—carried the wounded away to dressing stations. German bearers, taken prisoner, were now tending to Canadian wounded, and their skill and dedication in this enterprise were much remarked on.

The taste of these victories was soured by the knowledge of what was to come. The Germans wanted their hill back—without it they could neither control the area nor make use of the rail lines. One of their airplanes made a lazy back-and-forth survey of the hill, and within an hour their artillery set up a gut-shrivelling bombardment, unleashing thousands of gas shells. The Canadian troops were well protected against phosgene but the mustard gas was a different matter.

Frustrated by their mask-induced blindness, many men removed the mask just for a moment in order to lay a sight, set a fuse, or tend to a wound. When the gas touched their skin even for an instant it caused terrible blisters as if the flesh had been boiled in oil. Their shrieks were unbearable, their disfigurements terrifying.

The Canadians made an attempt to push into Lens but it was not much more than a diversionary manoeuvre, far more murderous for the men who mounted it than for the securely emplaced Germans. Over the course of the next three days the Germans staged no fewer than twenty-one counterattacks, each following so swiftly upon the last that Quentin experienced the separate clashes as a single titanic struggle.

He had stuffed his ears with cotton but even so the shells seemed to explode inside his skull. One landed a dozen yards from the trench, burying half of it in a torrent of dirt. Pratt, who had been closest, dropped to his knees and scrabbled through the debris for something—for what? Ammunition? Water? A personal keepsake? Some time later—an hour, three, there was no telling how long—another shell landed in almost exactly the same spot. This time Pratt himself was completely buried. Quentin, Stokely, and another man dug frantically through the dirt and debris.

"Oh, Christ," Stokely said. "He's had it this time. He was right here."

"There's nothing left of him," the younger soldier said. "They goddam vaporized him."

A voice behind them said, "What are you looking for?"

It was Pratt, just emerging from the dugout.

They all burst out laughing and started punching Pratt playfully and calling him every insult they could think of. Pratt, with the goofiest of expressions on his face, got in a few taps and bear hugs of his own. It was a cheerful moment that made it all the harder to take when, only a few days later, Pratt went out on a work party that came under heavy fire and did not return.

"The silly bastard," Stokely said. "He'll turn up again."

*No, he won't,* Quentin thought. And on subsequent nights huddled under his greatcoat he thought of Pratt and all the others who were dying by the hour, emptying another body's worth of blood into the bottomless lake of Hill 70, a place that wasn't even a place, a battle that in all probability would not even be remembered, except by those who fought it.

From his vantage point on the firing step it seemed to Quentin that this battle, this hill, would cost the enemy, at a minimum, tens of thousands of lives. The machine guns were scything them down by the hundreds. Then the stretcher-bearers and the burial parties would emerge under white flags and the Canadians would leave them alone for an hour to bury their dead. The Germans killed plenty of Canadians, too, including Stokely who caught a round in his throat and drowned in his own blood.

Quentin wondered if the Germans had any more feeling for each other than he had for Stokely. It disturbed him, how little he had. Perhaps he was still shut down after Pratt. Or maybe it was war-induced numbness that would wear off, enabling him to shed a few tears for his fallen friend. Not that they had been friends exactly. He and Stokely would never have been pals outside of these unusual circumstances. Still, it bothered him that he didn't feel more.

As a private in the trench he was not privy to what was in the minds of officers. If the object of the enterprise had been to take Lens, then it had failed. If it had merely been a diversion from some bigger offensive—a gigantic push on the Hindenburg Line, say—then it might have value. But in the trench it felt like just another stalemate: the Germans would keep Lens, the Canadians would keep the hill, and they would lob ordnance at each other until the war was over.

He wrote letters to his father and to Jack, telling them about taking their objective, careful to leave out any identifying geographical details. A couple of days later he received a letter from Jack.

Dear Quentin,

I will keep this short because I have written this letter a hundred times and a hundred times consigned it to the flames. If I go on at any length, this one too will end up in the fire. But with you over there facing death every minute, every hour, I feel I simply must come clean before it is too late.

I love you, Quentin—and not in the way one friend, even a very close friend, loves another. I love you in the way you loved—and I know you still love—Imogen Lang. I love you with an unquenchable longing. I think about you all the time and yearn every minute of the day to have you near. I want no one else's company but yours. I long to hold you in the morning, the evening, and all through the night for the rest of our lives. I long to kiss you.

How I tremble to commit these words to paper! (Burn this at once.) I am homosexual, Quentin. My gorge rises as I write the word, and tears burn my eyes. It is not a passing thing. I have never felt the slightest desire to kiss or hold a girl. My "infatuation" with "Emma Gilbert"? Pure fiction. I made it up so I could be like you, so that I could tell you about my feelings—oh, it was a thrill to do so—without your knowing I was really talking about you.

Do you remember the time we went for that midnight swim in Mirror Lake? The sight of your dripping body, shining in the moon-light! That whole night I lay awake tormented by desire, imagining climbing into bed with you, your arms opening to hold me close. Dear God, how I love you.

Forgive me for telling you. I know you don't want to know, but the truth is I can no longer live without telling you. Please forgive me the discomfort this will cause you, and know that I will always remain, until the day I die,

Your faithful friend,
Jack

For a moment, as he read, Quentin thought Jack must be joking, it couldn't be true. But the anguished honesty of the words was undeniable. He was shocked, completely taken by surprise, and yet slowly he began to feel utterly stupid. How had he not known? He remembered a remark Imogen made long ago, after an afternoon the three of them had spent together at the art museum. She'd said, "It's almost like he's in love with you." Ridiculous, Quentin had scoffed—he's dying of love for Emma Gilbert. "Haven't you noticed," Imogen said, "how he's always looking at you? Defers to you? He even rushes ahead to open doors for you." Quentin hadn't noticed any of this.

The only thought he'd ever entertained about men's bodies (other than their fragility before the onslaught of fire and steel) was to wonder how women could stand to look at them, let alone touch them—the squat, hairy creatures he shared barracks with repelled him with their apish gaits, their furry chests and backs and cracks, and the appalling genitals that ranged in appearance from turkey necks to a bunch of grapes in a dark revolting nest. Jack, how could you?

Quentin waited two days before replying, writing in the dugout on a blue aerogramme. He told Jack he was sorry he had been suffering so, but that under the circumstances he did not see how they could continue as friends; he could never return his "love."

I don't think less of you morally, but I shall if you do not seek treatment. It's clear from your letter that you do not want to be like this. Let that motivation stand you in good stead as you seek to change. If you do manage to change—really change—then I shall be glad to resume our friendship. But until that time you and I must part. This letter will be painful for you to read; it is painful to write. I hope, Jack, that you will become once again the man I have known and admired. Until such time I must remain,

Your former friend,<br>Quentin

As he folded the blue paper, a sob of self-pity escaped him. Jack was as gone from his life as Stokely and Pratt. As Imogen.


Quentin's object now was to survive at least until the battalion was relieved, without turning into too much of a thing. He prided himself on little when it came to fighting. He was not a great shot, he had a terror of ever having to use the bayonet, and he had no remarkable leadership skills. But he had become good at surviving. He could now tell how close a machine-gunner was and whether he was a threat. He could tell by the pitch of a shell's whine whether he was in immediate danger or not. His reflexes had even proved sharp enough, at least so far, to save him from the whiz-bangs. When they were on the move he knew whom to follow, where to march, to minimize the danger to himself. He knew to get to the front of a marching line. When there was a lengthy halt, and there were plenty, the front men were quick to move. If you were at the rear—a mistake many men made—you had an interminable wait before you started moving again. Tiny accomplishments, perhaps, but a lot of the other men seemed to have no instinct for survival at all.

One of the most important skills—and here he had to give credit to the staff officers and the training manuals—was keeping filth at bay. Those officers, the sticklers who had no experience of the trenches anyway, might have been thinking of appearances and their effect on morale. If troops stopped looking sharp, they started to look defeated, and this was not good for anyone except the enemy. Far more important to Quentin was that dirt and dishevelment very quickly made him crazy. A few bits of hay inside the collar, the itch of ground-in grime, could make the difference between an acceptable level of discomfort and weeping misery.

One day on his trip back from the water station he was forced by enemy fire to circle around an old slag heap. Behind it he discovered a pool of water. Twenty minutes later he crept back with his soap and shaving kit and bathed himself thoroughly. The difference to his mood was so marked he was tempted to keep the pool his own little secret but hadn't the heart. He told the others in his platoon and down they went, two by two, and came back shiny, slick, and chatty.

"Worth taking the place off the Hun for that alone," Lieutenant Pegram remarked. "Well done, Goodchild."

Another of his battle-honed instincts kicked in later that afternoon. The shelling started up again, and while the enemy ordnance seemed mostly targeting the Red Line, he suddenly discerned the rising whine of a shell coming his way. Really his way. He leapt from the firing step and ran.

He had two seconds, maybe less, not enough time to reach the dugout and open the flap. He made for the next bay, the shell screaming closer. Even in his terror, he sensed that he must bear more than a passing resemblance to Charlie Chaplin—running like hell, the whites of his eyes vivid, reaching the turn in the trench and clutching at a sandbag to swing himself around the corner. He had an image of Imogen, her smile, her thoughtful eyes, her soft voice, as they talked about Chaplin after a night at the movies. Image of Imogen. The phrase was in his mind as the shell exploded. His feet flew out from under him and he was lifted into the air, hoisted as if by a giant hand. He was flailing this way and that, and the giant had now apparently been joined by others. Each had taken hold of a limb, or his head, and they all pulled in opposite directions.

An Elizabethan execution, he thought. They attached your limbs to four horses with ropes or chains and then commanded the horses to pull in their separate directions. You were literally torn apart. The blast had sucked all the air from the trench, had sucked the air out of his lungs, and none was coming back. He had a ridiculous image of being sewn back together, of continuing life as a rag doll. But being deprived of breath, he knew, was something you didn't survive.

# 4

Imogen arrived early for her first appointment with Professor Ganz and had to spend twenty minutes in an anteroom guarded by a secretary with a grave moustache. She later learned his name was Penn—an ideal name for a secretary—and that despite the melancholy moustache, he had a sweet disposition. At exactly eleven o'clock, Mr. Penn set aside a stack of papers, rose from his desk, rapped smartly on the inner door, and opened it. "Dr. Lang is here."

A voice from within: "Excellent. Show her in."

Mr. Penn swung open the door, and Imogen entered, a little unsteadily—partly owing to nerves, and partly to being encumbered with the two buckets.

Professor Ganz snatched a tiny pair of spectacles from his face and stood up with Mittel-European alacrity. "Jonas Ganz," he said with a smart little bow. "I am delighted to make your acquaintance, Dr. Lang."

"I'm honoured to be here, sir."

"You are a woman of unique achievements."

"Well, I am a woman with three brains."

"Oh, please. Forgive me." Professor Ganz rushed around from his desk and took the buckets from her. He was a small man; Imogen towered over him like a giantess in a storybook.

"They're from Dean Dodson," she said. "One is for you and one for a Professor Welch."

"Please be seated," Ganz said, nodding toward the chairs arranged in a semicircle facing his desk. He set the buckets down behind his desk, detached the envelope, and sat down himself. He put on his spectacles again and slit the envelope with a letter opener, extracted the contents, and then perused them.

Imogen no longer felt so peculiar about delivering human organs to the esteemed director of the Henry Phipps Psychiatric Clinic. Ganz's office, while of a luxurious size and appointments, more closely resembled a pathologist's lab than an administrative office. Shelves crowded with specimen jars covered most of the walls. Brain sections marinated behind amber-coloured glass, and in larger, horizontal cases, four or five human spines reposed like musical instruments. She had come to exactly the right place—a place where she would not only be learning the latest theories and methods of patient care, but also be at the forefront of scientific research. Imagine helping to make some breakthrough, find some key that would turn the lock of psychosis and open up the mysteries of madness.

"Dementia praecox," Ganz said, putting aside the letter, "though since it's neither dementia nor precocious I prefer the term *schizophrenia*." He removed his spectacles and stared across the desk at her. His eyes, almost black, were unnerving. The irises were completely clear of both upper and lower eyelids, giving them the look of twin gun barrels. A sharp goatee lengthened his chin, and his eyebrows, black deltas, would have suited a stage mesmerist.

He stared at Imogen. "Do you have any opinions on the terminology?"

Something of a trap, that question, since it was Ganz who had introduced the term *schizophrenic reaction* into the American lexicon.

"I've read of cases," Imogen said, "where the first attack of psychosis did not occur until the patient was in his forties, so I suppose one couldn't really call that praecox."

"Just so, Dr. Lang. Just so." His tone was amiable, but his eyes remained black pits. If he had known her long enough for it to be possible, Imogen would have been certain that he hated her. But surely no man could be that sensitive about his height.

✳

The junior physicians' rooms were on the fourth floor and looked out over stately elms and a circular drive. "Staff rooms face north so the patients get the southern light all day," Donna Artemis told her. "Sunshine can make a huge difference to a depressed patient."

Donna had been assigned to show her around the clinic. They would not be roommates, exactly, but they shared a bathroom, as did the other two interns. "Male, unfortunately," Donna said. "Men are the inferior sex—I hope we're in agreement on that."

"Oh, completely," Imogen said. Donna was also twenty-two, but she had a tomboyish charm, and a kind of juvenile, bouncy energy. She talked at hyper speed, which Imogen ascribed to nervousness, at first, and then to confidence. Imogen's own nervousness made her ponderous and dull, but Donna's chatter precluded any lags in the conversation.

Donna showed her the features of her room. "Not much closet space, I'm afraid. And nowhere to eat or keep food. Breakfast is in the day room on the second or third floor, depending which ward you're working on. Over breakfast we talk to the patients about what's in the morning papers—give them a kind of bridge to reality to start their day. All our other meals are in the dining room on the third floor. Private patients have their own dining room."

Imogen couldn't get over the furnishings. She plunked herself down in a Morris chair, and adjusted it to an almost reclining position. "I could sleep in this."

"And you will, unless you already know German."

"Far from it, unfortunately."

"I can read French, Spanish, and Italian. I don't see why all the brilliant psychiatrists have to be Austrian. It's very annoying of them."

Donna was touching her toes—up, down, up, down—as she talked, as if she were warming up for a track meet.

"When did you get here?" Imogen asked.

"A week ago. But I did my MD at Hopkins, so it wasn't exactly far to come—maybe three hundred yards? I also did a third-year rotation in the outpatient department. All the med students here have to do that. Come on, I'll show you the rest of the place."

And so, chattering the whole way, Donna led her through the building, which was more beautiful than any hospital Imogen had ever set foot in. Marble and oak everywhere, and even the elevators were pretty with their brass filigree.

They started at the fifth floor.

"East wing is men, west is women. Wards are referred to by floor and wing: West One, West Two, et cetera. Obviously I can't show you the men's wards. Here we are. *Voilà*."

They were standing in an indoor roof garden.

"It's beautiful," Imogen said.

"We've got it all to ourselves at the moment. Everyone's at lunch."

Donna led her to the outdoor garden, on a wooden deck that overlooked the clinic's courtyard and patio.

"Access to this is restricted," Donna said. "Don't want any jumpers."

Donna showed her the auditorium with its gleaming Steinway and a church organ that was powerful enough, according to her, to levitate the entire building. "Dr. Ganz does not like to hear anyone banging around on it—or the piano—unless they can really play. *Ist verboten*."

They took the stairs down to the fourth floor. "End rooms—*suites*, I should say—belong to the first assistant and the senior resident. Three times the size of ours, at least."

"Male?"

"However did you guess? But the dispensary chief is a woman— Lila Quinn. You'll be impressed with Quinn, though some surgeon performed a radical humorectomy on her. Honestly, why would you go into psychiatry if you have no sense of humour?"

"He seems to hire quite a few women, then, Dr. Ganz."

"It's the war, sweetheart. A lot of men have enlisted, even if old Woodrow is refusing to send them anywhere. And let's face it, psychiatry ain't exactly high up the ladder."

"Oh, dear. And I actually suspected myself of having some merit."

"You do, doctor! You do!" Donna grabbed her elbow and shook it, an astonishing liberty. "Because I will tell you right now that I'm brilliant, and if you're here at the Phipps you're brilliant too."

"I thought all alienists were supposed to be crazy, not brilliant."

"I hide it well, don't you think?"

"Actually, I thought you were a patient."

Donna smiled. "I think I'm beginning to like you."

She pointed to a heavy oak door. "The corridor on the other side leads to the private patients. They each have a private or semi-private room. Some of them even bring their own nurses—don't you adore it?—as if they're domestics. Well, I suppose they are. Anyway, we have eight women on West Four, eight men on East Four. They're all personal patients of Dr. Ganz's or the assistant director, Dr. Mackenzie. You'll like Mackenzie—he's Scottish, which means he's unintentionally funny. So's the second assistant. Have you noticed? Every psychiatrist who isn't Austrian is Scottish."

The third floor housed the quiet wards. "I won't show you just now. You'll see them soon enough. They're small—only eight beds to a floor. East Three's the nicest. The quiet ward? Works as an incentive for them, I guess. As your behaviour becomes more normal you literally rise in society—Phipps society anyway." Donna pointed to the end of the hall. "Far end, histology lab."

"Do we get to do much lab work?"

"Oh, Ganz is all for lab work. Not crazy about it myself." She pointed again. "This end is the psychology lab—you know who runs that, right?"

"Robert Taunton, isn't it? The behaviour man."

"That's him. He even helped design the labs—right down to the wiring. We can pop in and say hello if you promise not to be stunned by how good-looking he is." She pushed open a heavy door and they went in.

A man was seated at a desk washed in the light of a huge bay window, pecking at a typewriter. He kept typing even as they stopped just a few feet behind him.

"Apparently," Donna said, "this peculiar behaviour of poking at a machine was rewarded at some time in his past and he keeps at it, poor thing."

When Taunton swivelled around in his chair, Imogen found herself looking at the handsomest man she'd ever seen. He looked her up and down and said, "Who are you?"

"This is Dr. Imogen Lang. Dr. Lang, this is Mr. Taunton, head of psychology."

"Pleased to meet you," Imogen said.

"You shouldn't be," Taunton said, not bothering to stand up.

Imogen didn't even have a gauge to measure how rude that was.

"I'm going to make you obsolete," he said. "I already have. You just don't know it yet."

"Mr. Taunton teaches courses in modesty and social grace," Donna said.

"Neither of which is required," Taunton said. "You'll soon notice, if you've a brain in your head, that my laboratory is the only place in this clinic where actual science takes place. Observations are made, theories are tested, truth revealed."

"He means assertions," Donna said.

"None that I can't demonstrate," Taunton said. "Unlike your Viennese voodoo. Now if you don't mind I'd like to get back to changing the world."

"Taunton is actually quite fun," Donna said when they were out in the hall again, "and he really is changing the world, unfortunately. I find his looks quite unnerving."

Imogen had nothing to say about that.

Donna showed her the lower wards, the lecture hall, and the gorgeous library on the second floor, the biochem lab on the first, and the occupational therapy rooms and outpatient department on the basement level. Afterwards they sat on a bench in a cloister that over-looked a walled garden with a terrace and pond. The tranquility was marred by a man's voice yelling for strawberries and cream.

"You said you did a third-year rotation here," Imogen said. "Dr. Ganz warned me I would be somewhat behind Hopkins graduates."

"Probably true. He's managed to get psychiatry into the med school curriculum at every level. Normal psychology first year, history-taking second year, outpatient third year, and fourth year we got to sit in on staff conferences."

"Here at the Phipps."

"Here at the Phipps."

"Dear God," Imogen said. "I'm going to be the class idiot."

"Quite possible," Donna said, and gave Imogen's elbow a gentle pinch. "I'm teasing you."

"Did you say you took a whole course in history-taking?"

"Dr. Ganz is maniacal on the subject. When you do your asylum rotation you'll see why."

Patients and nurses were beginning to file out into the garden—patients in their hospital-issue percale shifts, and nurses in white aprons and starched caps that were blinding in the sunlight. From somewhere nearby, the man was still yelling for strawberries and cream.

"Come on," Donna said, springing up from the bench. "Let's see if there's anything left for lunch—though apparently we're suffering a shortage of strawberries."

That night, Donna tapped on her door and introduced her to one of the perverse pleasures of her new world: academic gossip. She brought with her a tin of digestive biscuits and as they shared them, Imogen remarked that she had never met anyone with the near-supernatural confidence of Robert Taunton.

"Taunton," Donna informed her in a highly confidential tone, "is a very special case. Ganz chose him sight unseen."

"Why on earth would he do that?"

"Two reasons. First, he likes Taunton's scientific attitude—some people think bringing weights and measures into psychology adds a certain sheen of rigour."

"And the second reason?"

"He needed someone in a hurry. The clinic was about to open and his director of psychology was supposed to be Donald Lyme—he'd been at Hopkins for centuries, well respected, several books et cetera. Then one steamy night Lyme gets caught in a police raid on a brothel. Boom! Done for. Hopkins has an ironclad policy on that kind of thing."

"Not just Hopkins."

"This place, they want to know who you marry—and don't even mention the word *divorce*. Were you thinking Taunton got the job because of his looks?"

"I have no opinion about his looks."

"Of course not," Donna said. "That would be improper."


The next day, Mr. Penn handed Imogen a thick questionnaire entitled "Personality Investigation and Survey." This, he informed her, was given to all new Phipps interns, and she was to fill it out as soon as possible.

She took it to the library along with *Hugo's German Grammar* and a Kraepelin text in the original. The prologue was ominous.

What is the object of a personality study? It is an attempt to stimulate the student to take a serious look at the "ledger" of his daily functioning and see where his assets and liabilities are taking him. The survey is an approach to self-acquaintance, and it is personal to the nth degree when answered openly and frankly. It will be read only by the instructor.

Someone had corrected the last sentence in ink, so that it read "only by Dr. Ganz." Imogen no sooner resolved to be frank than she found herself stymied by the first section: *(Autobiographic Record—Outline)*, *subsection I (Family Background)*, *Part A (Father)*. It began harmlessly enough, asking for pure facts—nationality, religion, schooling, occupation—then moved into more ticklish territory—nervous breakdowns, alcoholism—then became impossible: *(Admirable traits, less admirable traits)*.

Imogen flipped ahead and found much that she wanted to dodge.

*What emotional tendencies would you say run in the family?*

*Age of talking?*

She supposed she could answer truthfully about having been tongue-tied and choosing to communicate by pencil until the age of seven. It was not, after all, like confessing to idiocy. But what was she to do with *Do you consider your moods useful or wasteful?* The honest answer was that she could waste whole months at a time in depression, that she had probably inherited this tendency from her mother, and that she considered it a major flaw.

As to the questions about masturbation, well, she would simply not respond. Dr. Ganz was a man, he was her employer. Let him interpret her reticence however he might, Imogen considered the question completely inappropriate.

But about her father. Her father was another matter entirely.


For her twelfth birthday, Imogen's parents had given her a bicycle. With this, they expected her to ride to her friends' houses, which she did, and to the local branch library, which she also did. Her carrier could easily hold six to eight books, depending on the ambitions and endurance of their authors, and any extras could be slipped into her satchel. Her father—unusually for his generation—encouraged his daughters to read widely and freely. One of Imogen's favourite little tricks was to surprise him with a fact of geography or history or science, especially at the dinner table. "Aren't you a clever girl to know that," he would say, and turn to his wife for confirmation. "Isn't she, Rose?" Imogen would flush with pride. Her father, the picture of the noble, knowledgeable male, was a man anyone would be happy to impress.

Imogen was a gifted student, and her public school teachers twice moved her up a grade, with the result that she was always the youngest in the class. The social repercussions of this were not severe—some mild teasing for being the smallest girl and therefore of little use for team sports. And even this changed after her growth spurt at the age of twelve. She soon became adept at basketball, a favourite among the girls. Of slightly more concern—to her parents, anyway—was that she might be twelve or thirteen but all of her colleagues, as her father referred to them, were fourteen or fifteen. Was she to be granted the same rights and privileges as the older girls?

On the whole, since she was intellectually so mature, the answer to this was yes, and so her parents allowed her to ride her bike to visit with friends after school, provided she was home for dinner on time. As summer neared and daylight lingered, she was even allowed to go abroad after dinner, provided her homework was done.

The policy was not outrageously liberal. Her friends, after all, lived in the same neighbourhood so she had no need to travel far on her two trusty wheels. The library, her parents considered, was the limit of their daughter's personally known world, and they had no reason to imagine Imogen was ever outside the neighbourhood without their knowledge. The only member of the family who was also out and about in the world, albeit a much wider world, was her father. Her mother was too depressed to go out much. Alice was a complete stick who studied law and worked part-time in her father's office, and her two young sisters were not yet allowed off the property.

Josiah Lang was gone for two weekends of every month, owing, he said, to certain clients in Detroit—union clients—who could not meet on company time. On those weekends Rose Lang barely stirred from her room.

Imogen would lie awake on Sunday nights listening for the sound of her father's return. When eventually he arrived home, she would hear the soft opening and closing of her mother's door and her tentative steps down the stairs to greet him in the thin, dry voice of the chronically ill. In answer to his wife's queries about his business in Detroit, he would usually offer no more than, "Too boring, my love. Far too boring to go into."

Imogen had lately come across the works of Rudyard Kipling, and was particularly taken with *Kim*. She admired the characters who knew useful things, such as how machines worked, the names of rivers, or local geography. She resolved not only to ride her bike through every neighbourhood within a fifteen-minute radius, but to memorize, Kim-like, all the street names too.

Late one Friday afternoon, having completed her homework, and with an entire weekend ahead of her free of responsibilities, she set out on a route that would take her through Washington Heights and Brainerd, into the relatively uncharted (by her) territory of Hometown.

She found herself in an area of smaller houses, some of them quite rundown, with yards overpopulated with shouting boys. It was late May, and even though it was near dinnertime the sun was still warm on her back and she was glad she'd elected to wear just a thin cardigan over her dress. It always felt like such sweet freedom to finally shed the heavy outerwear of the Chicago winter. You couldn't help but be happy to be alive and mobile. The air was fresh, a stiff wind having blown the usual soot and stockyard smells away, leaving only the aroma of damp soil and new grass.

Imogen was humming "I'm a Yankee Doodle Dandy" as she rode along. She had to suddenly brake for a tabby that darted out from a hedge. "Silly cat," she said sternly, and went right back to humming as she pedalled on.

Just after she turned off Cicero onto Eighty-Seventh, a plum-coloured taxi passed her and pulled to a stop a hundred yards up the road. Automotive taxis were still a rarity, and Imogen had never imagined anything so exotic as a plum-coloured one. She pedalled a little faster to get a closer look.

The driver climbed out and unstrapped a tan-coloured suitcase from the rack on the rear. As Imogen neared she committed various other details to memory. Driver: mustard-coloured shirt, black waistcoat, tweed cap. Passenger: tall man not unlike her father with his derby hat, perfect semicircle of moustache, nose of a Roman centurion. He reached into a pocket and handed the driver some money. The driver tipped his cap, got back into his plum-coloured conveyance, and drove away, marring the springtime atmosphere with oily exhaust.

The passenger picked up his suitcase and pushed open the gate of a picket fence. The gate did not quite latch behind him, and as he turned to push it closed Imogen saw that the man not only resembled her father, he *was* her father. Over the course of the next half-second several competing emotions vied for dominance in her breast. The first was surprise. Her father was in Detroit—how could he possibly be here at the same time? Imogen was about to cry out to him, when another emotion took hold. This was a subspecies of fear with which she was not familiar and that she would later come to recognize as dread, the dark plunging sensation that something is wrong, deeply threatening, but as yet unknown.

Thirty yards remained between them. Imogen stopped pedalling and let the bike glide. *I'm being silly*, she thought, *of course nothing's wrong*. She had just decided that she would call out to him, when the front door opened and a little girl came running down the front steps and yelled a word that reverberated over the entire street—over Imogen's entire world. "Daddy!"

Imogen's father set down his suitcase. The girl ran to him and he scooped her up and swung her around, the way he did with Imogen's younger sisters, the way he used to do with her. He spun with the girl, the two of them seeming to turn as slow as an hour hand.

In that moment, as she would describe it to herself much later, Imogen existed between two worlds—the one being destroyed before her eyes and some other world yet to come. Even at the age of twelve she had suffered disappointments and heartbreak—the death of her twin sister being the gravest of these—but this was reality itself, her universe and all it contained, undone at a blow.

She wished—a kind of prayer, really—to go back in time, just by the crucial minute or two that would restore her world. She had wished the same thing when she saw Laura laid out in her red-and-white dress. She remembered the wish that somehow that other world, the one with Laura alive in it, would go on and on and this new one, the one soaked in tears, would never come.

Imogen was falling between worlds as the little girl ran back along the path and up the steps and into the house, the screen door slamming behind her and the piping little voice calling to someone inside. As her father bent once more to pick up his suitcase and then turned back toward the little gate to fully close it, he caught sight of the strange creature gliding by—open-mouthed, goggle-eyed—his daughter on her bicycle.

He saw her, and Imogen in turn saw the look of horror on her father's face, horror that turned instantaneously into guilt—an emotion she had never before recognized on the face of a parent. It had never occurred to her that her parents could be guilty of anything. Guilt was something to which only children were susceptible.

Her father's right hand came up from the gate as if to grip her shoulder and hold her back, though she was at least twenty feet away and on a bicycle. Then, as daughter and bike rolled past, the guilt and horror passed from his face. He pushed the gate shut—Imogen heard the decisive click—and turned back toward the house.

She rolled a few yards farther. There was no traffic other than a horse and trap half a block away. She looped around and rode back and refused to look toward the offending house and its offending denizens. The tears had not yet come—they would come soon enough—so she could not help but see from the corner of her eye the pretty woman who held open the door and then closed it behind her father as he vanished inside.

Imogen rode home at a slow, wobbly pace, as if the bike, too, were wounded. She went up to her room and pushed the door shut until the latch caught with a soft click. Her eyes were still dry. A part of her stood aside, observing. She had read somewhere of "shock," how the body when traumatized goes numb, at least for a time, one of Mother Nature's mercies.

Her brain shifted gears from numbness into a peculiar state of accountancy. She thought about writing things out as she sometimes did when confused. She even visualized the pen and paper.

Am I the only one who knows? Her younger sisters, giggly and carefree, were clearly unaware that their father had another family. Alice? Alice might know. Of all the members of the Lang family, excluding the head of it, Alice was the hardest to read. And Mother. Perhaps the long-ago death of her daughter was not the sole cause of her wraithlike existence, the way she had of not being present even when she was. For that was how her husband must make her feel. Someone of no account.

We're nothing to him, Imogen said to herself. That is how he is able to have a second family. This provoked another question.

Which family is primary? Surely the other family was the shadow family, the family you could ignore—after all, he was there only two weekends a month. The thought brought no comfort. The little girl she had witnessed leap into her father's arms was not more than four years old, at least two years younger than the youngest Lang. There-fore he had gone to them because we were not enough.

What shall we do about it?

What do I say to him?

What if I say something and he chooses the other family over us?

Faced with these unanswerable questions Imogen sat on the edge of her bed, gripping the counterpane until she heard Alice come home, her keys rattling in the small tray beside the door, her briefcase thudding to the floor beside the coat rack.

Imogen waited until she heard Alice's steps reach the landing and turn toward her room, which was at the other end of the house. She threw open her own door and rushed after her. "Alice? Alice, I must speak with you." The adult phrase was new to Imogen's lips, and Alice turned to her, one eyebrow raised.

Alice had her father's long face, his wide-set eyes that seemed to look past you, his wide cool brow and long nose. Her room was foreign territory to Imogen, who had set foot in it not more than half a dozen times in her entire life. Although Alice was not quite ten years older than Imogen, she had seemed like an adult—solemn and all-knowing—from an early age. And she had nothing of the maternal instinct common in older sisters.

Imogen did not know how to begin, and realized as she perched on the edge of the window seat that she was afraid of Alice, even though Alice had never been mean to her, indeed barely noticed her. She wondered if Alice found her younger sister equally alien, and decided it wasn't possible. Alice was the sort of person to whom the inner workings of the world are obvious, and little sisters would be entirely transparent.

Alice sat at the vanity, unpinning her hair, which was a lovely chestnut colour, long and luxurious. "Well?" she said toward the mirror. "What did you want to tell me?"

"Well, um . . . I was out riding my bike," Imogen began, and faltered.

"Go on."

"I don't know how to say it. It's too awful."

"Suppose you just say it," Alice said, dropping pins and clips into cut-glass pots. She allowed her gaze to fall on Imogen again, via the far panel of her reflective triptych. "Don't worry about how you say it."

So Imogen told her. When she got to the part about the little girl calling their father Daddy, tears ran down her face and neck, and speech became impossible.

Alice opened a drawer in her vanity and took out a neatly folded handkerchief and thrust it toward her. Imogen took it and pressed it to her face, weeping until she had soaked it through.

Alice picked up a silver-backed brush and started swiping at her hair. "What were you doing on Eighty-Seventh Street and—where did you say? Cicero?"

Imogen wiped her eyes and blew her nose. She wanted to crawl onto Alice's lap and curl up there but knew it would not be welcome. "What?"

"What were you doing way over there? What business had you?"

"I—I was just riding my bicycle."

"Perhaps you shouldn't stray so far from home next time."

Imogen had not known what to expect from Alice, but it was not this. "You don't stay home."

"I'm not a little girl. I'm a law student and a working woman."

A silence fell. Imogen watched Alice stroke a portion of her hair with the brush. She released it and it cascaded shining over her shoulder and breast.

"But what is Father doing over there?" Imogen asked. "Why does he have another family? You're not supposed to have two families. Nobody does."

She waited, hoping that Alice would turn to her and assure her it was not true, their father had no second family—what he had was a twin brother. A twin brother he didn't like to talk about, and that's why the two families had never met. It even made sense; everyone knew twins ran in families.

Alice's silence confirmed her horror.

"You knew."

Alice lowered the brush to her lap and, gripping it in both hands, turned to face Imogen for the first time.

"Look. I'm sorry you saw what you saw. It would have been infinitely preferable had you never found out."

"How did you find out?"

"She shows up at work sometimes—even with her daughter one time. They pretend she's a client. What difference does it make? You know what you know and you can't unknow it. You're just going to have to live with it."

"But why?"

The quiver in Imogen's voice sounded piteous even to her own ears.

"There is no why. Men do what they do and women must endure it."

"But no one has two families," Imogen protested. "Whoever heard of such a thing?"

"It doesn't matter who heard of what when, Imogen. Men can do what they want, within the bounds of the law, and the feelings of twelve-year-old girls don't enter into it. You're young to learn this but every woman learns it sooner or later, unless they want to hang themselves."

"Does Mother know?"

A curt nod.

"How do you know she knows?"

Alice leaned forward and gripped Imogen's shoulders. She shook her once, twice. "Mother knows. You hear? She knows—and you are not to raise it with her, do you understand? You are not to speak of it."

"But how can she—"

Alice shook her again. "This is grown-up business, Imogen. You are not to discuss it with Mother, with Father, or with anyone. Certainly not with Father."

"He has another family," Imogen wailed.

"It's not another family. Father and Mother are married. He is not married to this other woman."

"But that girl called him Father," Imogen said, then corrected herself. "She called him Daddy."

"She can call him whatever she wants, but Father is married to

Mother and that's that. He isn't leaving, if that's what you're worried about."

"I wish he would leave."

"No, you don't."

"I do. I hate him."

"No, you don't. In any case, hating him won't do any good." Alice
turned back to the vanity. She dabbed something fragrant on a handkerchief and wiped her face. "There's nothing to be done, Imogen. Go
and read a book and forget about it."

"Why didn't you tell me?"

"Are you happy, now that you know? Are you delighted to have this
knowledge about your father?"

"No."

"That's why I didn't tell you."

"You go to work with him. How can you?"

"I have no intention of justifying myself to you. I work in Father's law
firm and that's that. Now go and read a book and forget this ever happened. You are not an orphan. Nothing in your life is going to change."


Imogen noted in the questionnaire that her father's admirable traits
included intelligence and discipline, but restricted her enumeration of
less admirable traits to absent-mindedness. For a time, she harboured
a good deal of resentment that Dr. Ganz required his young residents
to open up their entire lives to him this way. One could not be certain,
after all, that his intent was benign, and it felt—perhaps especially to
his female students—as if one had been commanded to disrobe by a
man who could ponder your nakedness at his leisure. And it could
hardly escape the notice of a student of psychiatry that the relationship mirrored that of an analyst to his patients.

Still, she settled into the Phipps easily enough. In person, Dr. Ganz
continued to be welcoming; he even seemed to take a particular interest in her comfort. After rounds, he always managed to find a moment

for a personal comment or suggestion. "I thought your remarks on patient so-and-so were well taken," he might say. "See what you think of Dr. Kempf's recent papers on paranoia and homosexual panic."

His manner was so friendly and unassuming that Imogen was convinced she must be missing some European sense of irony.

During grand rounds—how she loved that expression, the "rounds" implying the quotidian, the "grand" implying a nobility all the sweeter for being available even to interns as lowly as Imogen Lang—he would stop before a patient and consult a five-by-eight-inch index card handed to him by a stenographer. He would then summarize the patient's life prior to admission, the presenting problem, and progress to date. If the patients minded this, they gave no sign. It was always done with the utmost courtesy, beginning with a click of the heels and a slight bow. These summaries reminded Imogen of obituaries in their life-encompassing brevity, but also in the equanimity of the doctor's tone. "Miss Hastings, being highly excited, snatched up a meat cleaver and severed her brother's hand before she could be subdued," he might say, with the calm of a geometry teacher describing a theorem, Miss Hastings showing no inclination to disagree. Facts, after all, were facts.

And facts, Imogen was learning, were everything to Jonas Ganz. Diagnosis was as nothing compared with facts.

One day, when Imogen asked why she had to interview the paternal aunt of a patient who had had no contact with the aunt for ten years, Ganz invited her to take a stroll with him around the cloistered courtyard. The days were getting colder, and the air had a bite to it.

"I've made two appointments for her to come in," Imogen said, "and both times she has not shown up."

"Some cases require more persistence than others—or more flexibility. You may need to see her after normal hours. From what you've said, you're far from understanding what underlies your patient's apparent break with reality."

"Perhaps it's just lack of insight on my part."

Ganz smiled at her. "Doubtful. More likely it's a shortage of information. When I was a pathologist at Indiana State, I was giving a lecture to the ward physicians and one of them asked me, 'Dr. Ganz,' he said, 'you have outlined numerous possibilities and similarities and conjectures, but can you tell us where in the brain the cause of the disease is located?' And do you know, I believe it was at that moment that I realized I no longer wanted to be a pathologist working in a laboratory, I wanted to be a psychiatrist working in a clinic. I answered him instantly, without thinking. I simply pointed at my briefcase and said, 'Gentlemen, the cause of the disease will be found in there, in the files, in his life history.' Mental disease is above all a *reaction*. Each patient faces unique pressures—pressures to which you and I would react differently. Now, what is it about *him*, about *her*, about her *life*, that causes her to react the way she does? To discover this you must *observe*, you must *ask*, you must *record*."

"But this aunt is not in his life."

"Really? And who is on your mind when you go to sleep at night? When you feel weak or afraid?"

"Well, a lot of people—my family. Perhaps an old friend."

"People who are not here."

"Yes, but—"

"Collect your facts, Dr. Lang. Collect your facts and then decide what's relevant."

Imogen was not alone in her frustration. The other interns also tired of writing patient histories, interviewing not just the patients but their parents, their siblings, their employers, their friends. Patients, overcome with shame, never wanted to grant permission at first, but Imogen found that when they perceived her genuine desire to understand, most of them relented.

Another sore point was that Ganz often made them go out into the field to perform such interviews. "I'm sorry," Jasper Bylsma, newly arrived from the Netherlands, cried, "but I do not want to inquire of a butcher whether his apprentice is masturbating at work or not."

"Why would that be?" Donna Artemis said in a sly voice. "Sharp objects make you nervous, Jasper?"

In his passion for observation Ganz reminded Imogen of Sherlock Holmes, though without the fictional character's theatricality. When he summoned her to his office, and those .45 calibre irises were aimed in her direction, she could not help but feel that he was mentally photographing her for later summing up on an index card. *Miss Lang is a tall, ungainly female with marked insecurities that she attempts to disguise with excessively correct manners and locution, or witty remarks. Perhaps ashamed of her rough Chicago provenance, she adopts the manner of the cool clinician, but her hands are restless and her eye contact sometimes fleeting.*

One evening after work she changed out of her white smock and stepped into the vestibule to knock on Donna's door.

Donna opened it and greeted her with "*Guten Abend, Doktor.*"

"Does Dr. Ganz make you nervous?"

"Hah! Come and sit awhile." Donna opened the door wider, and indicated the desk chair. "You can have the uncomfortable one." She herself plopped down in the Morris chair and adjusted the back into a more upright position. A volume of Janet lay open on the bed.

"Every time he speaks to me," Imogen said, "I'm convinced he's about to tell me I should find a nice respectable man to marry and forget I ever heard about psychiatry."

"Has he ever *said* any such thing to you?"

"Not in so many words, but . . ."

"And he never will. It's just his face, Imogen. I've never met anyone whose looks are in such contradiction to their personality."

"He looks like he suspects me of something terrible."

"I know. It throws everybody, at first. But have you noticed that the patients love him?"

"*Love* may be a bit strong."

"But they're not afraid of him, right? Don't you find that remarkable, when he has us all cowering?"

"Yes, I suppose it is."

"It's as if they have some sixth sense that he can really help them—even if he can't. They seem to see right past his facial expression."

"Either that, or their world is already so frightening that a demonic stare is not so bad."

"I'll tell you what I *do* like about him." Donna adjusted the chair again so that the footrest came down with a *clack*. "You can spend an hour with him discussing the most taboo subjects and there is absolutely no sexual *frisson* whatsoever. You know how with most men—and I don't mean lechers, I mean any man—with most men, there's an unacknowledged spark between you. The male-female charge. There's none at all with him. And I for one am really, really grateful."

"That's probably different for you." Imogen envied Donna's gamine looks, her doll-like size and perfect proportions. You wanted to pick her up and admire her like some fascinating *objet*. "Not everyone is so attractive, you know."

"Yes, I know. Isn't it just terrible?" Donna grabbed a pillow from the bed and threw it at Imogen. "Blockhead. 'Not everyone is so attractive.' Listen to her."

Imogen hugged the pillow, a strangely intimate thing, and didn't know what to say.

Ganz was behind his desk, surrounded by his jars of brains, his displays of spines, and the aroma of his omnipresent cigars, about to give Imogen her first quarterly review. Although he never failed to address her with respect and even kindness, she still sometimes thought he must be putting it on, or that he must behave in the same manner to all his residents. Yet Donna assured her this was not the case, that he had given her several dressings-down. Still, Imogen had been anticipating this meeting with dread.

A helix of cigar smoke curled from the ashtray and wound its way upward with the precision of a spiral staircase through a shaft of sunlight. Dr. Ganz balanced a clipboard on his knee, from which he read aloud the comments he would be placing in Imogen's file. "You have adapted yourself marvellously well to clinic routine, your patient histories are excellent examples of thoroughness combined with clarity and concision—a trick many never master. The patients, even the most difficult, respond to you with warmth and trust, which does not surprise me. I note a special rapport with those who suffer from depression. Two of these—Miss Garner and Mrs. Krumholtz— were released far earlier than initial assessment indicated was likely." He looked up from the clipboard. "I hope you're pleased."

"Oh, yes, sir—very. I'm sure I don't deserve such . . ."

"Yes, you most certainly *do*," Ganz said with a smile. "In fact . . ." Here he read from the clipboard. "'The only liability I see in the future for Dr. Lang is an innate lack of confidence—surprising in one whose young life is so rich with achievement.'"

He put the clipboard on the desk and took up his cigar. "Would you agree with that?"

"Lack of confidence? Well, yes—but it's well placed."

He puffed on his cigar, making the tip fiery, and squinted through the smoke. "I disagree. And in this you must bow to my greater experience. I know a good physician when I see one. I know an excellent psychiatrist in the making."

"Then why do I feel at sea so much of the time?"

"Because you should. So should we all, now and then." He tapped his clipboard with a well-manicured finger. "I'm interested in this rapport you have with our depressives. Several of the ward psychiatrists have noted it."

"Really?"

"Dr. Mackenzie and Dr. Quinn have both commented on it."

"Dr. Quinn?"

"High praise indeed. I'm wondering where this comes from. Something you mentioned to me before, concerning your mother . . . I'm wondering if we might not venture in that direction."

Imogen hadn't exactly *mentioned* her mother's moods. She had noted them in response to that intrusive questionnaire—a confessional lapse she was now regretting.

"Well, um, yes—she certainly suffers from what I should call depressive attacks. Stays in her room for days, won't see anyone, loses interest in all her usual activities."

"And the apparent cause, in your view—if there is one?"

"Well, the proximate cause would be my father's behaviour toward her."

"And not the death of her daughter at the age of five?"

"That was a matter of fate. It was not done to her by anyone. My father is cruel." Imogen squeezed her intertwined fingers until they whitened. "Very cruel."

"And yet in your psychological profile you wrote of your happiness as a child."

"As a *young* child. Before I knew what he was really like, especially to my mother."

"He is disloyal to her?"

"Yes."

"With another woman."

"I don't like to say, really."

"Of course not. It's painful to think of one's mother being hurt. But you realize I do not ask out of idle curiosity."

"Yes, I know."

"One of the sidelights of our profession is we get to analyze each other. Sometimes it can be painful. But if we don't do it to ourselves we can hardly expect the patients to put up with it."

"No."

"Also, it's essential to be aware of one's blind spots and sensitivities. All of us wear tinted glasses, and it's important to know what shade."

Imogen felt a wall of resistance building up inside her. But Jonas Ganz clearly saw the analysis of the human mind as a rarefied skill that required constant development, constant practice. "To be a psychiatrist," he had said in the morning staff meeting, "is not just a profession, it is a way of life, a mode of thought, and a practitioner cannot consider himself an adept until it becomes second nature."

"My mother knows . . . the situation," Imogen forced herself to say, "but she never speaks of it. No one in the family does."

"But why does she retire to her room? Is she punishing herself, do you think? Or is she punishing your father, withholding her affection?"

"Herself. She's punishing herself."

"But she has done nothing wrong."

"No, but she blames herself. It's obvious what she must be thinking: *Am I not enough for him? Am I so repellent that he must seek physical affection elsewhere?*"

"Why does she not get angry at him? Yell at him. Throw things, perhaps."

"One obvious reason is because she cannot afford to suffer the consequences of his anger in return. Were he to withdraw his support she would be impoverished overnight."

"And a less obvious reason?"

"She doesn't express anger because she doesn't feel anger. She feels hurt, dismay, disappointment, abandonment, unworthiness, loneliness, loss, worry, heartbreak."

"Indeed, it would be difficult to function under such a burden of negative emotions. How is it you have the list on the tip of your tongue?"

"Because I feel them myself."

There it was. It had just slipped out. Those eyes of his, which at first had seemed so threatening, now just expressed curiosity, a willingness to accept without judging. Imogen had never made such a revelation to anyone. It felt illicit, as if she had got away with something but might yet be caught.

"You feel them yourself—the loneliness, loss, and heartbreak. How could you not? Because it's not just your mother who gets left behind when your father goes wandering, is it?"

Imogen shook her head. Pressure was rapidly building in her chest, gathering in her throat. She pressed her lips together to hold it back, but something inside her gave way; the cry escaped her lips and the tears poured forth. It should have been humiliating, but the relief was too profound.

With just a handful of words, deftly applied, he took her deeper.

"As if it were not enough that he withdraws his love and attention from you, he drives your mother into a state so unresponsive that in effect he has orphaned you. At a stroke you are rendered not just fatherless but motherless."

The truth of this was so piercing she could do nothing but cry harder.

Ganz waited for the tears to subside a little, before encircling her with the warmth of a revelation of his own.

"I too feel a particular affinity with patients who suffer from depression," he said, "and I think I know why this is so." He set the clipboard down on the desk, and fingered his stack of index cards, puffing on his cigar for a moment and contemplating the smoke. "By the time I had won my MD and had finished my apprenticeships with Kraepelin and Alzheimer, there were no positions available in Zurich, or none that I wanted. At best I would have remained a lecturer in pathology, earning little, with little prestige and no hope of advancement.

"I decided to move to America. My father had died eight months earlier, and my mother was understandably still grieving, but I did not let that stop me. My older brother had moved away to Paris, but my younger brother, Michael, would still be in Zurich to provide her with company and support. My mother begged me not to go, ostensibly for my sake—I would be lonely, America was so big, I knew no one, et cetera—but of course she was concerned, too, for herself.

"I was ambitious. I had a small offer from the University of Chicago and I wanted to take it. So, despite my mother's protests, I got on the boat. Shortly after my arrival in the United States, she suffered a severe case of influenza. She recovered from the fever, but it left her in a condition, as she wrote to me, of 'unbearable sadness.' And then Michael, my younger brother, died."

"How awful," Imogen said. "Your poor mother."

"Indeed. She sank into a depression so disabling she had to be hospitalized at the Bergholzi, where I had previously worked. Her psychiatrist was Dr. Forel, who had trained me. I maintained a close correspondence with him, and he informed me that he did not think she would ever recover. I'll never forget his exact words: 'recovery, in her case, is extremely unlikely.'"

"You must have been devastated."

"I was deeply worried, of course. But I did not concur with Dr. Forel's prognosis. You see, I had one telling advantage over him: I knew my mother. Knew her strength, her resilience. I always believed she would recover, and luckily, after a period of some eighteen months, she did."

"Which is why you are telling me about her?" It came as a shock that her august director would open up to a mere intern this way.

"Partly, yes. But also as a way of explaining that you and I have this in common. In part because my own mother so suffered, and in part because I know she recovered and this gives me reason for more optimism than another physician might feel. I believe patients sense this optimism, which is entirely unfeigned, and take heart. I hope the same for you."

Imogen felt her cheeks redden. "I'm not depressed."

"But you didn't finish your thought about your mother. You have a way with depressed people because you love someone who is subject to such sadness. But there is another reason."

"Because I'm prone to it myself, you mean."

"Well?"

She had been feeling so light after her tears, but now shame and embarrassment crept in. He could see it on her face; she could feel him reacting before he even spoke. He leaned toward her now, his posture, his gaze, saying nothing in the world was more important to him at this moment than how his intern Imogen Lang felt about her tendency to depression.

"Yes, I suppose I am prone to it," she said, trying to keep her voice neutral. "I try to be aware when it is coming on and take appropriate steps—try to ensure I eat well, and get enough sleep."

"And do such measures help?"

"Do we have to talk about this?"

"No. But you need to know that we can talk about it. I want you to know in advance that, should you feel so afflicted, there is no need to hide away."

"I feel as if we're discussing a limp, or a facial deformity."

"The analogy is not exact. Talk is of little help in such matters."

# 5

Imogen was just beginning to feel she had got her bearings at the Phipps when she was sent off to the Byberry State Asylum for a three-month rotation. Located in the countryside northeast of Philadelphia, Byberry was not one of the grander institutions. The main building was a long bungalow, and the nurses' residence, where Imogen was housed, was an ugly block of yellow brick. The surrounding cottages were not cottages at all but brick, multistorey buildings labelled A, B, C, and D. Still, being tucked amid low hills and rich farmland, the grounds did offer a certain tranquility.

The director was Dr. Ben Zachary, a friendly, shambling man of sixty with hair like straw, who reminded Imogen of the Scarecrow in *The Wonderful Wizard of Oz*.

"Well, if you're at the Phipps," he said to her on her first day, "you must be a very intelligent young woman. We get nothing but the best from the Phipps. Room all right, dear?"

"Yes, it's fine." *Dear?*

"Should be comfortable enough. The nurses eat better than the rest of us, for some reason—I keep meaning to look into it. Have you been inside a state asylum before?"

"No, I haven't."

"Well, let's just say we're not the Phipps."

He ransacked his desk for a set of keys and, when he finally found them, held them aloft like a trophy. With his wild hair and his baggy suit he didn't seem like a doctor at all.

He took her on a tour of the wards, keys jangling with every step.

A and C Cottages were not much different from the wards of a general hospital, but D Cottage was a different matter.

"Have to move quickly," he said, as he unlocked a door, "otherwise I'll never get out."

He introduced Imogen to the ward psychiatrist and the floor nurse but she didn't take in their names because of the cacophony of the patients, some wandering here and there, talking, gesticulating, sometimes shouting. Others stood stock-still, muttering, or simply staring.

"Obviously an area visitors don't see," Zachary said. "If they did, families would never allow anyone to be admitted and we'd end up with them roaming the streets."

Imogen nodded, and tried to look unruffled.

Two patients were sitting in corners by themselves, rocking violently back and forth. A wild-eyed man paced from one side of the day room to the other, making agitated gestures, then suddenly stopped to stare at the ceiling or floor. Many slumped in chairs, clutching books or magazines, unopened, on their laps.

As Zachary pointed out various aspects of the facilities, a handful of patients rose from their seats and shuffled around him, tugging at his sleeve.

"Doctor? Dr. Zachary? May I speak with you?"

But he breezed on by, pointing and chatting the whole time, as if the patients were so many leaves, blowing around him.

Imogen was glad he did not ask her any questions. She doubted she would have been able to reply—not just because of the noise, but because of the smell. The ward was clean, its surfaces shining, but the floors were old and wooden and all the carbolic in the world was not going to wash away the smell of urine.

"Well, how did that strike you?" he said when they were outside again. "Still sure you want to be a psychiatrist?"

"Oh, yes," Imogen managed. "Quite sure."

She breathed in deep lungfuls of fresh air, as they headed back to the main building.

Dr. Zachary pointed to B Cottage. "Our violent ward. We don't put interns through that."

"Do you have laboratories on the grounds?"

"Oh, yes—we do all our blood work in-house." He looked at her. "Or did you mean experimental labs?"

"Yes. Experimental."

"The asylum is not a research facility. We house the mentally ill. Some of them get better, but not a lot. Rest and quiet may be enough for those in A or C, but the patients you just saw are not going home. The minute some clinic or hospital sends us a cure, we'll use it, but until then we're what the unkinder critics like to call a 'warehouse.' Personally, I think it's no small thing to keep psychotic people safe and comfortable—it's a kindness society has not always provided."


Although the asylum's nurses and psychiatrists were friendly, Imogen missed Donna. She spent her evenings in her room, studying German and reading Freud and wondering if she might be able to apply his thinking to psychotic patients—a prospect for which Freud himself expressed little enthusiasm—and writing long letters to her friend.

"I don't know what I expected," she wrote. "I suppose I thought I could look into the eyes of a mad person and see the injured, suffering person hiding in there and coax her out. But mad eyes are so opaque—like windows onto nothing. At times it makes me question the whole idea of psychiatry. From what I see on the back wards here, the patients' best friends are the attendants. They're almost completely untrained, but some of them are marvellous, even with the most paranoid."

She told Donna about a legendary attendant named Molly Myers. She was a short, tubby little woman, who never had a harsh word for anybody, no matter the provocation. Patients were constantly asking to be transferred to her ward, because she was so kind and so good-natured—but firm and consistent. She teased the patients in a way no handbook would ever recommend. Imogen heard her say, more than once, "So-and-so, my dear, you're as mad as t'ree hatters today, but I loves ya."

"I suppose," she wrote to Donna, "the Irish accent helps."

One Monday morning, Molly was absent. Patient after patient came up to Imogen, asking, "Where's Molly? When is Molly coming back? I have to see Molly!" In the course of a few days, their worry rose to near panic. The ward psychiatrist finally relented and told them the reason why Molly was gone. One of her daughters had caught diphtheria and died—just ten years old.

A wave of sorrow washed over them, and even the more agitated lapsed into silence for a time.

Imogen was there when Molly returned to the ward. As she was signing in and checking the logbook, the patients gravitated toward her from all corners of the room like ducklings toward the mumma duck.

"I don't think they even said anything," Imogen wrote. "They just drifted over, one by one, and touched her arm or shoulder. And the tears just streamed down her face. Eventually, of course, she wiped her eyes and blew her nose and then said, 'Yer all nuts, the lot a ya, but yer good folks and I loves ya to pieces.'"

Donna's letters in return were full of Phipps gossip. Ganz had appointed Ruth Fein, a senior nurse whose single available emotion seemed to be self-pity, to his Mental Hygiene Initiative—unqualified, Donna noted, but at least it was keeping her away from the patients. And Lila Quinn was growing more waspish by the hour. The woman was a positive fount of turmoil, completely unemployable anywhere else, and remained at the Phipps solely because Ganz could not resist birds with broken wings. The good *Doktor* had a bigger saviour complex than all the other psychiatrists put together. She also wrote about her own growing passion for Freud.

Imogen was beginning to consider Freud the Einstein of psychology. Although she couldn't see a way to cure the severely schizophrenic with his insights, she thought there might be a chance on the middle

wards. "That's my trouble," she wrote to Donna. "I want to be brilliant in the lab and a saviour in the wards!"

There was a patient in C Cottage named Sylvia, who was about
thirty-seven. She had been in the asylum for six months, her third
admission. According to the intake report, she was a high school
teacher who had stopped looking after herself, stopped writing to
her family, stopped seeing friends. When she stopped showing up at
the school they sent someone looking for her and found her dirty,
highly agitated, and delusional.

As Imogen was leaving the ward one day, Sylvia was being led away
by a nurse for hydrotherapy. With her bombed-out eyes and grey
skin, she seemed as frail as a ninety-year-old. This, Imogen knew, was
the toll her inner voices were taking.

Molly Myers, who was also observing, said, "She fights her demons,
that one. All day long, and all night too if you ask the night nurse.
And it just takes it out of her. Some o' these poor souls aren't able to
fight, God knows, and some just breaks under the struggle. But not
Sylvia. She'll fight 'em till the day they die—or she do."

Imogen went to Dr. Zachary and asked if she could try treating
Sylvia with psychoanalysis.

Zachary closed Sylvia's file and folded his hands on top of it.

"All afire with Dr. Freud, are you, dear?"

"Well, not for *every* patient." *Dear yourself,* she wanted to scream.

He tapped the file with a stubby finger. "Why this patient in
particular?"

Partly it was because Sylvia just looked more normal than the
other patients. She had none of the facial distortions or tics that were
so common on the ward. Except for the exhaustion, she looked like
someone Imogen might know in the outside world. But she didn't
say that.

"I think Sylvia's a reasonable candidate because she has days where
she can be lucid for an hour or two."

Zachary shook his head. "Not enough."

"I know. But most days, Sylvia is aware of her condition. She's unique in that respect. Even when she's quite florid, she seems to know there's something wrong with her—that she hasn't always been like this."

"She doesn't blame electricity? Or the Marconi company?"

"No. She says, 'I know there's something going on inside of me, something that needs fixing.' She's motivated and she has this modicum of insight—I think she'd be a good candidate."

Zachary winced a little. "We don't want to confuse her even more, do we, dear. What would be your approach?"

"Dream analysis and free association, to begin with. I'd go gently."

"You'd have to. Won't do to force self-knowledge on people too weak to bear it."

"I'll proceed at her pace, not mine, Doctor."

"Very well. Tell the ward psychiatrist you've cleared it with me."

*The ward psychiatrist actually laughed at me,* she wrote to Donna a few days later. *I mean literally. I don't understand that attitude. Or maybe I do. These asylum psychiatrists are bitter men—they can't advance because, stuck out here in the country, there's nowhere to advance to. They're cut off from all the new developments, and I think they're in a kind of despair.*

She met with Sylvia three times a week. Even maintaining eye contact was beyond her patient at first.

"Can you tell me why you find it so difficult to look at me?" Imogen asked. This elicited a tight shake of the head.

It was only on her fourth session—and it felt like a major triumph—that Sylvia found the courage to answer.

"It's him . . . my voice," she said haltingly. "The loudest one. Meanest one. He's screaming in my ear—even right now, right this minute—that you are a witch. You're evil. You're here to poison my mind."

"Are you able to tell yourself it's not real? That what it says is not true?"

"He says the same about you. Your every word. Lies."

Session after session Sylvia resisted dream analysis. She would tell Imogen she had had the most horrible nightmare but refuse to tell her anything more.

"Did it involve someone near and dear?"

"I can't say."

"Was it full of action—or was it more like a mood?"

"Please, Doctor. I can't say."

"Why can't you, Sylvia?"

"I can't. Please, I just can't."

Sylvia received any probing question, no matter how gently phrased, as if it were a sabre thrust, cowering, folding herself up tighter in her chair. She could not talk about her childhood, her parents, her siblings—even in the most general terms. When Imogen asked, "Tell me about your father," Sylvia wrapped her arms around herself and rocked back and forth.

Free association proved slightly more successful—at least in bringing repressed material to the surface. But the moment Sylvia recognized it for what it was, her eyes would dim and she would curl up again. Over the course of two months, Imogen believed she saw some improvement but nothing that could remotely be considered a breakthrough.

*I should have known better*, she wrote to Donna. *I was so naive—not because it's hopeless but because there's simply not enough time. Two months is barely enough time for normal people to get to know each other. She's had no time to adapt to the process, and it was bound to fail. If Dr. Zachary were better informed he would have never let me make the attempt—Dr. Ganz wouldn't have. I don't think I did her any harm, but I feel totally humiliated. I can't bear the smirks of the staff psychiatrists and I can't wait to slink back to the Phipps.*

Donna wrote back to her by return post.

1. Of course you didn't do her any harm.
2. Dr. Ganz won't let anybody try anything that isn't mandated by the principles of his "psychobiology," which—you notice—are nowhere written down.
3. You have nothing to slink about.
4. Come back immediately.

# 6

After her experience at Byberry, the Phipps seemed to Imogen a temple of reason. Beyond its walls, the world was at war—even the United States was now officially a belligerent, though so far no troops had actually been sent overseas. But inside the Phipps, a psychiatrist could walk the corridors unruffled by the screams, the tears, the sudden mad pronouncements of its inmates, because reason was as unthreatened here as the oaken doors and marble floors.

Just as the smells and oppression of Byberry seemed to reflect the moribund nature of old medical thinking, the beauty and openness of the Phipps seemed a reflection of Dr. Ganz's common-sense approach to everything. The high, wide windows, bright with sunlight, mirrored his endless curiosity about the human mind and the myriad ways it might go wrong. The breezy roof gardens, the patio, the gazebo, the cheerful fountain—in short, all that open air—were at one with his openness to fresh ideas, new avenues of research, all the various possibilities for eventual, if elusive, cures. His patience and compassion were as quiet and contemplative as the wooden cloister, a place surely constructed to encourage the calm of quiet reflection.

In contrast to the despair of Byberry, Dr. Ganz managed to infuse his clinic with a crisp sense of optimism. "Treatment, research, and teaching," he often said, "these are the three aims of the Phipps." If Imogen made an error of judgment that perhaps provoked tantrums in a patient and the wrath of the patient's family, Ganz would say, "It's all right. You have learned something today, have you not? You have tried a treatment, it has had a certain outcome, yielded certain data.

You know more now; you are a better physician, and you will never stop learning."

The greatest demand he made of his residents, and he was unrelenting in it, was for detailed patient histories. At Byberry Imogen had seen for herself the "histories" that accompanied a patient from another institution. They were never longer than a single page and consisted of little more than a synopsis of the presenting problem.

"All mental illness," Ganz drummed into them, "is a reaction." Indeed, sometimes he seemed almost to be saying there might not be any disease involved, at least not in the traditional sense. "Even a schizophrenic does not entirely 'lose his reason,' as we are so fond of saying. If you believe the Democratic Party is plotting to murder you, it is not so unreasonable to stay all day in a darkened room. The premise is false, but the response itself cannot be said to be irrational."

Imogen found this idea did much to increase her tolerance for patient ramblings. She could assume incorrect premises lurked behind the mad verbiage and thus see it as less mad than ineffective, that the patient's reason, however vestigial, could be nursed back to health. All of Ganz's ideas encouraged optimism that, despite the absence of any actual cure, a physician could do much.

"Something in *this* patient's life," he would insist, "has made her respond in *this* way. Your task is to find out what has made her react the way she has. If you do not discover a specific inciting event, what you *may* discover is a *series* of events or sets of circumstances that help to explain *why* such a reaction might occur. If you have this in hand, believe me, the patient will recognize that you understand her better than anyone ever has, and you are a long way toward gaining her trust, her faith that you can help her learn more efficient ways of responding."

Imogen hoped that this was so—it had to be so—because what Ganz meant by a complete history was an exhaustive history. In a matter of days, you would know more about a patient than you knew about any member of your own family.

When she was eventually allowed to take the occasional male patient, Ganz assigned her one James "Jimmy" Worth. Jimmy had been working on his Ph.D. in mathematics at Johns Hopkins when he began to suffer from delusions, the most detailed of which involved a colony of mathematicians who lived on the dark side of the moon and were planning to take him there as soon as he was "ready." He was a good-looking young man, and also one of the brightest mathematicians Hopkins had ever produced. He had never shown any previous sign of schizophrenia, and it was thought this episode was most likely a transient event brought on by the stress of graduate work. A few weeks of hot baths and cold packs, along with deep, regular sleep, appeared to have set him aright, and Imogen worked with him for only three weeks before he was discharged. Even so, he took a strong liking to her and promised to come back and show her his thesis the moment it was accepted.

Her next serious therapeutic involvement was with Millie Nielsen, a twenty-nine-year-old salesgirl at Hutzler's department store, who had tried to kill herself by jumping into the Baltimore harbour in the middle of the night. She was unable to swim, and might well have drowned had she not been saved by an alert seaman on a Swedish freighter.

In the months leading up to her plunge into the harbour, Millie's behaviour had become increasingly bizarre. She had alienated her fellow sales clerks by repeatedly accusing them of plotting against her, and more recently she had become convinced the trolley tracks were speaking to her, commanding her to do terrible things.

Imogen spent hours with Millie's father, her mother being deceased, collecting the minute details upon which Dr. Ganz insisted. As a resident, she was expected to carry actual protocols with headings and subheadings beginning with birth itself and read them out: *Special circumstances surrounding? Instrumental delivery? Premature? First, second, third of how many children? Twin?*

And moving on a little: *Quiet or fussy baby? Easily disturbed by noise? Breast- or bottle-fed—feeding problem? Malnutrition? Illnesses—accidents—*

*convulsions? Age of walking? Age of talking (words and sentence formation)? Response to habit training?*

Millie's father, Reggie Cobb, was a high school janitor, and could not fathom why on earth his daughter's doctor was asking these things that were so very remote from his daughter's jump into Baltimore harbour. And that was before Imogen had even broached childhood and adolescence, under which she was supposed to record serious illnesses, operations, domestic upheavals, deaths in the family, economic strains.

Sitting across from her in the interview room, Mr. Cobb sometimes glowered, sometimes wept, as he tried to recall the minutiae of Millie's early years. Imogen pushed on to *Sleep habits: Bed alone? Night terrors? Sleepwalking?* and then to *Food habits: Fussiness over food? Vomiting? Gagging? Dawdling over meals?* At this Cobb cheered a little.

"Millie was one fussy little princess. Wouldn't eat anything but bologna sandwiches for months on end."

And then the less congenial subjects of *Toilet habits, Bedwetting, Emotional control: Tantrums? Sulking? Whining? Tears?*

Mr. Cobb looked upward as if to his deceased spouse for confirmation.

"Millie was a quiet little thing, mostly." He puffed on his pipe, perhaps trying to convey an image of the responsible father. "Yes, she was a good girl."

*Do any circumstances surrounding the above facts stand out as having a possible influence on your daughter's current habits and attitude toward life?*

Mr. Cobb snatched the pipe from his teeth.

"What, you mean what she ate for breakfast back in 1903? I'm telling you there's something wrong with the girl's nerves. With her brain. Not with her table manners. Her brain's all scrambled up."

Imogen gripped her pencil and moved on to *School background: Age on entering kindergarten or first grade—public or private—country or city. Repetition of grades? Special difficulties with subject matter? Friction with teacher? Age on leaving elementary school—grade reached? Age on entering high school—date of graduation? College? Business school? Special courses in music, arts, home economics? Give dates in chronological order.*

Dear God, all this, and she hadn't even got to sex. Residents were expected to glean not only the patient's level of information about sex but at what age they learned what, who from, and what effect it had on them. Millie, upon admission, was in no shape to answer any questions that did not revolve around her belief that the staff of the Misses' Shoes department on the fourth floor were closely allied with the elevator operators in a plot to bring her down. Still, Imogen did get her to agree to two hours of hydrotherapy, which would consist of a continuous bath strictly maintained at a temperature of 94 degrees Fahrenheit.

Dr. Ganz was well versed in the latest twists and turns in Freud's psychoanalytic theory, but he was not one to throw out any therapeutic technique that had been shown to work. The hydrotherapy facilities in the Phipps's basement were of the highest quality and so far Imogen had never heard of a patient refusing the continuous bath. During the blackest moods of her own adolescence, she had occasionally resorted to a hot bath herself.

It was amusing to see such a household remedy, albeit refined with the latest technology, at work in the country's most prestigious hospital. Of course, it was not a matter of a twenty-minute soak. The minimum duration was forty-five minutes, and two hours was standard, applied daily, sometimes twice daily where needed, for weeks on end. And it did work. It could calm the panicked, quiet the manic, and even somewhat settle the inner chaos of the psychotic. The nerve clinics would credit the soothing effect of vasodilatation; Freud suggested that it was a return to that acme of comfort, the mother's womb; Jonas Ganz liked it because it worked.

Millie emerged from the tub room after a couple of hours' immersion on her first day, her cheeks flushed as if she had just engaged in a game of tennis. She was tucked into a bed on the admissions ward and was sipping a cup of tea when Imogen came to see her again.

"There's no need for me to be in bed," Millie said. "I would really prefer the garden."

"I'm glad you're feeling better," Imogen said, "but all our patients spend the first twenty-four hours in bed. That way we get a sense of where you are emotionally, physically, mentally, in the absence of any kind of strain or excitement. Also, it creates a buffer between your convalescence and your experiences of the past few weeks."

"Are you going to be my doctor?"

"One of them. Dr. Quinn is the ward psychiatrist, so she is ultimately responsible for your care. Now I hope you're comfortable because I'm going to be asking you a lot of questions."

"That's all right."

"Some of them you may find intrusive, but I assure you that all the information will be useful to us in working out how best to help you."

"I may not answer all of them," Millie warned her. "I may not answer any of them."

As it turned out, Millie was voluble. She didn't even balk at the questions regarding her discovery of sex. At the age of eleven, she had been playing on the neighbours' porch with an older friend when they came across what Millie thought was a balloon. Her friend knew better and told her it was something you used when having sexual intercourse. Millie had never heard the expression before and wondered whatever could it mean? It's when a man lies on top of a woman, her knowledgeable friend informed her—you know, so that they don't have a baby. Imogen's gentle but persistent questioning elicited the information that Millie had been confused on the matter for several subsequent years, believing it was not the sheath that prevented conception, but the man's lying on top of the woman. Somehow that preposterous action prevented a woman from having a child.

"And did you come to a clearer understanding later?" Yes, she did, but only because she searched through the science section of the local library until she found a book on female health.

Imogen yearned to be asking her about her current situation, recent setbacks at work, in love, in family connections, but it was a *history* they were expected to construct, and that meant plowing on. *Onset of menstruation and attendant circumstances and facts. Onset of curiosity about sex, how satisfied. Any secrecy or shame associated with it?* Imogen doubted she would ever come across a patient who hadn't felt stealthy and ashamed about sex, certainly not a female.

So far, so good. But Dr. Quinn was standing at the foot of the next bed, eyeing Imogen up and down. She was young to be a ward psychiatrist, not much over thirty, small in stature, with a fine-boned grace somewhat marred by a slight curvature to her back, perhaps a mild scoliosis or an old injury. Imogen was about to embark on some of the most sensitive questions—*Sexual transactions after puberty? before puberty?*—when Dr. Quinn spoke up. "Your chart for Miss Obermeyer is not up to date."

"Yes, I'll be getting to it before the end of shift."

Imogen turned back to her patient.

"I note also that Mrs. Waldstein has not had a complete night's sleep in three days and yet no chloral, no bromide, nothing has been administered. Do you have some personal objections to the treatment of insomnia?"

"Mrs. Waldstein felt she was becoming habituated to chloral, so she's been having an extra bath in the evening."

"All decisions on medication go through the ward psychiatrist."

"Yes, well, you were not on duty, and—"

"I repeat: all decisions on medication go through the ward psychiatrist."

"Perhaps you're not aware, I do actually have an MD."

"Oh. Different from the others, are you? More experienced? Wiser? Ready to run the place? Just perform your duties as expected, if you please, and don't be so high and mighty."

Dr. Quinn let the chart fall back against the foot of the bed with a loud clack, and headed off to torment some other resident.

Imogen turned back to Millie, who had now screwed her eyes shut tight and gripped the edge of the sheet.

"Millie? Millie, it's okay. She's angry with me, not with you. May I ask you a few more questions?"

Millie pulled the sheet up over her head. Imogen watched it quiver for a few moments.

"I've got some very interesting questions for you now. They're extremely personal, and you may not want to answer but I hope you will."

The small voice came back from under the sheet. "Ask what you want, I don't care."

"All right. Tell me about infatuations with individuals of your own or the opposite sex. During your adolescence."

No answer.

"You can keep the sheet up if you like. What did or do you do for relief of the sex impulse? How do you attempt to regulate this?" Until she came to the Phipps, Imogen had never met a female who admitted to *having* a "sex impulse." *What forms of sex arousal are you now subject to? What is your sex goal?* Imogen was not even sure what was meant by "sex goal," and to make it more comfortable reframed the question as "What part would you like sex to play in your life?"

Millie wouldn't answer any of them. Eventually she lowered the sheet and said, "It's still here."

"What's here?"

"It."

"Do you mean me?"

"It."

"You mean I'm a thing. Because of the questions I ask? Is that it? To ask you about sex in that way seems inhuman?"

"It."

Later that night Imogen knocked on Donna's door with the patient history protocol in hand. Donna was in her dressing gown, a tatty old thing held together with what looked like a schoolboy's scarf.

"Can you explain Lila Quinn?"

"Oh, dear. A little frazzled, are we? Go fetch your cup. I'll share my hot chocolate."

Imogen came back with her cup and saucer.

"You take the chair."

Donna poured some chocolate from her own cup into Imogen's. She propped her pillow up against the desk and sat on the bed, her legs folded beneath her. She was such a fetching combination of curves and angles that Imogen had to suppress an impulse to curl up beside her as she recounted the afternoon's events.

"Yes, that's her favourite trick," Donna said, "humiliating an intern in front of a patient."

"I hadn't even done anything wrong."

"Even if you had, it's obviously bad form to tear a strip off a colleague in public. Have you ever seen her interview a patient?"

"No."

"It's terrifying. So harsh. Impatient. She must imagine she's a force for reality, but she just comes across as some kind of pull-your-socks-up sergeant-major."

Imogen sipped her chocolate.

"You're looking profound again," Donna said. "It's tiresome."

"Well, it makes me wonder about Dr. Ganz, that's all. Why would he keep such a person on staff? Why have her near patients?"

"Well, she's addicted to her work, for one. That woman does not go home until long after shift ends. She takes endless trouble over her patients, keeping up contact with their families and so on. She writes hundreds of papers. She's very involved in community mental hygiene—one of Ganz's pet projects. She runs a tight ship."

"And she's thoroughly nasty."

"And she's nasty—which can't be good for the patients, so you're right: why does he keep her on?"

"Perhaps simple kindness? She has that unfortunate scoliosis. I suspect she's in pain a good deal of the time and that's what makes her irritable. And lonely, too, don't you think?"

"I don't know about that."

"Well, she's a spinster at thirty-five or so. Doesn't seem to have anything but her work. I think she's terribly lonely and Dr. Ganz feels protective toward her. That's a good instinct, don't you think?"

"Maybe. Unless you run a psychiatric clinic."

"On another subject . . ." Imogen held up the protocol. "How do you get through this thing? How do you make yourself ask these questions? I'll never be a psychiatrist if I can't."

"I don't really see the problem, Imogen. You're a physician—you wouldn't have any trouble asking about polyps or diarrhea. Why should this be any different?"

"Because it is different. People don't routinely talk to a physician about sex. And we certainly don't ask about it. I mean I do it, but I'm blushing furiously the whole time."

"I had the same trouble on my rotation here last year. Everybody does. That's why half the women drop out. I nearly did, myself. Shall I tell you my secret?"

"Immediately."

"I just pretend I'm an actress, on a stage. I have to play the *part* of a psychiatrist who is not timid about asking these sorts of questions."

"And that works?"

"I don't even think about it anymore. It just began to feel natural."

"It sounds too simple."

"Why does that matter?"

Imogen smiled.

"What's funny?"

"You are."

"I am never funny. Withdraw that remark at once."

"You are, and it's adorable."

"Then tell me about your love life."

"I can't. I don't have one."

"You do. Tell me, you timid little mouse."

"No."

"All right. Let's try a little free association. Close your eyes and tell me the first thing that comes to your mind. Come on—I'll be Freud, you be the hysteric."

"No."

"Imogen, don't be boring."

"All right." Imogen closed her eyes.

"Cigar."

"Father."

"Duck."

"Quack."

"Sock."

"Mock."

"Punt."

"Runt."

"Hunt."

"Fox. And you are stacking the deck, missy."

"I am not. Penis."

"That's it. I quit."

They talked on into the night, talked as if they had been friends their whole lives. So delicious to open up to a lively, and beautiful, person like Donna. Donna told her about an ill-fated romance, a narrowly avoided wedding, her first sexual encounter, which took place on an extremely uncomfortable picnic table. Imogen told her about Quentin, and cried a little. "He could be lying in a trench somewhere, wounded and dying, and his last memories of me are me telling him to go away."

"Not at all, darling. He'll have seen the kindness underlying everything you said and did. He'll know you were trying *not* to hurt him, to protect him."

"Oh, I doubt that."

"Well, I don't, and I'm far more perceptive than you."

Imogen wanted to say, "Do you know, I grew up with three sisters—four for a while—but I feel like you're the first real sister I've ever had." But she remembered having said something similar to Quentin and felt it might be bad luck.

Millie's husband, Eustace, came in for an interview one night after work. He was employed in the packaging department of the Bromo-Seltzer factory, a pudgy little man with a rubbery face and thick round spectacles. He was only ten years older than Millie, but he looked and spoke like a much older man.

"My wife," he said, when he was seated, "was the most light-hearted girl you could ever meet, before all this happened."

Imogen asked him many of the questions from the family interview protocol. He answered them thoughtfully, as if he had long known doctors to ask such questions and it was only to be expected.

"I know she shouldn't be home alone while she's in this . . . condition," he said. "She starts talking to streetcars and next thing you know she's jumping in the harbour. I'm at work all day. Her father's at work all day. And her mother died years ago. But when do you think she might be coming home? It's awful without her."

"It may be quite some time yet."

"This hearing streetcars talking—sending her messages—that's not going to be forever, is it?"

"We don't know yet if these delusions are a symptom of a long-term illness such as schizophrenia, or a more passing ailment brought on by temporary circumstances. Millie is showing a mixture of emotional symptoms—her deep unhappiness, for example—and also elements of paranoia. We'll be able to tell more when she's had some rest."

"She definitely needs sleep. Last couple of months, she's just been pacing all night, saying all sorts of nonsense to herself. I tell her to come back to bed but it's like she doesn't even hear me. I don't even know this person she's turned into—she's not the woman I married, that's for sure. She will be getting better, won't she?"

"It's too early to tell. A week or two of good sleep could make all the difference."

"Because—" Mr. Nielsen removed his glasses, and pinched the bridge of his nose for a moment. When he had collected himself, he put his glasses back on and said, "Because—without Millie—my life isn't worth a whole lot."

After only a week, Millie's talk of speaking streetcars and plotting salesgirls became intermittent, rather than constant, and the colour came back to her cheeks. She became more cheerful and, with a good deal of coaxing from Imogen, began to take part in occupational therapy, as well as in social events arranged for the patients.

After two weeks, she pronounced herself "shocked" at her former behaviour, and her husband declared that Millie looked ready to come home. Imogen asked them to wait, to give the apparent improvements time to solidify. Millie reluctantly agreed to stay another week but no longer.

"I can't talk them out of it," Imogen said at the next staff meeting. "Her behavioural changes seem far too sudden to be real. But her husband desperately wants her home, and she wants to go."

"We are not police," Dr. Ganz said. "She is not here on a warrant. If she demands to go home, and her husband wants her, there's nothing we can do to stop it."

"Perhaps if you talked to her, sir."

Lila Quinn pounced. "You're a resident, not a first-year medical student. Impress upon these people your medical authority."

Imogen reddened. "I've tried, but they won't listen to me. Perhaps they'll listen to Dr. Ganz."

Ganz demurred. "Unfortunately, I leave tomorrow for Los Angeles and will be away for the next four weeks. Talk to them both one more time. Give it your best. And if they insist on her release, arrange for her to see you in the dispensary once a week for the first month at least. Her improvement is considerable—even the night nurse has remarked on it. Let's hope your fears are exaggerated."

Millie was released two days later, bright and chipper, into the welcoming arms of her husband. She told Imogen she would definitely come back for her first follow-up in a week's time, she would even look forward to it. She and her husband filled out the forms and signed the papers and left the building in a glow of love for each other and gratitude to the Phipps—in particular to Dr. Lang.

When Millie did not arrive for her appointment the following week, Imogen sent a bicycle messenger to her address, but he returned empty-handed. She woke that night and could not fall back to sleep. She stood by the window and watched the elms sway against the first damp gusts of a storm that soon broke, hurling fat drops of rain against the glass. She watched for almost an hour before returning to bed and a fitful sleep.

A letter arrived the next morning—not from Millie but her husband. It had been written the night before.

Dear Dr. Lang,

I am sorry to tell you that my loving Millie has this day taken her own life, as she has long wanted to do. She was always a cheerful girl until this sickness came along and took all her happiness away—and put in its stead a misery unbearable to see. But she will no longer have to suffer so, for this morning she wrote a note before taking the trolley to Twenty-Ninth Street and stepping in front of a train. In her note she blames no one but herself, as was ever her way, and says that she was only counterfitting happiness in order that she might come home and spend a short while with me before ending her time here on earth. She charged me to be sure and thank you for all your kind efforts and so I do. There was nothing you could have done better, Doctor, as the disease was implackable if that is how you spell it.

Yours sincerely,
Eustace Nielsen

# 7

It did not help that Lila Quinn was now not only her direct boss, but actively in charge of all the wards in Ganz's absence. Upon receipt of Eustace Nielsen's note, still in the fog of shock, Imogen sought out Dr. Quinn and asked to speak to her in private. They went into one of the special rooms off the main corridor.

"Well?" Quinn said, tucking a strand of hair behind her ear. For some reason she wore a nurse's cap even though she was not and never had been a nurse. "What is it?"

"Millie Nielsen has—has killed herself." Imogen handed her the note.

Quinn glanced at it, then said, "This goes in the file." She squinted at Imogen. "Are you crying? Don't you dare cry. In the first place it is not how a physician responds to news of a patient's death and in this particular case you've lost any right you may have had for tears."

"But it's such terrible news."

"Indeed it is. But hardly unexpected. Did I not tell you to impress upon the Neilsens your authority as a doctor and as a psychiatrist? Did I not tell you to be firm?"

"I was firm, and—"

"Not firm enough, clearly. The woman is dead."

"And that was not Dr. Ganz's advice. He said—"

"'We are not police.' I know what he said. Don't tell me what he said. Obviously we could not imprison her. But if you had followed my advice, the poor woman might well be alive today and this poor man"—Quinn waved the note—"might still have a wife."

Imogen sank to a chair and covered her face with her hands.

"No." Lila Quinn grabbed her wrists and pulled her hands away. "No, you *don't* get to hide and you *don't* get to cry. You continue to perform your ward duties like a professional—unless that too is beyond your capabilities."

Imogen did go back to the ward, but all that day she moved in a state of numb distraction. Others had to repeat things to her before she took them in. She forgot what she was intending to do from one moment to the next, forgot what she had intended for her patients, wanted only to hide in her room so she could tend to her self-blame in whatever way might be available. In the evening she curled up on her bed but could not sleep or read or do anything that might erase the images of Millie Nielsen, so happy to be leaving the Phipps, stepping in front of a train.

That same week Imogen was invited—well, actually ordered—to assist Taunton in the psychology lab. His graduate student had quit or transferred, and he needed someone to help test some new equipment.

He had acquired a contraption for measuring the grip strength and endurance of infants. It consisted of a miniature trapeze bar suspended over a table. The bar was hooked to a spring, which was in turn connected to a timer and a scale. Imogen spent two whole mornings helping him rig it just so, no baby involved.

"Just in time," Taunton said, when she came into the lab on the third day, "I've snared us an infant from the Lane Home next door."

Imogen went to the pram that was parked beside the centre table and peered in. "Hello, sweetheart," she said, and touched a warm cheek. "Aren't you a pretty one. What are we going to do with her?"

"Him. I don't know. Bake him in a pie?"

"Excellent idea," Imogen said. "I'll find us some knives and forks."

Taunton stopped fiddling with the spring mechanism and turned to her. "That's pretty funny, for a woman. I might have said that myself. Women are rarely funny, have you noticed?"

"That's only when men are around. We're hilarious on our own."

"I'm skeptical."

"Well, you've had no chance to observe, have you."

"Okay, wiseacre, hand me the kid."

"What's his name?"

"Max. But we'll call him Baby Edward in our paper."

Imogen lifted Max from the pram and placed him on the table beneath the grip bar. "I'd better keep my hands just underneath him, don't you think? For when he lets go?"

"He's fine. He'll just land on the pillow."

"And if the pillow slides off the table?"

"He'll probably sustain minor injuries, perhaps a little brain damage."

"Nothing to worry about, then."

"Just don't touch him until he lets go of the bar. The readings will be worthless otherwise."

"Yes, I think I've figured that out."

Taunton unhooked a three-pound weight from the bar and set it on a shelf. "Look, this isn't a meeting of the Suffragette Society I'm running. If you want the vote, swell—I'm all for it—but leave your attitude at home, all right?"

"Yes, master."

"God. Where did Ganz dig you up?"

"Out of the vast pile of Phi Beta Kappa applicants with degrees in science and doctorates in medicine."

Taunton looked at her. "Well, we know what your cardinal sin is, don't we. Where'd you do your science?"

"Chicago."

"Really—did you know Kimbel?" Taunton's face had changed, arrogance replaced by genuine interest, and Imogen felt the sweet stirrings of pride.

"I took psychology with him. He was positively loony about William James."

"That's Kimbel. Good God, what is that horrible smell?"

"Oh, dear."

Imogen pulled a clean diaper from the pram. "I'll take him to the ladies' room."

"There's a fire hose in the hall. Use that."

The ladies' room offered nothing that might serve to make cleaning up a beshitten infant any easier. Imogen delicately washed him off under a tap, which provoked from his twisty little mouth an aria of outrage. She wiped him dry using the clean portion of the dirty diaper. Taunton, a father of two, would know at least as much about changing diapers as Imogen, but it hadn't occurred to her to suggest he deal with it; women were women, after all, and men were men.

She swaddled the baby in the fresh diaper and tickled his nose a couple of times. The watery blue eyes rounded with surprise. He gurgled and reached up with tiny doughy fists. Imogen tilted her head and allowed him to grasp her hair and pull her face toward him. He cooed and she cooed back, a response that surprised her since she had not suspected herself of having any affection for babies and had always assumed she could get through life quite happily without them. Realistically, this was impossible; everyone had babies. Women who didn't were pitiable figures, prone to neurasthenia and secret addictions. Her heart was suddenly suffused with an ache—the realization that she very much wanted children and very much wanted a husband, provided he was nothing like Taunton. She looked into Max's pale eyes and said, "Would I be a terrible mumma, Max? Would you give me a B? B-minus?"

Max belched a bit of milky foam and said, "Hih."

"You're quite a disgusting little thing, aren't you? Say 'Yes, Doctor. Very disgusting. Horribly disgusting.'"

She pried his chubby fingers from her hair and carried him back to the lab.

"You took your time," Taunton said. "I hope you beat him."

"Soundly."

Taunton had her hold the baby under the trapeze bar, and when he grasped it she let him dangle using his own strength, keeping her hands just underneath to catch him. She thought he would hang on for only a second, but he surprised her.

"Twenty seconds," Taunton said when he let go.

"Clearly a circus baby, then." She gave Max a playful squeeze and said, "Aren't you the little Hercules."

"No, no," Taunton said. "You mustn't reward him."

"I wasn't rewarding him, I was just—"

"Just listen, will you? Remain neutral." He steadied the trapeze bar. "All right. Again."

They repeated the experiment five more times. Imogen, stung by Taunton's words, glared at him when he wasn't looking and rehearsed the bitter retort she would have liked to make. Had Taunton been ugly and a dullard, perhaps it would not have hurt.

"All right," Taunton said, when Max balked at any more grasping, "he's had enough. You can put him back in the pram."

Imogen did so. Max was asleep before she could tuck the coverlet under his chin.

"You're very quiet," Taunton observed.

"I'm being neutral."

"Ah, I see. Got your back up, have you?"

"I'm being neutral."

"Stew, if you must, but you still have to write up the results. That binder over there. Use my previous write-ups as a model. I'll check it when you're done."

Several possible responses vied in Imogen's mind. She was not a psychology student, she was a resident psychiatrist; Taunton had no authority over her. As far as she could determine, Lila Quinn was doing him a favour by handing him one of her staff to fill in for his assistant. That being the case, she should be spoken to with the respect generally accorded to a doctor and fellow professional.

She went over to the table and opened the binder. She could just walk out. That would surely earn a reprimand from Dr. Quinn. Then, too, Taunton could let it be known that she was a know-all who couldn't take instruction—a good argument made flesh for keeping women out of the medical-scientific community.

She glanced at Taunton's write-ups. They were clear, brief, and in a surprisingly feminine hand. This wouldn't take more than half an hour.

"I'll need your notes," she said.

"Yes, of course. I may have to interpret my scrawl for you."

He came over to the table and set his notebook open beside her. "Starts here." He pressed his index finger on the place. His hand was beautifully articulated, strong and elegant-looking. His skin glowed tawny next to the white of his shirt cuff. Despite her temper, Imogen wished she was wearing something more attractive than her clinic whites. If she were more attractive, her pique might upset him more. Don't be such a child, she told herself. Just get the thing done and get out.

"I'm sorry," Taunton said.

"Pardon me?" Imogen stopped writing.

"I'm sorry. For jumping on you earlier." His hand came to rest on her shoulder.

"I see. Well."

"I'm drawn to you, that's all. I see in you similarities to myself— spirit of inquiry, resistance to authority—and physically you are very distracting indeed." His other hand came to rest on her other shoulder, his warm fingers gently kneading her muscles. Imogen had received unwanted attention from men in the past, but never from anyone so physically attractive, and never from a teacher or employer. The only instruction she had received in such matters came from books in which the advice amounted to avoiding any situation in which you would be alone with a male. A stranger on a bus would have received a smart slap, but she was at a loss how to respond. She stared straight ahead. The faucets and counters of the lab seemed to glow in a heightened and useless way. Taunton's hands, his beautiful hands, felt good, his touch awakening longings she had almost forgotten, but they also felt wrong.

She wriggled her shoulders and tried to slip from his grasp without actually getting up and confronting him.

"Just hold still," he said. His voice was soft, now, all the sarcastic bite gone.

And now I've revealed myself, she thought. I didn't jump up right away, I didn't say "Stop" right away, and now it's too late. "Please don't do that," she said, but her tone, in contrast to her words, conveyed little that could be called negative.

His right hand shifted a little, a finger grazing the skin of her neck above her collar. The power of this feathery touch amazed her, nerves transmitting a shiver upward to the roots of her hair, a scalding flush to her cheeks, and a silky yearning between her legs. An ache seemed to open in her chest and she realized she had stopped breathing. "Don't." She stood, pushing her chair back and forcing him away.

"Why such hostility, Imogen?"

"Dr. Lang, if you please."

"Fine. Have it your way. You want to be alone, I'll leave you alone." He snatched up his briefcase and headed for the door. "But don't be surprised if you end up alone for a very long time."

After dinner she related this outrage to Donna.

"Well, there you are, sashaying around him, a nubile young woman, essentially begging him to ravish you—what do you expect, Imogen?"

"I call that a very rude thing to say."

"It was a joke, you fool." Donna got up from her Morris chair and put her arms around her friend. "You really are too innocent. Especially for a psychiatrist." She pulled back a little, round blue eyes scanning her face. "Is that why they named you Imogen? Because it sounds like 'innocent'?"

"It doesn't sound a bit like 'innocent.' And I was dressed in my whites, for God's sake. You can't get less provocative than that."

"You must have said something intelligent then. Some men find intelligent remarks erotic in the extreme."

"I did nothing of the kind. You know perfectly well I'm not capable."

Donna pointed at her with a prosecutorial finger. "You said something funny then."

"No. Well, maybe a little. And then he said, 'Women are so rarely funny, don't you find?'"

"Clearly we should blow up his laboratory."

"You're taking this very lightly."

"It's hardly a catastrophe."

"Do you want to be manhandled by your colleagues?"

"Sometimes."

"Well, you're just a trollop, aren't you."

"I don't really, of course. What did he do exactly?"

"He put his hands on my shoulders, and touched my neck. I could feel his breath on me."

"Did you find it arousing?"

"Oh, for God's sake."

"Did you?"

"All right, suppose I did—somewhat. A little. But one doesn't want to be aroused by a married colleague in the middle of a workday."

"Perhaps at night, then."

"Never."

"Come now. Admit Taunton's probably the best-looking man you've ever seen. You were aroused by his touch, but you'd—"

"A married man, Donna. It's not funny. I truly would never carry on with someone else's husband. It's a betrayal of our entire sex. A wife at home looking after his children? What kind of life can she have if she knows her husband is pawing the women he works with? If he tries to make love to every female who comes his way?"

Her voice had risen, and Donna frowned, assessing her friend. "This is about something else."

"Oh, don't psychoanalyze me just now, Donna. I couldn't bear it." Imogen had not told Donna much about her father other than that he was "not a good husband."

"You haven't had such experiences, have you? I mean, you were never jealous of Quentin, were you?"

"Quentin was the most trustworthy man I ever met. A truly loyal friend. You would adore him."

"So who made you so jealous that you react to a garden-variety male transgression with outrage not on your own behalf so much as on behalf of a woman you've never even met?"

Imogen reached behind her head and unclipped her hair so that it fell past her shoulders. She sat at Donna's desk chair and swivelled a little. "I've seen the effects of jealousy, that's all. The heartbreak and distrust. It's terrible, in case you didn't know."

"I can't say I've ever been jealous," Donna admitted. "I'm somewhat familiar with betrayal—I suppose that's why I never want to get married."

"Well, I do," Imogen said, surprised at her own vehemence. "I want a wonderful husband and at least two children—I want the fullest life possible."

"Full of what—that's what I say. But you're not talking about yourself, are you? You're talking about your mother."

Imogen looked at her. "I don't think you should use analysis as a weapon."

"Oh, my darling—not a weapon. A scalpel is not a weapon."

"It can be—when used carelessly. And who asked you for surgery?"

"Well, I'm not going to play dumb for you, if that's what you want."

"I just prefer not to make a case study of my parents, if you don't mind."

Donna got up and took hold of Imogen's shoulders and swivelled her a half turn. She kneaded her shoulders lightly, a tender echo of

Taunton's manoeuvre. "You don't have to talk about anything, if you don't want. Never ever." She kissed the top of Imogen's head. "You have beautiful hair. Shall I brush it for you, my princess?"

"I'm as far from a princess . . ."

"Go on. Get your brush."

Imogen retrieved the brush from her room and sat again at Donna's desk. Donna ran her fingers through the long tresses, spreading them over Imogen's shoulders in a wide cascade. As she brushed, she would hold a thick strand up and draw the brush along its length before letting it fall.

"Oh, that feels wonderful. I'll brush yours after."

"You don't have to."

"I want to. It's nice to do something physical with a person that doesn't have to be anything else."

"Well, I don't do this with everyone, you know."

Imogen reached up and took hold of Donna's wrist. They said nothing for a moment or two and then Donna resumed brushing. Imogen began to feel drowsy as a cat.

There was a knock at the door.

Donna laid the brush on her desk and went to answer it. She came back a moment later holding a handwritten envelope with a blue Special Delivery sticker attached. "I signed for it. Didn't think you'd mind."

Imogen took the letter and examined the return address. It was from Chicago, but she recognized neither the penmanship nor the address. "J.W.," she said. "I don't know any J.W."

Donna stepped away from the desk and sat on the bed to give her some privacy.

Imogen opened the letter and scanned it. *I'm sure you won't remember me*, it began. She turned it over to see the signature on the other side. The signature itself was illegible, but the writer had taken the time to print his name beneath it: Jack Wisdom. Imogen had to think a moment who Jack Wisdom was. Quentin's poet friend—the one who was always advising him to quit university and explore the North Pole, or take a train out west and work as a cowboy for a year. Her heart began to pound. She turned the letter over again and read.

Dear Dr. Lang,

I'm sure you won't remember me, but we met once or twice a few years back when you were seeing my good friend Quentin Goodchild. I am very sorry to have to inform you that Quentin was killed in action at Lens, France, on the 24th of August, 1917. I have made some inquiries and learned further that he was part of an important battle that advanced the cause of the Allies. Before he departed for France, Quentin asked me to inform you if anything should happen to him. Although we did not know each other well, Doctor, I close with the specific wish that should you want to contact me for any reason to do with Quentin—or, for that matter, anything else, I may be reached at this address.

Very truly yours,
Jonathan "Jack" Wisdom

Three weeks passed by, during which Imogen was not seen on the wards, in the dining halls, or in the courtyard—three weeks during which she did not stir from her room.

Late one afternoon she was lying in bed, awake—yes, painfully awake—but eyes closed, when she was disturbed by the smell of cigar smoke. The rattle of blinds being raised. She turned over and faced the wall, pulled the sheet over her face, the corner with *Henry Phipps Psychiatric Clinic* stitched in blue cursive. Her hair was greasy and from under the covers wafted the smell of old sweat, the acrid sweat of raw emotion. A deep ache pulsed in her forehead.

"Imogen?"

Donna's voice entered her brain as if a pencil had been jabbed in her ear. Imogen lay motionless, hoping it would go away.

"Imogen, Dr. Ganz is here."

Imogen opened her eyes and stared at the wall inches from her face. It had come at last; she was to be dismissed.

Then Dr. Ganz's voice.

"Thank you, Dr. Artemis. If you would be so kind—perhaps you could remain in your room a few moments with the door open."

Imogen heard the rustle of her clothes as Donna left the room. The scrape of a chair, and the odour of cigar grew stronger. Imogen lowered the covers to her neck and turned to look. If Dr. Ganz was horrified by her appearance he managed to hide it.

"Good afternoon, Dr. Lang. I have asked Dr. Artemis to keep the doors open so there can be no question of impropriety. Under normal circumstances, I would not visit you in your room."

"You've come to dismiss me."

"Not at all. Please put that idea from your mind."

"If you're going to dismiss me, please let's just get it over with." Imogen turned to the wall once more.

"I have no plans to dismiss you. I want to help you, if you'll let me."

"Dear God."

"You're horrified. 'My employer is in my private room and I am in bed. What could be more inappropriate?'"

"Mortifying."

"I'm afraid I can't hear you—could you turn this way, please?"

Imogen forced herself to turn once more onto her back but she could not look him in the eye. She spoke to the ceiling. "Mortifying."

"And yet I'm a physician and you are a human being in distress. What could be more natural?"

"I'm not a patient."

"Perhaps at this moment you are."

"Dear God."

"I will lay out the facts as they appear to me, and if you disagree with any of them you have only to say so. Three weeks ago you learned that a dear friend, a man you may even have loved, was killed overseas. A period of mourning is to be expected. You have taken to your bed, you have missed your shifts, your classes, appointments with patients, your studies . . ."

"I know how awful I am, Doctor, you don't have to tell me."

Dr. Ganz's voice was gentle. "I am not making a case against you; I merely state facts. Progress is easier if you know where you are. May I go on?"

He took the absence of a reply for agreement and continued in the same soft voice. "You have missed meals—a lot of meals, and anyone can see you are suffering from insomnia. Dr. Artemis reports that you have all but ceased talking to her."

"Exactly how many doctors do I have at the moment?"

"She says this as a friend. I'm sure you've noticed how fond of you she is? The rest of us certainly have. Your friendship has been a topic of admiration. She knows you better than any of us, but anyone who has the slightest acquaintance with Imogen Lang can readily observe that she is not herself. Do you disagree with any of this? Please feel free to do so."

"No."

"Will you face me as we speak? It would help me understand you better if you looked at me."

It was agony to face this man she respected so much.

"Thank you. There's no reason to hide from me. You've done nothing shameful."

"Hah."

"You disagree. Please elaborate."

"Dereliction of duty, for one. Abandoning my patients . . ."

"Have you been in any condition to help your patients?"

"No."

"So you have done them no disservice."

Imogen shook her head.

"You shake your head but I don't detect actual disagreement on this point—you perhaps showed them consideration by sparing them your own unhappiness."

"Uselessness, you mean."

"That is a self-accusation. Uselessness is not a word any objective observer could apply to a physician of your calibre."

"Not openly, perhaps."

"Do you suspect me of writing negative reports about you? You can be candid."

His expression was mild, waiting.

"No."

"So the bitterness in your remark would be directed where?"

"I don't really want to talk about this."

"It's often the case with terrible pain. We frequently accuse ourselves and perhaps one or two others in life of being whiners, but I find after extensive observation that this is rarely true. Human beings in terrible pain, pain that continues day after day, do not tend to whine at all. Quite the reverse."

"Because it's not acceptable behaviour."

"True. Self-pity is not an emotion anyone encourages. But is that the only reason?"

"It's boring. Pain is so incredibly boring. It doesn't bear speaking about."

"And?"

"And what?"

"What else about pain? Why do we not speak of it?"

"Because it's depressing."

"Yes. And I think we may say there is a unique feature about the type of pain we call depression. Depression is itself depressing. In depression we have a pain that causes more pain. Would you agree with that?"

Imogen managed a tight nod. "But I never said I was depressed."

"Again, you seek to avoid so-called whining."

"But really—I never said I was depressed."

"Nor did I. Diagnosis, as you know, is not high on my list of priorities." Dr. Ganz shifted on the chair. A waft of cigar smoke reached

Imogen's nostrils. Some still, quiet part of herself recognized it as the first thing she had *liked* in weeks.

"You have lost a dear friend; it's only natural to mourn."

"Yes," Imogen said with some ferocity. "*Exactly.*"

"So all this—" He waved a hand as if pointing out furniture. "The sleeplessness, the silence, the not eating, the isolation—these are expressions of grief?"

"Of course. Oh God . . ." She put a hand over her face.

"And yet I see no tears."

"Not at the *moment*. I cried when I read the letter."

"And since then? Have you been weeping a lot?"

"No."

"Why do you suppose that is?"

"Because I don't have the right."

"Really. *Don't have the right.* That's an unexpected turn of phrase. Can you explain a little?"

"Something Dr. Quinn said to me—when Millie Nielsen died. I started to cry and she told me to stop. I didn't have the right."

"I see. And how did that make you feel?"

"Hideous. I *already* felt hideous."

"And now you turn this phrase that made you feel so terrible against yourself."

"Because the situations are so similar. In both cases I did the wrong thing and in both cases someone ended up—"

Suddenly her throat was so thick she could not speak, could not swallow, and then with a loud sob—a choking sound—she began to cry.

Dr. Ganz took from his breast pocket a crisply folded handkerchief and handed it to her. She clutched at it blindly. After a few minutes he said, "Dr. Lang, will you come and see me tomorrow morning? Ten o'clock should be all right."

※

The next morning, Imogen bathed and dressed and tried to make herself as presentable as possible before going to see Dr. Ganz. After that first session, she met with him twice a week for an unofficial "consultation." They met in his private office, which was off to one side of his administrative office. Over the following two months she told him how she had hurt Quentin, how he had chosen war as his method of suicide, and finally, most reluctantly of all, she told him about her father and his covert second family.

Their meetings were by no means psychoanalysis; this was a purely cathartic endeavour—ventilative, to use Dr. Ganz's preferred term— and supportive. Reticent at first, Imogen eventually found herself speaking of things she had never thought she would reveal to anyone. She even told him the details of her tongue-tie, something she had minimized on his questionnaire and had never mentioned to anyone outside the family except Quentin.

Dr. Ganz's responses were sympathetic, clarifying. He made Imogen feel that he looked forward to their sessions, and found her worthy of so many hours of his time. He was not reticent about expressing his own feelings. When she told him about being tongue-tied, he sat forward and slapped his knee and exclaimed in his Swiss-German accent, "Aha! Of course! No wonder you are so patient and encouraging to those who find it difficult to speak. I should have guessed something of the kind but I confess it never occurred to me. Fascinating." He pressed the back of his pen hand to his forehead as if checking for fever. "Really, I am sometimes so imperceptive it frightens me."

She told him about Laura, her dead twin, and even showed him the death notice she carried with her. Dr. Ganz examined it and handed it back.

"So you carry your departed twin with you always—physically as well as emotionally. You speak of her with such warmth and sorrow I'm disinclined to use the term 'haunted.'"

"If she haunts me, it's only in a happier sense of the term. I envy Catholics their concept of the guardian angel—Quentin told me about it—you know, a benign supernatural being that is always at your side. Looking out for you."

"A charming conceit. And yet Laura is unable—or unwilling—to protect you from your current difficulties."

"No. In fact she disappears at such times." That sounded too crazy, and Imogen stammered a little trying to rephrase. "I mean, well, when I'm so terribly wrapped up in myself I don't think of her."

"And at such times she is replaced by—?"

"I don't know. Loneliness, I suppose." Imogen held back the tears. She had shed so many in this room.

"Interesting. I wonder if this isn't a case of Imogen protecting Laura." Imogen had to think about that.

"Protecting her in death," he added, "the way she could not in life."

A perfectly innocent sentence. An easy—even obvious—remark, and yet it travelled through Imogen's heart like a tiny, invisible javelin.

"I think that I shall never cry again," she said when she was able. "You've quite wrung me out."

"Oh, you will cry again. We will all of us cry again. But perhaps soon it will be over things that are present or to come, instead of the sorrows of the past. You said Laura got sick and died—what was the illness?"

"Scarlet fever. She was five years old."

"Scarlet fever. Scarlet fever is highly infectious. Did you manage to escape it?"

It is a memory disconnected from all others, so disconnected it might almost be a dream, but she knows it is not. The details are too vivid: the brilliant green of the linden tree at the window, the gold ceiling (who had painted the ceiling gold?), and most of all the bed, just a few feet from her own, where Laura had been sleeping—now empty. It is early summer, 1899. Imogen is five years old and her sister has been dead for twenty-four hours.

The sheet is damp and clingy with her sweat. Her head feels as hot as an iron. Sometimes she feels about to suffocate. Again and again

she wakes from a dream that an enormous animal is sleeping on her
chest, perhaps an elephant, a giant beast, otherwise harmless, completely unaware that it is killing the little girl beneath him, a girl who
hasn't the breath to cry out, whose arm is too weak to lift.

But now she is awake and the room is awash in green and gold and
the smell of linden. A dark shape looms over her. Her eyes can't quite
focus, or perhaps they are half-blind with sweat, but it takes her some
few moments to recognize the shape as her father. The smell of linden
is invaded by the odour of cigar that clings to him. A pale hand, impossibly large, impossibly cool and dry, presses her forehead.

The coolness of his hand is delicious. She wants to reach up and
clasp his fingers but her arms are too heavy to move, and in any case
the hand is soon withdrawn and her forehead burns all the hotter. The
bearded face turns away as her father speaks to some unseen other—
she knows it to be her mother, although she cannot see or hear her.

"It's quite hopeless," her father says. "This one's going to die too."


"Those were his exact words? He referred to you as 'this one'?"

Imogen nodded.

"As if you were one of a series, an item in a collection—a defective
item liable to stop functioning at any moment. Just like your sister."

"And Laura was an absolute angel. You couldn't imagine a sweeter
little girl."

"Which means what? It's acceptable that he calls you defective, but
not your sister?"

And on it went, the surgeon retrieving a blood-wet bullet here, a
dripping piece of shrapnel there, making a brief comment before
dropping it into a tray for disposal or further examination. Imogen
sometimes wondered if Dr. Ganz wasn't coaxing her out onto a ledge.

"Perhaps one could summarize it this way," Ganz said. "Until Mr.
Goodchild arrives on the scene, your sole experience of men is a
father who is cruel to your mother while pretending he is not, who

barely acknowledges your existence and dismisses you to the grave-yard when he does."

"Well, that's putting it harshly."

"I merely relate how you put it to me. If you want to revise, please do."

"He was kind to us when we were little. More attentive than a lot of fathers—reading to us, making us laugh."

"Thus having what effect when at the age of twelve you discover he has another family?"

Imogen could barely force the words out of her mouth.

"I'm sorry, I didn't hear."

"Made it worse."

"Yes, you had so much to lose," Ganz observed softly. "The kind-ness, the reading, the laughter. And given this excruciating experi-ence, why should we expect a young woman to leap at the first chance to get married?"

"To a wonderful man! A man I loved!"

"Platonically, you insisted."

"You don't understand how good Quentin was, how intelligent, how sensitive, how witty, how engaging. How much he cared for *me*."

"And what you don't understand is that none of that matters. He could have been any man. Why would you put yourself in danger by marrying him?"

"Quentin wasn't dangerous. He was sweet."

"Yes, yes, you keep saying: sweet, intelligent, thoughtful, *loving*. What could be more dangerous?"

"I don't understand you. Love—true love—is not dangerous."

"But you had no experience of harmless love. You had Josiah Lang—a man who had been the picture of kindness until you uncovered his deception. He ripped from under your feet your entire emotional world. Everything you thought was real, gone. One day you're a little girl riding her bike, and the next day you're what?"

"Nothing."

"He made you feel you were nothing. And then another man comes along promising everything a girl might want in a man. What are the chances she is going to believe him?"

"None."

"None." Ganz sat back as if winded. "Indeed."

They were silent for a time. Usually Dr. Ganz sat looking at her, placid, waiting, but now he tugged at his goatee and pursed his lips and shifted in his chair.

"What?" Imogen said.

"Nothing. I—I'm just struck by something. I think I have been guilty in the past of thinking that it is enough for a psychiatrist to understand *why* somebody makes the choice they do in a given set of circumstances. But perhaps when we truly understand we see not only *why* a person makes a particular choice, but how it is impossible for them to make any other."

# 8

Luckily, her return to the wards and the needs of her patients kept Imogen from dwelling on her own sorrow for too long.

Georgina Twill was a fifty-five-year-old woman who showed symptoms of dementia that had begun some four years previously, when she became irrationally jealous of her husband. He appeared to be a sweet-tempered man with an honest and open manner. But his daughters, lively young women of eighteen and twenty, began almost to credit the accusations of infidelity—until Georgina also started claiming she was being followed and reported on by "certain employees of Mr. Rockefeller." She began to hear voices of "evil creatures," who whispered "disgusting" ideas in her ear. By the time she was brought to the Phipps, she was getting lost in her own home, showed severely impaired short-term memory, and often could not remember the names of common household objects. On the admitting ward she became confused and prone to shrieking fits that disrupted the entire floor.

Imogen's exhaustive interviews with the husband and daughters ruled out alcohol or drug issues, and there was no history of mental illness in the family. Normal blood pressure seemed to preclude the possibility of a vascular cause, as did the absence of waxing and waning of symptoms. Her deterioration was now steady and swift. Despite Mrs. Twill's relatively young age, Imogen could see no other diagnosis than senile dementia, with its accompanying dismal prognosis, and Lila Quinn agreed. Mrs. Twill was transferred to a state asylum where she would almost certainly die.

Zen Moldar was a hollow-eyed, hollow-cheeked, thoroughly ema-
ciated forty-five-year-old when he was admitted. Imogen interviewed
his aging parents several times, although this was difficult, given
their limited English and her lack of Magyar. She learned that they
had recently moved to Baltimore from Boston, for work reasons, and
had removed Zen from the Worcester State Hospital. At home, he
took to wrapping the furniture in wet towels, painting himself different colours, and running screaming down the streets in the middle
of the night.

Imogen dug into his history via letter and telephone to Worcester.
He had been admitted more than two decades earlier at the age of
twenty-three, exhibiting bizarre and uncontrollable behaviour, such
as screaming until he would drop from exhaustion. Worcester reported
that paraldehyde, bromides, and hydrotherapy could calm him down,
but he could not be trusted outside the walls of the asylum and so he
languished on a chronic ward. Little wonder that he was disturbed,
Imogen thought, having been removed from Worcester, his home for
half his life.

She too prescribed paraldehyde, continuous baths, and bromides,
but Mr. Moldar was still unable to focus on any occupational therapy.
He resisted all attempts at psychotherapy, and spent his days sitting in
a chair, smoking and muttering, until one day Imogen saw him staring fixedly at a maintenance man who had come to mop up a spill.

When the maintenance man was finished, Imogen borrowed the
mop and pail and brought them over to Mr. Moldar, offering him the
mop. She had to wrap his fingers around it, but once she did, his features lit up with the first smile he had displayed since admission. He
got to his feet, carried the bucket to a corner, and began mopping.
He moved the mop back and forth in slow, thoughtful strokes and
squeezed it thoroughly each time he dipped it in the bucket. He got
even more pleasure out of polishing, and his ward soon gleamed like
no other. Although still delusional and disorganized in his speech,
Mr. Moldar responded well to the "cleaning therapy."

Imogen arranged for his transfer back to Worcester, where he would more than likely live out the rest of his days.

"The family has moved back to Boston," she informed the staff meeting, "and Worcester promises to let him clean to his heart's content."

"Under the circumstances," Dr. Ganz pointed out, "this can only be counted a happy ending."

One of the most surprising things Imogen learned about herself during this period was that dealing with depressed, even shattered, people was not in itself depressing. Helping them to find their way to happier thoughts and emotions—even if they were still denied a normal life—could be deeply gratifying.

Mrs. Alma Musky was completely psychotic when admitted. Imogen simply asked her her name and she screamed and rocked and tore at her hair. She had no idea where she was or why she was there. Imogen interviewed the husband and a daughter in her twenties, who revealed that, several weeks previously, the youngest child in the family, a fifteen-year-old boy named Joseph, had unexpectedly died. He had been involved in a high school football game in which he was tackled and hit the ground hard. Unconscious for several hours, he awoke in hospital feeling reasonably well and was released the next morning, but the day after that, when he failed to come downstairs for breakfast, Mrs. Musky went up to wake him and found him dead in his bed.

When the ambulance arrived it took two men to pry her away from the body, and when they were gone she remained in Joseph's room for the rest of the day and into the night. She could not be persuaded to leave, did not believe her boy was dead, and waited for him to come back. This went on for four days. "She wouldn't even come to the funeral," the husband tearfully informed Imogen, "because she didn't believe he was dead." Even the autopsy report, which cited cranial hematoma as the cause of death, could not shake her belief that "her perfect angel" would be coming back. She claimed he was sitting in heaven "right beside Jesus" and waiting for just the right moment to be resurrected. All of this was alarming enough, but she began seeing her son in dreams, beckoning her to join him, and now husband and daughter were terrified she was going to kill herself. She kept complaining of undiagnosed heart problems, which she said her son was "sending to her to hurry her along after him."

After three days of bromides, hot baths, and good sleep, Mrs. Musky calmed down considerably, but still could not accept that her son was not coming back from the dead. She could not even admit that he was dead. Imogen spoke at length with the husband and daughter, and suggested they not try to dissuade Mrs. M. from her delusions, that she was not going to respond to logical argument. "She has no history of psychosis," Imogen pointed out, "and I truly believe she just needs time—and a protective environment—for the truth to sink in. This kind of reaction to a sudden, unexpected death is not uncommon." In fact she had read about a similar case in Kraepelin. She asked them to bring in items strongly associated with the boy, and simply to sit with Mrs. M. and grieve with her.

After two weeks of this, the husband was in near despair. He had now lost not only his son, but also his loving companion. Imogen assured him she could see improvements. His wife was sleeping again, she was no longer complaining of imminent heart attack, and had not mentioned suicide. She asked him to bring in any letters that Mrs. M. had written her boy, or particularly treasured presents she had given him. The husband returned the next day with a letter she had written to Joseph when he was away at camp. The boy had liked the letter enough to hang on to it and keep it in his dresser drawer.

"Shall I read it to you?" Imogen said to Mrs. Musky at their session the following day. Mrs. Musky nodded, and the tears rolled down her face as Imogen read the words that told the homesick boy, then just eleven, how proud she was of him, of how he was not to worry if others were better at one sport or another than he was, that he was loved and missed so much that it was just not possible for anyone to be more loved.

"Not enough," Mrs. Musky managed to say through her tears. "Not enough."

"No, unfortunately no amount of love can save us, or the people we love, from dying, can it. But Joseph knew you loved him. You told him right here in this letter."

"Oh, I told him all the time. And I always will love him."

"Yes, and he knew it. He held on to your words, Mrs. M. Even if his life was short, it was full of love, wasn't it?"

"Yes," she admitted. "It was, it was."

"It was," Imogen said, intentionally echoing the past tense.

She allowed a few minutes' silence as Mrs. Musky wiped her eyes and caught her breath. Relief was visible in her expression, the way she sat—looking weak, drained, but no longer hunched and rigid.

"It doesn't have to be today," Imogen said, "but the cemetery where your son is buried isn't far from here. I could come with you when you feel ready for a visit."

That was how the two of them came to be standing, on a crystalline day of sunlight and puffy clouds, at the graveside of Mrs. Musky's fifteen-year-old son. Mrs. M. knelt beside the grave and stayed silent for many long minutes, but she never again spoke of her boy in the present tense, or of his coming back. She was discharged a few days later to a very relieved husband and daughter.

Dr. Ganz, however, did not appear pleased. "We have here a brief, reactive psychosis in a highly competent woman with no previous history of mental illness. How did you come to see fit to insert yourself into her life like this?"

They were at the staff meeting the day after Mrs. M.'s discharge, and Imogen had been prepared for the question. "I made it plain that this would be a one-time-only event, and that my best place to help her was in the hospital, but the moment was too opportune to miss. Yes, I could have asked her husband to take her to the cemetery, but he had already offered to so many times that she now perceived it as a threat."

"To visit the cemetery with her, though—it's a big step outside the doctor–patient relationship." Ganz spoke firmly but without anger, so Imogen was encouraged to say more.

"I see my role in this case as purely supportive, not analytical, not exploratory. I saw the trip merely as continuing our discussion in another location. I believe it was a breakthrough for her."

"Luckily," Ganz said. "But it could have been a major setback, and then where would you be? You would be one more cause of pain in her life, instead of the objective physician."

"Your little jaunt was not okayed by me," Lila Quinn put in. "Nor would it have been, had I been consulted."

"Hardly a jaunt," Imogen said softly.

Ganz looked around the table. "It may be that from time to time such a bending of protocol may be acceptable. But you must first have the permission of the ward psychiatrist, and if the ward psychiatrist is in doubt, he or she must come to me—is that clear?"


During Imogen's illness and recovery, Donna had managed to rise even higher in Dr. Ganz's regard. He now assigned her to look after his private patients when he was away—perhaps the highest mark of esteem he bestowed on anyone. Imogen noticed, with a pang of envy, how the other staff now deferred to Donna, sought her opinion and approval. Even Lila Quinn began to treat her as if she were the presumed second-in-command. Imogen was glad that her friend was doing well, but it was painful to feel that she herself had been set back by an inability to control her own moods.

It was not long, however, before there were faint rumblings of trouble for Donna, the roots of which went to the very nature of psychotherapy and psychoanalysis.

Ganz lectured his interns often on the difference. "It is crucial for you all to understand that these terms are not synonymous," he would tell them. "Crucial. Psychoanalysis is just one form of psychotherapy, utterly distinct from the others. It is based on Freud's theories that psychological trouble is caused by the repression of sexual memories or fantasies. Under pressure, the repressed material emerges into consciousness but in a distorted form. Analytic sessions focus on early sexual experiences, and the primary tools are dream analysis and free association. Gradually, very gradually, the patient comes to recognize his own distortions for what they are. I am full of admiration for Sigmund Freud, and you should be too, but underline these words in your notebooks, please: *We do not provide psychoanalysis at the Phipps Psychiatric Clinic.*"

Donna, it seemed, had neglected to underline. For one day at the staff meeting the ward nurse related, perhaps with some amusement, that one of the younger patients, a nineteen-year-old law student named Hobbes, who suffered from what looked likely to be schizophrenia, had begun using the terms "penis envy" and "Oedipus complex."

"I thought it peculiar," the nurse said, "because his mind is so overcharged at the moment that he is not even able to read. He can't follow a story in the morning paper, for example."

"Yes," Dr. Ganz said, "I've noticed that myself." He turned to Donna. "Dr. Artemis, have you been psychoanalyzing this boy?"

"Yes. He seemed such a good candidate, according to his background. Before his trouble he was a big reader, helpful to others, intelligent and thoughtful."

"Dr. Artemis, perhaps you didn't hear me, or perhaps you mistook my words for an offhand remark, so let me repeat them now: We do not provide psychoanalysis at the Phipps, do you understand?"

"But the private patients receive—"

Dr. Ganz raised his hand to cut her off. "We do not offer psychoanalysis because even in ideal circumstances, it is a lengthy treatment, usually measured not in months but in years. And it requires an intensity we have not the resources to offer. No one in this clinic can provide four hours of psychoanalysis a week to one patient without depriving other patients of proper care. And even if you were to make some headway, the patient would have to be dismissed before analysis was complete, which means he or she would have to start the whole painful process over again with a different analyst. Most importantly, the likelihood of analysis being of any benefit to a psychotic patient is virtually nil. Such benefit requires judgment, observation, and memory, precisely the faculties that are impaired in the psychotic, when not completely extinguished."

Dr. Bylsma, whose adjustment from Dutch to American medicine, and to Ganz in particular, was not perfect, raised a pale hand. "Sir, if I may?"

Ganz nodded.

"Ferenczi and Kempf, to mention just two, are quite convinced analysis can help with psychosis."

"Dr. Ferenczi has many ideas that are not acceptable to Sigmund Freud or to this clinic. I don't need to go into them here. As for Dr. Kempf, I admire him greatly, but he was fired last year from Indiana for practising psychoanalysis on psychotic patients, and is now experimenting with analysis at St. Elizabeth's. As of yet, he reports no significant progress. And I note that St. Elizabeth's routinely houses patients for *years*, which we do not and cannot do."

He surveyed the faces around the table. "To go back to this particular patient. Mr. Hobbes is *not* a private patient. Furthermore, he shows every likelihood of being schizophrenic. While I do not deny that he is capable of flashes of insight, for the most part he seems firmly in the grip of his psychosis. He is in no position to benefit from analysis even in the short term. Just last week, Dr. Lang raised the question as to whether he might not be better served at a state hospital where he could settle in for long-term care. So I repeat: Neither he nor any other public patient is to be engaged in psychoanalysis. By all means listen to him, talk to him, be supportive when you can—ventilative psychotherapy is one of the most powerful treatments we have—but Freudian analysis is not to be attempted. Any effort to do so will be considered insubordination."

Donna pursed her lips and stared at the table.

Imogen was a little worried about her. When she had emerged from her fog of grief, she'd heard rumours about Donna and a certain psychoanalyst. She had been sighted arm in arm with him at the theatre and in Patterson Park. Imogen resolved to ask her about it and did so the following afternoon when they were sitting across from each other in a tea shop.

"There is no affair," Donna sniffed. "He is my analyst, and beyond that, he is my friend and colleague. But we are not lovers."

Imogen knew Donna to be honest—sometimes brutally so—but she was far from sure her friend was telling the truth now.

"Is he the 'naval person' Ruth Fein saw you with last week?"

"Oh, he's thoroughly eccentric—*extremely* British. He quit the Royal Navy years ago, but he insists on wearing that damn uniform everywhere. His parents were in the Foreign Service, so he grew up in India, Malaysia, Hong Kong—all over the map—and moved over here ten years ago."

"I overheard Jasper Bylsma talking about someone named 'Snake' Walcott—that wouldn't be the same . . ."

"I know!" Donna exclaimed. "I know! He's quite beyond the pale! But he's also brilliant, and you're just going to have to meet him. I've told him all about you and he's invited us both to dinner."


William "Snake" Walcott lived and worked in a modest townhouse near the very pricey area of Eutaw Place. He was six foot four of red-faced, mutton-chopped garrulity and good humour, dressed, as Donna had said, in a British naval uniform. He greeted both women eagerly, telling Imogen, "Your reputation precedes you. Artemis here can't stop singing your praises."

He herded them into his front parlour, which was furnished with the psychoanalytic couch, a desk, many overlapping oriental rugs, and (Imogen estimated) about a thousand books. Sherry was served by a Chinese houseboy in a white jacket, a shiny ponytail vivid down his back.

Imogen pointed to the arrangement of couch and armchair. "You don't sit behind the patient?"

"Never. Sit where the patient can see me. Don't go in for all this disembodied nonsense. Grandiose. Counterproductive, too— patients spending years trying to sort out what the analyst is thinking. Let 'em see, I say. Let 'em see."

*Grandiose* seemed an odd objection, coming from someone dressed like the commander of a dreadnought, but Imogen was already trying to absorb the other oddities of the place. The glass cases that lined one wall housed a collection of motionless snakes. They varied in size from twelve inches to about twelve feet.

"Don't worry," Donna said, "they're stuffed. Dr. Walcott is a herpetologist, among other things."

The evidence was everywhere, from fanged skulls to rattled tails bleached white as chalk. They hung on walls, curled in corners, and lounged on top of a baby grand. A twelve-foot display case housed a motionless python.

News of Prohibition had apparently never reached the house of Walcott. When they were seated in the dining room, the houseboy ferried bottle after bottle of Château Talbot from kitchen to table. Walcott gulped his wine from a flagon that required constant refilling; the women's places had been set with sparkling crystal. Dinner was served by a silent maid who darted in and out of the room like a hyper-efficient sprite.

Walcott was a swiller of claret and a teller of tales, a veritable Niagara of knowledge and spewer of facts, ideas, and opinions. "Look, I worship Old Siggy, I truly do, but he wants to be the St. Benedict of psychotherapy, and it's just not on. We're all medical people at this table. Do we really want to confine ourselves to a monastic rule that applies *one* idea and a handful of techniques to every suffering being who comes begging for help? What do you say, Lang?"

Far from being offended at being thus addressed, Imogen glowed. At the Phipps, the men all referred to each other by their last names, often in a tone that conveyed both affection and respect, but always addressed the women as Dr. This, Nurse That. Had Jonas Ganz addressed her in this way she would have swooned with pleasure.

She put down her glass, which the houseboy instantly refilled. "Are you talking about new techniques," she asked, "or actual alternative therapies?"

Walcott winked at Donna, said "I like her" while simultaneously stifling a belch, and turned once more to Imogen. "A change of technique, depending on degree, may well amount to an alternative therapy. I talk of counter-transference—yes, she who must not be named. You can't sit back and pretend it isn't happening, but that's what Freud would have us do. Patient says, 'Hang on, Doctor, I'm sensing a certain disdain on your high and mighty part,' and we're supposed to emit a low, ambiguous noise—at most."

"But the point is for the patient to work through their feelings for the analyst."

"Six months into treatment it's quite common for a patient to say, 'I know I'm not as important to you as you are to me.' How would you respond to that, Lang?"

"If I were doing analysis—which we're not, at the Phipps—I wouldn't reply at all. I would acknowledge I'd heard it and wait for the patient to turn her own analytic power back on herself—Why do I think this way? Does it remind me of other relationships? Am I generally a suspicious person?"

"*Hah.*" Walcott slammed down his flagon. "But what have you really done? Here the patient has made an accurate observation. If you respond *your* way, *Freud's* way, you undermine her sense of reality— which is why she's there in the first place! A patient says, 'Doctor, why are you so cold? I feel that you don't like me—perhaps even hate me.' I tell her straight out, 'It's not that I don't like you or lack sympathy. But I cannot bring the same warmth as you to our sessions because

I have forty patients, and you have but one analyst. The imbalance is built in. *Voilà*. The patient is reassured that on this one point, at least, she is not crazy. Do it your way and you consign her to an endless undertow of suspicion."

"Do it *your* way," Imogen said, "and you short-circuit her ability to work things through for herself."

Walcott turned his florid face to Donna. "You neglected to warn me that your friend was so argumentative and apparently oblivious to a woman's proper place in the medical world."

Imogen's cheek grew hot. "Really, sir."

Donna, beautiful in the candlelight, placed a warm palm on Imogen's hand. "He's teasing you, my darling."

"Oh." Imogen dropped her gaze to the tablecloth. "Well."

"An analyst who refuses to admit his feelings," Walcott went on, "condemns a person who is already confused and anxious—perhaps even paranoid—to intolerable ambiguity. I have one patient who is exceedingly demanding—jealous of other patients, always wanting sessions when I'm not available, always angling for free treatment, often angry. Three weeks ago she said, 'I know you don't like me.' And I said, 'I get irritated by your constant demands. I find your jealousy of other patients tiresome. I'd rather you didn't behave this way. But I'm quite willing to keep seeing you as long as you want to keep coming.'"

"And how did she react?"

"With outrage. Tears. Accusations."

"Well, now who's replicating the patient's other experiences and problems?"

"I am—but with one big difference. I am setting my feelings before her in the bright light of day. Her exigent temperament causes her to alienate colleagues, suitors, even friends. They don't tell her why, they just abandon her."

"But you've prevented her from realizing it for herself. You're trying to force insight on someone who is not ready for it."

"Rubbish, Lang. I'm giving her a crystal-clear glimpse of her reality, and she knows it. Of course it hurt at first—she missed three sessions that week. But since then her behaviour has improved; therefore her relationship with me has improved. Our sessions now focus on her life outside my office, rather than her demands on me. Consequently I've every reason to think her *life* will improve. Friends will stay. Perhaps lovers too."

"You should work with Robert Taunton. You're clearly a behaviourist."

"Artemis! Save me from this horror!"

"She has a point," Donna said.

"She does," Walcott acknowledged. "And I dare say Mr. Taunton does too." He pushed his plate forward and placed his elbows on the table. "The art, Dr. Lang, is to know when a silence is likely to be productive and when it is not. Otherwise, our patients might as well book appointments with department-store mannequins.

"Eight out of ten patients come to me because of childhood trauma. Sometimes it's physical abuse—horrendous whippings, beatings, what have you. Other times, it's sexual. Papa gets into the whisky and next thing you know his four-year-old daughter is hemorrhaging from her vagina. Twenty years later, here she comes begging for help because she can't walk without pain, she has dysmenorrhea, and finds herself compulsively masturbating. Such patients, aside from the sexual assault, were damaged in their childhood by the lies and hypocrisy of those whose duty it was to protect them. By those who spouted loving words while ravaging their little bodies and souls, and heaping on them a legacy of guilt and anxiety.

"This does not mean they cannot be burdensome. I emit a sigh, and they sense I am fed up with their evasions and repetitions, and they get up the courage to say so. Freud would have me either deny it or not reply at all, thus *repeating the earlier trauma*." He stabbed the table with a stubby index finger for emphasis. "Those whose duty it is to heal are now inflicting new damage, thus *repeating the earlier trauma*. It's preposterous." He took a few glugs of his wine and wiped his mouth.

"So you make *your* feelings the subject."

"If feelings aren't the subject, Lang, I don't know what is. Tell her, Artemis."

"I'd much rather listen to you two. As you know, I only live to parrot everything you say."

"Lying shrew. Would it were so." He turned to the maid. "O'Brien, let's have some more of that roast beef. How's everyone for roast beef? Are we sated, all?"

The other two were indeed sated, but Walcott pronged two more slices from the proffered tray and sloshed them with gravy. He dug into them and, chewing with gusto, went on. "Just now I'm working on a theory of *mutual* analysis. Patient gets to analyze analyst."

"Who would get paid for such sessions—you or the patient?"

"Sly, Lang, very sly. It's an experiment." He held up his flagon as if for a toast. "*Experiment.* That is the one thing I will say in my favour: I never cease to experiment. But really, sometimes one yearns for some bedrock *science*, don't you find? Sometimes I fear we're all mere collectors of anecdotes."

The endless flagons were beginning to show their effect. Wine was spilled, a dish was brushed from the table.

"I have one patient," he said, "not only did her father regularly have carnal knowledge of her from the age of four until the age of thirteen, he passed her around to his two sons as well."

"She's now a hysteric, I take it?"

"And hysterics always make things up—that your point?"

Imogen refused to shrink under his aggression. "That they are prone to fiction is well documented. I merely wonder if the father would really risk involving his sons."

"He's faced no serious consequences thus far. Through the efforts of a concerned teacher, the girl was brought to the authorities where, with the greatest reluctance, she told them of her suffering. She was only thirteen, and they were skeptical, to say the least. But they asked her to describe her experiences in detail and she said, 'Papa's penis was red and blue and black.' *Aha*, you say, evidence of infantile fantasy right there! Hysterical mendacity! Well, the chief inspector, uniquely assiduous in my experience, took it upon himself to have the father's genitals examined. Lo and behold: red and blue and black. It seems the loving patriarch had had his organ tattooed in the image of the devil. We'll see what happens at his trial."

"How was your patient's demeanour when she told you all this?"

"Reticent. It took weeks for her to come out with it, and she was tearful in the extreme, poor girl. Not all hysterics are seeking attention."

"The devil, indeed," Donna said. "Now that you've upset and appalled my friend, perhaps we may talk of something else?"

"Not upset," Imogen said. "Just thoughtful." The expression, an echo of Quentin's rejoinder in biology class so many years ago, laid a sudden weight on her heart.

"Do you like music?" Walcott asked.

"Very much."

"Excellent. I have purchased a shiny new Victrola. Prepare to be astounded."


They adjourned to a room furnished with overstuffed chairs draped with scarves and shawls, and piled high with silk cushions—thankfully, no snakes—and he played them the adagietto from Beethoven's Seventh. Sombre and insistent, the music soon marched all thoughts of work out the door. Imogen resolved to buy herself a Victrola when and if she should ever have the cash to do so—and maybe even a house to put it in.

Walcott closed his eyes as he listened, his right hand inscribing maestro triangles in time to strings and trombones. When the music finished, the maid served tea and sweets, and Dr. Walcott plied Imogen with question after question about her studies and her background, which she answered circumspectly. He talked much of cats— he was considering breeding a particular type of cat, though his lodgings showed no signs of a feline inhabitant. He talked of hypnosis and near-hypnotic states, he spoke passionately about shell shock and how it took debating tactics that veered perilously close to violence to convince the military brass that shell shock was real. His passion on the subject was what had got him an early discharge from the military. His eyes watered as he told them of the horribly damaged men who were sent back to Flanders for more pointless punishment. And then, quite suddenly, his eyes closed and he began to snore. The streetcars having ceased to run, the houseboy summoned a taxi.

"Cats and snakes, indeed," Imogen said in the back seat.

Donna, almost as sleepy as her mentor, rested her head on Imogen's shoulder.

"Did you like him? You *must* like him. Tell me you do."

"He is definitely a force of nature," Imogen said. "Equal parts frightening and inspiring."

"Oh, Papa Walcott is a big pussycat."

"Papa, is it?"

"He *is* a sort of papa to me," Donna said dreamily. "I think everyone's analyst is, or should be, *in loco parentis*. Walcott certainly thinks so. He believes the analyst should give everything he can to the patient. He even lets me kiss him."

Imogen pulled away to look at her friend.

Donna gave her a little shove. "Don't go all prim on me."

"But I am shocked, Donna. Thoroughly shocked."

"It's not what you think. It has to do with my childhood."

"It's wrong, Donna. Will you have male patients kissing their female analysts? If their neurosis goes back to the breast will you suckle them?"

"Don't be pious."

"Well, don't you be such a trollop, then."

Donna rested her head on Imogen's shoulder again. "You know I love you, don't you?"

"I suppose."

Donna snuggled closer. "*Mumma*."

Fits of giggles ensued, which they tried unsuccessfully to suppress, and the driver turned around to scowl at them.

"You really are too naughty," Imogen said after he'd dropped them at the Phipps's gate. Banners calling on citizens to buy war bonds flapped in the breeze. "You'll get in terrible trouble one day, and as I'm not your pathogenic *mumma*, you will have only yourself to blame."

They walked arm in arm under the elms. Moonlight etched in light and shadow the elegant façade of the Phipps. The psychology lab on three gave off a dull glow.

"It's nearly 2 a.m.," Imogen said. "How are we going to get by the Duke?"

The Duke was the Phipps's night watchman, so named not only because his last name was Marlborough but because of his exceedingly upright, not to say humourless, manner.

"I expect you'll have to offer him sexual favours."

"Donna, *stop*. You frighten me sometimes, you really do. Shall we go in through the dispensary?"

"There'll be people there. Let's just go in the front."

There were no restrictions on the residents' comings and goings, officially, but two single women coming in at this time of night would raise eyebrows, and the Duke would be honour bound to record their arrival. Luckily, his modest, pulpit-like station on the first floor was vacant—he must have been making his rounds.

They avoided the elevator, moving as silently as they could on the marble floors to the staircase. As they were going up, they heard footsteps descending from the third floor. They paused, each on one end of a middle stair. It was not the Duke who appeared but Robert Taunton's new—and annoyingly pretty—graduate student, Sara Sands, wearing her coat but in her stocking feet—a dark-haired, dark-eyed beauty, clutching her shoes in one hand and a book in the other. Seeing Donna and Imogen, she froze in a shaft of light.

"My, aren't *we* working late," Donna said.

"Good evening, Doctor. I forgot something in the lab."

"Your shoes, apparently."

"No, no, my house keys. I just—" Miss Sands, usually a remarkably self-possessed young woman, was momentarily flustered. "I forgot my keys."

"Ah, yes—one's elusive *keys*. Good night, Miss Sands."

"Good night."

Imogen and Donna continued to the fourth floor. When they reached their rooms, Donna paused at the door. She put a finger to her lips and whispered, "Listen for it: elevator next, stopping at three, going down to the dispensary."

"No," Imogen said. "Really?"

Something metal clanked in the elevator shaft next door. They could hear it open on the floor below, then close.

Donna said one word: "Window."

Imogen opened her door and the two of them rushed to her window without turning on the light.

"Watch," Donna said. "He'll come from the dispensary side."

A moment later they saw the confident form of Robert Taunton, hat in hand, overcoat flapping, crossing in front of the building and heading toward Wolfe Street.

"Told you," Donna said. "The lecher."

Imogen got up and switched on the light and took off her coat. "That poor, dim girl—she must know he'll drop her the minute he gets bored."

"Oh, hell," Donna said. "Which of us knows any damn thing?"

# 9

For Imogen the following weeks and months seemed composed of nothing but rain. Her depression had lifted, but a deep sadness about Quentin remained.

The rain reminded her of a time she had arranged to meet him at the library. A Chicago cloudburst had threatened to shred her umbrella, but he had somehow managed to lose his, so that he arrived at the library looking as if he'd just had a good long soak in the tub fully clothed. Rain had plastered his hair flat, and when he removed his glasses to wipe them there were drops clinging to his eyelashes. Imogen had urged him to go home and change but he wouldn't hear of it and sat across from her making pencil marks in his poetry text and leaving patches of damp wherever his sleeves touched the table.

She felt the urge to talk about him, to share her affection for him with others in a way she had not before he died. Donna was deeply involved in her analysis with Walcott and, while she still wouldn't admit as much, Imogen was pretty sure they were lovers and was a little hurt that she wouldn't confide in her about it. Sometimes she waited up, hoping to hear Donna's key in the lock, only to fall asleep over whatever she was reading.

In addition to her work with patients, Imogen was now putting in longer and longer hours in the histology lab, comparing slides of brain tissue from schizophrenics with samples from normal people. It even seemed she might be on to something when she discovered irregularities in the part of the cortex associated with hearing—could that be where the voices came from?—but the differences vanished when she was given samples blind. When she didn't know a sample was from a schizophrenic the microscope refused to reveal any differences at all.

Engaged as she was by this work and by her patients, she still spent untold hours staring out her fourth-floor window. She was languishing there one Saturday afternoon when she saw a group of four people—two men and two women—approaching the front gate, all of them dressed in tennis whites, despite the gloomy skies. She recognized Robert Taunton and Sara Sands but not the other two. The gate was open, and Taunton and the two women went through. The other man took a short run and simply vaulted over the wrought iron fence, which was about four feet high, touching it lightly with one hand as he sailed over. The leap was graceful, effortless, and above all gratuitous—the gate was wide open. Imogen could not be sure why it captured her imagination so, but she couldn't stop thinking about it.

That night she rapped on Donna's door. It was past midnight, and Donna had just got in from an evening with Walcott. "You waited up for me? What's gotten into little Miss Early-to-Bed?"

"Will you help me tomorrow? I need to brush up my tennis game."


His name was Carl Kromer. Taunton was taking him on a tour of the premises and stopped into the histology lab.

"Dr. Lang, this is Carl Kromer. He's just finished his M.A. at Harvard and he's going to be doing his Ph.D. with me. Dr. Lang is a staff psychiatrist and also engaged in some interesting research here in the lab."

"You do both?" Kromer said. "Isn't that a little unusual?"

"Not really—not at the Phipps."

"True," Taunton said, "but the others are not so good at it."

"Maybe not so enthusiastic," Imogen said. "I put in the time, that's all. What is your dissertation on?"

"Cyclical behaviour—but it's a recent interest so I'm not sure I can pull it off."

Imogen was usually allergic to small talk but was aware of an intense desire to keep Carl Kromer there as long as possible. He had a sweet, open face and curly hair that resolutely ignored the part he had tried to inflict on it. She asked him what course work he would be doing.

"I've told him he doesn't have to attend a single lecture," Taunton said. "Just give me a first-class piece of research."

Carl talked a little about his excitement in coming to Johns Hopkins and working with Taunton, about the possibilities of turning psychology into a hard science. He grew increasingly animated as he spoke—looking back and forth from Taunton to Imogen, eyes alternately wide, and eager, and amused. When he talked of making a map of repeated human behaviour across intervals of a day, a month, a year, he inscribed a graph in the air complete with axes, dips, and spikes.

"It sounds as if you're already well on your way," Imogen said.

"That's what I thought," Taunton said. "I'll have to watch out, or he'll have my job."

He and Carl were just about out the door when Imogen, appalled at her own forwardness, called after them, "Oh, Mr. Taunton? Donna Artemis and I were looking for tennis partners—I don't suppose your new recruit . . ."

"He does. Quite well, actually—although he's intelligent enough to let me beat him."

Carl stood there adorably blushing and shaking his head.

Over the next couple of weeks Imogen played several matches with Donna, whose game was darting, aggressive, and occasionally slapstick. Afterwards, Imogen took care to always walk back past the windows of the west wing in hopes of catching a glimpse of Carl on the third floor.

"So he might see *you*, is what you really mean, missy." This from Donna, who kept pretending to be startled that Imogen was capable of what was clearly a crush, "dry old stick that you are."

"I'm not a dry old stick, I just don't chase after retired sailors."

"Oh, meow-*meow*." Donna tapped her friend's behind with her racket. "Still, if he does catch sight of you in that get-up the man's a goner. You look almost virginal."

"*Almost*, is it?" Imogen squinted up toward the lab windows, but it was impossible to see anyone unless they chose to park themselves right in the bay window.

Imogen could not be sure, and she certainly was not about to ask, whether Donna had prodded Taunton to finally make the invitation, but make it he did, and the four of them played several times over the next month. It soon became clear that Carl was the best player. It didn't matter how you mixed up the sides, whoever was partnered with him was going to win, a fact that eventually cooled Taunton's interest in playing, although he pleaded a pulled hamstring.

As with so many experiments, tennis did not yield the results Imogen wanted. It provided ample opportunity to admire Carl's physical grace and sportsmanship, but no chance to actually talk to him. She had hoped they could go for tea or *something* afterwards, but Carl lived on Park Street, two streetcar rides distant, and since he preferred to walk he always had to leave right after the match. Or so he said. The truth, Imogen told herself, was that he was probably just not interested, and why should he be? She was not the most scintillating creature on earth, and even if she had been, she was coming to believe what her mother had told her long ago: men simply didn't like working women. She was doomed to remain a spinster.

She was in this frame of mind one Saturday afternoon, when she was returning from a melancholy walk. As she was passing the Harriet Lane Children's Home she saw an odd sight. Carl Kromer was jumping and dodging through the ornamental shrubbery with a large object in each hand as if he were performing—not very well—a balancing trick. Imogen had not believed this man could ever look clumsy, but he did at this minute. Had she not known better, she might have mistaken him for a Phipps patient gone AWOL.

"Mr. Kromer," she said. "What on earth are you doing?"

"I am attempting to capture a rat. Several rats, in fact. Was attempting." He raised both his hands, displaying two empty cages. "I know. I look ridiculous."

Imogen shook her head solemnly. "Not at all."

Carl pointed an accusatory finger. "You're teasing me, you wicked person."

"Never."

He came out of the bushes, his face shiny with sweat.

"My researches have made two things abundantly clear. First, that my next mission must be to design a rat trap that actually works."

"And second?"

"Second?" He put his hands on his hips. Unlike slouchy, angular Quentin, Carl had a very four-square, almost soldierly stance. "Come to my lab and I'll show you. I mean, if you have a minute."

"Of course," Imogen said. Then, trying to sound casual: "I was heading that way, anyway."

Despite his high-energy aura, Carl was a slow walker—an ambler, as only the very calm or the very heavy can be—and Imogen, who had been accused by Donna of being a bit of a marcher, and by her mother of being a stomper, had to adjust her pace. Of course, Imogen thought, when you're a paragon of strength and confidence, what need to rush anywhere?

As they headed toward the Phipps he told her how he had come to his current experiments. "Taunton presented me with twelve rats and basically said: Do something. So for the next few days I just fed them bread and milk and stared at them. What struck me—and I know it sounds obvious—what struck me was how they just jumped around the cage and climbed around for a while and then were quiet again. I began to wonder what makes them active and what makes them quiet?"

"It's not a matter of just needing to exercise and then getting tired?"

"But why do it at certain times and not others? And why climb around a cage you already know every inch of? And why do they all behave in almost identical fashion? No one taught them to run around for an hour, sit still for twenty minutes, run a bit, and so on. And obviously they didn't *evolve* in these cages."

"No, but climbing must keep them alive, right? Get them food and so on?"

"The big question for me," he said, unlocking the lab door, "is why do they do certain things for certain durations after certain periods of time? So my first question was, how can I even measure such stuff?"

The psychology lab had been divided in two since the last time Imogen had seen it. Taunton's grasp-reflex apparatus had been moved to one side, and Carl's rat equipment took up the other. Books and files were stacked everywhere among the cages, and scattered among them were various parts of what had once been a bicycle. Taunton's side looked spartan by comparison.

Carl pointed to a table with a glass top and sides.

"I designed this thing. It sits on tambours so it isn't affected by our footsteps. It's not pretty, but you see the floor? It's covered with a rubber membrane, and if you take a look underneath . . ."

He squatted down and Imogen went carefully down on one knee beside him.

"You see that rubber tube? It connects the cage floor to that recording drum." He pointed to a metal cylinder. "That's smoked paper on it."

"It's a kymograph."

"Exactly. So as the rats run about, the tube makes a mark for each and every movement. And—the truly fiendish part—it's connected to a chronometer that simultaneously records the time on a chart."

They stood up, and Imogen remembered the graph Carl had drawn in the air the first time they met. "You'll be able to describe their activity levels throughout the day."

Carl nodded. "I can observe the effects of diet, fatigue, hydration . . . But it's time of day that interests me at the moment. So much of their behaviour seems spontaneous, I can't believe it's learned. It has to be driven from inside."

"What did Mr. Taunton say?"

"He looked at it for exactly two minutes, nodded once, and said, 'Not bad.'"

"Quite an encomium, coming from him."

"Really? Do you think?" It was the first time she had seen him exhibit anything like anxiety about his career.

"If Taunton isn't happy, he won't waste any time letting you know. Why do you need more rats? You have twelve."

"Oh, it's not the quantity. I want to see if wild rats exhibit the same cycles of behaviour—these creatures are domesticated."

"Well, it's fascinating work you're doing, but I'm due on Three West in about two minutes, so I'd better leave you to it."

"Thank you so much for taking an interest. Makes me feel almost . . . consequential."

Imogen smiled. "What was the second thing?"

"Pardon me?"

"You said your researches had taught you two things. You need to build a better rat trap, and . . . ?"

He put his hands on his hips again—a posture Imogen was beginning to realize was habitual with him—and consulted the ceiling for a moment, before looking at her once more.

"The other thing I need to do is ask Dr. Imogen Lang if she would accompany me to a concert."


The next afternoon they attended a concert in the park and afterwards went for tea and cakes in the boat pavilion. In the following weeks they went to movies, the occasional play, and even dancing, but it was their talks afterwards that Imogen loved the most, sitting across a table and unfolding for each other their life stories, their hopes and plans, their favourite books. They talked about the war, which was finally going well for the Allies. Carl had been in Germany the year it broke out.

"I was studying at the Technische Hochschule in Dresden—I thought I wanted to be an engineer."

"Well, that makes perfect sense. You like to make things, design things."

"All it taught me was that I'm a lot more American than I am German, despite my background. I mean, I loved the Germans in many ways—they were very friendly and happy people, the ones I knew—but there was this militaristic streak, and this ridiculous patriotism. They still hadn't got over the wars of the last century. Which isn't to say I think we should be shooting them now. A couple of my German cousins were killed last year."

"Oh, that's sad. I'm sorry to hear that."

"Have you lost anyone?"

"Yes, I—" Imogen faltered.

"Someone close?"

"Yes, a—a very good friend."

"Was she a nurse?"

"It was a man, actually."

Carl gave her a quizzical look.

"I know it sounds funny, but we really were just friends. At least I thought we were." And then it all came tumbling out—their parting, Quentin's declaration of love, his plan for suicide. It was the last thing she wanted to talk about, and yet she couldn't stop herself.

"Well," Carl said when she was done, "I can't fault a man for being in love with you."

Imogen didn't know where to look. It was certainly too soon for him to say something like this, but she could not call herself exactly displeased by it.

"And you shouldn't fault yourself for *not* being in love. You did the right thing."

"Difficult to say that, under the circumstances."

There was a silence, and Imogen was glad Carl made no attempt to break it.

"I just don't understand the point of all this slaughter," she said, after a time. "The *Lusitania* was a terrible crime, but this is all over ancient European grudges and it just seems like the male psyche run amok. I'm not much of a political person, but I truly don't think it would have happened if women were running things."

"You might well be right," Carl said stoutly. "They could hardly make a *worse* mess."

This was pleasant to hear, but it was not Carl's opinions so much as his expressiveness, his passion, and his eloquent hands that Imogen fell in love with.

Carl's arrival at the Phipps coincided with some spiky developments in clinic politics. While Dr. Ganz had initially been thrilled with lassoing Robert Taunton to run his psychology lab, he was disturbed when it turned out that Taunton not only believed in behaviourism, he believed in it to the exclusion of all other views. As his fame grew, so did his arrogance, and he ceased to be diplomatic about his opinion of Ganz's "psychobiology."

Taunton was writing books; Ganz was not. Indeed it was a running question among the staff—*Why has the chief never written a book?* Ganz was so full of ideas, so eager to back vastly different areas of research, so convinced that his chosen discipline was on the brink of a golden age, that it seemed perverse of him to keep his ideas to a small circle of associates.

Taunton invited Carl and Imogen—soon seen as a couple, if not exactly engaged—to supper one night at his beautiful house on Calvert Street. (His wife came from money, according to Carl. Big money.) They dined under a glittering chandelier—maid, footman, and butler close at hand. Mrs. Taunton's necklace rivalled the chandelier for sparkle, shooting tiny slivers of light in all directions.

The conversation revolved, as it usually did, around the Phipps.

Imogen spoke admiringly of Ganz's lectures on psychotic reactions and said, "I don't know why he hasn't put his ideas in a book."

"Very simple," Taunton replied. "Because he doesn't have any."

"I would have thought you would agree with him. Isn't he, after all, saying that patients *learn* to be schizophrenic?"

"No, he seems to think they *decide* to be schizophrenic. They can't face whatever reality is offering them at the moment, and so they retreat into insanity. You *could* call it a learned reaction, if you could demonstrate it. Has he been able to *induce* schizophrenic reactions in the lab? Can you *induce* a mania? If you could, you might be able to find a way to extinguish such behaviour by inverting the stimuli, but no. If you press him on it, he becomes huffy, and gets lost in his so-called psychobiology jargon."

"Robert, please," his wife said. "Our guests are not here for a debate."

After dinner, Mrs. Taunton at her husband's urging entertained them with a few songs at the piano. She had a high, clear voice, free of the hyper vibrato that bedevils so many amateurs, and Imogen was moved by her version of "Barbara Allen." Taunton stood behind her, hands on her shoulders, looking every bit the proud husband. Imogen thought of Sara Sands sneaking out of his lab at two in the morning and could not understand why a man married to so lovely a person as Evelyn would ever stray.

Over the next few months, relations between Taunton and his employer worsened as Ganz tried to get the psychology lab to develop experiments that might support his ideas. Taunton categorically refused.

"They're not even speaking to each other these days," Carl told her. It was winter now, and he had talked her into taking the streetcar all the way out to Roland Park where they could go ice-skating on the pond. Baltimore was suffering record-breaking low temperatures and ice-skating was suddenly the thing to do on a Saturday afternoon.

Carl was an energetic skater, constantly scooting ahead and then allowing Imogen to catch up, wriggling backward ahead of her so they could talk face to face. Skating was not a skill that came naturally to Imogen. A tendency to go pigeon-toed forced her to stare at her feet—distressing, when you wanted above all to look your best. When Carl had suggested the outing she had almost declined out of vanity. But he was such a *physical* entity, so clearly in need of action, motion, or sheer *doing*, that she couldn't deny him.

"Ganz scribbles a note," he told her now, "and Taunton scribbles a note in reply—they courier them to each other via graduate student." Carl did a loop around her and swooped back. "The chief is constantly urging him to design this experiment or that and Taunton tells him to mind his own business. Try to keep your ankles straight."

"They won't stay, I'm afraid."

"You're doing well, you're doing well. Your balance is good."

"I think I'm more suited to seated forms of recreation. Perhaps canasta or bridge."

"Ganz has no authority over what Taunton chooses to research of course, so he's just wasting his time. You should hear Taunton. It's not just about Ganz; he has nothing but contempt for psychiatry as a whole."

"Oh, I've heard him all right." Imogen had to swerve to miss a stumbling child and nearly upended herself.

"Stop looking at your feet."

"I can't see them anyway."

"Don't look at them. You balance by looking outward, not downward. Do you need to sit down?"

"Thank you, I'm perfectly fine."

"Taunton and Sara have got their hands on a movie camera from somewhere. They're planning to film one of their experiments with an infant. It's to do with how we learn to be afraid."

"You know, I think I will sit down. Keep skating if you want."

"Don't be silly—it's your company I'm after. I've never had my own psychiatrist before. Did you know my last name is actually Bonaparte?"

"We haven't had any Napoleons at the Phipps, so far as I know, but there was a Teddy Roosevelt at the state asylum. He was absolutely unreachable. It sounds funny, something like that, but it's the saddest thing in the world."

Carl skated to the little gate in the surrounding rail, opened it, and stepped through. He motioned for her to join him, as if she were unaware of the location of the gate or his current whereabouts. His rosy cheeks and curly hair—not to mention his plaid, flapping scarf—well, she could have kissed him right there in front of the whole skating crowd.

She came to a wobbly stop, skate tips meeting the wooden border with a clonk.

Carl offered his hand as she stepped through. "What are you smiling about?"

"You. You look sweet as a Christmas gnome."

"Elves, my dear, not gnomes. How are your ankles?"

"In exquisite agony."

They removed their skates and went upstairs to an open-air café where they bought hot chocolate and pastries from a man in a striped outfit. The day was cold and still, but it was warm in the sunlight, and warmer still under one of the gas-powered reflective heaters. Skaters circled the rink below them like a ragged carousel. The hills of the park were draped with a thin coverlet of snow.

"It makes me miss Chicago," Imogen said. "Except it was *always* this cold there."

"Stick with me, my dear . . ." He reached across the table and took her hand in his. "And I promise to keep you warm forever."

Carl's impetuousness was apparently contagious, because later, on the porch of the Phipps, in the darkness of the January evening, she allowed him to kiss her for a long time, and let his hands wander much too far before she finally put a stop to it. And not a moment too soon, for Donna Artemis appeared out of nowhere and said tartly, "You must be careful of psychologists—they're notoriously unstable."

"Not this one," Imogen said. "Carl is the only person I've ever met who has absolutely no neuroses."

"Well, this just gets more sinister by the minute. Be off with you, Satan. Dr. Lang is late for supper."

Donna was at first amused by Imogen's romance and charmed by her friend's excitement, if not exactly bowled over by the man who provoked it, but she soon seemed to build up a wall against him. Imogen wondered for a time if Donna was jealous. With Carl in the picture, it was Imogen's turn to be unavailable for tea, or a movie, or even a shopping trip. Perhaps it was only natural that Donna should resent the person who had stolen away her friend.

One Saturday afternoon she and Carl were taking a lazy stroll along Charles Street when they bumped into Donna coming out of Eichelberger's book store. The three of them adjourned to a tea shop three doors down. The conversation went well enough. They talked about the Phipps, and tennis, and Ganz (the chief was always a reliable subject), but Carl was a little taken aback that Donna was so acerbic in her remarks about Taunton. Donna, perhaps sensing this, asked Carl about his work, and he chatted happily for a quarter of an hour about his rats. But as he talked, Imogen sensed a slackening in Donna's interest, though she nodded, and kept a small smile fixed on her face. When Carl went to the counter to get some change for a tip, Donna got up to follow him. Imogen watched from the table, somewhat mystified, as they exchanged a few words.

The three of them parted on Charles Street. Donna had to hurry home to get ready for the opera Dr. Walcott was taking her to that evening, a career in psychoanalysis—or so Imogen teased her—apparently coming with a ticket to the high life. When they had walked a couple of blocks Imogen asked Carl what he thought of her friend.

"A nice enough woman," he allowed, "and very smart."

"Yes, she is that."

"D'you know what she said to me, over at the counter?"

"No. I did wonder."

"She said, 'So, do you love her?' Just like that."

"Did she? And you said . . . ?"

"I said I certainly do. And she said, 'You'd better. Because if you ever hurt her I'll probably have to kill you.'"

"Oh, that's just Donna. She's all bluster, you know."

"Well, yes—I don't think she was actually threatening me with death—but still I thought it an extraordinary thing to say. I mean, why would I hurt you?"

"It's just her peculiar way of telling you she loves me."

"It put me off, to be honest."

"You'll get used to her."


One evening in early June, Carl stopped into the lab where Imogen was co-ordinating research on possible linkages between clinical observations of patient behaviour and the composition of their blood. Most of her student assistants had gone home for the summer, so she had pages of tabulations spread out on the centre table so that she could further develop the bar graphs for comparison.

Carl was struck by the number of graphs, and the details they illuminated. "I had no idea of the scope of your work," he said, picking up one of the sheets. "Korsakoff's syndrome?"

"Yes, we're looking at what happens to blood composition as the patient withdraws from alcohol dependency. How does it compare to non-toxic cases of transient psychosis as the patient gets better. You can see rough similarities right away."

He picked up another chart. "Sedation and insomnia."

"There, we want to see what happens to blood chemistry as a patient gets more sleep. The ward nurses have been so helpful with their observations. They're getting quite curious about our results too."

"This is good work, Im." He tapped the chart with a forefinger. "This should be published. It would be helpful to everybody—clinicians, hospitals, drug researchers. You could expand it to the asylums—get a wider scale. You could—"

"I know. We could have everybody researching. That's what I'm going to propose to the chief when I hand this in—assuming he thinks it's publishable. So far he's only let me publish a single paper. He's had two more sitting in his inbox for months."

"On this research?"

Imogen nodded. "One on manic-depression. One on non-cyclic depression."

"Well, he won't sit on this one," Carl said. "It's brilliant."

"I don't know about brilliant." Imogen looked around at her charts and graphs. "It's just common sense."

Carl laughed and put his hands on his hips, looking her up and down as if she were a racehorse. "You are wonderful."

"Not really, but I'm—"

"Yes, really." He stepped closer and hugged her tight. "And I love you, Dr. Lang."

"Carl, you mustn't." She tried to pry his arms away but he was strong. "Carl, please—we're at work."

Just as suddenly, he let her go, stepped back, and dropped to one knee.

"Say you'll marry me."

"What?"

"Say you'll marry me, Imogen."

"Is it really what you want?" She had sensed this was coming for some time now, and knew what she would say. "You're not going to change your mind, are you?"

"Never."

"Because I'd want to keep working. I'm not cut out to stay at home."

"I wouldn't want you to. I consider your career just as important as mine." He took hold of her hand. "Truly. I can't imagine you not working."

"Did you always plan to propose in the lab?"

"It just came over me." He kissed her hand. "Please marry me, Imogen. I don't know what I'll do if you say no. I'll have to become a behaviourist and develop a heart of stone."

"Well," Imogen said. "We can't have that."

They did not set a date because certain financial and bureaucratic matters would first have to be addressed. For one thing, there was the university's policy against marriage between staff members. What if the board refused to make an exception? And Imogen's cost of living would go up when she moved out of residence: the expenses of meals, rent, and transportation would mount. She was still categorized—and paid—as an intern, despite the fact that she had completed all her courses and now performed the same duties and worked the same hours as any of the associate psychiatrists.

"I don't feel I can raise the issue with the chief," she said one day when they were walking downtown. "If I'm worth promoting, the idea should come from him, not me."

"I'm not sure what my career prospects are either," Carl said. "The chief considers me flighty."

"Flighty?" Imogen said. "How could anyone apply that word to you?"

"Because I used to be in engineering, and then I changed my mind and went into psychology."

"But *of course* you would study engineering. I've never met anyone who had such a passion for finding out how things work."

"Ah, but then I did it again, you see. When I got here, I told him and Taunton I was going to study animal learning and then I decided to study cyclical behaviour."

"I think you may be misreading Dr. Ganz's facial expressions—everybody does at first. I'm quite sure he admires your ability to strike out in new directions. He's much like that himself."

Carl paused to look in the window of a hardware store.

"Well, he's hoping I'll turn up something that will explain manic-depression. But he still thinks I'm flighty. Also, he knows Taunton and I are on good terms, and that counts against me."

Imogen considered this. She would not have thought Dr. Ganz would hold Carl's closeness to Taunton against him. Not until recently.

As Carl had mentioned, Taunton and Sara Sands had indeed got their hands on a movie camera. They had also once again secured the services of the infant Max a.k.a. Edward from the Harriet Lane Children's Home next door. Their other requirements, in terms of equipment, were one white rat, one rabbit, a fur coat, and a noise-making source. For this, they chose a four-foot iron bar which, when struck with a hammer, produced a loud clang.

With the camera running, they showed Edward the white rat. He smiled and, displaying not the slightest hesitation, reached for it. The rat was taken away, and he was shown the fur coat. This produced coos and gurgles. The same was true for the rabbit. In the course of several sessions, by making a loud clang every time a rat or rabbit or fur coat was shown to him, they managed to change Edward's response from coos and gurgles to tears and wails. He learned to fear these harmless things.

A few weeks later "Conditioned Emotional Responses" appeared in the *Journal of Experimental Psychology*—credited to Robert Taunton and Sara Sands—and the study of human learning and behaviour would never be the same. Taunton was confirmed as the shining star in the Phipps crown.

Ganz might have appreciated the lustre Taunton's revolutionary experiment brought to the institution, were it not for how Taunton gloried in his new-found fame, becoming even more arrogant in his attitude to anything that was not behaviourism. The fact that his photograph appeared on the July cover of *Time* only made things worse.

Things reached their nadir, that year, at the staff Christmas party. Taunton's department put on an elaborate skit—there was a house tradition for such entertainment—in which an "esteemed professor," clearly meant to be Ganz, answered every question about his psychological theories in what sounded like Chinese. After that, Dr. Ganz not only refused to speak to Taunton, he refused to speak *about* him.

Imogen felt she had to warn Carl. "I don't think he's so small a man that he will hold your *work* association with Taunton against you. But you probably shouldn't pal around with him in off-hours."

"He's my friend, Imogen. I can't just drop him."

But, she suggested, perhaps he could make his excuses for a few weeks until Dr. Ganz's anger cooled. "Tell him you're too busy seeing the woman of your dreams."

"My angel, you mean."

"Exactly."

"The woman I adore and yet want to ravish."

Carl put his hands on her waist but Imogen took hold of his wrists and kissed him on the nose.

"You can ravish me when we're married."

"We really must talk to Ganz about it," Carl said. "If the university is going to stand in our way, the sooner we know the better."

"I've been putting it off. The prospect makes me nervous."

"Really?" Carl scanned her face. "You know he adores you."

"He treats me the same as everyone else."

Carl shook his head. "He looks at you like a proud papa."

"Carl, he does not. He's my employer. He's just a fatherly sort of person. And don't smile like that."

"Like what?"

"With amused skepticism. It's extremely irritating."

"Consider it done." He covered his mouth with his hand for a moment and the smile vanished. "I shall obey you in all things."

"A sound policy."


Imogen fretted about talking to Ganz the entire next day, and continued putting it off until a quarter to five; he would be leaving for home in fifteen minutes. She ignored the elevator and rushed downstairs. Mr. Penn was sliding files into cabinets, tucking other items into his desk drawers.

"I need to see Dr. Ganz," Imogen said, breathless from nerves, as well as the stairs. "He's still here, isn't he?"

"He is about to leave for the day. Shall I book you an appointment?"

"No, it's not a—well, it's a personal matter, and—"

The door to the inner office opened and Ganz leaned out. "Mr. Penn, you may bring my car round front. I believe you have the keys."

"I do, sir."

"Dr. Lang—what brings you here?"

"I need to talk to you about something, if you have a moment."

"A personal matter," Mr. Penn put in.

"Yes, but an important one," Imogen said. "Please. If you can spare the time."

Dr. Ganz opened the door wider. "Of course."

She sat across from him, took a deep breath, and told him she and Carl were to be married. They had not yet settled on a date, but they hoped it would be soon.

"Mm, yes." Ganz stared at her, fingering his goatee. "I feared it would be something of the sort."

It was as if she had told him she had been diagnosed with TB.

"Oh, he's a fine young man," the chief added, as if overhearing her thoughts, "but it seems to me precipitous. He's only been here, what, a year?"

"A year and a half—and we are very much in love. I hoped you would be happier for me."

"Of course. I wish for you every personal happiness."

"But?"

"To be honest, Dr. Lang, I wonder if you aren't rushing into marriage as a kind of medication for your earlier unhappiness."

"My depression, you mean?"

"Your depression, yes, but I am also concerned you may underestimate the impact of your earlier loss—your friend who went to war."

It was disorienting, when she was feeling so lucky and optimistic, to be reminded of Quentin.

"He meant a lot to me," she said evenly, "and I will never forget him. As to depression, I'm not looking to marriage as a cure. Carl makes me happy—that's the simple truth of it. I love him. We're good for each other. But I don't see him as my saviour."

Really, she was thinking, could Ganz not be a *little* less the psychiatrist for once?

"But what if children should come along? How will you afford them?"

"That is definitely a concern—in fact, I was going to write you a letter on that subject—but what I really wanted to discuss was the hospital policy against marriage between staff members."

"It's a university policy, not the clinic's."

"Yes. But I thought, as you are director of the Phipps, it would be your opinion that would count."

"I could ask for a waiver, true. That doesn't guarantee it would be granted. This is a policy of long standing, and many able physicians and nurses have left the hospital's employ because of it."

"Then, if I may, I ask you to make a strong recommendation that the board make an exception. You know both of us well, you know our work . . ."

"I know you quite well. Mr. Kromer is a relatively recent addition."

"But you'll make the recommendation?" Imogen persisted, feeling pushy, but she had learned that clarity and persistence were the only things that worked with Dr. Ganz.

"I will—provided you think this over very carefully. It seems so hasty."

"I will think it over," Imogen said, "and I'll consider everything you say. God knows, I have every reason to value your advice."

He gave a nod. "Then please consider this: I have seen these marriages before and by and large they don't work. Oh, the *marriages* may work, but the *careers* suffer. The women's careers. Take a look around you—just here, at the Phipps. Look at the women who are doing well: Dr. Quinn, Dr. Fein, Dr. Artemis. Not one of them married."

"Donna is brilliant. Are you really saying her career here at the Phipps would suffer if she were married?"

"Marriage seems alien territory for Dr. Artemis. We don't know how she'd react. But I can name you half a dozen other women at Johns Hopkins whose careers were derailed when they got married. You're competing with physicians for whom medicine, psychiatry, is the be-all and end-all of their existence. They live in one world, not two."

"Well, that's an excellent argument for marrying *within* the staff, then."

Dr. Ganz smiled. "You delight me with your quickness, as always. But once you are married, it will be Mr. Kromer who comes first—not psychiatry, not medicine, not you. It will be your husband. And if you should be blessed with children, *they* will come first. You can't be changing diapers and running a psychiatric ward simultaneously."

"Not simultaneously. During working hours, one works. During off-hours—"

Dr. Ganz raised a hand to cut her off. "There will be competing demands on your time. Children are exhausting. So are schizophrenics, lab work, manic-depressives. If there comes a point where Mr. Kromer's career demands one thing and your career another, it will be your career that suffers, not his."

"Carl assures me he sees our two careers as equal."

"He is unquestionably a progressive young man. I've heard him argue the suffragettes' case quite persuasively. But the things a man says when he's in love may change in the course of time."

"Dr. Ganz, I don't go into this with the expectation of a *bad* marriage."

Ganz saw that his words had stung her, and softened his tone. "Forgive me for being so candid. I hope you will see my concern as paternal—in only the best sense of that term. Please think things over awhile, and when you have made up your mind I will do whatever I can to aid in your happiness."

# 10

*The deep pleasure of quiet, the uncluttered joy of being clean*, Quentin wrote in his notebook. *And the food is ambrosia compared to hard-tack and bully beef.*

He paused with his pen above the page, remembering the first morning he had felt like himself when he woke in the field hospital. The quiet had wrapped itself around his head so thoroughly that he thought at first his eardrums had been blown out. He made the slightest adjustment to his position, the slightest movement of his arm, and the sheets rustled, almost rasped. Wondrous. He ran his fingers along the sheet and made the sound again. The linen was blinding white and smelled of carbolic; he pressed it to his face. It smelled of health, of order and discipline. It smelled of optimism. In days to come, he would realize that it was not so quiet here, that you could hear the thunder of the front ten miles away, someone else's bad dream.

He had been carried unconscious from Hill 70 and taken to a dressing station. He was streaked with blood, most of it from a broken nose and a gash on his cheek that must have been sustained when he was thrown into a trench support. Other than these, he had no obvious injuries.

Hours later he was conveyed by mule-drawn ambulance to a casualty clearing station.

He had no memory of any of this; he had been told about it days later when he regained consciousness in the hospital. His head throbbed and hammered with a headache beyond anything he would have thought possible; he was certain he had taken a round in the skull. The advent of consciousness brought with it a paroxysm of vomiting that lasted—although he had nothing in his stomach to eject—for what seemed an eternity.

For several days he did not remember his name or where he was from. He sensed dimly that this was a pathetic state to be in, but the vise-like headache prevented him from worrying about it. The doctors and nurses didn't seem too concerned, having seen such amnesia countless times, and he gathered from the cries and moans that there were others worse off than he was.

Then one morning he woke up and had his life back; he remembered everything right up to hearing the approaching shell and running for it. Although it did not vanish entirely, the headache receded to a bearable level. He lay thinking about his childhood, his father and mother, his mother's death. He thought about his abandoned medical career, and about a novel he would like to write. He thought about Imogen, and tried not to.

Not long after, a letter arrived from his father, with a tiny clipping from the Lake Placid paper glued to one sheet. Underneath, his father had written, "I recall you had a friend named Wisdom. I hope this is not the same man but thought it best to let you know."

### BODY IDENTIFIED AS MISSING PERSON

A body discovered in a rowboat last week on Mirror Lake has been identified as a 24-year-old Rochester man who went missing Monday.

Jonathan "Jack" Wisdom was last seen at the train station in Rochester NY. The body was found Tuesday adrift in a rowboat off Mount Whitney Road by a concerned citizen who alerted State Police. A spokesman for the Medical Examiner's office said cause of death was a single gunshot to the head but there was no evidence of foul play.

Over the following days and weeks, images of Jack would come to him—his laugh, the exultant way he looked when he read a particularly fine line from Keats or Shelley. And he remembered what Imogen had said—so long ago it seemed decades—about how Jack was so attentive to him, the way a gentleman attends to a lady, how he looked at Quentin with devotion. And I, Quentin thought, self-regarding fool that I am, did not even notice. I, who prided myself on being some kind of virtuoso of romance, could not recognize love when it was right beside me. The letter of rejection he had written to Jack now seemed an unwarranted attack. He had punished the most loyal of friends for the simple crime of loving him.

But even the lacerations of loss, regret, and self-blame could not set Quentin back for long. *Obviously*, he wrote in his notebook, *because I am a supremely shallow person*. Slowly, all the good food and rest had their effect. The headache was still a problem first thing in the morning but tended to be gone by noon. It would be a long time before the scar on his cheek would fade, but the bruises along the left side of his body were shrinking like retaken territory. He grew daily more comfortable with walking and exercise.

At his request, Lieutenant Pegram had written to central command and filled out myriad forms, thereby securing for Quentin orders for scout training at Étaples. He would never have to live in a trench again, although the odds were still good he might die in one. It was a warm day in June when, after a comfortable train trip, he arrived at Étaples and was duly shown to the tent he would be sharing with a half-dozen other trainees.

"Where is everybody?" he said to the corporal who had driven him across the enormous grounds.

"Recreation hall. Decorating. Got a big social planned for this evening. May as well join 'em—you're still officially on leave until reveille."

Quentin arranged his trunk at the end of his assigned cot and spent the next hour at the baths cleaning up. He paused in the middle of shaving and held his hand in front of his face. Quivering. There was a fluttering sensation in his chest that had been getting worse all day.

The noise of battle was louder here. The earth shuddered beneath his boots. His tongue and throat dried up in a way they had not since leaving the front. Soldiers talked of leave all the time, talked excitedly of the meals they would eat, the beer they would drink, the number-less women they would conquer. But he remembered the pallor and sweat on their faces when they came back.

"Are you all right?" he'd asked a battle-damaged man named Jimmy Cooke, just returned from London.

Cooke had been a rock in his platoon, a man who never hesitated, never whined, but he looked at Quentin with worried eyes and said, "It's a bit hard, that's all."

"What, coming back?"

A tight nod. "It's like goin' over the bags," he said, and Quentin now knew this was true.

He finished shaving and made his way to the recreation hall. It was a lovely June evening, the sun drenching everything in amber. In the hall, men on ladders were looping blue-and-white bunting over the rafters. Others levelled an enormous sign that said WELCOME, BLUEBIRDS! Quentin racked up some billiard balls and passed the time by sinking a few. It wasn't long before some other men joined him and he lost several games that parted him from actual cash.

Dinner in the mess hall was noisy. He'd forgotten the racket hun-dreds of men could make. It made him edgy. He would be joining a new battalion after training, and didn't feel like making the effort to make friends with people he would never see again. It was a bad atti-tude, but he couldn't help it.

The nurses arrived at the recreation hall promptly at eight o'clock and an enormous cheer went up, the stadium roar that follows a home run. The band was not quite ready, and a period of confusion and hilarity set in—soldiers making whooping noises, nurses pairing off in confidential giggle-fests, an enormous crush of people around the bar. Quentin found himself heartened by the sudden wealth of femininity. The cloud of perfume conquered, at least for the moment, the acrid smell of cigarette smoke.

When finally the band started to play he pushed and slithered his way through the crowd and, reaching out blindly between two soldiers, tapped on the tiny shoulder of a dark-haired woman with her back to him.

"Oh, my stars," she said, when she turned and saw him—shouting above the hubbub, "if it isn't Private Goodchild of Rochester."

He shouted back, "Nursing Sister Morley of Bracebridge. I didn't even know it was you."

"Just randomly shoulder-tapping, were you?"

"I was! I was!"

"Well, are we going to dance or stand here yelling at each other?"

They squeezed their way out from the bar area and proceeded to hop and crash amid the dancing crowd like dice in a cup—waltzes, foxtrots, one-steps—grinning at each other. When it became impossible to actually dance, Quentin grabbed her hand and said, "Come on, let's step outside and have a proper chat."

"Chat," she said when they were outside. "You've picked up some words from your Tommy pals."

"Indeed—not all of them fit to print. Oh, you've been wounded."

In a gesture that he realized was thoughtless even as he made it, he brushed aside a fringe of her dark hair, revealing a jagged, pale crease. She didn't pull away, just closed her eyes and tightened her lips.

"Sorry," he said, "I was just—"

"It was at a casualty clearing station. Couple of shells brought the roof down on us. It was misery for the poor patients."

"And for you too, looks like."

She shook her head. "Others fared much worse. You've been busy yourself, I see. I thought duelling was illegal."

"Mortar. I got off with nothing worse than a nasty headache but everyone makes a fuss as if you're a hero."

"You are a hero, you nitwit."

"I'll have to steal some medals from someone. Couple of Victoria Crosses ought to do it."

She gave a small smile but a shadow crossed her face.

"You've lost some people, haven't you," Quentin said.

She nodded. "Two brothers. Both at Vimy."

"Oh, I'm sorry—that's hard. How are your parents holding up?"

"They're devastated, of course. I'll be seeing them pretty soon though."

"You're headed home?"

"Early October, supposedly. But these things are subject to change, as you know."

"Do you mind if we walk a bit? It's so nice to just talk and, I don't know, just *be*."

"Just *be*, exactly."

He looked around, and pointed off toward the setting sun. "There's a sports field over there. Should be pretty quiet now."

They strolled across the grounds like two old colleagues taking the air. The noise from the recreation hall diminished behind them, and the distant shelling had ceased for the night. Quentin told her about his training course.

"A scout? But that's so dangerous."

"No, cowering in the trenches when the shells are coming down is the scariest thing. You're just waiting for God to point his finger at you and say, 'That one.'"

"But you'll be out between the lines."

"At night. When the shooting's stopped—unless they see you."

She shuddered. "Terrifying."

"Hah. This from someone who's been bombed in her casualty station."

"Let's talk about something else."

"All right. How many soldiers have fallen in love with you?"

"None. Well, lots, I suppose. I mean, they think they have but it's not love, of course. I know from my own experience. When the doctor gave me a shot and sewed up my scalp I wanted to kiss him all over his face. I restrained myself, thank God. You're so helpless, so vulnerable, and suddenly there's somebody offering you a little sympathy and your heart just floods with gratitude."

"But you weren't in love."

"Can we talk about something else?"

"How many times can one change the subject?"

"I don't know." Her shoulders sagged a little, and for a moment she looked like a schoolgirl who has just failed a test. "Every subject's painful in wartime, if you talk about it long enough. Sooner or later it will remind you of someone who's died, or you've left behind, or who's hurt you."

The war had aged her. Quentin knew it had aged him too—and not just with the deep creases at the corners of his mouth, or the bruise-coloured shadows beneath his eyes. Often during the course of a day he'd catch himself sounding like a man three times his age. People in their twenties were supposed to be gay and carefree, not grumpy and pessimistic. *Curmudgeonly.*

"Curmudgeonly?" She looked at him with dark round eyes.

"Sorry. I was thinking out loud. Thinking what a grumpy old man I've become."

"You're just a man of the world, that's all. Happens to all of us. I'm a man of the world too."

Quentin laughed.

She touched his arm. "I'm sorry I never came to meet you on the *Metagama.*"

"That's all right. I assumed you had a battle-axe for a matron."

"Oh, matron was *evil*, but that's not what stopped me. It was just— I'm a coward, I suppose. I was worried I'd fall for you and that was not something I wanted right before stepping into the lovely fields of Flanders, thank you very much."

"I went every night—to the prow, like we said—and I waited."

"You didn't pine, I hope." There was a touch of flint in her tone; she was a no-nonsense sort of woman, despite her talk of love.

"Can't say I pined—I hoped you'd come, though. I wanted very much to see you again."

"You did tell me you were hoping to get shot, you silly twit."

He nodded. "I loved someone. Someone who didn't love me. I suppose it sounds pathetic."

"Not pathetic."

There was a silence. They had reached the abandoned baseball diamond and sat on a wobbly bench near third base. Sounds of merriment from the recreation hall were distant yet vivid, like the sounds from a passing paddle steamer on Lake Placid.

Margaret touched the back of his hand with one finger. "Did she have someone else?"

"No, she was probably just trying to protect me. She could see I was in love and she wasn't, so what was she to do? She knew if we kept on it would just get harder and harder for me, and . . ."

"Yes, I see. Oh, dear. And you're still in love with her?"

"No, I . . . Probably not. I think of her all the time, though. Wonder what she's doing and so on. But I've no plans to get in touch when I get back—if I get back. Do you have anyone back home?"

She shook her head. "Strictly solo. I mean, I had fellas before I volunteered but . . . I don't know. I wanted to avoid complications, I suppose. Look at that sunset!"

The sun was a wafer of fire bisected by a telegraph line. They looked at it in silence for a few moments.

"It must have been hard for her," Margaret said. "Breaking off with you, I mean. It would be hard to lose a friend like you. I bet she's regretting it now."

"Oh, she'll be busy with work. Surrounded by handsome doctors."

"She's a nurse?"

"A physician. She'll be a psychiatrist by now."

"She's brave—that's a difficult field for anyone, let alone a woman. What are your own plans when you get back?"

"I don't know—I've stopped thinking about it."

"What *were* your plans then?"

"Write books. Become an author. If I'm lucky. God knows how I'd support myself."

"Well, as long as God knows, you're all right then, aren't you."

Quentin felt his cheeks redden; her simplicity embarrassed him.

"When they send you home, you'll land in Canada first. Promise me you'll look me up. I'm going to give you my parents' address in Bracebridge—they'll know where I am—and you can come and stay with us."

"They don't even know me."

"Quentin, they've lost two sons. They will love you. Now take me to the bacchanalia. I want to dance until I faint."


The benefits of being a scout were many. Foremost among them was the escape from the forward trench, the firing line, and even from the reserve trench. Scouts had their own dugout far behind the reserve line, and only nine men sharing it. This relative comfort and safety allowed them to catch up on their sleep during the day, their highly specialized work of reconnoitring the enemy line being confined almost entirely to the hours of darkness.

They cooked their own meals and kept to themselves, except when the assignment involved snipers or a raiding party. On such occasions they prepared the way by crawling up to the enemy's forest of barbed wire and snipping an opening through it, before guiding the raiders through the craters and corpses of no man's land and getting them back again, lobbing the odd grenade by way of support.

Quentin dreaded the prospect of going on a raid. The raiders would breach the enemy parapet, cut the throats of sentries, hurl grenades into any dugout they could see, and murder anyone who made it out alive. Captured raiders could expect no mercy from the enemy, but successful raids could be even worse, because they provoked

retaliation—and escalation. This last factor had managed to somewhat cool the high command's vicarious ardour for raids, and so far
Quentin hadn't had to face one.

His fellow scouts were a congenial lot, definitely a different breed
from the random enlistees of the trenches. It wasn't that they were
braver, but that being a scout gave you the sense—almost certainly
delusional—that you had some control over your fate, that you were
dependent on your own senses, your training, your resourcefulness,
not simply upon destiny. And while you never knew what exactly it
was you'd be walking into (crawling into, more likely) you knew it
wouldn't be massed machine-gun fire. The scouts seemed a livelier,
more intelligent bunch than the pure cannon fodder.

One of them was even a fellow writer, an unpublished though
prolific (by his own report, at least) novelist. At thirty-two, Lance-
Corporal Stan McClintock was the oldest of them, but he seemed
much older, partly owing to his receding hairline and partly to the
shrapnel scars around his forearms. He had an old wreck of a typewriter squirrelled away in the dugout, and the peck, peck, peck of
Mac's industry was a source of amusement among his comrades.

*Being around Mac makes me want to write*, Quentin wrote in his notebook. *He makes it seem such a manly occupation. He's tight-lipped about it.
I asked him once what he was working on. "Novel. War." I told him I planned
to write a novel if and when this war might ever end. "Just write the goddam
thing. Don't for Christ's sake talk about it." I don't know how he can write
about the war when he's right in the middle of it—but that's probably why
he's a novelist and I'm just a talker.*

And there was "Ginger" Hayes, who had been in scout training with
Quentin at Étaples. They had learned how to crawl together, crawling
being the scout's primary form of locomotion, and an exhausting one
at that. No one could have guessed how many different crawling techniques there were, but at camp they had to practise all of them.

Ginger was the same age as Quentin, a delivery driver for a Toronto
bakery, with ginger hair, ginger eyebrows, ginger lashes, and even ginger

fuzz on the backs of his hands. Mac liked to tease him that ginger men had no souls and were very possibly descendants of an alien race that had crashed on Earth centuries ago. Ginger would just grin and shake his head. "Keep telling those tall tales, Mac. That's all writers are good for."

Ginger was a prolific writer himself—to his parents, his sisters and brother, to his many cousins, to his friends at the bakery, and most of all to his fiancée, Winona. It took two weeks to get a letter to Canada, and another two weeks to get a reply. Ginger had stormed into the dugout in a state of high indignation one day when he had learned that British Tommies could receive a letter two days after it was posted in London or Liverpool, though why this should have surprised him was mysterious. Whenever he had a letter from Winona, he would read it slowly, line by line, moving his lips as he savoured each word. Then, when it was done and he had folded it again and slipped it inside his tunic, he would curl up on his cot and face the wall and not say anything for a while. At such times Quentin would think what a letter from Imogen might have meant to him. What it would have meant to have her waiting for him to come home. What it might have meant to have her love to look forward to. He wrote wry, chatty letters to Margaret a couple of times but received no reply; he had no way of knowing where she'd been posted. He felt a definite attraction, and considered there might be a future with her. Perhaps one day it would even be love. He definitely planned to look her up in Toronto.

Later Ginger would come out of his reverie and leave his cot and be his usual chipper, resolute self. He seemed a man possessed of a secret source of self-confidence, perhaps a man with a deep, abiding faith in his Saviour. Ginger was definitely the squad favourite, right up until the moment one late afternoon when a shelling frenzy caught him in a communication trench. His armless torso, blown free of his clothes, was found naked twenty yards behind the parados. One of his legs dangled from a splintered tree, and his head, minus the lower jaw, lay upside down a few feet away.

✄

After the British tanks smashed through Cambrai, the scouts had less work than before. Not because the brass wasn't hungry for information but for the simple reason that the moon insisted on being full and bright. Quentin's battalion completed an afternoon's march, crossing a canal and taking up billets in the barns around Escaudoeuvres. A good night's sleep in a hay pile and a hot breakfast set them up pretty well the next morning.

"They won't need us," Nate Gormley said. He was a religious twenty-year-old from Ontario with a tendency to unjustified optimism. "They'll just send the tanks in again."

"No, they won't," Mac said. He was threading laces into his boots.

"They've got to. They'll roll right over the wire."

"I got news for you, Gormley. The only place those tanks are rolling is north. They're probably in Flanders already. And in case you haven't looked up, we've got heavy cloud coming in."

"Well, gosh all fish-hooks. Just when I was getting used to our vacation."

Lieutenant Bagnal, head of the so-called specialist unit, of which the scouts were a part, appeared at their barn door with a clipboard, always a bad sign.

The scouts got to their feet and saluted.

"All right, men. I trust we've sharpened our clippers?" he said, and went on without waiting for an answer, now and then glancing at his clipboard as he spoke. "The division objective is to retake the château at Avesnes-le-Sec, and the battalion objective is the surrounding high ground. The enemy have not been there long, so it should not be the most difficult task in the world. Indeed, if we take the high ground, the château must follow.

"We've got a short march at 1600 across the Erclin river to a sunken road running southeast from Iwuy. When we get there . . ." He raised an arm and pointed to the right. "Battalion headquarters is the mill known as Moulin de Pierre, Pete's Windmill. Here's where you come in: There's a wood on the east side of the château. This wood does not appear on any map and so has not been taken into consideration in the planning. Field glasses show a couple of machine-gun nests but they may not be the whole story. Any questions so far?"

"I have one," Mac said.

"Go ahead."

"What high ground?"

"Good point. The surrounding geography was at one time dead flat, but is now cratered with shell holes. We need to know what kind of cover they will afford. Obviously any part of that field is high ground compared to our sunken road, but closer to the château there is a slight rise with a copse of trees—enough to give you a view of the whole field. Your main job tonight is to get right up to that wood and that slight rise and find out exactly what we're facing. It's asking a lot, I know. HQ is well aware of the risk, but we know you can do it because you've done it before. Everything you learn will save lives in our assault tomorrow, so if it should cross your mind to ask why the hell you're risking your neck like this, that's why. Saving lives is what scouts are all about, right?"

"Yes, sir!"

"Come on, lads, that was pathetic. Let's hear it again."

This time they shouted. "Yes, sir!"

"That's the spirit. One point, weather looks to be perfect for a night out, so be wary of enemy patrols and work parties—or indeed enemy scouts. They know we're here. Corporal McClintock, I'll leave this with you." He removed a sheet from his clipboard and handed it to Mac. "Right then. Godspeed."

When he was gone, Mac looked up from the order paper. "Jesus. It's twelve hundred yards between us and them. Could be a long night."

They duly made the march to the sunken road. The enemy was aware of troop movements, though not their precise co-ordinates, and shelled the area for hours. These sunken roads were a peculiar feature of Europe that Quentin had never heard of before. They had started out as wagon tracks. The surrounding forestation had largely been cleared for farmland, leaving only a strip of trees running along the sides of the road as a windbreak. Under the pressure of decades—perhaps centuries—of traffic, the road had sunk until it was much lower than surrounding terrain. Treetops had long ago met overhead so that the overall effect was of a long green tunnel that could be charming on a sunny day. Although they provided good cover, a hard rain of any duration turned these roads into rivers of mud. And if the enemy sensed movement along them they were shelled relentlessly, often with gas, which would linger long after the shells had stopped.

Crawling is not an efficient way to get anywhere. It is also extremely tiring, calling upon muscles—deltoids, lats, and intercostals—that are not required for heavy work in everyday life. The weeks of practice at Étaples were proving invaluable.

When they had set out at 2200, the night had been moonless, starless, misty. They had removed all the pips, badges, and bars from their uniforms and blackened their faces with burnt cork. They wore gloves for clipping wire, but still blackened their hands in case they had to remove the gloves for other tasks. All shiny objects were their enemies. They would not even be wearing helmets, which tended to ring like Big Ben if they were struck with the smallest pebble. Bayonets were the only things they took that might gleam, and these they kept fixed but sheathed. In addition they each carried a dagger, an entrenching tool, and a revolver.

It was a rule of thumb in the army that major things went wrong with every operation. You could never be sure *which* thing, but at least one major foul-up was inevitable. Mac had requested that the battalion wiring parties be ordered to create an exit so the scouts would not be required to clip their own wire as well as the enemy's. Somehow the request was not conveyed. It took Mac, Quentin, and Gormley three hours to clip their way out of the sunken road before they could even get to no man's land.

There was almost no shooting. Every now and then a sniper let fly at a stray glint of light—perhaps the lens of a trench periscope—and there might be a brief exchange. This happened twice in the first half-hour of their venture, way off to the right of the line. That in itself was information. The enemy could be restricting their fire in order to avoid their own scouts who might be at work between the lines.

The night was so dark they had agreed to walk rather than crawl for the first four hundred yards. Unless the moon came out, or someone launched a Verey light overhead, there was no chance of the enemy spotting them. Eventually they got down and started to crawl. This too provided information. The formerly flat terrain was now gouged with holes and craters that would provide some cover for advancing troops but made the scouts' progress slow. They crawled ten yards or so apart from each other, within hailing distance via a sudden *psst*!

Quentin's face was inches from the earth, the smell of which had been soured with explosives. Now and then as he crawled he gripped the dirt in his hands. The earth, from which they had come and to which so many of them had all too swiftly returned, was home to a soldier when the shooting started. He clung to it as to the maternal bosom, wept into it, cried out into it, again and again, even though the loudest cries were inaudible beneath the hiss and shriek of steel.

A second thing went wrong. The art of weather prediction being imprecise at best, the moon remained hidden but a few stars came out. You could not see any great distance, but as Quentin was crawling over the lip of a mid-size crater he heard movement just ahead. A gleam of light on a German boot. And then another. He gripped the dirt.

He looked to his left and right. He was not sure if the others had stopped too. In truth, coming into the vicinity of an enemy work party was not the worst thing that could happen. The German line would be expecting the return of their men, and the scouts could slither along, undetected, in their wake. He hoped Mac and Gormley would make the same calculation but he couldn't see them.

Another fifteen minutes of crawling and his triceps were screaming. The wooded area was up ahead. He heard Germans begin muttering to each other as they got closer to "home." Quentin had only a
few words of German, but they would no doubt be anticipating a rum
ration and a smoke.

He could hear other voices now, most likely from enemy machine-
gun nests.

A German shouted something—a sentry challenging the work
party. A guttural exchange and then the brief glow of a cigarette.
Another bark and the cigarette tumbled to the ground. This was a
superb piece of luck, to have found the enemy's entrance through fifteen yards of barbed wire. Quentin lay on his back in a shallow crater
and tried to fix his position. He could just make out the steeple of the
Iwuy cathedral and beyond it what must be the Escaudoeuvres cathedral. He would be able to lead attacking troops to the spot in daylight.

He lay on his back, listening. Up close, the murmur of men in
another machine-gun unit in very close proximity. Attacking troops
would face withering fire. He could hear the slap of ammunition belts,
the slosh of water filling the Vickers cooling tanks. Farther off, the
rumble of transport and the tramp of carrying parties. It sounded
like a lot of trucks. He could hear no horse sounds, but the animals
would be picketed at a distance.

He crawled to the edge of the wire and clipped a six-inch section
and put it in his pack. Overhead, the clouds were thinning; the moon
was a faint smudge. He cinched his pack tighter to his shoulders, and
crawled away from the wire. He fixed his mind on the ration of rum
he would get when he returned to the line, imagining the trail of
flame it would make down his throat, the sweet detonation of warmth
in the pit of his stomach, the way it would calm his quivering hands.

His elbows and knees were scraped and sore and his breath was
coming in gasps. He told himself to slow down; it was always a temp-
tation to move fast on the way back, homing in on the illusion of
safety ahead. Five hundred yards stretched between him and the

sunken road. He could not see his fellow scouts, and that was good. If he couldn't see them . . .

A gunshot split the night, and a flare arced into the sky. Bullets thudded into the earth around him. He rolled into a crater—a deep one with a foot of water in the bottom. Harsh light carved sharp, swinging shadows into the gloom as a flare drifted down on its parachute. There was no way to know if the Germans had spotted him or one of the other scouts. He clutched his rifle close and held his breath, listening for cries of pain, but he could hear none above the chatter of machine guns.

No individual shots, no sniping—that was a good sign, seeming to indicate the enemy had not spotted anyone but were sweeping an area where they thought they saw something. The flare sank into darkness—Quentin badly wanted to run but forced himself to wait. Another flare went up, and he congratulated himself on having the discipline to keep still. The enemy held fire. The rum was banished from his mind now. He kept low in the crater.

Again the flare sank to earth and expired. The moon chose that moment to emerge; if he ran, they would see him. He sank back against the dirt and waited.

Then came a rustling sound and a stabbing pain in his leg as someone landed on top of him. Quentin rolled him off and kicked away from him. A German. Quentin had his Enfield trained on him; the German's rifle lay a few feet away. The two sat staring at each other across the crater with wild eyes.

The German was little more than a boy, eighteen at the most. An entrenching tool was strapped to his back; he must have got separated from his work party. He started to reach for his rifle, but Quentin jerked his own and shook his head. The German sat back.

Better to shoot him right now, Quentin thought. Those machine-gunners would hear it, but they were in a crater, the muzzle flash would not be seen. His finger tightened on the trigger.

The boy raised his hands and shook his head, eyes pleading. He looked like any new recruit, he could have been anything—a bakery driver like Ginger, a student, a poet. He spoke in a low, frightened voice, still with his hands up. "Prisoner, yes?" He nodded vigorously. "Prisoner?"

Keeping his rifle trained on the boy, Quentin stretched out the toe of his boot and hooked the German rifle by the strap. He pulled it toward him and laid it against the side of the crater.

"Please," the boy said. "I am good prisoner—will *be* good prisoner."

The Germans always seemed to have some English. Sometimes quite a lot.

Quentin told him to shut up. He was wishing he had fired at once. He didn't want a prisoner, even though battalion HQ would certainly love the opportunity to interrogate the boy. The two of them would have to traverse four hundred yards of no man's land, and it offered a thousand opportunities for chaos. But if he let him go, he would reach the German line before Quentin could get clear. No, no, the proper thing would have been to bayonet him at once, straight through the throat, preventing any cries.

The boy smiled a sickly smile and pointed upward. "Dark now. We go and no one shoot us, yes?"

Quentin pulled the stock of his rifle tighter to his shoulder. The boy turned his head to one side and closed his eyes. "*Gott. Bitte.*"

"Hey," Quentin said. He didn't want to talk; they were too close to the German line.

The boy was shaking, eyes clenched tight.

"Hey."

The boy opened his eyes.

Quentin held a finger to his lips.

It took the boy a moment, then he nodded.

Quentin pointed to his own chest, then back over his shoulder. I go this way. He pointed to the boy and then farther off toward the German lines. You go that way.

The boy nodded frantically.

"Wait." Quentin looked up toward the moon. When the cloud thickened, he shouldered the German rifle and once more put a finger to his lips.

The boy nodded.

"Go."

They turned away from each other and began the climb out of the crater. But with his back to his enemy, Quentin was gripped by a sudden terror. He yanked the sheath from his bayonet, turned around, and launched himself after the boy. He stabbed at his back and felt the blade glance off the entrenching tool before lodging in flesh and bone. It held there as the boy slithered back down the crater. He cried out but it was not loud—his lung was pierced—and sprawled face down snatching at his back for the blade.

Quentin pulled but the bayonet caught on something—bone? ligament?—and pulled the boy with it so that he fell on his back in a twisted posture, head lower than his feet. Quentin stood over him, bayonet poised and dripping.

The boy made horrible gurgling sounds.

Quentin took hold of his arm and righted him so that he was lying upright with his back against the crater wall. He coughed weakly. The moon came out, and black blood glistened where it covered his mouth and chin.

Quentin took out a field dressing. He pulled the boy forward by one arm, reached around, and pressed the field dressing against the wound. Hot blood soaked his hand. He must have opened an artery as well as the lung.

The boy was trying to speak.

"Don't talk."

Quentin looked up. The sky was black and freckled with stars. The moon was now entirely clear of cloud. He sat back against the crater wall facing the boy, his rifle across his knees.

The boy was crying now. The lung wound was too severe to allow much noise, but the tears slid from his eyes and shone on his cheeks.

"Try not to cry. Breathe slower, if you can." He pointed to the sky. "I'll take you back when it's dark again."

The boy lay looking at him, his breathing rapid and shallow. Aside from this only his eyes moved, their bright whites extinguished every now and then by a slow blink.

Quentin stared at the sky, urging it to cloud over again. Cumulus the colour of charcoal edged closer to the moon.

The boy moved—or rather, his right forearm moved. An index finger pointed to his bloody mouth. "*Vasser. Bitte. Vasser.*" He could only whisper. "*Vasser. Bitte.*"

Quentin shook his head.

"I have no canteen. No water. When it's dark again I'll take you back, see?" He pointed to the sky again but the boy's half-hooded gaze did not change.

"*Bitte.* Please."

"Soon. When it's dark."

"*Ich* . . ."

"Shh. Quiet now."

"*Bin* . . ."

"Stop trying to talk."

". . . *tod.*"

"You're fine. You're not going to die."

The tears overflowed the eyelids like a slow fountain. So much blood, so many tears, the boy's thirst would be terrible.

The eyes closed. The lips, black and sticky with blood, kept moving. Quentin could no longer hear him, but it didn't take a lip-reader to make out the silent syllables.

"Soon," Quentin said. "You'll see your mother soon."


He had to sit and watch the tears drying on the dead boy's face for another half-hour before it was dark enough to climb out of the crater. There was shooting as he made his way back, but not at him.

He had learned not to flinch at rifle fire; you would never hear the one that got you.

A panicky sentry challenged him and he gave the code word and was allowed through. Mac and Gormley were waiting for him.

"Where were you?" Mac said. "We've been back nearly two hours."

"Got stuck in a crater with a German."

"You killed him, I hope." This was Lieutenant Bagnal, who had just appeared behind Mac. "Your rum, man. You look as if you've earned it."

Quentin took the metal cup of rum, spilling it with all his shaking.

"Steady, man. Easy does it."

Quentin brought the cup to his lips and drank all the rum down. It was a bigger ration than usual and should have felt glorious.

Bagnal pointed to Quentin's blood-soaked left arm. "Is that yours?"

Quentin shook his head. "Got him with the bayonet."

"Well done, Goodchild. Well done, indeed. Bit hard on the nerves, though, right?"

Quentin nodded. "Yes, sir."

"Very well, your report?"

"I could hear transport, sir, but not huge transport, only field guns, I think. Did the others tell you about the work party?"

"They did. Damn lucky you all got back alive."

"I followed them and saw where their own path through the wire is. I don't know if the others saw it."

"They did. It's excellent intelligence, Goodchild. Bad luck for you three, of course, as you'll be guiding us into the show. Anything else?"

"The wood, sir. Judging only by the sounds, I'd guess there are eight to ten machine-gun emplacements in the wood."

"Hmm."

"They have a clean sweep of the entire field. Every man of us will be mowed down."

"That will certainly be my advice to HQ. Whether it has any effect is another question."

Quentin reached into his pack and handed the lieutenant a six-inch piece of German wire. It was thicker than the British-made stuff, with longer barbs.

Bagnal smiled. "Course, we have no way of knowing if you boys are stockpiling these. It's not like they're date-stamped."

"It's from tonight, sir."

"I know it is, Goodchild. I was joking. Now off with you and your colleagues. Try to get some sleep before zero."

Mac had already scoped out a patch of ferns off to one side of the sunken road where they could stretch out and led the way. When they got there, all three of them lay down.

"Moon's out again," Gormley said. "But at least it's not raining."

"It'll be raining steel soon enough," Mac said.

Quentin sat up again. "I killed a boy. In a crater."

Mac looked over at him. He was lying on his back with his hands behind his head, his elbows forming brackets for his face.

Quentin told them how the boy had fallen on him, the rest of it. He heard the panic rising in his voice as the miserable story spilled out of him like blood. Guilt squeezed his stomach.

"You did what you had to do," Mac said.

"I bayoneted him in the back. I told him he could go and then I bayoneted him in the back."

Mac reached over and grabbed his elbow, hard. "Listen to me. You think where that Hun's at now he gives a damn whether you stuck him in the front or the back? We're here to kill Germans. It's our job. You did what you're supposed to do."

"I should have taken him prisoner."

"Christ, man, listen to yourself. You were two guys scared shitless in the bottom of a *crater*. One of you ended up dead and I for one am delighted it wasn't you."

Quentin shook his head. "It was cowardly. Unfair. He was just a boy—maybe eighteen, more like sixteen."

"It's *war*, Goodchild. Not college football. Did Bagnal seem worried to you? Nobody gives a damn. It's what war *is*."

"He was crying like a little boy. He wanted his mother."

"Shut up, Goodchild. I mean it now. No one wants to hear this shit."

Some months earlier—it wasn't even on the battlefield, it had happened back among the transport lines—the enemy had let fly with a barrage of high explosives. When the shriek of the shells finally stopped, the air was alive with the cries of the wounded. Some calling for help, some wailing in agony, and one man with his arms blown off begging for someone, anyone, to put a bullet through his head. But somehow worse than all of this were the high, inchoate shrieks of the animals. A donkey on fire ran from one side of the road to another until finally someone managed to shoot it. A horse with its belly ripped open staggered by, trailing intestines. And now Quentin added the boy to these images.

He turned over on his side and pressed his hands between his knees.

Their artillery opened up forty-five minutes before zero hour. Unfortunately they overshot the mark and did not take out the machine guns in the little wood. Quentin was stopped before he had gone twenty yards. He felt a thudding sensation and a searing pain in his side but didn't realize the extent of his trouble until blood poured into his eyes. "I'm hit," he said to the man next to him, and collapsed in the mud.

The machine-gun fire was so intense, the terrain so flat, that the stretcher-bearers had only one place they could carry the wounded. The company medic had them lined up on the ground behind the windmill. When a wounded man died, he was carried out of the safety zone and his spot was given to someone who was still breathing.

They must have administered morphia at some point because Quentin awoke lying on his back in a dreamy state. He was aware of pain but it wasn't bothering him. His right leg was wrapped and splinted but he had no idea why. There was a bandage around his head, and another around his chest that showed a bright scarlet bloom.

Must be a lung wound, he said to himself, and thought what a beautiful colour. The colour of flags.

The man next to him was muttering a continuous stream of words. Quentin assumed it was a rosary or some other form of prayer but when there was a lull in the shellfire he could just make out the multiplication table. He was on the nine times table when he stopped. Seconds later he was removed and another man was lowered onto his spot.

"Mac!"

Mac's head lolled in his direction. His chest and stomach were covered with blood but he seemed unaware of it. "This is something, isn't it, kid?"

"I'll see you in London, Mac."

"Naw. I've had it."

"London. London."

"Do me a favour, kid. Look after my novel."

"You'll look after your own novel. It'll be a great novel."

"No. You look after it for me."

"Sure, Mac. But really . . ."

"Hell of a thing, eh?"

"Sure is."

"Hell of a thing."

Mac lost consciousness, and a few minutes later the stretcher-bearers took him away.

# 11

It was not long after Imogen's discussion of her marriage plans with Dr. Ganz that Robert Taunton's wife discovered his affair with Sara Sands, and demanded an immediate end to it under threat of divorce. The betting at the Phipps was that Taunton would drop his paramour, but he surprised everyone, including Imogen, by moving out of his house and into an apartment on Calvert Street, where the divorce papers were duly served.

As if that were not enough, the case turned into a scandal that made for sensational headlines, partly because of Taunton's celebrity, and partly because Evelyn Taunton had somehow got hold of a dozen letters her husband had sent to his lover—letters that were noted to be remarkably passionate for a behaviourist.

Perhaps Taunton was counting on Dr. Ganz to save him—after all, he had brought much glory to the Phipps—but, mortified by the scandal and the relentless publicity, the president of Johns Hopkins demanded Taunton's resignation, and the chief, recognizing an opportunity to rid himself of the thorn in his side, made not the slightest effort to intervene.

Taunton was no sooner out the Phipps door than Dr. Ganz appointed Carl head of the renamed Psychobiology Laboratory. It came as a complete surprise, but it was not unmerited; Carl had completed his Ph.D. in record time, and his prolific papers were getting a lot of attention in the psychology journals.

Imogen took no pleasure in Taunton's fall; in fact, she felt sorry for him as well as his wife. But she could not help feeling that the tide of fortune had turned in her favour. Really for the first time since she was a child she could reflect on her life and know that she was lucky, she was happy, and the future seemed edged with gold.

Ganz eventually came through with a waiver allowing them to marry, and they decided on a simple ceremony—at city hall with a clerk from the local water department as sole witness. This elopement provoked Imogen's father to write to her for the first time since she'd left Chicago. "Apparently you did not consider that a man wants to be present at the marriage of his own daughter." *Well, you have at least one supernumerary daughter to make up for it*, she felt like replying, but did not. She also received a telegram from her uncle Mason offering to forgive the remainder of her unofficial student loan, but she would not hear of it. He shot a second telegram right back: STUBBORN AS YOUR PAPPY STOP.

A few weeks after their honeymoon (Cape May, all multicoloured gorgeousness in October) she realized that it had been several days since she had thought of Quentin. She allowed herself the pang of sorrow this realization brought, but it surfaced with a certain resignation, acceptance even, that she hoped might be the beginning of wisdom. Quentin had wanted to end his life and he had succeeded—or one of the mad architects of the war had succeeded for him—and she could acknowledge her role in his death, but would no longer blame herself for it.

Carl was a—well, "breath of fresh air" was far too anemic a phrase for Carl Kromer. He was all enthusiasm, all energy; he was optimism incarnate. No sooner did he have an idea than he wanted to test it in the lab. *Boom*: write the paper, send it off—next idea, please. Imogen was thankful that her own interests—despite Ganz's restrictions on clinical treatment—were now turning toward psychoanalysis. She did not want to be in competition with her husband, especially when she had yet to publish her second paper. The work was done, but she had been waiting months for Dr. Ganz to approve it. Psychiatric residents could not submit anything for publication without clinic approval, and if they did, the journals would not print it.

Carl's experiments on the endocrine system, behaviour patterns, and "biological clocks," as he liked to call them, had profound implications for human psychology. Even small hormonal changes could wreak havoc on energy levels and mood. Menstrual upsets were the most obvious example, and postpartum depression a more frightening one. Carl's discoveries offered hope for the development of medications but, much like theories of predestination, tended to undermine one's confidence in human agency.

"Those medieval doctors were right," he liked to say. "It's all about the balance of humours. It just happens there are a lot more than four."

If he was a blizzard in the intellectual realm, he was a force-10 gale in the physical. One thing Imogen Lang had been absolutely certain of never becoming: sex-mad. She was thoroughly aware of America's current fixation on Ivor Novello, Rudolph Valentino, and Harry Houdini, but she did not share it. Smouldering gazes and oily hair seemed funny, even repellent, to her. Carl's curly hair and humorous eyes were far more exciting to anyone with an ounce of discernment.

In high school she had experienced a crush or two, even three, but these were matters of idealization, not lust. She had been kissed several times, too, but she had remained a virgin and had never felt any compelling reason to be anything else, until she'd met Carl. Not only had she allowed Carl to touch her almost anywhere he wanted, she couldn't wait for him to do it. Nor could she keep her hands from roaming all over his body, with its perfect proportions and ropy muscles. Their kisses were breathless, panting collisions that left her feeling both ravished and ravisher.

It was amazing to her that she had managed to remain a virgin right up to their wedding night. It had not been easy. For some weeks she had drawn the line at touching each other outside their clothing. That line being crossed, her fallback position was no direct touching beneath the belt. Well, the belt line quickly collapsed and by then their erotic temperature had climbed many degrees.

No orgasms. That had become her next unspoken boundary, and it lasted little more than a week. Carl was, after all, good with his hands. He was also as avid for Imogen's pleasure as for his own, perhaps even more so.

She had thought at first the sheer weirdness of it would prevent her from sinking any deeper into absolute harlotry—the alarming heat of his balls, for example, or the sensation of his penis in her hand. It was just too strange—harder than flesh had any right to be, the silky sleeve scorching to her fingers. One evening she burst out laughing, couldn't stop herself, and Carl, perturbed and throbbing, wanted to know why.

"Nerves," she replied weakly. Just nerves. But what she had actually been thinking was: *Penis envy, what a mad conceit.* She adored Freud by now, but no, Herr Professor, who could possibly envy the pompous little troll lurking in a man's trousers?

And then one night she allowed Carl to smuggle her into his apartment. They worked themselves up on the couch until Carl was beside himself and she just could not abandon him on that ledge. Also a part of her just wanted to see the thing go off. What an experience that was: Carl's ragged cries, semen roping and flying everywhere, coating her fingers with slippery heat that rapidly went sticky. Horrifying. And yet . . . captivating.

"Well," she said, as Carl lay gasping, "that was interesting," and they rolled against each other, giggling.

Even after that she would never have thought that she could become so consumed by anything as grotesque as sex. But their wedding night changed her thinking, and the many nights that followed confirmed her in her wickedness. For she had no doubt that she had now stepped into realms of sexual behaviour that did not much occur outside pornographic novels, case histories, and French postcards. She found herself daydreaming about her husband's penis, for God's sake, right there in the lab, in the middle of the workday.

She'd be staring out the window, seeing not the elms or the carpet of fallen leaves or the November rain, but only that rod of flesh, imagining it in her fist, and in her mouth, and in its proper place. It was the oral business she couldn't get over, because she had never imagined herself having anything to do with anything so bizarre. Yet now she thought about it at all hours of the day—the shape of him, the feel of him on her lips and tongue, the taste.

A behaviourist like Taunton would no doubt say that this degree of lust was a conditioned response. Just as little Edward had learned to fear a harmless rat, Imogen had learned to crave Carl's body because he rewarded her with orgasms so exquisite they demanded a whole other word of their own.

"My God," she said, after he had brought her to yet another heart-stopper with the tip of his tongue. "How did you get so good at that?"

She clutched his arm before he could answer and said, "No, don't tell me. Never tell me. I don't want to know about you and anyone else. Ever."

"You don't have to worry, sweetheart." He looked at her with amused affection. "You just inspire me, that's all. It's all your fault."

"I've never been with anyone else. You know that, don't you? So this is rather frightening."

"You're my darling," he said, stroking her hair, "and I plan to love you always."

She kissed his shoulder and willed herself to be comforted. Because it was true: she really didn't want to know, but she couldn't stop wondering. No one was born knowing how to bring another human being to ecstasy; Carl must have been giving and receiving orgasms by the dozen with those beautiful German girls. The tooth of jealousy nipped at her heart but she fought it off, would not allow herself to be jealous of the past.

"Marriage agrees with you," people kept saying those first few months. Ganz said it, Ruth Fein said it, Lila Quinn said it—Lila Quinn!—and even Donna, unsentimental Donna, said it. It made Imogen blush, because she thought, *They know*, and what they were really saying was, *Well, my dear, you certainly look well f***ed!*

"How is the physical side of things?" Donna said one afternoon when they had bumped into each other in the Phipps library. They didn't get to see each other much now that Imogen had moved to an apartment with Carl.

"The physical side?" Imogen looked about to see if there was anyone else in the library but they were quite alone.

"Little tart," Donna said, and squeezed her wrist. "It's depraved, isn't it."

Imogen nodded. "Extremely."


Carl was a big walker. Their apartment on Reservoir Street was a good three miles from the Phipps, but he never even considered taking the streetcar. Imogen soon learned to enjoy the walk at least one way every day.

On weekends they would walk up to Druid Hill Park. Imogen particularly enjoyed this outing because Carl liked to ride on the park's whimsical narrow-gauge railway with its decorative Moorish and Chinese "stations," thus giving her a chance to sit down. In contrast to Chicago, you could enjoy the outdoors in Baltimore into early December. But Imogen was bothered by the park's rigid segregation of facilities into "coloured" and "whites only."

"Chicago won't allow that sort of thing anymore," she said. "It's not as if they're still slaves."

"I don't think anybody minds being separate," Carl said, "as long as things are equal."

"That tennis court doesn't look equal." Imogen pointed across the lawn where two Negro couples, vivid in their tennis whites, were playing a game of doubles. "It's rundown—and there's only the one court. The white area has six."

"This is the South, Imogen. You don't see any Negroes in the Phipps, do you?"

"No—because the private patients wouldn't tolerate it, and their fees are the only way the place can stay open."

On Saturdays they would walk to Lexington Market, so colourful and noisy, and stop into Henny's to purchase coffee and tea. Carl was not a materialistic person, but he was finicky about his coffee. He had a small grinder with a crank, and its crunchy whir greeted Imogen as she woke most mornings. That was the only aspect of the kitchen in which he took any interest. Like all men, he expected meals to be set before him on a plate and expected that plate to be washed and put away while he was doing something more interesting.

Carl saw their careers as equal, but he never offered assistance in the kitchen, nor did Imogen expect him to. Before they got married, they had both come to rely on the food services provided by the Phipps and Johns Hopkins and, faced with the prospect of meal preparation, Imogen had been obliged to write home to her mother's housekeeper, Mrs. Bidwell, for some simple recipes.

Carl was good about fixing small things around the apartment—a sticking drawer, a loose tile, a jammed window. He took pleasure in such projects, just as he enjoyed his various contraptions in the lab.

One Sunday morning in February—after a week of frigidly un-Southern temperatures—they rose early and went up to Druid Lake. The sun had still not cleared the treetops, and there was no one else around. They clamped blades to the soles of their shoes and skated around the lake, hand in hand. Eventually Carl took off at great speed, torso low, right arm swinging. He spun around and called back to her various insults—Lazy! Slug!—but Imogen preferred her more contemplative pace.

As she completed another circuit, she noticed they were no longer alone. The low sun was now directly in her eyes, but she could make out a man in a long dark coat as he stepped onto the ice. A few moments later he was gliding toward her with his hands behind his back—a small man, with a dark goatee, sharply pointed, skating with a preoccupied air. He started when Imogen called to him.

"Dr. Ganz, how nice to see you."

"Why, Dr. Lang, how delightful to see you abroad on this beautiful morning."

"Yes, rather more like Switzerland than Baltimore with all this ice."

"Indeed. Perhaps it was an attack of nostalgia that provoked my little outing. Mary thought I was quite mad. Is that young Kromer pounding toward us?"

"It is."

"A good researcher *and* an athlete—a combination to be treasured."

"Hello, my treasure," Imogen said as Carl scraped to a halt beside them. The three of them stood talking, their breath visible in the cold.

Dr. Ganz inquired after Carl's latest experiments, speaking in the dry tones of his lectures. "It would be of inestimable importance," he said, "if we could discover the organic processes underlying the formation of habits—but wait—don't tell me now. Why don't the two of you come to my house for dinner tonight? Come at six. That way we can enjoy a long conversation before dinner."

"Perhaps we should make it another day," Imogen said. "We wouldn't want to be an unpleasant surprise for Mrs. Ganz."

"You won't be. Mary will be charmed by your company."

"You're not left-handed, are you, Doctor?"

"Carl," Imogen said, "why would you ask a thing like that?"

"The chief was skating clockwise. Most people skate counter-clockwise."

"What power of observation," Ganz said. "I am right-handed, as it happens, and like everyone else I usually skate counter-clockwise. But I am writing a monograph on habits, and wanted to note my own reaction to breaking one. It's quite a distinct sensation—a tightness in the chest, which one suspects is anxiety. But please. Enjoy your recreation and we'll speak more of this tonight."

That evening, Imogen had a difficult time deciding what to wear. It was a lucky thing that the Phipps required, and provided, clinic whites, because the economic realities of being a student, followed by the slow repayment of her debt to her uncle Mason, had turned shopping for clothes into a luxury she could rarely afford. She tried on a dress of sage-green cotton voile, but it seemed too light for the season. She was fond of her blue check gingham, but it was out of the question for a dinner party. She finally settled on a silk messaline in midnight blue with a Russian-style blouse hanging loose from the shoulders.

"What do you think," she asked Carl, "too much?"

"Perfect. Absolutely perfect."

"I think you may be biased."

"That doesn't mean it isn't perfect."

"It is just dinner. I don't want to be overdressed."

"You look lovely and confident and stylish. And I'm going to look a complete oaf beside you."

"Nonsense."

Carl was one of those perfectly proportioned men who can buy a suit off the rack and with minimum alterations have it look like Savile Row.

They took a taxi to number 9 Rugby Road, a four-square mock Tudor of stone and stucco, convincingly half-timbered, in stately isolation at the crest of a low hill. This allowed for a good sweep of driveway, and showed off the surrounding snowy folds of Roland Park. It was a country mansion compared with their own poky little place, and Imogen experienced for the first time the dull pinch of the heart that comes with the realization that one has come down in the world and might not be rising anytime soon.

Mary Ganz answered the door, greeting them warmly and taking their coats and scarves.

"We've landed on you unexpectedly," Imogen said. "I hope we're not a terrible inconvenience."

"It was a surprise," she said, hanging up their coats, "but a delightful one. Jonas always has such warm words for you both that you would blush to hear them."

"We're tremendously lucky to work with him," Carl said.

"Oh, I'll have to let him know you think so." She leaned toward them and added in a whisper, "He sometimes worries he's perceived as something of a martinet. Now follow me—*le grand chef* is in the sitting room."

Dr. Ganz sprang from his wingback chair to greet them.

"Dr. Lang. Mr. Kromer. I'm so glad you could come. You've met Mary before, I think?" He put his arm on his wife's shoulder as she came to stand beside him, and the two of them—both trim, both diminutive—resembled a pair of matched dolls. "It's always a good thing to get to know one's colleagues in a setting outside of work, don't you think?"

"Depends on the colleague," Carl said.

"Carl, really . . ."

"Well, it's true. I was only being honest."

"May I pour you a drink?" Dr. Ganz said. "We have gin, rye, bourbon . . . Don't worry, I haven't broken any laws. All of these were laid in before they passed the Amendment."

"Jonas has been socking away the wine like Molière's miser."

"It's a matter of civility, Mary. One must be able to entertain, one must have society."

"I know, my love. And you know I approve."

Imogen asked for a gin and tonic, Carl a bourbon. Dr. Ganz added ice to their glasses from an insulated caddy with dainty silver tongs. His wife declined.

"Mary has been visiting the families of new patients for the past three months," Ganz said. "It has affected her views concerning the consumption of alcohol."

"One just sees so much damage," she said. "I would say, eight times out of ten, alcohol is a powerful force for harm in the homes of the mentally ill."

"Not that it's a cause per se," Ganz put in, "except in a case of Korsakoff's."

"No, no. But you have a father who drinks his paycheque, or drinks and then gambles and loses the housekeeping money, or drinks and becomes violent . . . or worse. The stresses and strains to one's mental and emotional balance can be considerable. Excuse me for a moment, I must just check on dinner."

Ganz watched her leave, and raised his glass in a silent toast. "Light of my life. Could not do without her. Mary's very active in the Mental Hygiene Society—doing a lot of work with Ruth Fein, arranging for talks, community programs, and so on."

"The two of you will always have much to discuss—just as Carl and I do."

Carl nodded. "I don't know how so many of the medical and scientific people do it—go home to spouses who understand nothing of their work. How do they talk to each other?"

"Some of them don't, I suppose. I know a lot of medical men—and one assumes women—who are happy to leave work at the hospital."

"Not me," Carl said.

"Nor me," Ganz agreed, and of course this was Carl's cue to talk about his current experiments on activity cycles. Ganz could not have been happier. In contrast to Robert Taunton's work, Carl's findings on endocrine levels could have immense implications for the affective disorders. Imogen too was thrilled to have this chance to discuss her husband's work, as well as her own, with her chief, and to find Dr. Ganz so warm and welcoming.


The twins were born the following winter, a couple of weeks after Christmas, a boy and a girl with Imogen's round eyes and Carl's curly hair. Imogen had a powerful urge to name the girl Laura and, having thought of Laura, was beset by an equally powerful urge to name her son Quentin. Once these names were glowing in her mind, all others seemed dull.

But she could not do it. There had been only one Laura and so it should remain. And to name the boy Quentin would be a final slap in the face to the young man who had loved her so unhappily: *No, I couldn't marry you, but I've named my son after you.*

Charlotte and Aubrey, as they were eventually named, were in the eyes of their new mother entirely perfect—quiet yet curious, toothlessly good-humoured, and, what was most important, fond of a good sleep. Imogen was granted only three weeks' unpaid leave from the Phipps ("Entirely out of my hands," Ganz pleaded) and in order to add another two had to deduct them from her vacation time.

When Carl came home in the evenings he would coo over the twins in the most adorable way, and hoist them in the air and spin them around as they gurgled and drooled, and cover them with kisses. He constructed toys for them, after hours, in the lab—a tin "automaton" that might delight an eight-year-old, a wooden pedal car that might come in handy when they were four—until he finally hit upon an ingenious pair of hand puppets that he fashioned out of old mittens. The twins could not use them yet, but the parents could and provoked many smiles and wriggles of appreciation.

"You don't think they're just being polite?" Carl said.

"Not at all. They appreciate good costumes and fine acting the same as anyone."

"My God, I am a lucky person," Carl exclaimed. "So lucky!" And at such times Imogen, too, thought her happiness as complete as happiness could be.

When it came time to go back to work she made inquiries and found that the cost of hiring a white nanny was prohibitive. She interviewed three Negro women and although all three had good references and an agreeable manner with the children, she chose Myra Temple, largely because she had a very soft voice that the twins would find soothing—and also because Imogen liked her name.

"She certainly is negroid," Carl said after they had interviewed her.

"I don't think the children will mind."

"But won't it be confusing for them? They may start wondering why they're not the same colour."

"We can't afford a white nanny, and even if we could I'm very taken with Myra."

"You don't think we should reconsider your going back to work?"

"We've discussed that, Carl."

"Staying home is the normal thing, you know. It wouldn't diminish you in any way."

"It would diminish my career. Instantly and permanently."

"I'm not so sure. The chief thinks you're wonderful, you know that."

"Carl, I'm going back to work."


And going back to work proved to be even more pleasant than she had anticipated. To occupy her mind once more with patients on the wards and biochemical analysis in the lab was a deep pleasure compared with the repeated evaluation of infantile ingesta and ejecta by consistency, colour, and volume. The peace and quiet of the lab, the sense of doing work of some value, the talk with colleagues, restored her sense of self.

But she was also glad to come home at the end of the day. She loved Charlotte and Aubrey with a sea-surge of devotion that amazed her. Taking the streetcar toward Reservoir Street, she would find the cases of auditory hallucinations, say, or protease reactions in the brains of schizophrenics, receding and being replaced by the bright, milky faces of her children. To take them from Myra and hold them in her arms was a release of pure, unalloyed love.

"They the sweetest babies I ever did see," Myra said.

"It must be your influence, Myra. No one in my family is so sweet-tempered."

"Mine the same, Doctor. No, I reckon the good Lord just handed you and Mr. Kromer these two little angels he musta had goin' spare."

For a good six months after returning to the Phipps, Imogen could feel that she and Carl were something of an idealized couple—especially among the nurses. Here were two who had truly mastered the world of medicine: good jobs in a prestigious institution, a happy marriage, and children.

"Everybody loves you," Donna told her one day when she came to visit her in the lab. "You show them everything is possible—everything the suffragettes have been yelling about."

"Well, I don't know that the Phipps loves me," Imogen said.

"You're joking. Everyone knows you and Carl get invited to the chief's home for dinner. That's the highest honour available in this place."

"Do you know what my job title is?"

"Associate psychiatrist, I should have thought."

"It isn't."

"What then? Third assistant?"

"I'm still classed as an intern."

"That can't be right. There must be some mistake."

"Believe me, I've asked. There's no mistake. Do you know how embarrassing it is when I'm corresponding with other institutions? The chief pathologist at McLean wrote back and said, 'I beg your pardon, I thought I was communicating with the head of your histology lab, and now I see you are an intern. Please direct my inquiries to someone with the proper authority to answer them.'"

"How humiliating. You must thrash this out with Ganz at once."

"Oh, I've tried to raise it with him, but you know how he is—when you raise anything that involves money he gets extremely tense. He seems far more comfortable talking about sex than money."

"That's true of all psychiatrists."

"It wouldn't be so disturbing if he didn't seem so warm to me sometimes—almost like a father. He can't be unaware that this tight-fistedness feels like rejection."

"Well, look how he treats me. One minute he's praising me as brilliant beyond compare, the next minute he's practically calling me a delinquent little whore."

"Donna, he's *not*. He's just concerned that you aren't respecting Phipps policies."

"Which are what, for God's sake? Do *you* know where he stands on psychoanalysis?"

"Yes. He sees it as valuable in general but far too expensive and time-consuming for public patients at the Phipps. Which is why I study it in my off-hours."

"But you know he's making a fortune analyzing his own patients."

"He can't be. They don't stay long enough."

"Where do you think he goes every summer?"

"Los Angeles. He likes it there."

"Hah! He likes it there because the McCormick family pays him two thousand dollars a week to psychoanalyze the son they've got locked up in his own house."

"The McCormicks? You mean *the* McCormicks?"

"The ones who manufacture every tractor on every farm in every country on earth. Those McCormicks."

"How do you know he gets two thousand a week?"

"Because Snake gets the same when he treats him."

"But I heard the McCormick son is totally psychotic—beyond all reach."

"You heard right."

"Two thousand a week. That's more than I earn in six months."

"Private practice, sweetheart. Do you realize how many people—people who can afford it—would pay for psychiatric treatment if it didn't involve going to an asylum or a hospital? The so-called nerve doctors are getting rich and they've never even heard of a 'schizo-phrenic reaction.'"

Donna swept up her coat and bag and kissed Imogen on the cheek. "Write him a letter, darling. Point by point, telling him your situation. You've got children now, for pity's sake, you can't live on intern money."

"I know you're right, I just . . ."

"Just what?"

"I don't know. I just feel this block against doing anything that might upset him."

"You don't want to annoy Daddy, you mean."

"Me? *You* should talk if we're getting on the subject of upsetting Daddy. You do it on purpose—why do you suppose that would be?"

Donna laughed. "Don't you love being a psychiatrist? It makes everything so simple."

Despite the issues of money and status, the next few years of Imogen's life seemed to fly by. Not only did she manage to avoid even a single bout of depression, she was actively happy most days, waking up in the morning to the sound of Carl's coffee grinder or the squeals of the twins, and looking forward to the rest of the day. Her work on the blood chemistry of schizophrenics looked promising, and she enjoyed overseeing the work of the occasional graduate student. On the wards, she found it deeply rewarding to help a patient through a transient psychosis, a suicidal depression, or the inevitable crash from a period of mania.

Although she enjoyed the logic and quiet of the lab, she gradually discovered that talk therapy was the highlight of her workday. There were many hours of no progress, of course, but the occasional moment of insight, when a patient came to recognize a truth about herself she had long denied, made up for those. She read and reread the works of Freud, Jung, and Ferenczi, and without adopting the full range of psychoanalytic treatment (which would be sure to anger Dr. Ganz), managed to incorporate their thinking into her own clinical skills.

Home life was exhausting—especially once the twins became mobile and discovered every breakable or dangerous object within their ever-lengthening reach. She took the usual pictures of birthdays and milestones and discovered in the process that she was a perfectly terrible photographer. (Carl, of course, was an instant expert.) It was fascinating to watch the twins' personalities become more and more distinct—Aubrey essentially sunny and chatty, Charlotte quieter and more watchful but also more imaginative. Best of all, they loved each other's company—almost always preferring to do things together. As they got older, Imogen began to fret more and more about their health—the spectre of scarlet fever loomed large in her worries—but the two of them managed to reach the age of five without suffering anything worse than chicken pox.

Myra was a constant, cheerful presence in the children's lives during the week. On weekends and the occasional evening, one of Carl's graduate students, a young woman named Cynthia Bee, would babysit. She was a plumpish brunette with a big laugh and a self-deprecating sense of humour. Carl had brought her home for dinner more than once, and Imogen took to her right away. One of Cynthia's most attractive qualities was that she loved children and showed great interest in Charlotte and Aubrey—tossing them about and tickling them and making up silly stories for their entertainment.

Being blessed with such an abundance of happiness made Imogen want to share it. She made efforts to keep in touch with her mother, sending her the occasional letter and tiny square photographs of the children. Her mother's letters in response were characteristically dry and factual, but Imogen thought she detected a certain peace of mind in them as well. This may have been wishful thinking on her part. She invited Rose several times to come and visit in Baltimore, but her mother always found a reason to put it off for "another time."

Money matters became more urgent when their landlord announced yet another increase in their rent. Carl, like Donna, advised Imogen to raise the issues of position and salary with Dr. Ganz. "You work hard, he respects you, you deserve better," he said more than once, and Imogen promised to do it soon.

Recently Carl had lodged a half-amused complaint that she never showed any interest in his work. This was unfair; they discussed his work quite often. The truth was Imogen had trouble keeping track of

Carl's multitudinous experiments—he worked on so many projects at once, wrangling a platoon of graduate students to assist him.

She decided to remedy this one afternoon by visiting him in the psychology lab. They rarely dropped in on each other, even though their labs were both on the third floor. Carl was delighted to see her, immediately introducing her to a cadaver-pale graduate student clutching a clipboard, who was tending to an array of bubbling cylinders along one wall.

"This is Mr. Codwell. Mr. Codwell, this is my wife, Dr. Lang."

Codwell gave a sickly grin and, clutching his clipboard even tighter, turned once more to his bubbling cylinders.

"What's the experiment of the day?" Imogen asked, looking around.

"Mr. Codwell and I are hoping to put together a paper by next week on the phenomenon of sudden unexplained death in man and animals. I told you about the voodoo deaths, remember?"

"Oh, yes. Men dying within days of being cursed by the witch doctor."

"Turns out it's more common than I thought. Anthropologists are finding it in Australia, New Zealand, and Africa, as well as Haiti. And in our own culture as well. Do you have the time—can I explain in full?"

"Yes, of course—that's why I'm here."

"Well, in our culture you'll find responsible surgeons won't operate on patients who are truly terrified of the procedure. Such patients have been known to die on the table before the first incision. You also get sudden deaths from fright, the sight of blood, hypodermics, sudden immersion in water, and no one knows why."

Carl's eyes brightened and his hand motions became more emphatic as he spoke, and Imogen was glad she'd come by. How often had he listened to her as she rattled on about the subtleties of blood samples, the miseries of a patient, or the beauty of psychoanalytic theory?

"Up to now, anthropologists have thought that in the case of witch doctors, the victim is so terrified that he suffers a continuous outpouring of adrenalin. They can't run tests in the field, unfortunately, but they surmise that the individual would hyperventilate, have a rapid pulse, and show hemoconcentration from loss of fluids from blood to tissue. Ultimately the heart would speed up until finally it contracted altogether and you'd get death in systole. Our studies on rats may throw light on the underlying mechanisms in man—in our own culture, as well as in Haiti or wherever. I should mention by way of prelude that a similar phenomenon has been observed in rats."

Imogen looked over at pasty Mr. Codwell and the bubbling cylinders. They were a good twelve feet distant, and the glass was somewhat fogged, but she thought she could make out tails and paddling feet.

"A fellow over at Yale was studying rats' eating habits and, in order to prevent separate food sources from being inter-contaminated, he had to shave off their whiskers. Well, a peculiar thing happened: most of the rats began incessantly pushing their noses into the corners of the cages or into their food cups in a kind of corkscrew motion. Eight days later the rats were dead."

Carl illustrated this by mimicking a screwdriver action with his right hand. "Why are you smiling?"

"No reason. It's fascinating."

He gestured toward the cylinders.

"In our studies on responses to stress we've been measuring endurance by means of swimming survival times."

Imogen followed him over to the cylinders, and Mr. Codwell stepped nervously aside, gripping his clipboard. The cylinders, about thirty-six inches in depth and four inches wide, each contained a rat frantically paddling.

"We have a jet of water shooting into the centre that prevents them from floating, and the collar on top makes it impossible to escape. We're tracking the relationship between endurance and water temperature. We've found a direct correlation between average survival time and the temperature of the water. Their swimming times range from ten to fifteen minutes at 65 degrees Fahrenheit, to sixty hours at 95 degrees, to twenty minutes at 105 degrees."

"I'm sorry," Imogen said. "These are averages?" Her mind had snagged on the phrase "survival times" and could not get free. A darkness pervaded her stomach, as if she had swallowed a litre of something not meant to be swallowed.

"Averages, yes. We found marked variation in individual swim times. I mean, some rats died within five minutes. Others swam as long as eighty-one hours. The elimination of these large variations posed a real problem and—"

"I'm not sure I understand. A rat swam in one of those cylinders for eighty-one hours?"

"Yes, several of them."

"Three and a half days straight."

"Remarkable, I know. Then it occurred to me to examine the effect of trimming the rats' whiskers on performance in the water. I wondered if they'd show the strange behaviour of the rats in the metabolism experiments. We shaved a dozen of them. Well, the first rat swam around in great excitement for about forty seconds, then dove to the bottom where it began to swim around, nosing its way along the glass wall. Died two minutes after entering the tank. Didn't come to the surface a single time. Three of them responded in this way. The other nine swam forty to sixty hours. Those were domesticated rats. Wild rats performed much worse—all thirty-four died within fifteen minutes of immersion."

Imogen fixed her gaze on Carl's mouth as he spoke, the full nether lip slightly wet, the slightly uneven incisors. She dared not look at the bubbling cylinders with their miniature, paddling cargo.

Carl continued in full flow. "Conclusions are preliminary at this stage, but it seems trimming the rats' whiskers destroys their most important means of contact with the outside world and this is disturbing enough to cause their deaths. Especially the wild rats. Now we come to the interesting bit.

"Are we in fact dealing with a flood of adrenalin as the anthropologists surmised? Turns out we're not. We rigged up our own EKG, you see, and far from showing increased heart rate, it shows a marked slowing of the heart. We've got the results taped up over there." He pointed to a wall covered in long, narrow sheets of paper.

"At the terminal stage, the heart stops in diastole, not systole, and autopsy shows an enlarged heart filled with blood. We removed the adrenals from the next batch of rats and got the same results, so we know absolutely that death is not adrenalin-related.

"Here's what I think. Adrenalin is the hormone of fight or flight, but the situation of these rats hardly seems to demand either. Rather, it's one of hopelessness. These are animals in a situation against which they have no defence. In fact, the wild rats seem to give up as soon as they are firmly grasped in the hand.

"So, how do we show that the sudden death depends on the emotional reaction to restraint or immersion? We eliminate the hopelessness. What we did, we repeatedly held them briefly then let them go, immersed them for a few minutes then took them out. Very quickly the rats learn that the situation is not actually hopeless. They become aggressive again, try to escape, and show no sign of giving up. And what do we find? Lo and behold, the wild rats swim just as long as the domesticated, or longer."

"Eighty hours," Imogen said.

"Sixty to eighty, yes. Amazing, isn't it."

"Yes. Truly." Imogen looked at her watch. "My, I completely lost track of the time. Must run. See you at home."

"Oh." Carl looked crestfallen. "You're not impressed."

"No, no, I just lost track of the time."

She struggled to pull open the heavy door, then leaned against it. "It's suicide, isn't it? The rats that don't surface? They're committing suicide, don't you think?"

"Suicide." Carl cocked his head to one side, assessing Imogen, rather than what she had said. "Yes, I suppose it is."

In the hallway, Imogen started back toward her own lab, got halfway, and stopped. She looked back toward the elevators. She fought an urge to go upstairs to the fourth floor and throw herself on the bed in her old room. She would pull the covers up to her chin and curl up and face the wall and not come out for days and days. But of course her old room was occupied by a new intern.

She went into the ladies' room and sat in one of the stalls, overcome by a heaviness of spirit. The story of the rats had crushed her, and she could not get out from under it. Various phrases flared up in her mind: *no defence, escape is impossible, hopelessness*, and above all, *eighty-one hours. Swam for eighty-one hours.*

"Are you all right in there?" It was Ruth Fein's voice.

"Yes. Thank you." Imogen tried to lower her voice.

"Are you sure? I thought I heard moaning."

"Cramps. That's all. Cramps."

"Well, perhaps you should lie down somewhere."

Imogen waited until Ruth was gone, and then waited another five minutes to be sure, the sad phrases sinking in her mind like tiny hopeless bodies.

# 12

"They're rats," Carl said, "in case you didn't know. Not people."
They were sitting up late in the cramped little kitchen on Reservoir Street. Myra had gone home long ago and the children were asleep.

"I know that, Carl."

"I am not doing it for pleasure—I'm doing it for knowledge. It's not frivolous."

"Sweetheart, I know that too."

"Sometimes as scientists we inflict pain on animals so that we can learn how to prevent it—or cure it—in human beings. You're a doctor, for God's sake. I don't understand why you are so shocked."

"I'm not shocked that it is done," Imogen said, "I'm shocked that *you* are doing it. It's just not how I've imagined you."

"And now you think I'm a monster."

"No, I just—"

"Just what?"

"I can't stop thinking about them. Surely you see how cruel it is. How unutterably sad."

"You can't think such things and do the experiment."

"Well, how urgent is this research into 'sudden death phenomenon'? It seems a rare and occult problem, hardly a pressing concern."

"Now you're betraying your ignorance. Obviously insight into these emotions will give us insight into the biology of such things as shock, depression, and—as you so dramatically suggest—suicide."

"Yes," Imogen said. "I can see how that might be." Then, abandoning the field of battle: "I'm going to make myself a hot chocolate before bed, would you like some?"

Carl said no, but she made some for him anyway, and they passed the rest of the evening in comparative tranquility.

One of the constraints of having children was that Imogen found it hard to attend any after-hours lectures, but when it was announced that Sándor Ferenczi was going to be giving the Tuesday evening talk at the Phipps, she made plans to go with Donna. Carl, who had no interest in Ferenczi, stayed home with the children.

The lecture room was directly beneath the lab, and at 5:45 she locked up and was halfway down the east stairwell when she met Donna coming the other way.

"Why are you coming up? It starts in a few minutes—we won't get a seat."

Donna sagged against the stair rail, looking as if she had been shot. "I've been fired."

"Good God. What for?"

"For daring to refer patients for psychoanalysis. You know, you reach a line with Ganz—there are certain areas of his impenetrable Swiss skull that are surrounded by trip wires."

"But he believes in analysis, he just—"

"I meant authority. If he senses his Olympian authority is being questioned let alone contradicted he goes berserk."

Imogen reached out and squeezed Donna's arm. "Come on. Let's go for a walk."

"You don't want to see Ferenczi?"

"I want to see you."

"Oh, Imogen." Donna suddenly leaned forward and kissed Imogen full on the mouth. "You're the only person in this place who was ever kind to me."

Imogen, unnerved by the kiss, backed up the stairs. "Wait here. I'll just get my coat."

They walked through the evening crowds down Wolfe Street and over to Patterson Park. Baltimore was enjoying a long, beneficent spring and Imogen liked the idea of a stroll around the boat pond, but the area was not safe once it started to get dark. They decided instead on Kauffman's Pharmacy and Soda Fountain, where they sat at the counter. Donna was too upset to order anything, so Imogen ordered them two strawberry phosphates.

"This place reminds me of Willard's," she said. "A pharmacy I worked at in Chicago."

"It's probably where I'll wind up working," Donna said. Her high-boned, slightly hollowed-out face looked beautiful when sad.

Imogen squeezed her hand.

"You'll do fine. You were already planning to go into private practice."

"I'm not ready. I haven't completed my own analysis yet. Snake says I need another six months to a year. To tell you the truth I don't think I can finish it with him."

"Why is that?"

"He's too crazy."

"Well, really, Donna—shouldn't the name 'Snake' have provided you with some small clue? Not to mention the naval uniform."

"He's a brilliant man, Imogen. A terrific analyst and an even better supervisor. The stuff he points out to me when I'm having trouble with a patient . . ."

"You've been analyzing patients at his clinic?"

"Yes, of course."

"Well, that'll be the reason Ganz is so angry. You're essentially advising people to come to you for treatment outside the Phipps. You must see it's using the Phipps to further your private business."

"He's making a private fortune off the McCormicks. I don't see the difference."

"They sought him out—he didn't *refer* them to himself. It's not the same thing."

Donna took a pensive sip of her soda, and Imogen waited.

Eventually Donna said, "I can't get over how much this hurts. Personally. I feel worse than I ever felt about any romance, that's for sure. It's a rejection, obviously, but losing a job—it's one's place in the world. To have it suddenly torn away . . ."

"You did have some warning," Imogen said gently.

Donna continued as if she hadn't heard. "Also—and despite things I may have said—I have a lot of respect for Ganz. His achievements are undeniable. And it meant such a lot to be accepted as part of the Phipps. I suppose I took it for granted. Mind you, I can't tell you how much I will *not* miss his idea of a patient history."

"He *is* obsessive on that score."

"He's a bloody tyrant. All that time probing for *fact, fact, fact*, when there's no guarantee any of it is relevant. When you've got schizophrenics growing up with siblings who are completely normal—how can you call it a *reaction* to anything?"

Imogen let her friend go on, uttering sympathetic murmurs from time to time. It felt good to offer a kindness to her friend who always seemed supremely confident, invulnerable, even a kind of champion. She was aware too of some filament of resentment glowing in her heart—that Donna had provoked her own ouster, thus depriving Imogen's day-to-day existence of her company.

"Well," Donna said with a sigh, "it might be a good time for you to push for a raise. With me out the door, he certainly won't want to lose you."

"Don't worry about me on a day like this."

"I can't help it—I'm practical."

"Supremely. Very feet-on-the-ground."

"Donna Artemis," Donna said ruefully, "salt of the earth."

✄

Donna had for once read the chief correctly. Having lost one good psychiatrist, he was not prepared to lose another. When he received Imogen's letter outlining her case, he summoned her to his office and responded with a series of proposals. Behind him, on a shelf, the brain she had brought him from Chicago so long ago floated in its amber jar, still with its Rush label of *Dementia praecox*.

"I have corresponded with the treasurer's office and they have agreed to change your official designation to assistant psychiatrist, but they tell me there is nothing they can do in terms of your salary. Unfortunately, we are under severe budget restraints, and they are treating the departure of Dr. Artemis as a chance to save money."

"Dr. Ganz, you know my situation. I am still paying off what I borrowed to attend medical school. Carl and I have two children to feed and clothe. We have only a tiny apartment, and we'll be moving into an even smaller one at the end of the month."

"Oh," Dr. Ganz said, as if this were cheerful news. "Where is it?"

"On Dukeland Street."

"I don't believe I know it."

"No. Well, you wouldn't. But even with the lower rent, there are things we just can't afford for the children, or ourselves, on our current pay. You know I want to stay here, but I may have to seek a position elsewhere if my income doesn't increase."

A slight nausea stirred inside her as she spoke.

"Now, now." Dr. Ganz raised his small hands in a calming gesture. "I've not been entirely idle on your behalf. I *can* make it possible for you to take every other Thursday to teach on a topic of clinical discussion—starting immediately. I've also asked Dr. Quinn to arrange with you a schedule of group teaching. And I will get to work on the matter of publication."

"When do you foresee my being able to publish?"

"I can't put a date on it just yet."

"The research will be out of date soon."

"Yes, yes, I'll see to it."

What was there to "see to"? Her results and write-ups on depression had been sitting in his inbox for years. All that was needed was permission. Publishing without his approval was out of the question. The moment it was discovered she had submitted papers without institutional approval she would be fired, and rendered permanently unpublishable.

"How much would the teaching pay?" she asked weakly.

"Each lecture comes with the small honorarium we normally grant guest speakers. And you would be developing new contacts, expanding professionally."

"Dr. Ganz. The last time my pay increased was when the twins were born. If my work is not valued, then perhaps it's just as well if I move on."

"Imogen, please."

It was the first time he had ever called her by her first name. Ganz took a deep breath and held it, as if deciding whether to continue, then let out a sigh. "There is something coming up that may be of interest to you. It would suit your research talents, and it should pay quite well. But it involves a bit of travel."

"What is it, exactly?"

Dr. Ganz swivelled his chair and opened a drawer. He pulled out a book, shut the drawer, and handed the book across the desk to Imogen.

"Have you heard of this man?"

# 13

The author was Rupert Bingham, director of the Trenton State Hospital, and the book was *Towards a New Treatment of the Insane*. Imogen had not heard of the book, but she had heard of Bingham—she had even met him once, at a conference in Boston. They hadn't talked much, just long enough for her to form an impression of a rather odd individual. Bingham was about forty-five, pale and puffy, with sad, suspicious eyes.

His book was an explication of the focal-infection theory, the idea that, contrary to the concept of psychogenesis, the cause of mental illness might well lie in infections of the teeth, tonsils, colon, or other sites. It was a theory that had been gaining ground in Europe, notably in England, where it had several distinguished champions. But Bingham's book was dry and full of jargon, which may have been why it hadn't attracted much notice.

Imogen read late into the night, Carl softly snoring beside her. In painstaking detail, Bingham laid out the context in which the theory of focal infection had developed. After thousands of years there had been discovered to date exactly one cure for madness, a drug called Salvarsan, which followed on the Germans' discovery that syphilis was caused by a spirochete. Paul Ehrlich found that if he dosed the patient with this compound—even someone in the tertiary stages of the disease, who was hallucinating, delusional, with the beginnings of paralysis—he could cure them. Overnight, half the long-term beds in the asylums emptied out. The cure made headlines around the world, and it was the beginning of the near certainty that all mental illness would eventually be found to have a biological cause that could be treated. (It had also been one of the reasons Imogen had dreamed of working in a laboratory as well as with patients.)

It made perfect sense that other forms of mental illness—manic-depression or schizophrenia—could stem from similar infections. The teeth and tonsils, Bingham pointed out, were proximal to the brain; infection could easily migrate from one locus to another. Or it might be located in the bowel, the womb, or other large organs, where it would infect the whole bloodstream and thus the brain. Imogen found his thinking both clear and reasonable. He was not ruling out psychogenic causes of madness, but seeing them as likely catalysts rather than causes. A broken heart or a financial reversal, say, might cause endocrine reactions that in turn sparked a chronic low-grade infection to become virulent.

Bingham gave credit to Frank Billings and others for their work, but Imogen quickly realized that what made Bingham unique was his position as the director of a major state hospital and his determination to transform it into a research centre. At Trenton, he was treating chronic patients with radical dental extractions, sometimes removing all of their teeth, and abdominal procedures that included hysterectomies, bowel resections, and, in extreme cases, removal of the gonads. The results were astonishing. Trenton now claimed a cure rate of 87 percent, an unheard-of figure.

Imogen couldn't wait to hear more from Ganz on the subject, but he was unavailable until five o'clock. They met in his private office.

"Here is the situation," he said. "The budget for the Trenton asylum is up before the state legislature. Dr. Bingham has lately taken to the newspapers and magazines announcing his results in public, rather than in the appropriate journals—no doubt hoping to encourage approval."

"He's certainly getting dramatic outcomes," Imogen said, "assuming the numbers are correct."

"Exactly. And the legislature wants to be sure they are accurate before approving an increase, so the board has asked me to appoint someone to conduct a scientific study and deliver a report."

"This would mean evaluating discharged patients to verify results?"

"Yes. It could be quite time-consuming. But you'd be well paid, and your report is guaranteed an interested audience. Remuneration and publication could come together nicely. Would you like to take it on?"


Carl came home late, when the twins were already asleep. Imogen told him her news as she was setting out his supper for him on the kitchen table. She expected him to be happy for her—for what it meant to her career and, not least of all, what it would mean for the household income. But he astonished her by becoming angry, even raising his voice, something he had never done with her.

"Trenton? You're going to Trenton? That's half a day on the train—you'll have to stay overnight."

"It's about five hours. I checked the schedule. There's a train every hour on the hour."

"You'll still have to stay overnight."

"At least two nights, sometimes three, I imagine."

"It may have escaped your notice," he said, "but we have two children to raise. Bad enough you insist on having a job and leaving them in the care of a Negro."

"Oh, for God's sake. Negroes have been caring for white children forever."

"That's not the point. The point is, you are going to vanish from their lives for three days a week and you don't even seem to care."

"Of course I care. Do you think I want to travel every week? You think I'm dying to work in a state asylum? I'm doing this for the children and for us. We need the money, Carl."

"But you've already agreed to take it on, and we haven't even discussed it. You've never even mentioned Trenton State Hospital to me."

"I only just heard about it. I'll be conducting a major study. It will get me published, possibly even noticed, and that will mean a higher position."

"Ganz promised you this? A higher position?"

"Not exactly. But I'll never get one if I don't publish. You know I have to. You publish all the time."

"Because I do a lot of experiments."

"Because you don't have to go through Jonas Ganz. He's been sitting on my research for years. Literally years, Carl, and I don't know why. It's not personal— he does it to other people, too—but he won't be able to sit on this, because someone else is paying for it. The Trenton medical board. They need independent verification of Bingham's results and they're willing to pay."

"And you're just going to take off. Just like that. Leave me, leave the kids."

"Carl, this is upsetting for me too. I hate being apart from you."

"Apparently you don't."

"Please don't say that. I don't want to be away from the children either."

"If that's true, why did you rush back to work a few days after they were born?"

"Carl, it was five weeks, not a few days." Thinking, dear God, it was years ago. Can he really be harbouring such resentment all this time?

"They'll be in kindergarten five days a week," she said. "Myra can pick them up and look after them in the afternoon and early evening."

"And I'm to be their nanny the rest of the time."

"No, you're their father *all* of the time. If you don't think that carries any responsibilities then you're not much of a father, are you?"

She'd said it gently, but it provoked white heat.

"You dare say that to me? I take my responsibilities seriously, Imogen. It's why I work day in and day out—all the extra hours I work—it's to try and make some kind of life for us. Don't you dare lecture me about responsibilities."

Carl was sullen for days, leaving the house early and coming home even later than usual. Imogen took to keeping his supper in a double boiler for him to heat up when he got home. In his absence, she read the children stories, hiding her sorrowful heart behind the works of Hans Christian Andersen, Beatrix Potter, and Lewis Carroll. She read to them from the beautiful edition of *Alice* that Quentin had given her, and when they fell asleep she rested her fingers on the inscription Quentin had written in his machinelike script, *To Imogen, with all my love.*

That Friday, Carl came home around nine. She heard him setting out his dinner and then putting the dishes in the sink but when he came to bed he opened a book and barely responded to her. It was as if she had damaged her exuberant husband with the brute force of her selfishness, and it pierced her with guilt.

She reached over and touched his arm.

"I'm sorry," she told him. "I'm sorry I didn't discuss the Trenton offer with you before accepting it. I should have, and I'm sorry."

Carl gave a noncommittal grunt. His gaze remained on his book but she could see he was no longer reading it.

"If you really want me to, I'll tell the chief I can't take it. He knows I need some time to arrange child care and to read up on Bingham's work and so on—he won't have told the Trenton people yet. If my taking this job makes you think less of me, I won't take it."

Carl closed his book and looked at her.

Neither spoke for a while. Then he said, "I won't think less of you. I don't know why I reacted the way I did. I think I was just shocked and scared. I mean, I was unprepared, you know."

She squeezed his arm. "I'm sorry."

"And I hate being apart from you. And I'm terrified the kids will be miserable and I won't know what to do."

"They adore you. They'll be perfectly happy."

"They won't. You know that."

"Look, they love Myra, and Cynthia can look after them if you need to get out once in a while."

"I know. But they're going to miss you terribly."

"They'll get used to it. It'll only be for a few months. I'll always be home on weekends, and I'm going to try to never be gone more than three days at a time. But still. I've come to see it from your side and I'm prepared to give this up if you think I should."

"Well," Carl said, "first of all, you're right that we need the money. Second of all, you're right that it's an excellent career opportunity. Third, I reacted with panic and I'm sorry too."

They leaned toward each other and in the fragile warmth of mutual forgiveness kissed and lay quiet in each other's arms.

"Well, you're in for it now," Laura remarked. She had not shown up for some time, but trains and trams offered broad dark windows, where Imogen's ghostly twin could travel beside her, dressed like her, with Imogen's features, Imogen's face. She could lean her translucent head with comely weariness against the pane, never mind the landscape rippling by at forty-five miles an hour if you were taking the Clocker from Baltimore.

"Who was it who said she never wanted to be apart from her husband? And abandoning her children," Laura went on in her breathy voice. "What kind of feckless mother does such a thing?"

The connecting door rattled open and the conductor came through announcing Trenton in ten minutes. Imogen sat up and rubbed her head where it had been resting against the glass. She was already missing her children, Aubrey with his endless questions, and Charlotte so serious and cautious and sensitive.

Laura was still lingering in the window—faint, but with impish smile intact.

"I don't see why you'd want to upset a husband who is not only supremely talented at his work, but also makes you feel positively glorious in bed."

As the train began to slow for Trenton's Penn Station, Imogen was remembering Carl's touch, his muscles, the way he held her. Whatever else her feelings about this trip, she was not looking forward to lying by herself in a cold bed.

She took a cab from the train station to Trenton State Hospital. They had to stop at the gatehouse and wait for an attendant. He duly consulted a list on a clipboard, made a check mark, and opened the gate. As the gatehouse receded behind them, Imogen's heart began to lift. The hospital's driveway curved through an alley of oak trees and emerged into beautifully landscaped grounds—almost a park. It was a warm fall day, and the trees were bright gold and rusty red, the grass brilliant green.

The main building was massive, the front door guarded by six Corinthian columns. The cab stopped between the fountain and the front steps, and the driver held the car door open for her. Imogen paid him and reached for her suitcase, but he insisted on carrying it up the stairs—a welcome kindness, since she counted thirty-six of them on the way up.

The interior was grand in the neoclassical style, with much marble and stone and a sense of rock-solid stability—not the worst environment for people with a shaky sense of reality. She pushed open the door to the medical director's office and introduced herself to the receptionist.

"I'm Dr. Lang—I've just arrived from Baltimore. Dr. Bingham is expecting me."

"Yes, yes. He'll be right with you. Please have a seat."

Imogen was not sure what would constitute a proper reception. She was, after all, a kind of independent auditor. One should not, she supposed, expect too much warmth. She sat in a hard oak chair that offered a view of the oak counter and the huge oak clock that indicated she was exactly on time. Ten minutes went by, during which she began to feel rather oakish herself, thick and heavy with the fatigue of travel. It was only four o'clock but all she wanted was dinner and a book and bed.

After fifteen minutes she got up and asked the receptionist if Dr. Bingham had been made aware of her arrival.

"He's expecting you. I'm sure he'll be along any minute."

Imogen waited until he was half an hour late before speaking to the receptionist once more. "It appears the director has been detained. I wonder if perhaps someone else could show me where I'll be staying?"

The receptionist scanned Imogen's features as if trying to organize them into a face. Finally she said, "Dr. Bingham will be here any minute. Let's just be calm and wait for him, shall we?"

"I have been waiting. I've been travelling most of the day, and I—"

The door banged open and Dr. Bingham came in, greeting the receptionist but not Imogen. "Iris—any messages?"

The receptionist got up and followed him into his private office, closing the door behind them. Imogen felt the heat of anger rising in her neck and face. She took a deep breath and told herself to remain calm.

The door opened and the receptionist came out. "You can go in now."

Imogen dithered a moment about what to do with her suitcase before deciding to take it in with her.

Rupert Bingham's office was three times the size of Dr. Ganz's, brightly lit by tall windows. The walls were lined with fat volumes of medical texts, mostly on surgery. Bingham sat at a massive, extremely neat desk, examining some papers. He put them aside when Imogen entered, and came around the desk to shake her hand.

"You've been kept waiting," he said blandly. "I apologize. Surgery went longer than expected."

His handshake was limp, damp, cool—as bland as his features, which showed no trace of any current, or for that matter historical, emotion.

"We'd thought it was a simple bowel resection, you know, a couple of punched-out ulcerations, but it turned out to be a diffuse folliculitis, involving the entire mucous lining."

"A dangerous procedure then."

"Not as dangerous as leaving it untreated. But, come—let me show you around—or are you too tired? Would you rather rest?"

"No, no—a tour sounds just the thing after sitting all day. What about my suitcase?"

"You can leave it here. I'll have it sent to your quarters."


Bingham led her along the echoing marble hall to a rear exit. The grounds, beautifully landscaped in the Romantic style with curving paths and shady ponds, looked tranquil in the low September sun.

They walked down a winding, rustic lane lined with elms, oaks, and maples, and Bingham pointed to an elegant stone house, set all by itself on a small hill. It had a circular drive and an ornate veranda. "The medical director's house," Bingham said, as if referring to someone other than himself.

"How lovely. That veranda must be heaven on hot summer days."

"My wife enjoys the house very much, and it's been a healthy environment for the boys to grow up in. That big building coming up on the right is where the attendants live. We have apartments for the married couples, of course, but mostly it's much like a school dormitory. Then we have the nurses' homes."

"The grounds are so beautiful."

"You can thank Dorothea Dix for that. Trenton State was the first hospital built when her reforms came in. That way are the doctors' houses," he added, pointing. "We have nine psychiatrists on staff at the moment."

The houses were charming, cottage-like affairs, with tiled roofs that seemed optimistic considering the New Jersey climate.

Bingham led her back toward the building where most of the wards were located.

"How is Dr. Ganz doing these days? He seemed a little subdued when he visited here last month."

"Oh, the chief's fine. He's always fine, you know."

"Yes, he was a great inspiration to me," Bingham said without enthusiasm. "I don't think I'd have got half as far if I hadn't had Jonas Ganz to guide me."

Dr. Ganz had felt it was incumbent upon him to make a preliminary journey to New Jersey to get a quick look at the site of Imogen's investigations. He'd told her that his glance into the surgical records had been anything but reassuring. Although he was satisfied that every measure was taken to keep the operating room antiseptic, operations on the bowel, even by the finest surgeons, remained extremely risky. A few of the numbers had stuck in Imogen's head, bright as crossing lights: Of 133 total colectomies, 44 had died. Of 148 patients who had had their colons reconstructed, 55 had died.

"I think it's wonderful what Dr. Ganz has done for psychiatry in general," Bingham was saying. "I hope to do the same or better for asylums." He stopped on the path and waited for Imogen to catch up. "We're not a warehouse. Trenton State Hospital is just that—a hospital. People get better here, as your survey will show."

The path curled around a copse of trees and then a vista of sky and hill opened up, with a row of small, red-brick buildings on one side and, on the other, a large, dark structure that abutted the stone wall surrounding the grounds. Bingham pointed to the smaller buildings.

"That's our butcher. Then the baker, the shoemaker. That's the laundry over there, and the one with the smokestack is our powerhouse."

"Such a vast enterprise," Imogen said. "Don't you get overwhelmed by it all?"

"I'm solely the medical director. Another man is in charge of the physical plant."

She detected a note of annoyance in his response. Normally the medical director was in charge of every aspect of an asylum, no matter how large. It was unusual to have two directors.

A gang of starlings was pecking about in the shade of an elm and making clicking sounds, as if they were cracking jokes about the food. As Imogen walked with Bingham toward the large building, she became aware of a background noise, an aural blur that became more distinct in its components as they approached the stone façade. These were the wails of men, groans and cries in every register. Some were singing, most were yelling, several haranguing. Someone was crying, "Pardonna me! Pardonna me!" Another sounded as if he had his lips right up against one of the barred windows, shouting individual words in a clipped, clear voice as if teaching an unseen crowd English from the dictionary, one word at a time. "Crack! Crackpot! Crack shot! Crack corn! Craft! Crafty!"

Bingham took no notice. He started up the steps as if they were heading into a library. "Our home for the criminally insane. I needn't take you into the cell area."

"Are any of your surgical subjects drawn from this pool?"

"Not possible. There's no way to secure informed consent from someone who has been ruled not responsible for criminal actions."

They entered the building and proceeded along a hallway. About halfway down, Bingham pointed to a pair of heavy doors at the end. "Criminal wards are beyond. Don't worry—there's always an attendant controlling the door on the other side. No one gets out who shouldn't."

His words echoed against the tiled walls.

"This is your room." Bingham took a key out of his pocket and opened a door numbered C106. "It's pretty spartan, but you should be comfortable enough. We have the odd medical resident stay here and no one's ever complained."

The room contained a narrow bed, an armoire, and a dresser much scarred with cigarette burns. The dimensions were those of a cleaning supplies closet, which it clearly once had been. No windows.

Imogen said nothing. Her suitcase was already parked beside the bed.

"Facilities are just down the hall. Don't worry—you'll have the place entirely to yourself, but do be sure to keep the door locked at all times."

He handed her the key, which Imogen accepted numbly, and led her back outside. All the way back across the grounds he talked about the money his procedures were saving the state, but she didn't take any of it in. She could still hear the howling. She was still seeing that room.

Bingham took her through the rear entrance of the ward building, shepherding her along one floor after another. He introduced her quickly to each ward nurse, who in turn introduced her to a patient or two. The wards were neither better nor worse than those she'd seen at Byberry. They smelled of urine and floor polish, nicotine and paraldehyde.

A highly animated patient, a man of about sixty with a perfectly bald head, fired questions at Imogen. She could tell they were questions by the interrogative lilt, but his speech was so impaired she couldn't understand the words. She smiled and said, "Perhaps I'll see you again," as they moved on.

Another man, impeccably dressed in what had once been an expensive pinstripe, sidled up to her, gripping a newspaper. He looked about to deliver a political comment, perhaps a diatribe about state funding, but he too had impaired speech. Having suffered from being tongue-tied herself, Imogen was sympathetic to speech problems, but simply could not make out what he was saying.

On another ward, a young patient waved to her the moment she entered, a look of recognition lighting his eyes. Imogen was sure she had never seen him before. He had the dark hair and clear eyes of a young person—perhaps twenty-five or twenty-six—but his cheeks were sunken like those of a moribund eighty-year-old.

He jumped up and started talking as he crossed the room. "Dokser Lang! Dokser Lang! Is me! Jimmy! Jimmy Worse!"

This, she realized with a shock, was Jimmy Worth.

"Why, hello, Jimmy. I haven't seen you for a long time." She would never have recognized the caved-in face. Twenty-five, and he looked ancient. "I thought you lived in Baltimore."

"No!" Jimmy said. "I got sick again! Sick! Sick! Sick!" He gave her a great wide grin that showed raw red gums and not a single tooth.

They have no teeth, Imogen nearly said aloud. None of them have any teeth.

"Former patient of yours?" Bingham said when they were outside again.

"Yes. He was extremely bright—doing advanced mathematics at Johns Hopkins—when he suffered his first attack. The delusions calmed down after a few weeks, but I can't claim it was in response to any treatment I gave him."

"No, it wouldn't be—because his problems are not psychogenic. He had massive dental infections and pyorrhea of long standing. We pulled all the teeth and cleared all that up."

"He still seems rather florid, don't you think?"

"Oh, there's a lot more work to be done. We'll be putting him through all the tests and I've no doubt we'll find focal infection in the bowel. Perhaps even endocrine involvement. He gets headaches, you know—headaches are always a sure sign."


That first day at Trenton was as anxious and lonely as any Imogen could remember. She had dinner in the staff cafeteria, and the nurses and physicians were friendly enough. They were impressed, even intimidated, that she was a staff psychiatrist at the Phipps. ("You work with Jonas Ganz? What's he like?") They expressed cautious interest in the eventual outcome of her study and wished her well with it.

"You'll have a hard time tracking down some of the patients," one nurse said.

"Oh, you mean the follow-ups? I'll have the assistance of two social workers for that."

"Which social workers—did he tell you?"

"I'm to meet them tomorrow."

"I'm sure they'll be very good. That'll make all the difference."

Imogen tried to keep up polite conversation but found herself yearning to be home at her kitchen table having dinner with the twins. She missed their chatter about all the newsworthy events of their day. Myra took us here! Myra told us this! Myra said cough drops are bad for you, is that true? She wanted to be reading them to sleep and listening for Carl's key in the door. My God, she thought, as the nurses talked on, I'm not a professional person at all.

If dinner was uncomfortable, sitting alone in her grey little chamber was worse. Having the whole corridor to herself did nothing to make her feel secure. Every so often would come a piteous cry, or a howl, or a wail—*Pardonna me! Pardonna me!*—followed by suggestions, expressed in the harshest terms, that the howler immediately kill himself. Other cries were not words at all.

She tried to read to distract herself, but the words on the page of her novel refused to form sentences. She put the book aside and switched out the light and tried not to mind the creak of the springs, the sag of the mattress, the desperate cries of the mad.


An office had been set aside for her, just off the records room, and it was a definite improvement over her sleeping arrangements. A wide window offered a view of brilliantly coloured maples, where black and grey squirrels spiralled and somersaulted.

Imogen had her own lockable file cabinet, a good-sized desk, and even a typing table complete with a shining new Underwood and reams of paper.

"This is Mrs. Boxer," Dr. Bingham said, as he ushered in a roly-poly woman in a rumpled brown suit. "Our statistician."

The woman smiled at her, displaying a palisade of snow-white teeth.

"Feel free to call on her for anything you need." Bingham handed Imogen a thin file, tied with black ribbon. "In the meantime, Mrs. Boxer has put these figures together. They should give you a good grounding."

When he had gone, Mrs. Boxer showed her the layout of the records room, the protocol for signing out files, and handed her the key to her office. She was a cheerful, bustling sort of woman, the kind of person you'd want to look after children. Imogen asked her if she had any.

"Two girls, twelve and fourteen. And you, Doctor?"

"I have a boy and a girl, five years old. Twins."

"Mother of twins and a doctor too. You must be a very special person." Mrs. Boxer closed a file drawer and blew some invisible dust off the top. "Dr. Bingham is a very special person too, as I'm sure you know. A brilliant, brilliant man. I was in a terrible state. Not fit for anything. I'd seen a nerve specialist for months—couldn't do a thing for me. I come here, Dr. Bingham takes one look at me and says, *Well, it's no mystery why the neurologist can't help you. What you need is the dentist.* Before you know it he's pulled out must be I don't know how many teeth—a dozen or more—and I haven't had a problem since. Discharged me a few weeks later."

She clacked her dentures together—*clack, clack, clack*—by way of proof.

"And here I am. Started in the front office, filing and so on. I'm just a natural for filing—I like things shipshape—and then eventually they put me back here looking after all the files and keeping track. I could not be happier, and here I'd been so sick you've no idea and it was such a relief to realize it was all my teeth and not my head. Or not just my head, anyway. Goodness me, I've talked your ear off—you're going to think I'm still a lunatic."

"Not at all," Imogen said, "but I suppose I should get to work."

Mrs. Boxer bustled ahead of her, swiping at invisible dust.

"I'll leave you to it then. You take a look at those figures, Doctor. I think you'll be impressed."

Imogen went into her office and closed the door. She looked out the window at the sparrows and squirrels. In the distance, two male patients, crooked and bent, were raking leaves. They reminded Imogen of a painting she had seen somewhere.

She sat at the desk and undid the ribbon around the folder and began to read. Within minutes she found mistakes: subtotals that did not add up to their given totals, percentages that did not add up to a hundred.

"It must be my arithmetic," she said quietly, and went over the figures again.

It was not her arithmetic. She flipped back to the first page. It was stamped and signed by the chairman of the hospital's medical board. Was it possible he'd approved work of this calibre? If he was counting on these figures to secure a raise in funding he'd be laughed out of the committee.

She read on, checking a column labelled "condition at discharge." Almost every patient discharged was listed as "cured." Anyone even slightly familiar with mental illness and its treatment would know that the largest number should be "improved." She went over the columns of names and found patients that had been counted as cured more than once. Readmission had apparently not cancelled out the earlier "cure."

Imogen closed the folder, and sat very still, hands folded on the desk before her. Mrs. Boxer, however good-natured, was clearly going to be of no help. The implications of this darkened the room, as if the blinds had been lowered.

# 14

When he had first returned home from the war to live with his father in Rochester, Quentin had been subject to fits of uncontrollable weeping. His exterior wounds had healed, all infection fled, but there remained within him a reservoir of sorrow that the peaceful surroundings of home seemed, surprisingly, to pressurize. He would be reading, or trying to write, and suddenly the tears would flow.

The scar from the bullet wound in his side was badly puckered, but the two in his chest had healed nicely, and the scars on his legs were not so bad. But he suffered from a continual sensation of being out of true, which he was, and although he had long imagined himself fully recovered from Hill 70, the doctors warned him that internal injuries from that blast might yet develop into kidney and liver problems. Even now, in the spring of 1924, climbing stairs made him gasp for breath and he walked with a tentative, measured gait entirely unbecoming to a young man. It was difficult for him to turn his neck, so that if something off to one side caught his attention he had to turn his entire body to attend to it. In the scheme of violence visited upon the bodies of war victims, he had got off lightly. But he felt unready for the world, that he needed yet more time in the peace and quiet of his father's house—weeks and months to think, to gather himself back together, and above all to write.

Before being shipped back home, he had made extensive but ultimately unsuccessful efforts to retrieve Mac's manuscript and look after it, as he had promised. Since Mac had been writing about the war, partly by way of homage to his fallen comrade, Quentin set out to do the same. After many false starts and many setbacks he had little more than a hundred pages to show for his efforts, and those hundred seemed to him entirely inadequate. The problem was not discipline exactly. He sat himself down at the desk every day and put in several hours, but for most of those hours he wrote nothing. Almost immediately he would sink into a kind of nether zone—not daydreaming exactly—where he remained in a strange paralysis of non-thought.

This particular day he had set himself the task of describing his last few weeks overseas.

After two months in the hospital at Étaples he had been evacuated out of France and deposited at Woodcote Park Convalescent Hospital in Epsom, sixteen miles southwest of London.

Woodcote Park had once been a grand estate but, despite its bucolic-sounding name, looked like any other army camp. A hundred huts clad in galvanized steel had provided beds for as many as five thousand patients, but as the war wound down, their numbers had dwindled to some fifteen hundred by the time Quentin arrived.

His head wound turned out to be the most minor of his injuries, being the work of a ricochet that plowed a three-inch-long furrow in his scalp but broke no bone. The bullet that had sliced its way into his left lung had necessitated a complicated and dangerous operation at the casualty clearing station. This had saved his life but left him battling pulmonary infections that threatened him with slow drowning as he convalesced. Shell fragments that had hit him after he lost consciousness had broken the tibia, fibula, and femur of his right leg.

"Another quarter-inch," the field surgeon informed him, "and it would have severed the femoral artery and you'd have died in the muck. You're a lucky man." War, Quentin had often noted, tended to rearrange one's ideas about luck.

His foot-to-thigh cast was removed soon after his arrival at Woodcote, but he was so weak, and his leg so unreliable, that he spent most of his time lying in bed listening to the English rain hammer on the roof of the hut, an unsettling sound that seemed never to stop. The men called the place, none too affectionately, Tin City.

As a convalescent hospital, Woodcote offered an aggressive program for rehabilitating shattered limbs. The nurses took stern delight in fitting Quentin into a Victorian-looking contraption of weights and straps that pulled and squeezed his leg into positions it would have been unlikely to adopt even before his injury. He had only been cast-free for a few days before he and several other "gimps," as they called themselves, were ordered to take daily "strolls" with a cheerful and voluble NCO who was himself a patient.

Quentin was just beginning to think himself truly on the mend when he came down with the flu that raged through the camp, killing nearly three hundred men who had managed to survive the combined efforts of Messrs. Krupp, Vickers, and Shrapnel to murder them. Quentin emerged from the illness fifteen pounds lighter and half-suffocating with yet another lung infection.

By the time the spring rains eased off he was better. Just keeping down the awful food seemed a signal accomplishment, and his mood grew brighter as his physical strength returned. A period of uncharacteristic sunshine did more than anything to cheer him, and soon he was able to enjoy stumping along the green hills of the park on his own. For a week or so he even began to feel optimistic, an emotion with which he had grown unfamiliar.

It didn't last. As the days wore on, he found himself slipping into a kind of numbness. The nurses and doctors, the support staff and his fellow patients, seemed to drift in a plane quite apart from his own and from which they could not touch him. It was not entirely unpleasant—there was enough aggravation at the camp to make numbness welcome—but it felt "wrong," in an almost physical way, as if a veil were hanging between him and everyone else. A disquiet, a detectable sense of dread, had set up a low drone in his consciousness.

The war had been over for months but the patients at Woodcote had yet to be demobilized, were still soldiers, still subject to military rules. Morale was appalling, the atmosphere that of a train station when service has been delayed without explanation and with no hint of when it might resume. The men snapped at the nurses and snarled at the NCOs and especially at the few military police on site. Some blamed British bureaucracy for the delay, others blamed a shortage of Canadian ships. Whatever the reason, Woodcote Park was housing fifteen hundred agitated souls who wanted to go home. Extensive efforts were made to keep them entertained. Every night saw a film or musical revue or some other performance in the recreation hut. The men were allowed into town between 1600 and 2130 hours every day. They weren't prisoners; they just felt like prisoners.

When they went into town they could not ignore the fact that the British had fallen out of love with Canadians. Appreciated as they had been for coming early and decisively to England's aid, beloved as they had been for their heartbreaking sacrifices at Passchendaele, and worshipped as they had been for their costly breakthrough at Vimy Ridge, by the late spring of 1919 it was clear the colonials had out-stayed their welcome.

Former British troops, many of them jobless, were not happy to see well-paid Canadian soldiers buying drinks and trinkets for their women. Accusations were made that the Canadians were not casualties at all, they were only venereal cases. Many were, although these were a minority at Woodcote and had to wear a Saxe blue uniform to distinguish them from the "real" wounded.

One warm June night two Canadians were arrested in the Rifleman pub and hauled off to jail. Quentin had spent the evening in a different pub with a hut mate named Sam Hawsey. They were heading back to the hospital to make the nine-thirty roll call, both limping, when the sea-like sound of an angry crowd flowed over the crest of a hill near the high street, soon followed by the men themselves—hundreds of

Woodcote patients. Quentin and Sam were pulled into the crowd and whirled along with it into Ashley Road. They ended up at the front of the mob that now pressed up against the wrought iron fence surrounding the Epsom police station.

No plan or organization was discernible, and yet the crowd seemed to move and breathe like a single organism. They wanted the two jailed Canadians released at once. Over and over, the men chanted, *Let them go! Let them go! Let them go!* and even Quentin tingled with excitement—you couldn't not feel it, despite its distinctly unwholesome tang. He recognized several men from his hut—men he knew to be sober, serious individuals—yelling, laughing, their eyes shining. But when he called out to them, they just kept yelling and laughing and paid him no mind.

More and more men flooded over the hill, filling the road, far more men than the local police could hope to handle. Four constables emerged now from the ivy-covered station and stood in their blue uniforms and ridiculous helmets halfway between the iron gate and the front door. One of them, a sergeant, stepped forward and tried to reason with the crowd. He yelled, but the mob drowned him out with *Let them go! Let them go!*

Some of the Canadians clambered over the fence, dodged around the sergeant, and charged the other three constables, who began swatting at them with their billy clubs. That enraged the crowd, and now men swarmed through the gate. Quentin was pressed up against the fence so that his chest wound screamed.

"Best get out of here," he yelled to Sam.

"Hell, no!" Sam yelled back. "Fuckin' imperials—who do they think they are?"

The front yard of the station was a full-blown riot scene. Two of the soldiers now sported police helmets. The constables were submerged, bareheaded, in the chaos. The crowd surged past them and flowed around to the back of the station. Windows were smashed. One man wrestled with a constable on the ground and came up with his club.

For no obvious reason he came back toward the fence and poked the sergeant with it. When the sergeant turned around, the man swung the club into the side of his head. The sergeant crumpled. It was clear by the way he fell—no hands thrown out to break his fall, legs folded beneath him in impossible positions—that the injury was grievous. Even the man who had clubbed him saw this. He stood staring, his mouth a black circle, then backed away. He dropped the club and pushed through the crowd, his blue uniform vivid against the churning sea of khaki.

Quentin had lost track of Sam—he might have been inside the police station or helping others to attack it from the rear. He clutched the arm of the man next to him and pointed to the sergeant. "We've got to get him out of here."

"Right."

Quentin went through the gate but the man held back.

"Come on, man. Get over here and grab his arms."

The man did as he was told. Two other men, perhaps shaken into sense by this new level of violence, joined them. Together the four of them carried the policeman to a nearby house. Another man was sent to summon an ambulance. The terrified neighbour—a pasty woman in housecoat and slippers—was in no rush to let them in.

"Please," Quentin shouted. "We have an injured policeman."

The curtains of the front window parted an inch, and a moment later she opened the door.

"He needs a cold compress," Quentin said as they lowered the sergeant to the sofa. When she didn't move, he said, "Hurry—a dish-towel in cold water."

She brought him a face-cloth in a basin. Quentin squeezed the water out and pressed it gently to the sergeant's head. The depression in the temple region was deep enough that he could feel it through the wet cloth. If he regains consciousness, Quentin thought, he'll be lucky to remember his own name, let alone how to count. His skin, already pale against the dark hair and moustache, turned paper white.

His breathing grew shallower and irregular and then stopped alto-gether. The other three men muttered their excuses and left. Quentin sat in an overstuffed armchair, easing his leg, while the lady of the house eyed him from her seat at her dining room table, where she was smoking furiously.

Seeing a photograph on the mantel, Quentin said, "Your son?"

The woman nodded, and took a long pull on her cigarette, making the tip glow.

"Artillery?"

She exhaled a jet of grey smoke and said, "He died at Vimy."

"A hero, then. Anyone who got through Vimy owes it to British artillery and men like your son."

"You wouldn't know it—way your lot is always going on about it. 'Canadian miracle' and all."

"I know it."

She stubbed out her cigarette with some violence.

"High-explosive shell. They say he didn't suffer."

"That's a mercy, then."

Parents of men roasted alive in tanks, or screaming as they tried to gather their intestines back in, were told the same thing. Nobody suffered.

The ambulance men finally got through the crowd and confirmed the death. Quentin gave them his name and information, and they carried the dead sergeant away on a stretcher.

"So why'd they want to do that, then?" the woman said. "Kill a p'liceman only trying to keep order. I thought we was all on the same side."

"I don't know why," Quentin said. "War doesn't bring out the best in people."

"Can't blame the bloody war. The war's over."

"Yes," Quentin said. "Yes, I heard that too."

Over the next few days he was questioned thoroughly and repeat-edly. He told the police everything he had seen but he could not identify the man who had killed their comrade. Their skepticism, at first sulphurous, eventually gave way. In the end, they arrested every Canadian soldier who showed billy club injuries and a man was charged with murder—the only one of the injured men who was wearing a blue uniform.

Quentin tried several times during his convalescence to contact Margaret Morley. It seemed decades ago that they had danced in the crowd at Étaples. He wrote three letters care of the Canadian Army Medical Corps but received no reply. It was possible she was still on duty. She had given him her parents' address in Bracebridge, Ontario, but he didn't want to intrude on them when he was only an unfamiliar name. He asked one of his Woodcote nurses, a Miss Jenkins, for help locating her fellow nurse but she kept forgetting his request. It was frustrating, but he could hardly blame her, overworked as she was and surrounded by bad-tempered soldiers.

"I've given up," he said to her one day as she strapped him into the leg extension apparatus. She was a plain girl, awkward and graceless, and with an all but affectless bedside manner.

"You can't give up. Only another month of this and your leg will be fine."

"Not that. I've given up waiting for you to locate my nurse friend. I'm writing to her parents today."

"Well, if you know her parents . . ."

"I don't, but she gave me their address. Ouch!"

"Sorry." She readjusted the hip strap. "All right. You get to work and I'll be right back."

He flexed his leg, then extended it. Flexed, and extended. It hurt much less than it had at first, but his rate of progress had slowed, making it hard to stay interested in such a repetitive task. And Nurse Jenkins still had not got the strap right. It chafed every time he straightened his leg.

She came back clutching a piece of paper, and when he stopped for a breather, she thrust it into his hands. It was a typed notice, curled at the edges and with pinholes in the corners. The date at the top indicated it was months old. Quentin would have still been in the field hospital in France, barely out of the anaesthetic.

A memorial service will be held on Thursday morning for our gallant nursing sisters killed last week on the hospital ship *Laurentian*. As you know, the ship was clearly marked, and yet the Germans saw fit not only to sink it but to attack the lifeboats. All 210 souls perished, including the following three sisters: Florence Harper (Toronto), Jeanine Watts (Markham, Ont.), Margaret Morley (Bracebridge, Ont.). Service will take place at 11:30 a.m. All patients and personnel may attend save those handling any emergencies.

Quentin looked at Nurse Jenkins. "You knew all along."

"Not all along."

"Good God. It was months ago. I wish you'd told me."

"Yes. Well."

"Could have saved me writing all those letters."

"You've been very unwell. I thought it was for the best."

"No one wants to live in a fantasy."

"I do," she answered with an uncharacteristic note of passion. "I spend a great deal of time imagining I'm someone else in some other place—even at another time."

She rattled on about movie stars she worshipped, and Quentin stopped listening. He thought about the cancelled future of Margaret Morley, the thousands of people she would have helped, and how her parents, who had already lost their sons, would grieve for their lost daughter. He thought about the loss to himself. It was odd. He had not had time to fall in love with her, but now that she was dead he covered his eyes and wept.

"See there," Nurse Jenkins said. "Exactly why I didn't want to tell you."

At the time, he had wanted to hit her but now, in the late summer of 1924, in the sad tranquility of Rochester, New York, he wondered if Nurse Jenkins had not been right: that ignorance, the simple purity of ignorance, was the only sure defence against sorrow.

There came the day of his departure on RMS *Ascania*, the relatively calm crossing, a few days in Montreal where he was officially demobilized, and then the train to Rochester. His fears that he and his father would find themselves at odds soon proved groundless.

Dr. Goodchild, now retired, was changed by the reappearance of his damaged son. Perhaps it was mere gratitude that his flesh and blood had survived, but there was a tenderness in his attitude toward Quentin that was new. Where before he had been gruff, he was now solicitous and kind. He took to referring to Quentin as "boy," or "my boy." *Shall we go for a stroll, boy? Sleep well, my boy? Fancy a porterhouse for dinner, boy?*

Dr. Goodchild spent much of the day reading the papers and writing letters to the editor, to the mayor, and the White House, for he was still waspish where others were concerned. Quentin put in his hours at a desk in the spare bedroom. For lunch they walked to Woolworth's and sat at the lunch counter, sharing a crossword puzzle. His father was good at these, if a little competitive. As weeks and then months went by, he never once asked Quentin what he planned to do with his life, or if he had thought about getting a job. Quentin found it a surprising, but welcome, change in a man who had never been averse to cracking the whip.

For the first time in their lives, in other words, he and his father became friends. In the warmth of this shared domesticity, Quentin felt his war anguish slowly beginning to recede. The bouts of tears, the nightmares and the fits of shaking became less frequent. He no longer woke in the morning wondering which hospital he was in, or what surgery awaited him. After a mostly silent but agreeable break-fast the two men would retire to their separate chairs and not talk again until it was time for lunch.

But the writing went badly. Quentin would get a few pages in, and he would be overwhelmed with sorrow—sorrow that rapidly turned into an anger so white-hot he could not be coherent in his thoughts, let alone on the page. He felt peculiar, and useless, and out of place. One day, out of desperation, he decided to invent a fictional author, one who felt no need to write about the war.

This little mental trick changed his life. In the guise of this invented author, he began writing vignettes about a peculiar stranger who shows up in a very proper, conservative town and causes havoc with his penchant for blurting out passionate statements in settings where they are most unwelcome. Although he had started with no plan for a novel, slowly the vignettes accumulated, and other characters came alive. With these in hand, he worked out a general storyline with a few peaks and valleys. He wrote and rewrote and gradually, reluc-tantly, began to admit that he might indeed be a novelist.

As soon as he completed the first manuscript he put it away in a drawer and started another. Like the first, it was short, uncluttered, and focused around an odd, passionate protagonist who alienates almost everyone he meets—except other misfits. He made lists of possible pseudonyms. A year later, with two complete novels in hand, he began contacting publishers. It took a few months, but eventu-ally he was taken on by an editor named Griffin Burke at Essex Taylor Bradkin.

He felt the possibility of happiness beginning to blossom within him. His father noticed, and was heartened by it. "I begin to see my old Quentin," he said one day. "You'll never know what joy it brings me."

Their shared contentment was not to last long, however. The old man had never mentioned it to Quentin, but he had been diagnosed with metastatic cancer and had elected to forgo any surgery. The end came in the form of a spinal tumour. He began to complain increasingly often of his aching back and eventually had to be taken to the emergency room in agony. Ten days later he was dead.

# 15

"Why on earth would Bingham do that?" Carl wanted to know. "Why would he stick you in a broom closet in the criminal wing? Surely it's not in his interest to antagonize you. He's hoping for a favourable report, right?"

They were lying in bed, speaking softly. Imogen's train had got in at nine-thirty, when the twins were already asleep. She had had to suppress an urge to wake them up and hug them.

"Bingham is a strange man—he's cold and clammy. He looks at you but doesn't see you. Very flat affect, except when he talks about his surgical procedures. He doesn't seem worried about a favourable report—he's too certain he'll get one."

"Those asylum directors are an eccentric bunch. A Harvard friend of mine has worked with three of them and says not one of them would be employable in a regular hospital."

"It's the isolation. Bingham's been in place at Trenton since 1916. He still calls X-rays roentgenograms."

She told him about the statistics Bingham had provided.

Carl, a man who knew the value of good statistics, shook his head and said, "Again—why would he do that? Why give you bad numbers?"

"It's possible he's never looked at them. Either that or he didn't notice. He just sees what he wants to see. If Mrs. Boxer tells him the numbers are good, he assumes they are—which means I'm going to have to dig up all my own numbers. Or at least keep a close eye on Mrs. Boxer. Oh, and did I tell you about the social workers? Bingham assigned me two social workers to do the follow-up visits on discharged patients. These two ladies waltz in and they're just like Mrs. Boxer— mouths chock full of brand new false teeth."

"Former patients."

"And supremely grateful ones. They talk, seriously, about what a miracle-worker Bingham is. They think he's a saint *and* a genius."

"Well, who's going to do the follow-ups then?"

"I'll have to."

Carl looked at her. "Imogen, for God's sake—you'll be away months!"

"I know."

"I thought you were just going to be checking files and putting numbers together."

"So did I." She rested a hand on his shoulder but he pulled away.

"God damn it, Imogen."

"Please don't be angry. This has to be done right, and I'm not going to have any help from Trenton. If anything, they'll be in the way."

Carl turned away from her, and switched out the light.

Imogen woke early to the sounds of the twins chattering in the kitchen.

"Mumma!" they both cried, when she appeared in the doorway. Hot little hands clutched at her fingers. "Mumma, where were you?"

Imogen dispensed what they ultimately conceded was a satisfactory number of hugs and kisses. Pure joy to ruffle their hair, to inhale their warm, biscuity smell. How is it possible, she wondered, that I ever manage to forget I have this happy life? Even if nothing else should ever go right, I have this home, this joy.

"Where's Trenton?" Charlotte demanded. "Why did you go to there?"

"You remember, darling—I have work to do."

"Are there children there?" Aubrey asked with a worried look.

"I'm sure there are," Imogen said, "but I didn't see any. I'm working at the hospital—remember I told you about that?"

"I remember," Charlotte said.

Imogen made oatmeal and placed a bowl before each of them. The twins talked excitedly about Cynthia Bee. Cynthia had taught them new games and taken them to the park and horse riding and on the carousel and all kinds of things.

"Cynthia says on Monday or Tuesday she'll take us to the dinosaur museum. She says they have tiny horses there. Horses this big." She indicated six inches or so off the table. "Will you come with us?"

"I won't be able to, dear. I'll be going back to Trenton Sunday night."

"Why?" Charlotte said.

"Why?" Aubrey echoed.

"Because I have more work to do. I'll be going there every week."

"When is Sunday?" Aubrey asked in a small voice.

"Three days from now."

"Three more sleeps?"

"No, two sleeps, love. Three days. Come on, now, eat up. We've got to get you to school."

"Good morning," Carl said, taking coffee beans from the cupboard and measuring them into his grinder. "How are the two terrors of Dukeland Street? Are they behaving?"

"They're positively angelic," Imogen said. "I should go away more often."

"No." Aubrey slammed his spoon on the table. "You stay home."

"I feel the same way," Carl said mildly, "but Mumma has to work, and that's that."

After Carl headed off to the Phipps, Imogen walked the twins to school; Myra would pick them up at noon.

She had anticipated great pleasure at being back in her laboratory, but found that the work did not engage her. Lately her results on blood chemistry and psychosis were merely supportive of work that had gone before. And since there was no telling when, if ever, Ganz would allow her to publish, it all seemed pointless. She still had only a single publication to her credit.

She did enjoy lunch in the third-floor dining room. A couple of her former patients greeted her warmly. It was one of the sadder realities of her Trenton mission that it had meant transferring her patients to other psychiatrists. After the abject souls adrift in Trenton, the Phipps patients seemed only mildly eccentric. They also looked supremely healthy, but that may have been because they still had teeth. After lunch, she met with Ganz in his office. He was in an uncharacteristically jolly mood, holding forth on the pleasures of train travel.

"I find there is a certain tranquility to long-distance train travel, don't you? One has no telephone, and I have only once received a telegram en route. One's existence takes on a parenthetical character. One is freed from the usual responsibilities, and the narrative of one's life is suspended. All in all, an experience that encourages reflection."

The word reminded Imogen of her "conversations" with Laura.

Dr. Ganz tapped the ash from his cigar and examined the tip. "Of course, the trip to and from Trenton—it's not going to be the same thing, I expect."

"No, but I enjoy it—it's very good for reading."

"And what are you reading these days? Other than the collected works of Rupert Bingham."

"I've become rather fond of Jeremy West. I've read two of his books now. They're quite unique—in atmosphere, anyway. They manage to be both dreamlike and highly realistic at the same time, if that's possible."

"Jeremy West. I've not heard of him."

"I think you'd like him. Donna would too." She immediately regretted mentioning Donna, but Dr. Ganz would not be nudged from his cheerful mood.

"The elusive Dr. Artemis. You still see her, do you?"

"We have tea now and again."

"I miss her," Ganz allowed. "She was a lively presence."

"Yes."

"But we must talk of other things. Tell me about Trenton."

She told him everything she had told Carl, in more detail. She struggled to maintain an even tone; she wanted to appear, and to be, fair-minded. Ganz listened in silence, gazing up at the ceiling as she spoke. When she was finished, he stubbed out his cigar and said, "Well. A less than auspicious beginning."

"To be fair, I suppose shoddy statistics don't necessarily indicate a bad intention."

"No. Nor do they imply unacceptable outcomes."

"Clearly I'm going to be away longer than we expected."

"Without question. You'll have to do your own follow-ups with the patients—and some of them may be quite far-flung."

"I found Bingham himself a little odd. You worked with him at Worcester, didn't you?"

Ganz gave a curt nod. "I found him able enough . . ."

He let the phrase hang in the air.

"But?"

"Perhaps I shouldn't say anything more—I don't want to sway your judgment one way or the other."

The afternoon seemed long and empty. Instead of pressing ahead with her write-ups, Imogen spent an hour or more staring out the lab's bay window at the falling leaves, and at the cars that came and went in the circular drive. Precisely at five o'clock she put on her coat and stopped off in Carl's lab down the hall.

"I'm heading home now. What time will I see you?"

"I won't be late. Six-thirty or seven?"

Cynthia Bee emerged from one of the research rooms, carrying an empty cage, and they greeted each other.

"I hear you've been enormous help with the twins," Imogen said. "We're very grateful, both of us."

"Oh, I love to see them," Cynthia said. "They're such delightful little darlings."

"Well, they're quite mad for you," Imogen said.

She stopped off at the butcher's on the way home and bought two pounds of pork tenderloin. As she waited for him to wrap it up, a sadness rolled into her spirit. She began to count the ways in which she was not good: I am not a good wife; a good wife does not abandon her husband and children for three days out of the week and expect to do so for the next six months. I am not a good mother, because I let other people—Myra, Cynthia, and Carl—take up my responsibilities. I am not a good sister, in that I don't keep in touch with my siblings; I am frankly not even sure if I love them. I am not a good daughter because I've upset my parents by becoming a working mother, and in a field—psychiatry—that garners scant respect in the civilized world. I can't even call myself a good psychiatrist at the moment, having handed off my patients for the duration, all so I can pursue this dubious mission in Trenton, New Jersey.

I am a good researcher, she allowed herself. I know how to isolate a theory and test it and collate results in a logical, convincing manner. Not that anyone else sees it, thanks to the vague obstructionism of Jonas Ganz.

Good God, she thought, taking the package of pork from the butcher and putting it in her string bag, I'm not even a good Jew.

The tenderloin was to be her effort to be a good wife at least for the short time she would be home. Carl, she knew, would be living on cheap steak and cheese sandwiches while she was gone.

The children brightened her mood by greeting her deliriously. After Myra had departed, she sat on the couch and watched them playing with Charlotte's dollhouse, an ingenious three-storey affair that Carl had spent many weeks building. Highly detailed—it even had tiny electric lights, something many real houses did not yet have—and beautifully proportioned, it threw open a door into the children's imaginations. She loved to watch them making up dialogue, two tiny dramatists moving their miniature characters from room to room. Carl had even managed to find a Negro maid figure that Charlotte in particular liked to voice.

"Did you put your toys away?" she would say to Aubrey, mimicking Myra.

"No, I'm the father."

"No, you're the boy. Did you put your toys away? Do I have to go check?"

"I put them away."

"You a good boy. Lemme give you a big ole kiss."

"No! Ugh!" Aubrey trotting his tiny figure into another room and hiding under a bed. "You can't find me!"

"Where could that bad little boy be?"

"You said I was good!"

"That was before."

"Oh."

"Now you're bad."

"Why?"

"Because you just are."

"I don't want to be."

"But you are, okay?"

"No. Why don't you be bad?"

"Because I'm Myra!"

It was fascinating to Imogen how they slipped in and out of the two realities, and in and out of character as necessary to impose desired destinies. And it was hard to miss their moral certainties and hesitations, the embryonic superegos struggling with conflicting desires to boss or submit, to take or to give. But she did not want to be too much the psychiatrist with her own children. She left them to play and went into the kitchen to start dinner.

The weekend unfolded much as she'd hoped. Carl came home and happily devoured his dinner. She read to the children, and the feel of them lying against her, enthralled by a story and falling asleep against their will, restored something deep inside her that had been in danger of breaking.

Saturday was given over to their morning routine of marketing, and then in the afternoon she and Carl took the twins to the zoo. The day was unseasonably warm, and a tiger cub, much to the chagrin, even outrage, of his elders, jumped into the moat that separated them from the gawping humans. The senior tigers growled at him, and finally one of them hauled him out by the scruff and lectured him in deep-throated Tigerese. Aubrey cackled with delight, and Carl was amused as well.

And yet when they turned out the light, Carl did not reach for her and Imogen knew that he had not forgiven her.

On Sunday he stayed home to do some reading in much-deserved peace, while Imogen took the twins to the park to play on the swings and teeter-totters. It had turned cold overnight, and windy, and their matching scarves flew out behind them. Imogen felt like the children with the dollhouse, directing a tiny distant avatar of herself into first one role, then another. Now I am a psychiatrist, now I am a researcher; now I am a wife, now I am a mother. Now I am good, now I am . . . not.

She had just enough time, when she got home, to make lunch and then catch her train. Carl was on his knees in the dining area, attempting to fix a radiator.

"Lunch is ready," she called for the second time, when she and the children were seated.

"I want to finish this," Carl said, banging at something with a wrench. "I don't want to freeze like last winter."

"You could fix it later," Imogen said. "I have to catch my train soon."

"I'm not stopping you."

The children ate quietly, tired after their morning out, and no doubt a little disheartened at their mother's imminent departure. When they were done, Imogen sent them off to their room.

"Please don't stay angry with me," she said quietly. "I thought you'd gotten over it. It can't do any of us any good."

"You're doing what you wanted to do. I react how I react."

"Carl, please. It's hard enough without this."

"Hard, is it?" He put aside the wrench and turned to face her, still sitting on the floor. "Then why are you doing it, Imogen? Why are you depriving the kids of their mother? Why deprive me of my wife?"

"Carl, we've been over this. You know why—the chance of publication, advancement. I'll be bringing in more money. That's for all of us. Why does it have to be a source of friction?"

"Because it's not what women do."

"You don't mean that."

"It's not what *wives* do. *Mothers.* You should be here, Imogen. With your family. You know it and I know it."

"Carl, it's not like I *hid* anything from you. You always knew I wanted to keep working. Why is it suddenly a problem *now*?"

He turned back to the radiator, wrench in hand.

"Carl, please don't be like this."

"Just go and catch your damn train."


The Clocker was crowded, and the woman seated next to Imogen smelled strongly of lily of the valley, a scent that never failed to give her a headache. Before they had gone very far, Imogen took out her new Jeremy West novel.

She was disappointed to discover that it was not in fact a novel but a collection of short stories. She found novels as a rule more absorbing, and she had hoped it would take her mind off Carl.

The first story was narrated by a man who has nothing but contempt for the "gamine little flapper" who lives in the rooming house next door to his Village townhouse. He has an acerbic wit that he deploys to describe the young woman, an actress struggling to make it on Broadway. She has the looks for it, he allows, but also points out that "like all flappers" she is dim-witted, conceited, and promiscuous. He knows this because she is beautiful and because she is an actress— and everyone knows what actresses are like. He does not say so, but he is clearly counting on that well-known promiscuity to make his day when he asks her to have dinner with him.

He takes her to a fashionable restaurant on Fifth Avenue and orders an expensive bottle of Bordeaux, "not that she was capable of appreci- ating it," and "stokes her vanity" by asking questions about her expe- riences onstage. The young woman is sharply critical of her own skills, and full of praise not just for the current stars but for her col- leagues in the rooming house, most of whom are theatre people. The narrator sees this "fake humility" as just another actressy tactic to make herself superior.

As he is walking her home, they pass a dog walker with a long- haired dachshund straining at the leash. The young woman suddenly becomes very quiet, and the narrator asks her what's wrong. She explains that her dog, also a long-haired dachshund, died not long ago. It's a warm night, and they sit on a bench in Washington Square and she begins to tell him about Timmy.

At this point West's story swerved in a new direction, much as his novels did. It became about the dog.

The girl talks about Timmy's affectionate character, his love of play, his canine obsession with sticks and balls, his catholic taste in food, his Lothario tendencies toward female dogs five times his size, and above all his bottomless capacity for love and loyalty.

All very sentimental, one might think (the impatient narrator cer- tainly does), except that it is the girl's character that West illumines through her description of her pet. She comes across as a creature of infinite loyalty herself, loving and gentle, as she nurses Timmy through a long and debilitating illness until finally he has to be put down.

Her description of the dog's last days brought tears to Imogen's eyes and, indeed, when the girl finishes her story she cries and cries and the narrator holds her close. As he offers her this comfort, he slips his hand inside her coat and fondles her breast. The girl says nothing but soon gets up from the bench and dries her eyes. They finish the walk to the door of her rooming house on Waverley Place. She thanks the narrator and says good night.

But when he asks her to dinner again, she makes excuses—as she does when he asks her again. And again. The story closes with his fulminating, in his bitter yet amusing way, on the "secret contempt that beautiful women harbour for every other member of the human race."

Imogen closed the book, keeping her place with an index finger, and thought about what she had read. A portrayal of self-delusion, to be sure, but what had moved her more than anything was the "dim-witted flapper's" description of the death of her dog. Her vulnerability, her grief, and her discovery of the ineffable sadness of life contrasted powerfully with the scheming narrator—though even he, by the end of the story, becomes quite sympathetic, his prejudice and resentment all but guaranteeing him a life of misery. A sad story, all in all, but not a depressing one.

She glanced outside at the telegraph wires as they rose and fell from pole to pole. The soft light of early evening gleamed on a swamp, green with lily pads, and illumined the backs of houses and their tiny yards criss-crossed with washing lines. Lamps were beginning to come on in some of the houses.

She read several more of the West stories before reluctantly putting the book into her bag; saving a few would draw out the pleasure. The lily-of-the-valley lady was gone—Imogen had been too absorbed to notice her departure—and the train now smelled only of oil and steel. Her mind turned to the conversation she had had with Mrs. Boxer before leaving for Baltimore the previous week.


They had been in Imogen's office in the records department, Imogen seated at her desk, Mrs. Boxer standing nervously in the doorway.

Imogen asked her to sit in the only other chair, which she did, perching on the edge, hands clasped primly in her lap.

"Mrs. Boxer," Imogen began, "in order for this study to have any validity—and in order for it to be of any use to this or any other institution—it must cover a large series of cases. Dr. Ganz and I have agreed that it should consist of the following—and don't worry, I shall provide you with a typewritten copy of the particulars.

"We want to document the long-term effects of Trenton's surgical interventions for focal infections, both abdominal and dental. So I'll need you to supply me with three series of patients who were admitted in 1920."

"Three series in 1920. I see."

"Group One must be the first hundred patients, regardless of diagnosis. Group Two will consist of the first hundred functional cases—that is, patients whose trouble had no obvious organic or toxic basis. So, no syphilitics, no epileptics, no one suffering from brain damage, no drug or alcohol cases. If you are in doubt, please ask me."

Mrs. Boxer nodded. "So, the first hundred patients, regardless of diagnosis."

"Yes."

"And then the first hundred functional cases."

"Correct."

"I see."

Imogen consulted her notes. "The third group has to be another hundred patients, but these are to be people who are currently under treatment. Those will show us the immediate effects of surgery."

"One hundred current patients."

"Yes. Admitted consecutively. We don't want to pick and choose among any of these three groups. Selection is strictly consecutive."

"Strictly consecutive. Yes, I see."

"Now I want a fourth group: patients who have received all phases of treatment for focal sepsis—in other words, patients for whom the hospital has done everything it could. Every surgery that Dr. Bingham wanted them to have."

"You want a hundred of these too?"

"Well, there may not be a hundred. As you know, many people find surgery a terrifying prospect. Others may agree to one treatment but not another. You might feel all right about having some molars removed but draw the line at abdominal surgery and so on. So let's say up to a hundred. Patients who have had every recommended surgery."

"I'll do my best."

"Finally, a special group to be selected by Dr. Bingham himself— patients that he considers have shown the greatest improvement. As many as he likes, up to a hundred."

"Oh, he'll have some good ones for you there. You'll be amazed."

"Excellent." Imogen handed her a typewritten sheet. "Here is the summary of what I've just told you. I'd like to be able to get started on these when I come back on Monday."

"I'll do my best."

"Any questions?"

Mrs. Boxer put on her glasses and peered at the typesheet.

"This may take some time, all this."

"It's a lot of work, I know. As long as I have a good batch to get going with on Monday."

"Five hundred cases. Five hundred files, my goodness."

"It may not be five hundred. Because the last two groups—"

"Yes, but still."

"I don't need them all on Monday, Mrs. Boxer. Just some."

"I'll do my best," Mrs. Boxer said doubtfully.

"I'm sure that will be more than adequate."


Mrs. Boxer greeted her cheerily on Monday morning. "Did you have a nice few days with your family?"

"Very nice, thank you. And how have you been, Mrs. Boxer?"

"Oh, my husband is a grumpy sort, especially if he doesn't get what he wants. Which is most of the time, unless I constantly submit to him. Leonard is a man who suffers from inflamed appetites. Or rather, I suffer from his inflamed appetites."

"Ah. Well. I hope you managed to enjoy your weekend anyway. Did you have any luck with the files?"

"Oh, yes. First group's all done."

"The purely consecutive group from 1920, all diagnoses?"

"That's the one. On your desk, dear."

"Excellent. But please call me 'Doctor.'"

"Doctor. Forgive me. Sorry—I'm not used to doctors being young and pretty."

Imogen went into her office and closed the door. She stood at the window for a moment. The trees had lost more of their leaves, and those that remained were duller than they had been the previous week.

She sat down and opened the first of the boxes labelled *Consecutive Cases, 1920*. She began to sort them into diagnostic groups: Functional, Organic, Epileptic, or Constitutional (meaning patients whose intellectual development was retarded, no matter the cause). Even using the status cards attached to the top sheets, that took most of the morning.

At noon she walked over to the main building to eat in the doctors' lunchroom. She approached a communal table with a plate of lamb stew and mashed potatoes. Dr. Roper, a man of about forty with dark hair slicked straight back à la Valentino, had been holding forth, but he went silent as Imogen took her seat. She detected a new coolness in the atmosphere, and folded the *Trenton Chronicle* beside her plate in case it should be needed to ward off conversation.

Dr. Roper spoke up. "How is the assassination going?"

"Assassination?"

Dr. Roper dug into his stew and surveyed his own folded newspaper. "That's what you're here for, isn't it? To assassinate our director?"

"Actually, no. I'm here at the request of your medical board to do a statistical analysis of your surgical results."

The sense of being attacked set Imogen's heart racing.

"We are an asylum for the insane, Dr. Lang. Since when are 'results' even expected? Surely every result other than early death or lifetime incarceration must be counted a victory."

Imogen's mouth had gone dry. She took a sip from her water glass. "My study is for informational purposes. The board—and your legislative funding committee—want to know if their spending is warranted. It's the same for all state hospitals."

Roper framed an invisible rectangle in the air, as if picturing a headline. "'The Great Phipps Clinic Speaks.' I can see it now."

"You seem to be assuming my findings will reflect badly on your institution."

"I didn't say that. You did."

"You accused me of assassination."

Roper ate a few mouthfuls of his stew, and dabbed at his mouth with his napkin. "We have figures of our own, you know. We can count, believe it or not. It's a little unusual to have a Grand Inquisitor come to question our numbers."

"I'm not here because I question your numbers. I'm here because other hospitals and psychiatrists wonder if your numbers can be accurate. Unfortunately, some quite astonishing figures have been floated in the lay press, but there've been no independent studies to confirm them. Perhaps mine will be the first to verify results that sound extremely encouraging."

"If true."

"Pardon me?"

"Encouraging numbers, if true."

"Are you trying to tell me they're not true?"

"I'm trying to tell you you're about to do a great deal of damage." Roper pushed his plate away and stood up. "Tell me, what do they do at the Phipps Clinic for people that smear themselves in their own excrement?"

"I don't—"

"I'll tell you what they do. They send them to us—to the state hospitals, the asylums—because chronic schizophrenics are as hopeless as hopeless human beings get. And those asylums lock them up for thirty to forty years. Why? Because there is no treatment, that's why."

"We take our share of schizophrenics—"

Roper talked right over her.

"No known treatment. Nobody's even trying to treat them. Rupert Bingham is the only man brave enough to try something new, rooting out infection in the teeth, the gut, the tonsils, the glands—wherever it may be hiding. He roots it out and these people go home. Yes, Dr. Lang of the Henry Phipps Clinic, Johns Hopkins Hospital and University, we send people home."

"I know you do. It's my job to find out what condition they are in five years later—among other parameters. If they are doing well, that will be wonderful news."

"And if they're not?"

"And if they're not, then obviously further studies would have to be done, and different treatment modalities applied."

"No. If they're not, you're going to take away the one thing we give our patients and their families, which is hope."

"That's what the spiritualists say, as they empty the pockets of people in mourning."

"Which is exactly what people in mourning need!"

"But your figures are not claiming hope. They're claiming cure. Don't you want to know the truth? Dr. Bingham does. He's wholeheartedly behind this study."

"That's Dr. Bingham. You'll do what you want, no doubt. But don't expect me or anybody else in this place to thank you for it."


Imogen resolved not to let Dr. Roper get to her. She didn't know him, had no reason to value his opinion. She thought of her medical and scientific heroes—Freud, Pasteur, Semmelweis—and how they had persisted with their studies and experiments despite insults and isolation. Over the next few weeks she bent her mind to the task of further classifying the stacks of cases before her. Her preliminary categories were four: Recovered, Improved, Unimproved (at large), Unimproved (in hospital). She had to follow up on the fates of a hundred people admitted to Trenton five years ago—and that was only the first selection.

Just finding out where a former patient was currently living was difficult. People moved—sometimes out of state, leaving little trace behind. The dead were the easiest, since their demise was a matter of public record. More than thirty of the first hundred patients, it turned out, were no longer among the living.

Luckily, Carl seemed to have reconciled himself to her travelling back and forth. He greeted her with a bear hug each time she returned home, told her he missed her (without actually complaining), and engaged her in much-needed sex on Saturday night. When it came time to part on Sunday, he kissed her goodbye. Even the twins seemed to adapt, thanks in large part to the help of Myra and Cynthia.

But Imogen was itching to get on with the job of interviewing former patients and when, after three or four trips, she had just a few remaining files to sort, she telephoned Carl to say that she would have to stay an extra day, perhaps two; there was just so much work.

She had expected him to be annoyed, possibly even angry, but he took it in stride. In fact, he expressed sympathy that she had to face such an arduous task with so little dependable help. She would have liked even more sympathy. She would have liked to tell him how the staff psychiatrists hated her, and how sloppy the record-keeping was, but it was too expensive to do so over the telephone.

"Is everything all right with the twins?"

"Everything's fine."

"You must be at your wits' end."

"No, Myra and Cynthia have been wonderful. It's been much easier than I thought it would be and I'm sorry I've been such an ass about it."

His apology soothed Imogen's wounded heart. She was a lucky woman with a good job, two beautiful children, and a loving husband. Her eyes watered at the sudden uprush of emotion and—not long after she hung up the phone—she changed her mind. She would not stay an extra day; she would catch the four o'clock back to Baltimore.

Her buoyant mood changed her attitude about the work. Instead of feeling it would never end, she could now see that she had made good progress. If she and Mrs. Boxer kept this up they would certainly have a rough itinerary organized by the following Monday.

Optimism infused her with energy, and she made plans to visit those former patients who had been found to live reasonably nearby. She had purchased a road map of New Jersey, and as she settled into her seat on the train, she consulted it to find out how far away were such places as Rahway, Haddon, and Fort Lee.

There was no dining car on the train, but a steward came around with a basket of sandwiches and cold drinks, and in any case she was too excited about heading home to eat very much. In the face of Carl's apology, she began to feel a little guilty about her own anger toward him. Surely he hadn't deserved it; he was far more understanding than most men. She thought, too, of his brilliance in the lab, how he was making a big name for himself—and the Phipps—by helping to turn psychology into a real science instead of a branch of philosophy. She thought of his laugh, which was frequent, loud, and contagious, and his love of play, which made him so popular with the twins. She couldn't wait to be home again.

She arrived in Baltimore still basking in that glow. The taxi was thick with the smoke of the previous occupant's cigar, and she opened the window, leaning her head out, letting the night breezes of Baltimore wash over her. It was nearly eleven o'clock. The streets were quiet in a way that the streets of her native Chicago never were. But over the past near-decade those once-foreign scents of magnolia, tea olive, and salt water had come to smell like home. The night was much warmer than the day had been in Trenton, and she undid the buttons of her fall coat.

The house on Dukeland Street was dark. It was a banal little structure compared with the house she had grown up in, and housed two other tenants, but even so she approached it with affection. Home. She slotted her key in the lock and turned it as quietly as possible. It opened with a clunk that made her jump but was probably not loud enough to disturb the slumbers of husband and children.

She stepped inside and set her overnight case by the front closet. The air was redolent of the beef stew she had prepared in advance for Carl to eat while she was away. She opened the case and took out her nightgown. Then, feeling quite shameless, she took off her clothes in a shaft of moonlight that made her skin glow platinum. She draped everything over the back of a living room armchair and walked barefoot across cool linoleum. The door to the master bedroom (grandiose term for a room roughly half the size of her girlhood refuge) was closed. She and Carl rarely closed it unless they needed privacy from the twins, but Carl sometimes shut it when the house was feeling drafty. She gripped the knob and turned it and pushed the door open. The room was pitch-black, the heavy curtains drawn. Her side of the bed was the near side, however, so she was confident of reaching it without tripping on anything.

She reached out in the blackness for the covers. But instead of the covers she clutched instead a woman's breast. Imogen jumped back with a gasp and knocked over a bedside lamp. It hit the floor, and a woman let out a cry.

"What—what's going on?" Carl's voice was thick as he fumbled for his own bedside lamp.

"Someone grabbed me! Charlotte, sweetheart, was that you?"

The light came on and Cynthia Bee covered her face with her hands. "Oh, dear God."

Carl, his face puffy with sleep, stared at his wife as if she were a horrific accident.

"Imogen. Imogen—what are you doing here?"

Imogen backed away from the bed until she bumped against the closet.

"I thought you were coming home tomorrow," Carl went on stupidly. "I got home late, and . . ."

In treating her patients, and especially in dealing with their families, Imogen had often heard people describe their emotional reactions to a life-changing moment—a murder, a suicide, a train wreck—moments of terrible shock, world-destroying heartbreak, catastrophes of fear or loss. Commonly they said things such as "my head was all in a whirl," "I was such a jumble of emotions," "I couldn't speak, I was in such a turmoil." She found that all of these were true.

Imogen the Observer hovered somewhere behind and above Imogen the woman, able to witness it all, to witness and take note of Carl's face, distorted with shock and shame, of Cynthia's mortified blush. Imogen the Observer could hear what they were saying (Cynthia: *I'm sorry, Imogen. I'm so sorry. You didn't deserve this.* Carl: *I think we'd best call a taxi for Cynthia. Maybe you could step out, Imogen, so she can get dressed*).

Imogen the Observer could even think of biting replies to their every word, could see the resemblances they all bore to figures out of drama, out of myth, and most of all out of farce. Didn't Charlie Chaplin have a scene somewhere where he wakes up beside some hulking slob, dreaming it's a beautiful woman? The mistaken identity, the slapstick crash of the lamp, the blinding revelation—all the stuff of comedy. How unjust that the deceived person must always look ridiculous, no matter how much his or her misery might be contrived by other persons.

Imogen the Observer could also note the similarity of her stunned present-day self to the twelve-year-old girl wobbling away on her bicycle down a leafy Chicago street having just discovered that while she had only one father, that father had a secret daughter.

Imogen the Observer noted all these things but Imogen the wife, the lover, and the mother had no words at all, and even if she had they could not have escaped her throat. This Imogen turned from the two people who had done this to her with a pang of envy. They did not feel as she did. They might feel embarrassment, perhaps even guilt, but they did not feel this infinity of emptiness.

As she left the room, she trailed a finger across the closet door, the bedroom wall, the bedroom door, and all along the wall of the corridor, like an invalid uncertain of her balance. She scooped up her clothes from the living room chair and carried them to the bathroom. There, an automaton engineered to carry out only the simplest motions, she dressed herself.

She closed the lid of the toilet and sat down, gripping her face in her hands and rocking back and forth in the manner of a chronic psychotic, and perhaps for the same reason: the body's effort to provide comfort to a tormented soul. Now her mind did begin to whirl. Black bolts of thought flashed and ricocheted across the confines of her skull. *Why did I get dressed just now? Is she gone? Why did Cynthia do this to me? Have I been hateful to her? To Carl? In* my *bed. With* my *children just across the hall. What was their plan for the morning? Good morning, children—I'm your mother's replacement. Why did I get dressed just now? Has she gone? I should get up, I should go to the living room, I should scream at them. Where can I sleep? I should go to a hotel. I'm exhausted, this is my house, why did I get dressed?*

A timid knocking rattled the bathroom door.

"Imogen? Imogen, I need the bathroom."

"Get out of my house, whore."

"What? I didn't hear you. I need the bathroom."

Imogen jumped up and opened the door.

"I said get out of my house, you whore."

"Imogen, I'm sorry—really, truly—but—"

"I trusted you with my children. My husband."

"I know. I'm sorry. But I need the bathroom."

"Frankly, I wouldn't care if you were bleeding to death."

She closed the door and locked it and sat back down, rocking and now weeping, rocking and weeping.

Then Carl's muffled voice. His "rational" voice. His words were indistinct, but the low register, the measured flow of the syllables was exactly the tone he adopted whenever he wanted to, as he put it, "talk sense." She heard the front door open, and close, and the house went quiet. Who can I run to? Imogen was thirty-one. Did thirty-one-year-old women run home with their broken hearts to their mothers? Their fathers? No doubt some did. No doubt some even found comfort there. But not from her mother. And certainly not from her father.

Voices again. Cynthia's. Carl's. And then the sound of a motor car driving away. The front door closed, and Carl's footsteps came down the hall.

"Imogen?"

"Go away."

"Imogen, I don't want to shout through the door—we'll wake up the children."

"Oh, yes. You're so concerned about the children." She stood up and opened the door. "Fucking your whore not ten feet away from where they sleep."

Carl's face registered shock at her choice of words. Imogen never used such words, even though he had often encouraged her to do so in bed. She pushed past him and went to the living room. She sat in the armchair that faced a small bookcase and the fireplace that did not work. On the mantel, the family portrait photograph made her stomach churn; it looked to her like a historical photograph, a picture of people from long ago—happy, by all appearances, but people she did not know.

"It's my fault," Carl said, coming into the room. He had got dressed too, she noticed, the two of them now in their armour. "There's no need to be harsh with Cynthia."

"Harsh. You think I'm harsh."

"Petty, then—about the bathroom. She had to go outside in the backyard."

"The poor creature. How tragic."

"Shall I make us some tea?"

"I don't feel like having tea with you for some reason."

Carl went down on one knee and reached for Imogen's hand. She snatched it away. He let out a sigh and got up and went over to the other armchair. They didn't have a sofa; the room was too small.

"I'm sorry, Imogen. I truly am. This was not a regular occurrence."

"I don't believe you. Inviting her into my bed? It implies a level of comfort and familiarity."

"It was not the first time, but it was not a regular occurrence, I swear. It was just—I had to work late, and she was looking after the twins, and I was so lonely without you."

"I am sleeping in the criminal wing of a lunatic asylum and *you're* lonely."

"All right, all right, I know. It's my fault and I'm sorry. Truly, Imogen. I never wanted to hurt you."

"That can't possibly be true. The first time we're apart for more than a day or two you have sex with someone in our bed—a student, for God's sake. How was that not supposed to hurt me?"

"I wasn't thinking, Imogen. I'm so sorry."

Imogen got up and picked up her case.

"I'm never sleeping in that bed again—in fact, you can burn it. I'll sleep with the twins for now."

"Don't do that, sweetheart. I'll change the sheets."

Imogen went to the bathroom and took her nightgown from the hook and slung it over her arm. She went to the children's room and once more got undressed. As Imogen climbed into the narrow bed, Charlotte groaned and curled up in a tighter ball.

✳

Carl slipped out early in the morning, before anyone was up. Imogen, stunned and numb, made the twins' breakfast and walked them to kindergarten where Myra would pick them up later. By nine-thirty she was in Ganz's office, bringing him up to date on her progress at Trenton. Dr. Ganz sat behind his desk with his chair at an angle to her, apparently having learned over the years that his gaze was unnerving even when he didn't intend it to be. But his posture, and his intermittent murmurs of approval or annoyance (Imogen had long ago learned to distinguish one from the other), indicated serious attention.

"But how disgraceful," he said, looking up at the ceiling. "If you cannot trust Trenton staff to follow up with in-home visits, what will you do? Some of the former patients must live quite far afield, no?"

"They do. I'll have to purchase an automobile. It will be less expensive than renting, in these circumstances."

She could hear the dryness in her throat. Anguish, already high, was rising in her chest.

Ganz looked at her with concern.

"Still. A considerable expense."

"Fords have come way down in the past year or so. And you can purchase on time, which should make it manageable, if not ideal."

A thin vibrato had set up on the edges of her voice, the sound of barely controlled panic. She could feel her mouth moving and her hands gesturing, but they seemed disconnected from her. She was talking of Mrs. Boxer and the files, of Trenton and motor cars, but all she could see in her mind's eye were the flashing bodies of Carl and Cynthia—kissing, hugging, licking, sucking—her husband and his student engaged in the sweet, shivery things she had thought were for her and Carl only. Overnight, she had been transformed into one of his little white rats, pink paws frantic as it swims for its life.

"Dr. Lang? Imogen?"

"Sorry," she said. "What were you saying?"

"You're very pale. Are you feeling all right?"

"I didn't sleep well last night. The train, you know . . ."

She hadn't slept at all. She lay curled beside Charlotte with her back to the door, tensed for the sound of it opening and Carl coming in. He did not come, but her eyes remained open, staring into her daughter's curls that smelled of shampoo. She could not imagine ever sleeping again, not in this agony. She pressed a palm to her chest. Amazing that there was no blood, no physical evidence.

She draped an arm over Charlotte's hip, and tried to be calmed by the world-filling love she felt for this person so miniature and flawless and yet the product of so disastrous a union. For she had no doubt now that her marriage to Carl was a catastrophe on the same level as her discovery of her father's duplicity. As she lay there listening to her child's oblivious breathing, possible futures unreeled before her. She could leave Carl—God knows, it was certainly her immediate impulse—but it would mean penury, ignominy, failure; a divorced woman was a pathetic woman. And to take the twins away from the man they adored, to destroy their faith in the world at such a tender age, no matter how misplaced that faith might be? Unthinkable.

The brightest future she could imagine was one in which Carl merely pretended to love and to care and she merely pretended to forgive and forget. They would become two actors endlessly acting, two puppeteers never allowed to address each other directly. Not only would their true selves never connect, they would never again be unified, integrated persons within themselves.

Hours passed and the twins' room slowly began to lighten. The covers, the bedposts, her children's sleeping forms gradually took on shape and colour. Charlotte, without waking, stirred and turned over, draping a hot arm across Imogen's waist. Five-fifteen. Five-thirty. She tensed at the sounds of Carl getting up and leaving the apartment. Soon the children would wake, and the entire day would scratch and scrape at nerves already raw from sleeplessness and humiliation. And that would be Day One.

She would go along with it; Imogen knew herself well enough to know that. She would go along with it for the children's sake. She would accept that hers would be a life in which happiness played no part.

"Mumma!"

Charlotte's wide blue eyes took in her mother with wonder, and so the charade began.

But what was Dr. Ganz saying to her? *Are you feeling all right?*

Imogen opened her mouth to speak, although she had no idea what she was about to say. What emerged was scarcely a word at all. Her throat opened to say the word "I," which until this day, this moment, had been an unproblematic word. But now, in this world of falsehood, there was no longer an I. The person whose talents and weaknesses and history had formed a coherent enough whole to merit the first person singular was now no longer "singular" but in pieces.

Her throat emitted a sound like a hiccup. She tried again to speak but some muscle round about the diaphragm let go and she collapsed forward in convulsions of grief.

Dr. Ganz was taken aback. Over her wails, she heard him approaching from around his desk.

"My goodness," he said, "my poor girl. Whatever is it? What has got you in such a state?"

At that moment, even with mortar shells of misery bursting inside her, Imogen loved him. She heard in his words and his worry that he was not being the psychiatrist at this moment, he was being the fatherly, even motherly, person he was behind the Swiss correctness and the ice-chip eyes. He came near enough that she could smell his signature cigar-and-bay-rum scent. She felt the lightest touch on her shoulder, a butterfly alighting for a moment, then nothing. His instinct had been to physically comfort her, but no doubt remembering himself he stepped back.

He let her cry—neither of them had any choice about that. Eventually the torrent of tears began to subside and Imogen accepted, yet again, the crisply pressed white handkerchief he waggled before her tear-blinded eyes.

"Well, well," he said. "A good ventilation, I would say. Clearly you were in need of it."

Imogen blew her nose and wiped her eyes. "Dear God."

"It grieves me to see you in such pain, Imogen. We've known each other a long time. You arrived when I was still quite new at this job, the Phipps was still new, and you were the girl with three brains—you remember?"

His gentleness alone would have been enough to bring on fresh tears, but it was his use of her first name—and that "girl"—that pricked her heart afresh. She wept a little longer.

"Dear God," she said again.

Dr. Ganz went to his office door and told Mr. Penn to cancel something or other. He went back around his desk and seated himself at his former angle.

"By all means tell me if I'm wrong, but I think these tears have not much to do with Trenton State Hospital. Only love could be the cause of such pain. Perhaps only a husband."

"A husband who—" Her voice caught once more but she took a moment to steel herself. Dr. Ganz waited. "A husband who hates me."

"*Hate* is a strong word."

"It's quite true. Although I'm not sure Carl knows it himself."

"Interesting." Dr. Ganz, making the transition back to psychiatrist, though not, bless him, to employer, lifted the lid from his desktop humidor and extracted a cigar.

"One of the hazards of our profession," he went on, "is a tendency to over-interpret the ordinary ups and downs of life. I'm sure you know."

"Yes. I do know."

"Mm. And knowing this, why do you say he *hates* you, and not choose some other, less extreme, word?"

"You mean like *indifference*? Unfortunately, when you are a rat in a swimming jar it makes no difference if the man who put you there hates you or is indifferent."

"Mm. Please don't feel compelled, but you know you can rely on my absolute discretion, and I would like to help any way I can. Would you care to tell me what has happened that has made an attractive young woman, a brilliant physician and loving mother, feel like a rat in a swimming jar?"

# 16

The waiter, clad in the French manner in black and white, came and took their order—quiche Lorraine for Quentin, sole meunière for his editor, Griffin Burke—and went away again. Griffin talked on as Quentin looked around at the decor of Le Papillon. The mauve banquettes, the etched glass and potted plants, managed to look quite French but the patron, a shy man named Nick (much hounded by his fearsome wife, Alex), was decidedly Greek. Le Papillon had the virtue of being both moderately priced and located just a few yards along 48th Street from Essex Taylor Bradkin, where Griffin plied his inky trade.

"What are you working on these days?" Griffin asked at last. He always asked it lightly, as if the answer were of no consequence, but the question filled Quentin's heart with trepidation. It was impossible to summarize a work in progress without feeling one's genitals shrivel.

"I'm not sure. It'll be something totally different, I know that much."

"Not an obsessive love story?"

Quentin shook his head.

"People seem to like 'em, Quentin. Oh—reminds me." Griffin opened his briefcase and pulled out a plump manila envelope. He handed it across the table. "Your fans."

"Not always. Some of them want to tell me a thing or two."

"Oh, everyone hears from the loonies."

Quentin put the envelope on the banquette beside him. The waiter came with their meals, and asked if he could bring them anything else.

Griffin inhaled the aroma of his sole meunière with a theatrical toss of the head. "Dear me, I could use a glass of Meurseult with this. A bottle, in fact."

"I know, *monsieur*. The law is a great pity. *Bon appétit*, gentlemen."

"Why can't we be civilized like other countries?"

"Which countries would those be?" Quentin asked.

They ate in silence for a while. The food was far better than anything he'd ever eaten in Lake Placid, and he enjoyed spending time with his editor, feeling himself part of an industry, a literary community. When Griffin asked him how life was treating him upstate Quentin surprised himself by saying, "Actually, I've been thinking about moving to Manhattan."

"That would be swell if you did. I could introduce you to all sorts of people, and it would make our work together a bit easier."

"I think I'm ready for a bit more company these days."

"Let me know if I can do anything to help—you know, keep an eye out for an apartment or whatever."

Having stalled a little, Quentin now allowed the talk to move on to possible follow-ups to his last novel.

"What about a war story?" Griffin said. "Been some decent efforts lately, but I think you could really knock one out of the park. You could write it under your own name, maybe."

"That's the last thing I want to write about."

"Of course. Sorry—I'm sure it was terrible."

"No one would believe it, if I wrote the truth."

He heard the tremor in his own voice and knew that Griffin heard it too; he certainly changed the subject fast enough.

"I've become fascinated the past few years with psychoanalysis," Griffin said. "I tried to talk Brett Essex into grabbing translation rights to Sigmund Freud but he hemmed and hawed and Boni and Liveright snatched them up. I got on to it a couple of years ago. Friend of mine had a nervous breakdown. Fellow who works in a difficult field—a sensitive, cultured man with a beautiful English accent.

Suddenly couldn't face people, couldn't do his work, couldn't do anything but roll on the floor and cry."

Griffin hesitated, took a drink from his water glass, and set it back
down, then dabbed at his mouth with his napkin.

Quentin knew his editor was trying to be discreet, but he also knew
he was talking about another writer. He could even guess which one,
English accent and all.

"Anyway, somehow he ended up in the Phipps Clinic in Baltimore—
have you heard of it?"

Quentin kept his face neutral. "Yes, I believe I have heard something."

"Part of Johns Hopkins."

"Yes, sure. Supposed to be a good place."

"I was impressed, I can tell you. Nothing at all like you hear about
the state asylums. More like an expensive hotel crossed with a college. So I visit my friend and we sit outside in this courtyard they
have—charming little place with cloisters, fountain, birds . . . the
whole deal. Most intriguing of all, at least to this old fogey, his psychiatrist was a woman."

"Really. Who was that?"

"Aha! Now his ears perk up! She was a delightful person, very infor-
mal. Smart as a whip. And pretty?"

"What was her name?"

"My, my, you are interested, aren't you? She had an unusual name—
Donna Artemis. Isn't that lovely? Dr. Donna Artemis. I gather she
did fine work with my friend. He saw her in private practice after he
was discharged. Still does." Griffin leaned across the table and adopted
a confidential tone. "Tell you the truth, I wouldn't be surprised if he's
in love with her. And he got so excited about psychoanalysis, he got
me excited about it. Have you read any?"

"Not a word. Not interested."

"You're not fascinated by the idea of the unconscious?"

"Only in the sense of hidden motives—hidden even to the person they're motivating. The last thing I want is someone else's idea of how people work."

"Mm, yes. I suppose I can see that."

"Sorry. I didn't mean to sound so pompous. I'd probably enjoy reading Freud—but he'd kill me as a novelist."

"Oh, well. Just an idea."

Quentin sat back and took a sip of his water. "The place, though. That's a different story. The place is definitely interesting."

So interesting that it was only a matter of days—well, a little less than two weeks—before he found himself in Baltimore, a city he had previously given no thought to visiting. He told himself he was there because he was embarking on a new kind of writing—more texture, more context, more rooted in the here and now—that called for a new way of working. Which was why he had come to Baltimore and the Emerson Hotel.

On the train he had begun jotting notes for his story. *Young man in love with his psychiatrist—she doesn't know—believes it's just part of the "treatment"—he remains unshakable—whole effort not to be cured but to win her love.* Such a storyline was completely in keeping with the novels he had already published, stamped with his signature combination of obsession and misunderstanding, "leavened," as one critic had put it, "with near-suicidal loneliness."

Quentin didn't think his books were that sad. Certainly the readers who wrote the letters Griffin had given him did not think so. Most of them were young men who seemed profoundly relieved that there was "someone out there who knows what it's like." Quentin was grateful to them for buying and reading his books, but it was really his pseudonym they were writing to, and he restricted his replies to postcards.

When he got to the hotel, he unpacked his suitcase and laid out his shaving kit in the bathroom. He had every intention of just going for a walk—a constitutional to stretch his legs after the long train trip, nothing more. He would not try to see Imogen, or to contact her in any way. He went back downstairs to the lobby and asked the uniformed desk clerk to secure him a telephone line. The clerk picked up his own phone, spoke into it briefly, and said, "Number four, sir," pointing to a row of wooden booths.

Quentin entered, shut the folding door, and sat down. He picked up the receiver and a woman said, "Number, please."

"I don't have the number. It's the Phipps Psychiatric Clinic on North Wolfe Street."

"Just a moment, sir. I'll connect you."

He wondered how many operators had listened in on tales of madness and catastrophe, or overheard the ravings of psychotics.

"Phipps Clinic."

Quentin had prepared for this. "Good afternoon. I'm addressing correspondence and I just need to know if I have the details correct for Dr. Imogen Lang. She is in fact a physician at the clinic?"

"That's correct, sir."

"Six hundred . . ."

"Six hundred North Wolfe Street, Baltimore, Maryland."

"And would she be in today?"

"No. Dr. Lang is only here on Thursday and Friday."

It was Tuesday; there would be no risk of bumping into her. He left the hotel and walked out into the late afternoon sun. The streets were thronged with people heading home from work. He didn't mind; it was all research. Many of the workers were women. They waited at the corners for their streetcars, many clutching novels or magazines, oblivious to the swirling crowds as only those who face them every day can be. When the streetcars arrived, the Negroes entered by the middle doors, white people by the front. There were many streetcars, but also more horses than in New York or Chicago. Crossing the avenues Quentin had to watch where he stepped.

Eventually he took a smaller street to get out of the crowds. It did not look a particularly prosperous street, and yet it was lined with stately, if compact, townhouses. And even though it was October the southern air was fragrant with flowers. The breeze from the harbour was cool, damp, benign. A cheerful atmosphere, all in all, and he was happy for Imogen, that she had lived so long in so pleasant a city.

He took a zigzag route toward the Phipps and did not even have to consult his hotel map, having memorized the location without trying. He wanted to see the building where his slowly germinating novel might be set.

The neighbourhoods became less cheerful the closer he got. The apartment buildings went from modern to weathered, then to dingy, and the homes turned into rooming houses. Here the coloured people far outnumbered the white, and he wondered for a moment if he had not taken a wrong turn. But no, North Wolfe Street was just ahead. As soon as he saw the sign a tremor started up in his injured leg.

The Phipps was a handsome building of red brick that matched the other Johns Hopkins buildings in that respect, if not in style. Over the portico, in incised letters: The Henry Phipps Psychiatric Clinic 1912. The place would have still shone with newness when Imogen had arrived in 1916.

1912. It seemed a lifetime away. Any time before the war now seemed antiquity, back before human beings knew the true depths of stupidity they could plumb, before they knew that boys could be ordered into the fire of a hundred machine guns. What different people we were back then, Quentin thought—what a different person I was, marching off to war with the stupid idea of killing myself by proxy.

And then, witnessing blood and death up close, he had come to love life. All the soldiers did. They had all come to adore the animals that withstood the man-made hell, the birds blackened with smoke and soot hopping along the parapet, the solitary green shoots that sprouted in the blood-soaked mud of no man's land. It was for this reason they had adored Gerhard Goetheimer and all the squirrels, lambs, and dogs that became battalion mascots. They adored their luck. Gerhard's luck had ultimately run out at Avesnes. A letter from his lieutenant had informed him the goat had been killed by a whiz-bang.

Two women emerged from the front door of the Phipps and broke Quentin's reverie. Thrown into momentary confusion, he backed away.

"Were you looking for the dispensary?" one of them asked. She had a hard face but her voice was kind.

"Well, um. I don't have an appointment."

"That's all right. If you need to see someone just go inside and take the stairs on the left down one flight."

"Thank you."

He tipped his hat to them and started up the stairs. He had not intended to go inside but now he felt compelled by social convention.

The interior of the building impressed, as it was meant to, but he was more excited by the knowledge that Imogen had walked these marble halls for years, and still did. He went downstairs as instructed and entered through a door marked Out-Patients' Waiting Area. It was an oddly shaped room of many benches, only a couple of which were occupied at the moment: one by a ragged-looking woman in the care of a policeman, another by a child who was kneeling on the bench and rocking violently, obsessively, back and forth beside his pale, thin mother on whom exhaustion hung like a shroud.

Quentin sat on a bench toward the back and wondered how many thousands of patients had passed through here. The air smelled pleasantly antiseptic, but he had a sense that there yet lingered in the atmosphere coils of paranoia, strands of delusion, not to mention the boundless sorrows of the suicidal. How odd to think that he had once numbered himself among them. Who would have prescribed the trenches as a cure?


Quentin left the clinic through the dispensary's side door and went back to his hotel. That glimpse of the waiting room had whetted his appetite for detail. He would have to know how the Phipps Clinic worked on a day-to-day basis. He wanted to inhale the place, memorize it, make it his own.

Next morning he called and asked to be put through to Dr. Artemis. He was informed that Donna Artemis no longer worked there, and all inquiries from the public would have to be directed to the office of Jonas Ganz—would he like to be connected?

As Jeremy West, he wrote a letter on hotel stationery, explaining that he was writing a novel set in a fictional clinic not unlike the Phipps and wondered if a brief tour might be arranged. He sent the letter by messenger and was surprised when Dr. Ganz responded that very afternoon in the affirmative. He would conduct the tour himself, provided Mr. West could be at his office at noon sharp the next day. After that, he would be out of town.

Quentin showed up at the appointed hour and thanked Dr. Ganz for agreeing to his request. "I was frankly surprised, sir. I expected to be flatly rejected."

"Another novelist might have been, but as it happens I have read two of your books and found them most interesting and entertaining."

"I would have thought—as a man of science and the overseer of a complex institution—you wouldn't have time for any fiction, let alone mine."

"No, I am fascinated by fiction, as I am by all works of the imagination. Novelists, and of course the great poets, spend as much time thinking about human psychology as we do. Your books, in particular, interest me on that score. I have nowhere encountered a better rendering of states of obsession, depression, and even mania."

"Dear me. That doesn't sound very entertaining."

"Immensely entertaining. Immensely. Now we haven't much time so let's get to it, shall we?"

They left Ganz's office, turned left in the marble hall and left again immediately after.

"Our library," Ganz said. "We are quite up to date with all the latest books and journals."

"What a beautiful room. Makes me want to sit right down and study." The expansive windows, the angled spokes of shelves, and the heavy oak tables made for an inviting atmosphere of learning and contemplation. Quentin had a vision of Imogen seated in the window light, head bent over a book, making careful notes. How many times had he seen her in just that pose back in their student days in Chicago.

"We encourage staff to contribute to the journals, although lately so many of them seem to want to write books and not articles. I am envious of your own productivity."

"Oh well, you know, novels. Novelists don't actually have to *know* anything." He did not really believe this; he was just trying to prolong his reverie by being agreeable.

"But novelists have to *observe*, Mr. West, you have to be constantly observing both the inner and the outer man, whether you're aware of it at the time or not. You're collecting facts, facts, facts, and then you make of them what you will."

Ganz led him back along the corridor toward the lecture room, talking animatedly about the lecture series he had inaugurated, but Quentin was only half-listening. He was picturing Imogen seated in the audience, taking notes. She would be happy, doing that.

They left the lecture hall and Ganz produced a set of keys and attacked a massive oak door with them.

"The reason I asked you to come at noon is because the patients will all be taking their meal upstairs. Patient confidentiality, you know."

"Yes, I understand completely."

"This is the men's semi-quiet ward. All the wards are pretty much alike, eight patients to a ward."

Ganz spoke briefly to a woman in an office on the right, nodded to a maintenance man carrying a tool kit, then they were in the ward itself. Quentin let out a bark of laughter.

"Something amusing?"

"It's so lovely! It couldn't be more different from the last hospital I was in. Woodcote, it was called."

"Woodcote? I don't believe I—"

"It was in Epsom. After the war. A lot of tin huts rattling in the English rain."

"The war, of course. I noticed you were limping. I hope they treated you with the honour and dignity you deserve."

Quentin went quiet. He had slipped out of character; Jeremy West had not fought in the war. In the secret biography he had given his pseudonym, he had been ruled "psychologically unfit" for active duty. Neurasthenia. It was only by thus surgically removing the war from his authorial memory that he was able to write at all. Quentin Goodchild, at least as far as literature was concerned, had been rendered mute by the war. He did not like to deceive this curious and engaging man who had employed Imogen for nearly a decade, but the deception was small—he was, after all, the real "Jeremy West."

"Forgive me," Ganz said. "I didn't mean to pry."

"Not at all. Is that a porch I see beyond the far door?"

"It is. I insisted our patients have ready access to the outdoors—within the bounds of safety, of course."

They pushed through the door and stood overlooking a garden with a terrace, a pond, an elegant cloister. Quentin imagined Imogen down there, dressed in her hospital whites. She could never resist a garden. They went back inside through the dayroom, left the ward, and went upstairs to the next floor.

"Our histological lab. Pity Dr. Lang is not in today—she'd be able to tell you what precisely she's working on."

Hearing her name caused Quentin to stammer so that Dr. Ganz looked at him quizzically.

"Sorry," Quentin managed. "I'm a little confused. In my preliminary inquiries I understood Dr. Lang was a psychiatrist, dealing with patients."

"At the Phipps we practise psychobiology, so it's not uncommon for a psychiatrist here to do lab work in addition to treating patients.

Dr. Lang is also in charge of the laboratory, supervising medical students and so on."

"Psychobiology?"

The single word launched Ganz into a lengthy and enthusiastic explanation, as Quentin knew it would. It gave him time to take in Imogen's domain. Here was where she had spent countless hours and days. Among these beakers and tubes, these microscopes and slides, she would have been happy or sad, fretful or angry. How many times would she have stood right here, in this spot where he was standing, and turned to look out this very window at that very elm—budding in spring, bare in winter—thinking about her life, her future, and perhaps every now and again sparing a thought for the young man who had loved her—or boy, rather—the boy he had been before the war.

"Can you give me some idea of what the current work is? Here in the lab, I mean? I need a few specifics for my novel."

"Of course. Here's her lab book."

It was a hardcover notebook, spread open on a tabletop lectern affair for ease of writing while standing. The pages on both sides were held open by clips. Dr. Ganz unclipped the left side and leafed back a few pages. Quentin's pulse quickened at the sight of Imogen's handwriting.

"Yes," Ganz said. "She's working here on possible links of stroke to mania."

"May I see? Just to see what the notes look like?"

"Of course."

Dr. Ganz stepped smartly aside, and Quentin placed his hands on Imogen's book. He turned the pages slowly, scanning them, picking out a word here, a phrase there. *Hemorrhages. Hemoglobin. Spontaneous.* He let his fingers trail lightly over the writing. I am a ghost, he thought, haunting her world.

"I think perhaps you are allergic to something in this lab, Mr. West. Your face has gone very red."

"Yes," Quentin said. "Horribly allergic."

"Come. Let me show you our hydrotherapy facilities and a few other things and then I have a luncheon appointment with a colleague."

The next day, Quentin went to 800 North Broadway to meet with Dr. Donna Artemis. She was not at all what he had expected from her formidable name. Petite, boyish, even elfin in appearance, she engaged him with a directness he found unnerving.

"Mr. West, you have forty-five minutes," she told him, checking her watch. "What do you want to know?"

She plunked herself down in an armchair, slipped off her shoes, and drew her feet up, folding them under her to one side so that the pale toes peeked out beneath the hem of her skirt.

"I need to know basic things. Nuts and bolts about the daily life of psychiatric residents at the Phipps."

"Why come to me? Why not speak to people who actually work there?"

"I've already met with Dr. Ganz, who was kind enough to give me a Cook's tour. But I thought someone no longer employed there might feel free to be candid."

"Why would you think that? There's nothing secret about the place." She waved her hand against her own objection. "Oh, never mind. Just go ahead."

He asked her about her background and that of her colleagues. He asked about the hierarchy, and about Dr. Ganz himself—what was he like to work for?

Dr. Artemis never took her eyes off him. All through the interview she watched him like a cat. He sensed himself being evaluated and found wanting. It seemed probable she had read one of his books and despised it.

"In the short term, on a day-to-day basis, Jonas Ganz is a dream to work with, a perfect dream—kind, thoughtful, knowledgeable, et cetera."

"And in the long term?"

Her eyes held him. Judging.

He didn't expect her to answer. Ganz was the most powerful psychiatrist in the country; she wouldn't risk saying anything negative. But she surprised him.

"Impossible. His insistence on gathering facts—endless facts, facts, facts—gets in the way of diagnosis and treatment. As does his delaying of diagnosis itself. And if you ever figure out what his position is on psychoanalysis, do let me know, won't you? Because nobody else has. One day he's all for it—he's an absolute Freudian. Next day he decides the unconscious is not nearly so interesting as the pattern of the carpeting in the patient's living room."

Dr. Artemis was apparently a woman wedded to candour. In answer to his questions she went on to tell him why she had left the Phipps, and what her own thoughts were on psychoanalysis. Quentin asked her if she liked being an analyst, and what it was like, emotionally.

"Lonely." Those eyes. Holding him, daring him to doubt.

"Lonely? But you're in a room with patients all day."

"Exactly. It's lonely."

"Please elaborate."

"Hah! Psychiatrists say that forty or fifty times a day. 'Please elaborate.'" She lit a cigarette and exhaled a column of smoke that she scanned, chin uptilted. "Patient and analyst are embarked on two different quests: the patient seeking the relief of pain, the analyst inflicting more of it through the process of transference."

She explained the term quickly, impatiently, tapping her cigarette with a trim forefinger. "Forget analysis. They don't practise analysis at the Phipps. You said you wanted nuts-and-bolts stuff."

"Tell me about living arrangements. Did you have your own room?"

"My own room, yes. But I shared a bathroom and entrance with another resident."

"Did that cause problems?"

"Not for me. I was lucky. I shared with a lovely woman—a complete darling—very earnest and serious and studious, but also with a good sense of humour. That's important, because the patients could be upsetting, and relations with senior staff could be frustrating, to say the least.

"We studied together, the two of us, trying to learn German. Commiserated, giggled, you know. And she was wonderful with the patients—particularly the depressives."

"How so?"

"Well, aside from being sensitive, intuitive, she was something of a depressive herself. Not a depressive, just sad. She'd had an unfortunate romance with a young man. It hadn't ended well, and when he joined up with the Canadian forces to go to war she felt she had driven him to it—to a kind of suicide. Silly girl."

She stubbed out her cigarette and turned away from him toward the window.

Quentin had expected Donna Artemis to be acquainted with Imogen, but nothing like this. He wanted to hear more without appearing too interested.

"In a situation like that—you're both young, away from home . . ."

"Oh, *far* away. And not just geographically. We both had terrible families."

"Don't misunderstand me, but you don't seem like one's picture of a psychoanalyst."

"What's that supposed to mean—Viennese? Bearded?"

"I'd pictured stern. Guarded."

"Perhaps you were expecting wisdom, and you're disappointed."

"No, I didn't mean that."

"I should hope not."

Quentin smiled. This woman would have made him nervous even if she hadn't mentioned Imogen.

"Since I'm not psychoanalyzing you," she went on, "I don't have to play the sphinx and sit here saying nothing about myself. You're asking me questions and I'm answering them, so the professional reserve you're talking about is out the window. In any case, if you were expecting wisdom you won't get it from psychoanalysts. It's a very good trick, this job, because the patient is the one doing all the work. We're just catalysts."

"To go back to your shared digs, if I may. In that situation, did you use your new-found skills, your training, to understand each other? To help?"

"I don't know how much help it was. You can't dispense psychotherapy like a cough drop. But yes, we analyzed each other in a playful way. Mostly we were just a shoulder to cry on. Not that Imogen was prone to tears." Her hand flew to her mouth and covered it. "I shouldn't have said her name."

"It's all right. I'm not planning to do portraits." Oh, the sweet ache of hearing Imogen's name from someone else's lips.

"We were like sisters. Unique, in that respect. The other residents weren't close. But we commiserated with each other, you know. She could calm me down when I got too worked up about things. And I cheered her up now and again. She was devastated when she found out her soldier friend had been killed. Absolutely devastated."

Quentin nearly cried out. *Killed? She thinks I'm dead?* Somehow he managed to deliver his next question with no wild display of emotion. "Do you still see her?"

"Not as often as I'd like to. She got married, and I went into private practice so . . ."


All the rest of that afternoon, Quentin wandered around in a peculiar, disembodied state. Even before learning that Imogen believed him dead he had been feeling like a ghost. But the words of Donna Artemis had left him hollow and drifting, a scrap of paper batted about by the lightest breeze. He walked the avenues of this strange city, neither knowing nor caring where he was headed. He was dimly aware when the streets filled up with secretaries and executives leaving offices, workers leaving factories. His feet took him through areas where everyone was coloured, and through others where no one was, through residential neighbourhoods and business districts and eventually down to the harbour.

The chill damp air of the waterfront brought him back to himself a little, as did the intense odours of water, fish, and creosote. He sat on a bollard and watched a pair of tugs guiding a rusty freighter away from the wharf. Slowly the numbness wore off. He looked at his hands, pale and stippled by the cool of November. Imogen believed him dead. Imogen was married. He had not had the presence of mind to ask Dr. Artemis what year she had received this "news," or how she was informed. And by whom? Not being next of kin, she would not have received official notification. And although there had been thousands of mix-ups concerning the dead and missing, his father had never been misinformed. But what could any of it possibly matter? What did it matter that Dr. Imogen Lang of the Henry Phipps Psychiatric Clinic was married, or that someone she used to know, a long, long time ago, was dead?

# 17

Dr. Ganz was shocked at Carl's behaviour—shocked first of all because he found it morally repugnant, but also because, as he put it, "He has hurt you, and I cannot conceive of a person less deserving of such treatment." He was disappointed, even bitter, that Carl, whom he clearly saw as a shining star in the Phipps firmament, could bring such dishonour to his institution.

"You will be thinking of your children above all," he said, "but as your employer and—I hope you see me this way—as your mentor, I must warn you that, however much marriage may have put a strain on your career, divorce would be far worse. People—that is, not just patients but medical boards—prize stability and dependability above all else, especially in psychiatrists. Otherwise I would insist that Mr. Kromer find work elsewhere."

"I'm not contemplating divorce," Imogen said. "I couldn't do that to the children."

But she also knew her own limits, and knew that she would not be able to continue as Carl's wife as long as the treacherous Cynthia Bee was beside him in the lab. Carl had promised to get rid of her as soon as possible.

Over Thursday and Friday, Imogen went through the motions of her normal routine, although she slept in the children's room, much to their noisy delight. She found it impossible to get back into her lab work, knowing that Cynthia was in the building. She imagined the lovers' tearful goodbye, the hugs and kisses perhaps leading to more. But no, Carl came home on the Friday night and told her that

Cynthia would be transferring to Columbia. "She won't lose her semester," he added, as if Cynthia's academic success were paramount in Imogen's mind.

The worst was Saturday. Normally the weekly outing to the market was one of her favourite activities. Sharing it with her husband, selecting fruits and vegetables from the sellers, listening to the children's chatter, grounded her. But Carl did not come along this time, and the vendors who smiled at the twins seemed engaged in premeditated mockery. Look at the lovely young family, *haw, haw, haw.*

Cynthia was gone, and now all that remained was for Imogen to get over her heartbreak and carry on. The current wisdom suggested this was simply a matter of accepting reality, as if accepting reality were easy. How do you accept that your husband holds you in contempt? That the person you'd most trusted has betrayed you? That everything you'd thought was real was an illusion? She yearned for a woman to talk to, but her mother would just write back that that's the way men are, dear, and Donna—Donna did not seem to even understand marriage, or at least to feel any need for it, being content to live through a series of affairs. In any case, she had never really taken to Carl.


On the train to Trenton that Sunday, Imogen examined all the ads in the paper, and on Monday visited a Trenton dealership to buy a Ford automobile. The salesman "threw in" four free driving lessons, and Imogen rapidly overcame her fears—so much so that her instructor soon lost his own courage and had to beg her to ease off the gas pedal. Imogen didn't bother to clear the expenditure with Carl; she just went ahead and bought the thing which, all-in, would cost no more than five dollars a month plus gas and oil.

The salesman had made much of "the thrill of the open road," and on this score the car absolutely delivered. A sense of invincibility took hold of Imogen behind the wheel and she looked forward to her time in the car, often rolling down the front windows despite the chilly breezes. She went shooting across the New Jersey landscape, winding her way through the splendid hills, scooting past little towns, geometric fields, and indigo lakes. The car whisked her up the hills and down with an effortless sense of flight. She flashed along the smaller roads, taking curves and straightaways through alleys of magnificent maples. She soon considered the horse-drawn conveyances that forced her to slow down vexatious in the extreme.

Imogen had two former Trenton patients to see in or near Rahway, and had to stop at a gas station for directions. Winifred Dawes, forty-two, a former schoolteacher, now a sales clerk in a local Woolworth's. Admitted to Trenton State Hospital in 1920 for severe depression, she had had four infected molars removed and, after a stay of two months, was discharged as "cured." She'd had previous admissions for bouts of mania, and her hospitalizations at those times had lasted three and four months. Given her history, Imogen had to wonder why the admitting diagnosis had not been manic-depression, a cyclic pathology that goes, intermittently, into spontaneous remission.

By prior arrangement, Imogen met Miss Dawes at her apartment on her day off, which was Monday. The place was neat and clean, almost antiseptically so, as was Miss Dawes herself. No, she said, she'd had no trouble since her discharge from Trenton. She had found work—to be sure not work as rewarding as teaching six-year-olds to read, but paid work nonetheless. It suited her, and was far less likely than teaching to aggravate her "nervous" condition, as she called it. This was the longest she'd ever gone without going back to hospital, and she had to credit Dr. Bingham for that. She had never lasted more than eighteen months in the past, and now it had been five years. Who would have thought a few teeth could cause so much trouble? Certainly all her previous doctors had missed it. Imogen stayed long enough to satisfy herself that Miss Dawes was healthy and then moved on.

Her next stop was a small house perilously close to the railway tracks. Although old and in need of repairs, its yard was neatly trimmed and bordered with well-chosen plantings. Beside the front door was a polished cedar plank inscribed with the words "God bless our home."

The door was answered by Mrs. Doris Trout, who was fiftyish and so diminutive as to barely reach Imogen's elbows. But her wide brow, prominent cheekbones, and strong nose looked as if they had been carved out of wood.

The Trouts did not have a telephone, and Imogen had to apologize for arriving unannounced and explain why she was there. "Is Ronnie at home?"

"Yes, Ronnie's here. He's in his room, where he always is. You'd better come in."

"Your husband's at work?"

"Yes, at the train yard."

The front door opened directly into the living room, which was furnished with cheap items variously patched and draped. Interspersed with these were more solid-looking side tables, a coffee table, and, beside the front door, a handsome box made of walnut.

"You said you wanted to ask me a few questions first?"

"Yes, that's right." Imogen already had her notebook and pen in hand. "I mostly need to know how—in your view—Ronnie's doing."

"Well, he's thirty-two and he can't get work, even though there's lots of jobs around, so that should tell you something."

"He's been home now for five years, is that correct?"

"That's right."

"And how was he when he first came home?"

"He still wasn't right—in the head, I mean. But much better than he was when he went in. He wasn't seeing and hearing things that aren't there, for one thing. He wasn't muttering to himself all the time. And he could manage a good night's sleep."

"But he was unable to find work?"

"Oh, he tried, he really did. He's very handy with tools and things. He made those tables," she said, pointing, "and that box over there for our scarves and mittens and so on. He's not a master carpenter, but quite capable of putting things together. He'd always worked before he went off."

"If he was so much better, why do you think he was unable to get work?"

"Because he's got no teeth, of course. They pulled 'em all out at Trenton, on account of they was all infected and causing his brain to go wrong. Well, people put two and two together, you know. They see a man of thirty with no teeth and they know where he's been, doesn't matter how sane he might look at the moment. Everyone knows they yank your teeth out at Trenton. So anybody's got no teeth they know right off."

"The records show he had extensive dental surgery."

"He's toothless. Completely toothless."

"Was he not fitted for dentures?"

"Hah. A full set of dentures? You know how much they cost? We haven't got that kind of money."

"How does he eat?"

"I chop everything up small. And give him lots of mashed potatoes and such. It's not his fault. People just see you got no teeth they think you're . . ." She made a circling gesture next to her temple.

"I see."

Mrs. Trout pulled a handkerchief from her sleeve and dabbed at her eyes.

"May I see him now?"

She nodded. "You'll have to visit in his room. He don't come out of there, not anymore. Except to use the bathroom. Hasn't set foot outside that room for months and months. You'll have to forgive the smell. It's hard to get him to bathe—well, he won't bathe—but most days I can get him to wash his face. The bathtub talks to him, see? The pipes, the drains."

Mrs. Trout led Imogen down a short dark hall. A stench of old sweat and filthy socks emanated from a room on the left. She rapped crisply on the door.

"Ronnie?"

"Come in!"

She opened the door, and the smell made Imogen gag.

"Ronnie, this is Dr. Lang. She's come all the way from Baltimore to see how you're doing."

He was standing about twelve inches from a wall that was covered, floor to ceiling, with handwriting, block printing, and strange symbols in many different shades of ink.

"Baltimore," he said, then muttered it several times. His speech was remarkably clear, considering his toothless state, but he didn't turn to look at Imogen, just kept staring at the wall.

"Thanks," Imogen said to Mrs. Trout. "I'll talk to him alone, if I may."

"Suit yourself," Mrs. Trout said, adding, "You'll be polite, won't you, Ronnie?" She withdrew, closing the door behind her.

"Hello, Ronnie. Is it all right if we talk for a while?"

"Talk away," he said, still without looking at her.

"Perhaps you could sit on the bed and I could sit on the chair."

"You can sit. I can't sit right now. You can sit."

He gripped a thick pencil in his right hand, squeezing it so that his knuckles whitened.

"Will you tell me what you're working on?"

"Yes. It's a reality map. Realities, I should say."

He flexed and unflexed the fingers gripping the pencil.

"Tell me more," Imogen said, looking at the wall. "That central circle, is that the earth?"

"Yes."

"And you have another circle around it."

"The reality that encloses our reality. The one we only sometimes see. When we're really happy. Or really sad. It can be happy or sad. It's weather. Well, not weather."

"And you have another line much higher."

"I'm not supposed to talk about that."

"Why not?"

"It's Ercaluit. It's where the Ercalui live. Well, not live. I'm not sure if it's a separate reality, or an element in this one. They're like fish in water there. I think it's a separate reality."

"What are they like?"

He gave a deep sigh, folded his arms across his chest, and bowed his head.

Imogen didn't want to lose him. "They make you sad?"

He nodded.

"Are they mean?"

He nodded again. "Beautiful. Imagine the most beautiful woman you have ever seen, the most beautiful angel. That's how beautiful they are. Just to see them is to want to be with them. But they're cruel as well. Beautiful and cruel. They invite me in and then tell me I'm not worthy. Of course, they're right. I'm not worthy."

"Not worthy?"

"They put it stronger than that—a lot stronger. If I told you what they say, it would burn your ears. I am filth to them."

As he talked more, the damage to his speech became more obvious. A prospective employer might easily mistake him for an imbecile.

"Why are you not worthy?"

"I can't talk about it." He shook his head and choked back a sob.

"All right. I notice you're not looking at me. Do you find it hard to face people?"

"Some people. Sometimes. I mean, I can look a little."

He jerked his head in her direction and looked away again. His face had the collapsed, elderly look of the patients Imogen had observed at Trenton.

"How was that?" Imogen asked. "Was that difficult?"

"I can't look at you. I can glimpse you but I can't look. I'm sorry."

"That's all right. Why can't you look? You can tell me, I won't be mad or upset."

"Your eyes would suck my soul out of my body." He said it simply, as if stating an allergy to pollen.

"Do a lot of people have that effect?"

"No. Some. I saw a wedding ring. You're a happy woman, I can tell."

So much for "the wisdom of the mad," Imogen thought. No one who actually knew any psychotics thought they had any special insight; mostly their preoccupations made them dumb as bricks.

"Your mother tells me, and I can't help but notice myself, Ronnie, that you refuse to bathe."

"The Ercalui scream at me if I try. They say I don't deserve to be clean. That I can't be clean. You can't clean shit, you know. You can clean shit *off* but you can't clean shit itself."

"Since you know they are cruel, Ronnie, do you think perhaps you could learn to disbelieve what they say?"

Ronnie did not respond, but reached up the wall and waved his hand from side to side. "Macrocosm. Up here? That's macrocosm." He glanced back over his shoulder at Imogen, then away. "You see? Macrocosm."

"All right."

"And down here . . ." He squatted and pointed to something written in tiny letters. "Microcosm."

"You feel that's significant?"

"Microcosm." He slapped the wall. "Microcosm."

"Do you think you'll be going outside anytime soon? Will you leave the house at all?"

He shook his head.

"You mean not anytime soon? Or never?"

"Can't. Can't."

"Why is that, Ronnie? Why can't you?"

"They scream at me. They tell me to do terrible things. Horrible things."

"And in this room they don't?"

"Not as loud. Not as often."

"What sorts of things do they tell you to do?"

Instead of answering, he stood up and started writing on the wall, squeezing letters between lines of larger words: *Earth, Fire, Universal Key*. Imogen got up from the chair, and he whirled around with a look of terror. He smelled awful—a mixture of death and charred meat.

"It's all right, Ronnie. I won't come any closer."

"No. Please." His eyes were shut tight.

"I'll leave you alone," Imogen said. "I don't want to upset you—I just came to see how you're doing. But I'd like to ask you just one more question, if I may."

He turned his back to her, and she could see him trembling from across the room.

"Will you think about the possibility of going back to a hospital?"

"Why? I'm all out of teeth."

"It wouldn't have to be Trenton, necessarily. There are other places you can go. Places where they don't pull teeth."

He inscribed a symbol at the exact height of his forehead—a circle enclosing a triangle, which in turn enclosed a minus sign.

"What does it mean?"

"It's Ercaluit."

"Will you tell me what it means?"

"Yes. It means . . ." He leaned close to the wall so that his nose was almost touching it. "It means—there's no one here."

"In this room, you mean?"

"No. No, it means there's no one *here*." He tapped the wall three times with his forehead. "In this *body*."

Imogen said goodbye to him then, apologizing for upsetting him and thanking him for his time. She told his mother before she left that Ronnie could well be a danger to himself and others, that he should be examined by an asylum psychiatrist.

"I seen him worse," Mrs. Trout said. "Way worse."

※

Over the next few weeks, Imogen crisscrossed the entire state of New Jersey. The first snow flurries twirled over small towns, cities, and villages that were little more than a general store and a couple of houses at a crossroads. She visited patients in Lumberville and Raven Rock, in Yardley and Clarksburg, in Nelsonville, Englishtown, and Freneau. She drove highways 1 and 2 and 13. She drove the Lee Highway, the Lincoln Highway, the Victory Highway, and the Lackawanna Trail. She drove south as far as beautiful Spring Lake, home of a chronic depressive who killed herself between the time Mrs. Boxer located her and the day Imogen managed to visit. She saw the not-so-beautiful Belmar and the gorgeous Jersey Shore and the thundering Atlantic on a stormy day that whipped up stormy emotions in the chambers of her heart. She drove upstate almost to the New York border and saw patients in Sussex and Vernon, Campgaw and Oak Ridge. And of course there were patients much closer to Trenton. In fact she discovered that, owing to lax record-keeping, four patients discharged as "cured" were actually inmates in the back wards of the hospital itself.

Every week she summarized her findings in brief patient reports and sent copies to Dr. Ganz and to Dr. Bingham's office, keeping the originals for herself. Dr. Ganz quickly realized the import of her research. "God in heaven," he said, "this is not what we'd hoped for at all. Not at all."

Dr. Bingham, however, seemed bizarrely oblivious of her findings, even happy with her work. He took a more friendly attitude toward her, greeting her in the hallways and every now and again stopping by her office for a quick word.

"Morning, Doctor. How is everything going?"

"Fine, Dr. Bingham."

"Making progress?"

"Oh, yes. Good progress."

"Need anything?"

"No, I believe everything's well in hand."

"Excellent report on Tadeusz Retkowski."

Tadeusz Retkowski was a former patient, discharged as "improved," who had been repeatedly warned by state police over the past few months to stop impeding traffic by walking out half-naked onto the road and shouting at cars, drivers, and horses. He had attacked a local bank manager with a slingshot and was more than likely to find himself back in hospital within months if not weeks.

"Keep up the good work," Bingham said, slapped the door frame, and bid her good day.

Imogen found it peculiar, and entertained the thought that Dr. Bingham might be helping himself to pharmaceutical supplies. He did not even comment on her discovery of the four "missing" patients in his back ward. To be sure, her overview was not yet complete, but nothing now could make Bingham's work on focal infections appear anything more than a complete failure—at best.

His wife seemed similarly impervious to reality. Abigail Bingham was a Southern lady through and through, with a Southerner's veneration of family, loyalty, and tradition. She seemed to be under the impression that Imogen was working *with* her husband, and made a great fuss when Bingham introduced her. Imogen had been dropping off reports in his office and had been hoping to sneak away unnoticed—the reports once again being far from flattering—when the inner door opened and the two of them emerged dressed up for an evening out. (Imogen had noticed that the couple appeared regularly in the pages of the *Trenton Chronicle*, attending one charitable function after another.)

"My deah," Mrs. Bingham said, "you simply must come and have suppah with us one of these nights."

"Thank you. That's very kind of you."

"Nonsense, it's nothing but the merest good mannahs! You'll have to forgive the Director. His head is always on such lofty mattahs as scientific research, and simple mattahs like food and good company simply escape his notice."

"Well, thank you. If I would not be imposing . . ."

"Of course not—the very ideah. Now I know you only grace our hallways toward the beginnin' of each week. How would next Tuesday suit? Would Tuesday be convenient for you?"

"Yes. Tuesday would be fine. What time should I come?"

"Oh, the Director is an early risah so we take a early suppah. It's uncivilized but science ignores so many of the social niceties. You come at seven, and we'll have time to enjoy a propah visit before we dine."

"Seven o'clock. Tuesday."

"We'll be lookin' forward to it, Dr. Lang, we most surely will."

Throughout this exchange, Dr. Bingham stood in his wife's shadow, an ambiguous grin on his pink round face.

To visit the Binghams—at least to visit the Binghams knowing what Imogen knew about the medical director's treatments and his outcomes—was to visit a reality as separate as that of toothless Ronnie Trout and his wall maps. Their home was majestic compared with any other residence on the hospital grounds. The interior, with its burnished oak and walnut, its ornate mouldings and heroic fireplaces, was an asylum within the asylum. Imogen hadn't realized how used she had become to the clamour and wail of the criminal wing until she found herself wrapped in the quiet of the Bingham residence.

Before dinner they sat in the drawing room and Imogen answered the many questions of Abigail Bingham. She found herself captivated by the older woman's manners. Mrs. Bingham presented each question as if it were a little gift—a bonbon to be unwrapped at your leisure. "You have an eldah sistah? And what is her age and station, if one may inquiah? A lawyah! Heavens, you are an accomplished family of fine women, are you not? I feel an absolute slugabed by comparison—an absolute slugabed."

Rupert Bingham took on a glow as she talked, smiled her way, and nodded silent agreement with her observations. Imogen was struck by how shy he seemed. It was not what she had expected in a man who had pursued such bold, even radical treatments, and promoted them with unabashed vigour in such unscientific journals as the *Saturday Evening Post*.

At the supper table he came into his own. They were served by an Irish maid who stood, attentive and motionless until called on, by the sideboard. From the moment the opening course of French onion soup appeared the tone of the evening changed, with Mrs. Bingham now adopting the role of her husband's Boswell. She would broach a topic in a way that invited an expansive response from "the Directah," allowing Bingham to slip into an anecdote like a flattering self-portrait into a frame.

"My deah, tell Doctah Lang about your arrival at this august institution. Tell her the first thing you did. He's so modest, you see, I have to prod him."

"The first thing I did? The first thing I did was to hold a bonfire. It was at the far edge of the grounds, towards Stuyvesant. I had the staff empty the basement, empty the wards, and empty the storage rooms of all restraint devices. There must have been a dozen Utica cribs but also manacles, straitjackets, and bed cuffs. We had the patients help carry them out in a fantastic parade and toss them into a huge pile. Doused the whole thing with kerosene and set it ablaze. That was 1916. I was determined to drag this place out of the Dark Ages and into the light."

"And the second thing you did?" Here Mrs. Bingham turned once again to Imogen and added, "The Directah can't beah the slightest indignity toward people under his care."

"The second thing I did was to close these grounds to the public. Do you know what the locals were doing? Every Sunday they would show up, toting their picnic baskets and their blankets and their children, and they would set up under the elms or in a patch of sun and watch the patients as if they were at the zoo! You'd see children— and even some adults—mimicking the spastics and so on. It was an absolute disgrace. I told the commissioner we're an asylum not a circus. We house people here—not livestock—people."

"You were a real reformer then," Imogen said.

"I have devoted my life to it," he said. "My sole ambition is to put psychiatric treatment firmly on a foundation of rock-solid science."

For the rest of the evening Bingham overcame the modesty his wife had attributed to him and talked as if he were speaking for the ages. After they had finished their beef Wellington and their peach Melba, he pushed back his chair and folded his arms across his stomach and delivered himself of remarks that he clearly considered penetrating, pausing only when his wife lobbed him another softball. Later, in her room, Imogen wrote down the comments she could remember.

*Dentists in this country have a lot to answer for. A lot to answer for.*

*I am sick of the view—ever more current—that certain mental disorders can occur independent of any changes in the brain. From this view we unhesitatingly dissent.*

*Before Frank Billings and I developed focal infection therapy fewer than 25% of patients improved enough to leave state asylums permanently—and even those were due entirely to spontaneous recovery.*

*All devitalized teeth, especially those with root canal fillings, should be extracted immediately. All progressive dentists support this view.*

*I've made mistakes. But all of them were cases of not going far enough. I hesitated, in the early days, to resect more than a foot or so of large intestine. This was far too conservative.*

*The modern operation is safe for the patient. The modern surgeon must make the patient safe for the operation.*

*If a patient has twelve infected teeth it is bad medicine to extract only eleven. You harm without benefit.*

As Imogen was leaving, Bingham invited her to attend one of his surgeries. Excited by his own magnanimity, he became uncharacteristically animated and insistent. "No, you must come, Dr. Lang. I think it's essential you see what we do here, don't you? Besides which, I should very much value your comments and opinions."

"I'm afraid surgery is a long way from any expertise I may possess."

"Still. You must come and see. It's what we do best here. It's what we're known for. You can't go to New York and not see the Statue of Liberty."


The Trenton State Hospital had three surgical service areas, two for women and one for men. Imogen had no need to ask why the discrepancy; it was clear from Bingham's own writings. If removing tonsils, teeth, and lengths of colon didn't work, it was a certainty that "the female organs" must be involved.

The operation she was to witness was a straightforward colectomy and anastomosis on a thirty-four-year-old patient named Penny Clark, who had a history of chronic schizophrenia. At Bingham's invitation, Imogen waited, gloved and gowned, in the operating theatre where she could watch the nurses prepare. They were extremely efficient and capable. The room itself was a bright, sunny space with huge windows and three skylights. Overhead, a sky of electric blue was traversed by a procession of clouds as smooth as whipped cream. Sunlight flashed on the chrome of the instruments and caused the white sheets and gowns, even the white floor, to glow as if lit from within.

Shouting erupted in the outer area. A woman's voice—distorted by toothlessness and no doubt a heavy bromide—yelled no, no, no over and over. It's not fair! It's not fair! Her words slowed, became more slurred, and then stopped altogether. She was wheeled into the operating theatre, dreamy and docile. Dr. Bingham followed, majestic in gown and mask, greeting everyone cheerily, his eyes merry above his mask.

"Have you all met Dr. Lang—our formidable and lovely colleague from Baltimore?"

They had.

"Dr. Lang is a protegé of Jonas Ganz himself, so we must all be on our toes."

He walked round to the head of the operating table.

"Miss Clark? How are you this fine morning?"

The patient answered with difficulty that she was sad. Distorted by sedatives, it came out as s-s-s-ssad.

"And perhaps a little anxious, no? But I assure you that I have the finest surgical team on the East Coast in this room and we'll be looking after you all the way."

"No-o-o-o."

Imogen assumed this was a patient under court committal and that the necessary consent had been signed by next of kin, because clearly this woman was here against her will.

"Not to worry. The procedure is simplicity itself, and one that I have employed many times with excellent outcomes. We'll just be cutting out a bit of infected bowel and joining the two healthy pieces back together. Nothing simpler."

He nodded to the anaesthetist, and the mask was lowered. The woman was now just a shape under sheets, the mask obscuring the last individualizing features. A few drops of chloral were administered, and when unconsciousness was certain, Bingham asked for a pulse. The anaesthetist already had a finger against the carotid vein.

"Seventy-six."

"Blood pressure?"

"One twenty-four over eighty."

"Excellent. Part the draping please." The nurse folded back the surgical drape to expose the woman's abdomen. As Dr. Bingham turned back from his tray, scalpel in hand, the pale plain of her belly, tiny shadowed depression of navel in the centre, looked to Imogen the most vulnerable thing she had ever seen.

"This may be routine for the rest of you, but I'm going to give a running commentary for the benefit of our visitor. Dr. Lang, can you see all right?"

"Yes, thank you."

"As you know, for an inguinal colectomy, incision is on the left and exactly the same as for an appendectomy on the right, meaning we split the muscles, à la McBurney, without dividing the fibres."

A firm stroke, as with a pen nib, followed by the welling of scarlet ink. "No more than two inches is required. I'm taking a middle approach about two inches above the anterior superior spine at the ilium. There's a slight risk of prolapse, but the fecal reservoir is preserved, avoiding the risk of incontinence."

He clamped the bleeding at the edge of the wound, and swabbed the area.

"Note that the fibres of the external oblique muscles run parallel to the incision. You'll see as I split the fibres lengthwise . . ." which he now did, ever so gently, "we expose the internal oblique. Clever Mother Nature, you observe, runs these underlying fibres at right angles to the external."

He made a small incision, little more than a nick, and lengthened it with careful tearing. "Beautiful. Look at that. We're now looking at the transversalis fascia and the peritoneum. Retractor, please."

The retractor held the muscles apart, allowing Bingham to make a small incision in the peritoneum. Imogen winced. The peritoneum was the membrane that held the viscera in place, one layer being attached to the wall of the abdomen, the other folded around the entrails themselves. To pierce it was one of the most dangerous manoeuvres in medicine, with a high risk of infection. Peritonitis was excruciating, and nearly always fatal.

Bingham secured the cut edges with a pair of clips and inserted his forefinger into the opening.

"Seeking the sigmoid flexure . . . usually easy enough to find. Now hauling it to the surface."

From out of the tiny opening he pulled some eight inches of pinkish-grey tubing.

"Now pulling on the upper end until no more bowel will come out, at the same time . . . tucking the lower sigmoid back inside. Excellent. We have a good length of colon here, but it's crucial to pull the mesentery taut. We have to see the blood vessels."

The mesentery was part of the peritoneum and was roughly to the colon what the placenta is to a fetus. Dr. Bingham glanced at Imogen. "All right so far?"

"Yes. Fine."

She was struck by the change in Bingham. His eyes, framed between the surgical cap and mask, had lost their usual wounded look. Furtiveness replaced by calm. Instead of the hunted he was the hunter, on the trail of the focal infection that was driving this young woman (she was barely two years older than Imogen) into misery and madness. If that required him to yank out a loop of her guts and examine them on her belly, so be it. He was in his element here; he was in control. He would not be one of the countless psychiatrists defeated by the implacable mysteries of psychosis. If Imogen's only experience of Rupert Bingham had been this operation, he would have enjoyed her complete confidence.

He bent low over the patient's belly to examine the mesentery, then called for Pagenstecher. "It's the heaviest thread. I always use it to fix the bowel in place, and the Hagedorn needle—you need that full curve." He held it up for Imogen to see. He described what he was doing as he continued. "Holding the loop of gut in my left hand, we go down through all three muscles and the peritoneum, and leave about six inches of thread on top. Now I put it through the bloodless area of the mesentery I already selected. And up through the muscles and skin on the other side. Then back down through the wound and passing the needle through the same hole in the mesentery and— *voilà*—up through the wound. Tubing, please."

The nurse handed him a three-inch section of clear tube. Bingham disengaged the needle, and placed the tubing on the abdomen under the thread. The nurse handed him a second piece and he did the same on the other side. "This is just to keep the thread from cutting into the skin," he said, and tied off the suture. He looked across the patient at Imogen. "What do you think, Doctor?"

"It's brilliant."

"We stand on the shoulders of giants, Dr. Lang, giants—Moynihan and Paul to name just two. This stitch holds better than the usual strip of gauze wrapped around a glass rod and it doesn't get in the way." He spread the loop of gut with both hands. The mesentery was an intricate webbed fan of blood vessels. "Beautiful," Bingham said. "She's nice and trim. In obese patients the mesentery is a cloudy mess. Clamps please, Nurse."

One by one, the nurse handed him four surgical clamps, which he attached to the gut in pairs forming a wedge shape. "Paquelin, if you please."

The nurse handed him the knife of a cautery unit, the blade glowing dull red.

"It looks normal to me," Imogen said. "I don't see any growth or infection."

"Ah, but I do. That pink tinge? It's much pinker than normal. In a matter of weeks or months it would be flaming red. But even I can't see it sometimes. That's why we have one of the most advanced labs in the country. This woman's colon is swarming with a staph infection, and the only thing to do is cut out as much of it as we can. The distal portions, luckily, are disease free, as they must be. Few rules are so binding on the surgeon, Dr. Lang, as the one prohibiting the resection of unhealthy tissue. You'll notice I cut very slowly to prevent hemorrhage."

A whiff of seared meat rose from the table as he cut through first one side of the loop, then the other. The nurse held out a chrome pan, and he placed in it—with a clang—the severed length of gut, two clamps still attached. Now the openings of the sectioned gut, even though squeezed by the two remaining clamps, lay fixed on the abdomen like twin gun barrels. Over the next hour Bingham clipped, ligated, cauterized, and stitched. When done, he washed the gut with bismuth and called for a Paul's tube for drainage. He fixed this to the abdomen with a couple of stitches, packed the wound, and dressed it.

"I'm not going to close up now. Everything remains exterior for at least three days, sometimes as long as a week. We have to ensure that the stitches will hold even in the presence of digestion."

"But isn't that incredibly dangerous?" Imogen said—it wasn't really a question.

"As you saw, our antiseptic measures border on the fanatical, and our mortality rate is no higher than anyone else's. Yes, there are risks—internal bleeding, incisional hernia, leaking stitches—but the danger must be weighed against this woman's prognosis: the risk of a negative surgical outcome versus the certainty of a lifetime on the ward. I love surgery, Dr. Lang, I adore surgery. Surgery—whatever else it may be—is an adventure of the spirit, a trial of one's mettle, but I firmly believe there's no enemy that can't be conquered if a man's heart is set on victory."


From the operating room at Trenton State Hospital to her home on Dukeland Street, Baltimore, was only a half-day's journey—not so far, in the grand scheme of things. In some ways, it was no distance at all, a mere step through a mirror, but in this mirror-world Imogen found herself trapped in a bad dream from which there was no waking. Carl's contrition had soon mutated to anger and resentment, as if he were not the betrayer but the betrayed.

No doubt the atmosphere at work had changed for him. Jonas Ganz, Imogen was gratified to hear, was no longer cordial in his relations with Carl. Where before he had been friendly and interested, he was now merely civil. Invitations to have dinner at the chief's house stopped cold. Ganz no longer popped into the psychology lab to pay his respects, although he did still stop by Imogen's lab. Imogen thought this served Carl right, and he should have expected much worse for seducing a student.

Once having got over the initial shock, she had assumed that gradually her hurt would heal and their married life would resume its normal cheerful temper. She had withdrawn her demand that Carl dispose of the marriage bed he had sullied. They could not afford a new one, and Carl's hours at the lab did not allow him the time it would take to build one. Imogen had wanted nothing more than to set fire to it, but she accepted that this was impossible and, swallowing her pride, once more slept in the same bed with her husband. If she had thought he would recognize this concession for the sacrifice it was, she was soon disillusioned. Where she had hoped for some semblance of gratitude, she was met with his turned back.

Carl behaved toward her with stiff correctness, nothing more; there was no warmth in his "good mornings" or "thank yous" beyond that between people who happen to work in the same building. No smiles. He never inquired about her progress with the Trenton study, and showed not a flicker of interest when she couldn't help talking about events at the asylum. In contrast to his previous irrepressible chatter concerning his own work, he now came home humourless and mute. The only exception to this implacable cold—and it was an exception she valued highly—was in his attitude to Aubrey and Charlotte. He still played with the twins as eagerly, as joyfully as ever, listened to them attentively, and told them silly stories about a mischievous rat who disrupted his lab and wrote poems for him to find every morning. Still, Imogen could not watch these displays of love without pangs of abandonment. His coldness was so selective that it screamed, *You, my dear, are not worth loving.*

Her certainty that she had done nothing wrong began to waver. Perhaps she had failed him and was too self-centred to be aware of it. Perhaps it was sex. Perhaps he had been so unfulfilled that he was driven to look elsewhere for satisfaction. Now that Cynthia Bee was gone, he resented his wife for depriving him of his pleasure. Or it could be even simpler. No man or woman likes to be caught being his or her lowest self, and no one can be expected to thank you for shining a light on his lapses. Whatever the cause, Carl's cold anger caused Imogen's own love, already blighted by betrayal, to wither to its roots.

When the four of them were together as a family—at the market, in the park, at dinner—Imogen found it difficult to be loving even toward her children.

"Carl," she said one night after the twins had gone to bed, "you are behaving toward me as if I've done something terrible. I don't know why that should be, but I do need to know if you plan to continue this way."

Carl was hidden behind a wall of newspaper. "I don't know what you're talking about," he said, and noisily turned a page.

"Carl, look at me."

He lowered his newspaper halfway.

"Carl, I'm trying to forgive you for what you did to me—to us and our family. I want to forgive you and for life to go back to normal. But I receive nothing from you except hostility and resentment."

"Hostility and resentment. Sounds like normal married life to me."

"It's certainly not how we were before all this . . ."

"Before you abandoned us for Trenton."

"I didn't abandon anyone. I took a temporary job because we need the money and I need the publication. If you showed the slightest interest in my life, you'd know that what I'm doing is extremely worthwhile. When it's published this study will ultimately save lives."

"So being a good wife is beneath you, I suppose. No, no—Imogen Lang is far too grand to be a mere wife."

"I'm not a *mere* anything. Neither are you. I'm a wife, a mother, and a psychiatrist—a working woman, yes. I was a working woman when you met me. You said many times I was just what you wanted, I was exactly right for you. You claimed to think women should work."

"Women. Not mothers. You're a mother, now, Imogen, a mother. It's a full-time job."

"No, it's not. The children are at school for half the day and asleep for ten hours at night and Myra looks after them for half days. There's no reason I shouldn't have a career, and certainly no reason to defend my career to you. We've been over all this. Why are you harping on it now?"

"Because I'm the one who has to be home with the twins. I'm a man, Imogen, a man—someone who goes out into the world and earns a living. That's what men are for. I should not be called upon to be nanny and nursemaid and housekeeper—it's menial labour, for God's sake. I have more important things to do with my time. Unlike you, I'm not travelling around the country counting mad people."

"Can you not hear yourself, Carl? Can you not hear what you are saying to me? One minute you're accusing me—falsely—of deeming motherhood beneath me. The next minute you're calling it menial labour and far below the likes of you."

"Women have traditionally seen raising children as their main purpose in life."

"Suddenly Carl Kromer is a traditionalist? Whatever happened to the free-thinking progressive I married? The man who insisted he saw the two of us—and our careers!—as equal. Suddenly I'm just obsessed with the worthless occupation of counting mad people, as if counting mad people can't begin to compare with the importance of counting rats. You know what I'm studying and you know why it matters."

"Some women find their children—yes, and even their husband— more important."

"But you were reconciled to this! Carl, I was so relieved when you apologized and said you were wrong to object and I should absolutely go ahead and do the study. I thought to myself, 'Yes, my man is the real thing—a husband who can treat me as an equal without feeling something has been stolen from him.' Why, oh, why have you now reverted?"

"I only agreed to this ridiculous situation because we had Cynthia
to look after the kids, Imogen. Well, you got your wish and now she's
gone, so I get to play babysitter."

"Oh, God." Imogen lowered herself to a chair, the arm of it anyway,
as the real meaning behind Carl's words sank in.

"What? You're being melodramatic again. Honestly, Imogen.
Sometimes."

"I understand it now. I must be stone blind not to have seen it before.
You were *happy* to see me go—happy! You couldn't wait, could you.
You were already having sex with your student."

"Now I'm Satan because I want sex."

"Because you want it with someone who is not your wife. With
someone who is your student. You are not going to tell me you were
deprived of sex—you know you weren't. Our physical life was excellent right from the start."

"Was very good *at* the start. Look at yourself, Imogen. You must
have put on thirty pounds since we got married."

"I've had children, for God's sake. Your children. And Cynthia Bee
is hardly a model of feminine perfection."

"At least her tits don't sag." Carl flicked his newspaper back up and
rattled the pages.

Imogen stayed seated for some time, not moving, staring at nothing, while her husband remained barricaded behind his paper. Eventually she made her way to the bedroom where she sat on the edge of
the bed. She sat for a long time, staring at the closet door, just as she
had done as a child. Now and again the notion came to her that she
should get up, she should go for a walk, she should at least move, but
there was nowhere to move, nowhere to walk, nowhere to look that
did not hurt.

# 18

As Quentin began writing the first chapters of his novel, he found himself stymied in ways he had not previously experienced. He was now aiming for more texture, a greater feeling of actual people in real places, and discovered that he hadn't taken enough notes to achieve this. He wanted to know what kind of houses doctors lived in, what buses they took—the small details of their everyday lives.

He arrived in Baltimore on a Wednesday evening, and the following day he was waiting outside the Phipps, seated on a bench with a copy of the *Baltimore Sun* to screen his features, should the need arise. The day was chilly and damp but he didn't care. He had brought a book of crossword puzzles to occupy his mind in case the wait should be long, but he found his mind already so occupied with Imogen that his verbal skills abandoned him. It occurred to him that his "need" for novelistic detail could well be just a need to see Imogen. Obsession, if not love, he thought, was probably a form of stupidity. He felt guilty for lurking like this, and his leg, in all the places it had been broken, began to ache.

Shortly after five o'clock she appeared on the front steps, the only woman he had ever seen who truly merited the adjective "statuesque." She stopped at the top of the stair, as others emerged from the building and passed her by, and rummaged through her bag, apparently having forgotten something. The clouds parted and a shaft of late afternoon sunlight lit the steps. Her hair seemed darker than he remembered, or perhaps it was only a trick of the light. And she seemed even taller. Her height, her solidity had always given him pleasure—he could not have said why—adding a regal element that contradicted her innate diffidence. It felt wrong to be looking at her and he was afraid of how she might react if she recognized him. This, he knew, was not likely. As far as she was concerned Quentin Goodchild was dead. So even if she discerned a resemblance in this much older man with his hesitant gait, it would be a huge leap to think Quentin was actually alive.

She passed by him, still rooting through her bag, and walked up the path leading to Wolfe Street. Quentin fell into step about fifteen yards behind her. He wanted to speak to her but could not summon the courage.

On Wolfe Street, Imogen joined a queue and boarded the number 22 streetcar. Quentin dithered until the last moment, before jumping on. The car was full but a young man offered Imogen his seat, and to see this stranger accord her this courtesy gave Quentin pleasure. He kept his face averted as he passed her. As the streetcar started to move, he gripped the bar and looked at the back of Imogen's head and at her profile, the curve of her cheek, reflected in the window. She pulled a book out of her bag—he could not see the title—and began to read. It was exciting and unsettling to observe her in her daily routine. He who was dead to her was watching her live her life and, like a benign spectre, he tried to send her waves of affection. Should he speak to her? No, it was too . . . he did not know what it was too much of, but he knew it was too much.

Imogen did not look up from her book when the conductor called out the names of stops. A phrase came to Quentin from long ago, something she had said: peace and contentment. Looking up at him from a book, the sunlight shining on her hair, gilding her cheek, and saying, "Peace and contentment. That's what I get from reading. A good book on a sunny day, a pretty garden—what could be more perfect?" And here she was a decade later finding peace and contentment on a crowded streetcar, oblivious to the clanging bell, the driver calling out stops.

Gradually the Negroes left the streetcar until there were only white people on board. Even so, none of them sat in the rear third of the car. Quentin took a seat a few rows back from Imogen, on the other side of the aisle. When the conductor called out North Street, she put the book in her bag and stood up. Quentin turned his face to the window as she stepped by him toward the middle doors. When the streetcar stopped and the doors opened, he rose and followed her out. *Now*, he would speak.

But the opportunity vanished. A streetcar was just arriving on the far side of North Street, and Imogen hurried across the intersection, unaware of the ghost trailing behind her. Quentin was stopped as he boarded.

"Transfuh," the driver said, and repeated it when Quentin did not understand. "Can't be gettin' on the thirteen from the twenty-two without you got a transfuh." Quentin had to pay the full fare again, and felt the stares of impatient passengers. He kept his head down as he took his place a few seats behind Imogen. She was once more engaged with her book.

When she got out a few stops later he followed her on the opposite side of the street. She turned down a smaller street. The houses were modest here, some of them rundown. The one she went to was larger than some of the others, but there were three mailboxes by the front door, indicating other tenants. As she was collecting her mail the front door opened and a little boy and girl came out, calling, "Mumma! Mumma!" and clutching at her. She reached down to tousle their hair, and a coloured woman appeared in the doorway. Something Imogen said made her laugh and she shooed the children inside. Imogen followed them in and shut the door behind her.

Quentin walked on for a couple of blocks, then turned back the way he had come. He intended to catch the streetcar but when he got to the stop decided to keep walking—treading the pavement, smelling the grass, seeing the streets, the sky, the ground of Imogen's world.

By the time he reached his hotel it was night, and he treated himself to an expensive meal in the hotel restaurant. He was in a celebratory mood and yet a thread of shame ran through his excitement. No matter how affectionate it might be, there was something a little unsavoury about the way he had followed her.

By way of redemption he spent all of Friday in the Baltimore public library outlining his novel.

On Saturday, he followed Imogen and her family to the market. If a good opportunity presented itself, he would speak to them—this was his resolution when he started out, but he rapidly abandoned it. There were four of them, as together as four petals on a flower, and he knew there was no place for him in their world.

He took a seat up front where he could steal glances at them in the driver's wide mirror. The little boy sat on Imogen's lap, the little girl on her father's. Twins. He remembered something he had forgotten: that Imogen herself had been born a twin, that her twin had died of a fever. He remembered the sorrow in Imogen's face when she had told him about it. Now she straightened the cap on her little boy's head and kissed his brow, causing him to squirm. Imogen laughed and looked up, her eyes making contact, via the mirror, with Quentin's. Quentin blinked and looked away, and when he glanced back up at the mirror she was saying something to her husband.

He had done a little more detective work and now knew her husband's name and that he also worked at the Phipps and was the author of many papers on innate behaviour. Quentin recalled Imogen's admiration—hero worship, really—of the great figures in medicine. This man would have her respect; the two of them would enjoy the pleasure of shared experience. They would have common friends and colleagues, know each other's days to the hour and minute, understand each other's ambitions and frustrations. Love would be easy.

Imogen's daughter, contented and secure on her papa's lap, pointed at something outside the streetcar and both parents smiled. He didn't see the physical charms of Kromer. His features were bland, and he had something of a know-all look about him. Like so many men, you only noticed him because of the woman he was with.

The two of them had lapsed into a shared quiet now. Imogen's features took on the slightly sorrowful cast he remembered so well—her lovely melancholy, he'd always considered it. Lovely because eloquent. Lovely because temporary. Lovely because curable by him, or at least the young him. But she had others to cure it now.

The streetcar rumbled into the market area and the Kromer family roused themselves. They would be getting off here for their Saturday shopping. Quentin turned in his seat to watch—little girl aloft in father's arms, little boy guided down the streetcar step by Imogen who, somewhere along the road, had become her own guardian angel. And so he remained seated in the streetcar and watched them wade into the colourful crowds of shoppers and sellers, another happy family forming a tribe unto itself, needing no other.


When Christmas came, Imogen and Carl agreed not to exchange presents—to save money, they told each other. The only thing that made it bearable was that Carl elected to leave them and spend the holiday with his parents in Pennsylvania. The twins' disappointment quickly turned to crankiness and despite the toys, the tree, and Imogen's attempts to be cheerful, they had more than the usual number of spats.

In January Imogen continued to shuttle back and forth between Baltimore and Trenton. Although there were times when the pen and paper in her hand seemed to belong to someone else, or when the words she was typing would go in and out of focus, she kept working. How was it possible that her increasingly damaged heart was not visible for all to see? How could it not be as vivid as fire? Her husband hated her. The man with whom she had thought to share her life could now not bear to be in the same room with her. And by a bitter alchemy this disdain was transmuted into self-loathing. She was an ugly, unwanted woman with sagging breasts and a depressive personality. Who could blame a vigorous young man for his contempt?

Her self-respect could only be salvaged by her career; she would finish the Trenton report and she would publish. Sometimes, on board the train, she forgot which direction she was heading. In a way it didn't matter; her emotional arrival point was the same. If travelling away from Carl, she was bound for the tortures of jealousy and suspicion. Cynthia Bee had moved away, but jealousy was like an allergic response in that, once triggered, it is all too easily triggered again with less and less provocation. Her days in Trenton were soured by the near certainty that Carl was engaged in wild sexual encounters with every female who came his way. Knowing that this was irrational, that he was far too busy for such liaisons, made no difference.

The train was taking her home, but it was to a home in ruins. Carl only spoke to her when it was something to do with the children. He resolutely kept up the façade of normalcy, and even happiness, when the twins were around. Also in public. And she found herself responding in kind. Her acting talent sickened her. If Carl had made the slightest effort to repair things between them it wouldn't have hurt so much, but he made none—no kind words, no affectionate glances, not so much as a raised eyebrow of inquiry—so that these public displays of false intimacy were all the more excruciating. See? he seemed to say, I know how it is done, I know how loving husbands treat their wives but I am not one. I can do this forever, he seemed to be saying, how long can you stand it?

At home she had the children to remind her she was needed, she was loved. Sometimes she hugged them so tightly they would cry, "Mumma, I can't breathe!" At Trenton she had her report to remind her that she had a career, a possible future. She struggled on with the inadequate help of Mrs. Boxer. She worked the phone and the typewriter and watched the snow build up on her office windowsill—New Jersey had a different idea of winter than Maryland—and at last her work was done.

Over the past few weeks, slush and ice had made driving more harrowing, but even so, Imogen hated to part with the Ford. She sold it to one of the Trenton residents and lugged her carpet bag for the last time out of her little closet in the criminal wing, hearing for the last time those wails and curses and cries. Fifty-three pages of charts and figures and statistics, page after page of analysis, supplemented with four bound volumes of case reports, all of it amounting to a thorough indictment of Rupert Bingham's "detoxication" treatments. She had not yet written the conclusion, but it was inescapable. His claims were empty boasts, his cures were fictions. She said goodbye to Mrs. Boxer, who, having slowly come to realize the damage Imogen was going to inflict on her "saviour," gave her a curt nod in return.

It was heartening to know that her work would improve the lives of hundreds of patients, that it would even save some of those lives. But as she made her way to the asylum gate, she glanced over at Bingham's house and felt a surge of pity. Of all afflictions, self-delusion had to be one of the worst. Bingham had committed the crime of believing himself to be a great man, of being blind to his own blindness. Had this failing been confined to his own fortunes that would be one thing, but it affected all the patients who came under his care.

As she stopped to switch her bag from one hand to the other, Imogen felt she should say goodbye to Dr. Bingham and his wife. It was the correct thing to do, and it was nearly noon; he would be home for lunch. On the other hand, Bingham had been avoiding her these past couple of weeks, the armour of his denial having, apparently, finally been pierced by the power of the evidence she had amassed. She would be leaving no friends in this place. She trudged on toward the gatehouse, where the taxi duly arrived a few minutes later. As they drove away she turned for a last look at the grand gate of stone and iron—for so many a dread portal—to the Trenton State Hospital for the Insane.

※

A dreary winter rain was pouring over Baltimore when Imogen's train pulled in. Even though it was late afternoon, she went straight from the station to the Phipps. Dr. Ganz was delighted to see her, urging her to sit down and summoning Mr. Penn to bring them coffee.

He examined the latest pages of the typescript, shaking his head as he did so. He tapped the last chart and said, "This is devastating. You're absolutely sure your numbers are correct?"

"Yes."

"So much for his 85 percent cure rate."

"It's 12 percent," Imogen said. "And only 8 percent are even improved—less than a third of what most state asylums are reporting."

Dr. Ganz bent his head to the papers once more, absently stroking his beard. "And he can't even say it's because they refused treatment, or their families took them out before he was finished."

"Far from it. The patients who received all the treatment he recommended have in fact fared the worst. Forty-three percent of them are dead."

"Yes, I'm looking at it right here."

"Only 13 percent can be considered recovered, and 40 percent of them are still in hospital."

"Devastating," Ganz said again. "The more treatment they received, the worse the outcomes."

"It's all the abdominal procedures. He seems to have no idea of the difference between the mere presence of bacteria and an actual infection of the tissues. But he operates on them and they die of post-operative shock, pulmonary edema, cardiac dilation—not to mention severe diarrhea. The colon I saw him resect showed no obvious sign of infection, and the patient had not been complaining of abdominal pain. She died too. Peritonitis."

They sipped their coffee in silence for a few moments. Dr. Ganz put the papers aside with a sigh.

"Well, on the bright side—if there is a bright side—you've completed a first-class piece of research. You must be very pleased."

"I'm certainly relieved it's over."

"But more than that! It's a sterling piece of work—a milestone in your career."

"How soon do you think we can publish?"

"How long will it take you to write your conclusion?"

"No time at all. I could have it to you within a day or two. And then you'll allow me to seek a publisher?"

"Well, there's a bit more to it than that."

"I don't understand—what else could there be?"

"Just a formality or two. My agreement with Trenton's medical board is that the report cannot be considered complete until Dr. Bingham has had a chance to read it and make any comments or corrections he feels necessary."

"But he's been reading it from the start. He knows very well what's in it, and so far he's made minimal comments."

Ganz dipped his head and stared thoughtfully at his desk. "Yes, he has been rather silent in response to my letters."

"Chief, I don't understand why we need Dr. Bingham's signature on the report. In fact, any involvement by him would seem to undercut its value as independent research."

"He does not have to agree with its conclusions—that goes without saying—but there must be reasonable agreement concerning the cases we've studied and the statistical methods used."

"I can't see him rushing to agree to that."

"Indeed he has not. I've written to the board asking for a meeting to be arranged, so the three of us can go over everything."

"Very well. You'll have my conclusion by tomorrow or the next day."

"Excellent. Thank you." Dr. Ganz rose from his seat and showed her to the door. "And once again, congratulations!"


Imogen went to the lab and sat at the big desk. She had been rethinking her introduction on the train and wanted to rewrite it before she forgot. She typed and retyped the pages. It was crucial to word it in a purely objective way, and yet not compromise a clear statement of the findings. These were findings of fact, not bias, but until they read the study, no one else would know that. It was nearly nine-thirty when she got up from the desk and stretched to ease her back.

Outside, the rain hammered down on the streets of Baltimore. It rattled on the roof of the taxi and caused the aged driver to mutter curses at the wipers, overmatched by such a torrent. Two stalled street-cars blocked their way for ten minutes.

"I'm very anxious to get home," Imogen said. "Do you suppose you could turn around and find another route?"

"I'm not going to do a U-turn. It's illegal."

"Surely not, under the circumstances."

The driver twisted around and glared at her.

"Are you telling me how to drive?"

"I simply want to get home, if that's all right."

"No woman tells me how to drive." He faced front once more. He said nothing further but Imogen could sense him fuming. The streetcars were eventually dislodged, and the driver responded to this release with a burst of speed and much careening. Still, when finally they reached Dukeland Street, he carried her carpet bag right up the front walk.

She tipped him, and as he thanked her, rain spattering off the bill of his tweed cap, she noticed that many of his teeth were missing. He might be a former resident of Trenton, she thought, and realized that for the rest of her life she would wonder this about anyone with missing teeth.

She went inside and set her bag down and shut the door behind her. She stood for a moment contemplating the stillness of her home, its familiar front-hall smells of floor polish and children's boots. She took off her coat and hung it in the closet. The children's boots were not there.

She was struck by a sense of déjà vu. The house felt wrong—as wrong as it felt the night of Cynthia. It was overheated, and there was no motion whatsoever in the air. Carl always slept with the window open—she had never known him to close it—and the house being draughty, you could usually feel cool damp fronds of air wafting in from outside.

She went into the kitchen and switched on the light. Carl's coffee grinder was not on the counter. On the rectangular mat beside the back door there were still no children's boots, or shoes of any kind. She proceeded slowly, numbly, along the corridor with one hand extended to meet the doorknob of the twins' bedroom.

She flipped on the light and saw the two beds, neatly made.

Gone.

She crossed the corridor and threw open the bedroom door.

Gone.

A note on the bed.

Imogen stood immobilized in the doorway. A wave of nausea rippling through her. She went to the bed and sat on the edge—carefully, as if it might shatter. She picked up the note and switched on the lamp.

Imogen,

Don't worry—I have not stolen the children. You and I are not happy together and never will be. Therefore I have moved out and we take up once again our separate lives. Call me at LA 2495 when you get home and you can arrange to pick up the twins.

Carl

She read the note again, and then a third time. She got up and opened the closet. Every shirt, every tie, every hat of his was gone; nothing of him remained.

She began to pace back and forth across the bedroom, to the window, where the rain slid down in rivulets, to the closet, to the doorway, and back to the hated bed. It was nearly midnight; Carl would be asleep. She went to the living room, left hand pressed to her heart until she used it to snatch up the telephone.

Carl answered sleepily. "Hello?"

"Bastard."

"Imogen. You're home. I—"

"If you live to be a hundred and five," Imogen said, "you will never know the depth of my hatred for you."

She hung up blindly, the bulky handset crashing to the floor.

"I will not cry," she said as she stumbled once more along the corridor to the bed and collapsed across it, already weeping at the world receding behind her, and howling at the life to come.

# 19

The snow came late that year to Lake Placid. December usually meant the hills would be blinding white against a startling blue sky, but here it was the end of January and they'd had only a few soggy flakes of snow that dissolved the moment they touched the ground. Although the temperature had dropped to the point where Quentin required his woollen overcoat, the smell of wet leaves and soaking pine was rich and constant, so that the feeling of autumn persisted almost as if the little town had for once been granted a dispensation from winter.

He walked the wet streets, umbrella tapping the sidewalk, up before most of the residents, with the reliable exceptions of the milkman and the baker's deliveryman. He preferred to rise while it was still dark, liked to be abroad when the first light oozed from the hilltops, and the mist still hovered above the lake. A couple of miles, and then home to a breakfast of eggs and toast and coffee.

His father's death had left him with a modest inheritance—a place to live and an income that was just short of enough to live on. His books more than made up the difference. Not many men were so fortunate—few soldiers and even fewer writers. But he was often impossibly lonely. He wished for Jack Wisdom's company—a wish that was always accompanied by a spark of anger and a stab of guilt. He had been too harsh, he had not thought things through. He thought of Stokely and Pratt and Mac, but he knew that, with the possible exception of Mac, it wasn't the individuals themselves he missed, but his affection for them. Outside the trenches, Jack Wisdom was the only man he'd ever loved; other friends were mere acquaintances by comparison.

He yearned far too much for human contact. And for women. He thought of Margaret Morley's black hair and pale Irish features; he thought of Imogen. Often enough he found himself rapt at the images in the Sears catalogues his father had left behind. It baffled him that a mere drawing, a mere line, the merest oblique C of a nippleless breast could excite him so.

His plan was to finish this novel and then move to Manhattan, just as he'd said he would. Since his return from Baltimore he had been working on his Phipps story, his female psychiatrist. Despite the surface debt to Imogen, he found that writing the story took him away from thoughts of her. His character did things the real Imogen had never done, said things she would never say, and so the two—in his mind, as the pages piled up—bore less and less resemblance to each other.

One of the simplest tasks—selecting a name for his heroine—proved to be one of the most difficult. Eventually he settled on Grace, and even wrote several chapters calling her Grace, but found his Jesuit-moulded mind could not get past the religious overtones. He changed it to Gwen. It felt truncated and insufficient after Imogen, but he liked the Arthurian overtones.

Gwen, unlike Imogen, was in love with Bannock, an extremely manly man—a man with a taste for danger. Bannock enlists in the United States Army roughly thirty seconds after Woodrow Wilson's declaration of war—not out of any fantasy of suicide but for the pleasure of shooting barbarians. Gwen, although terrified for his life, accepts that he must go, knowing that he would be miserable on the sidelines.

Soon after she joins the Phipps, a young soldier is admitted—a possible schizophrenic, possible transient psychotic, and, according to the army medical officer who transferred him, likely malingerer. There is no question of shell shock because he has not yet left Fort Meade. Quentin chose not to describe the young man, whose name is Hansen,

but Gwen perceives him as extraordinarily beautiful. The question—
the only question as far as the army is concerned: is he faking?

At first Gwen has no doubt that he is suffering from mental illness.
No one could fake the Byzantine flights of speech he comes up with,
the dizzying illogic, the sudden paranoid "insights" followed by weeks
of immobility, and not actually be mad. And yet Hansen enjoys lucid
periods, all too brief, during which the charming and useful young
man he might have been comes vividly alive. He is a big reader, can
remember the plots and characters of Charles Dickens and quote pas-
sages of Shakespeare, not to mention Imogen's favourites, Lewis
Carroll and Jonathan Swift. But then it is as if a trap door opens and
this smiling literary man drops from view, to be replaced by the drea-
rily insane individual who occupies the same bed on West One.

The story had reached the point now where Hansen's delusions and
hallucinations begin to seem suspiciously poetic. Gwen starts to per-
ceive a coherence and beauty in them that goes far beyond the ironclad solipsism of the psychotic, but just as she starts to think he is
faking she also begins to suspect she is in love with him. This at a time
when men are returning from the front horribly mutilated—missing
eyes, jaws, limbs—and disfigured beyond all understanding. Those
who aren't physically burned and broken are mentally so, quivering
wraiths barely able to clutch a cigarette without dropping it.

Quentin was mulling whether to kill Gwen's boyfriend off or have
him come back hideously wounded. What he wanted above all was for
Gwen to protect Hansen by finding him insane. What would happen
beyond that he did not know, and he sensed an impasse just up the
road. Unless you counted the elements of war, which were peripheral
to the main story, it was very much a Jeremy West book.

The great advantage of being Jeremy West was that Jeremy West
was not in love with Imogen Lang. A state devoutly to be wished
because Quentin could lose an hour, even two, imagining life not
just with Imogen but with her children. He saw himself—wickedly,
he knew—in her husband's place, amusing them, teaching them,

comforting them when they were ill or hurt or sad. He imagined reading to them in bed—he in the middle with an enormous illustrated copy of *Alice in Wonderland* propped on his chest, a twin cuddled on either side, doing funny voices for the March Hare and the Red Queen and the Mock Turtle. And in the other bed—for there must be two little beds in the twins' room—lies his wife, Imogen, who looks on smiling, or listens with eyes closed, savouring Carroll's gorgeous nonsense, her children's rapt attention, her own colossal good fortune in being at the centre of this blessed, loving family.

He had been immobilized over his typewriter by these thoughts for a good ninety minutes one day when he shook his head, gave his face a dry wash, and stood up. He stretched, looking out the window—hill, town, lake—and gave a yell for no reason but to clear his head.

A copy of the *Lake Placid News* lay on the table. He picked it up and scanned the articles. Al Jolson had come to town to perform a benefit for the Girls' Industrial School. The University of New Hampshire winter sports team had arrived, apparently confident that snow would surely follow. One headline concerned the appearance of a black bear in Ausable Forks. *Bruin Pays Early Call on Village*, the subhead ran, *Routed by Four-Pawed Dog Without Argument*. Most days, Quentin enjoyed the local news, right down to the notices to creditors, but since his return from Baltimore he found it trivial, precious, priggish, and a great many other things that irritated him.

He sat down again and rolled a fresh piece of paper into the Royal and wrote the following to his editor: *Dear Griffin, I'm definitely moving to New York. Where's a good place to live?*

# 20

Three weeks into February, winter seemed barely to have grazed the city of Baltimore. People strolled about in summer-weight suits, and in many places—Johns Hopkins among them—the grass was still deep green. But Imogen had never been so cold. Never, growing up through all those Chicago winters, had she found it so difficult to get warm. At night, after the twins had gone to sleep, she would curl up on the couch fully clothed and under an eiderdown, and still her fingers, her toes, the tip of her nose were frigid, as if she had just staggered in from a sleigh ride. She recognized this as a transformation wrought by the chemistry of high emotion. It made her think of all the ice queens and frozen caves of myth and fairy tale, literary material she had come to re-explore through the works of Freud and Jung.

This same dark magic had transformed her beloved Phipps, her former castle, into an icy keep. The inviting red brick of its exterior was now the colour of rust and blood, the gleaming marble that had promised stability and protection was now comfortless. The hundred feet of hallway between her lab and Carl's might as well have been miles, and the marble itself seemed despair transformed into matter.

Her colleagues—to a man, to a woman (except Lila Quinn)—were kind. None of them said anything directly, but she registered the unlikely notes of cheer or warmth they added to the most routine exchanges with her. She had become that pitiable thing, the abandoned woman. She thought about picking up and moving away, anywhere but here, but she had always thought she would stay at the Phipps, and had never put out a single query about work elsewhere.

She had recently been surprised by a job offer that arrived, thanks to a friend of Donna's, from the state courthouse (juvenile division) in New York City. It paid reasonably well, but the work—assessing the psychological states of children and parents for court purposes—did not excite her. She would have no connection to an educational insti-tute, no connection to the famous Phipps. But she kept bumping into Carl at work and it was agony.

She met with Dr. Ganz in his office and asked him outright why Carl had not been fired.

"Oh, dear," Ganz said. "You are under enormous strain, aren't you."

"I'm in an impossible position. The entire staff know that he slept with his graduate student. I had almost reconciled myself to living with that. But now that he's abandoned me the looks of pity have become unbearable."

"Oh, not pity, I think. Empathy. Concern. You must know that you are very well liked—and very highly regarded—in this place. I think it only natural people should sympathize with you and wish for you happier circumstances, don't you?"

"When Robert Taunton left his wife you got him out of here quick enough. You and the board were adamant that his behaviour was grounds for dismissal—as were all the other institutions that refused to hire him."

"That's true. You know what I personally think of Mr. Kromer's behaviour."

"And what about the man Taunton replaced?"

"Donald Lyme."

"The minute it came to light he'd been in a brothel he was out that door."

"Yes, but—"

"And that didn't even involve a student!"

"Lyme broke the law. That's why he was banished. He wasn't right for the job anyway—far too theoretical, too meditative."

"But that's not why he was fired."

"Look, Dr. Lang, it grieves me to see you in such pain, but there are other considerations."

"What considerations? What are these *considerations*?"

"Mr. Kromer has become very valuable to this institution."

"Robert Taunton was the most famous psychologist in the world. You couldn't *wait* to let him go."

"Mr. Taunton's work, his writing, were very much out of harmony with our aims here at the Phipps. His behaviour—unlike Mr. Kromer's—was reported in all the papers. He damaged our reputation. There was never any question of his remaining on staff."

"But this is different?"

"Well, yes. Perhaps you have forgotten, but when your husband's indiscretion—"

"That's a nice word for it."

Dr. Ganz cocked his head to one side, eyebrows raised.

"When your difficulties came to light," he said, "I did my utmost to deal with them in a way that would cause the least turmoil for *you*. I arranged for the transfer of Miss Bee, and spoke sharply to Mr. Kromer about my disappointment in him. I certainly *considered* dismissing him but I had no indication that it was what you wanted nor any reason to suppose it would serve you best. If he were unemployed your circumstances would be all the harder, would they not?"

"Well, by moving out he has created two households where there was one."

"Just so."

"It's perhaps not professional of me to mention it, but you must see, sir—this is agony for me."

"I do. And it pains me. Truly. But it is now several months since the affair with—"

"Two months."

"I believe it is closer to three. In either case, enough time has elapsed that dismissal would now be seen as being at your say-so, rather than on the wishes of the officers of this institution."

"Do you want *me* to go, is that it?"

"Not at all. You mustn't think that."

"Because I can't bear this."

"You underestimate yourself. You're a resilient person. A strong character."

"Am I?"

"And look. I *do* have some good news." He held up a typewritten letter.

Imogen took the letter and scanned it. It was from the Trenton Hospital medical board.

"At long last," Ganz said. "Dr. Bingham will be here within the week. We'll thrash out our differences and the way will be cleared for publication. It's not all darkness."


The agony Imogen experienced at work was all but matched by the agony of being at home with two young children. She had underestimated how much their happiness depended on Carl's being at hand. With her father gone, and with her mother so upset, Charlotte became whiny and even reverted occasionally to sucking her thumb. Aubrey was sullen, listless, and, in contrast to his former sunny disposition, tearful.

The dreaded question *When is Papa coming home?* became gradually less frequent, but when it did surface it did so with anger and tears.

"You told him to leave," Charlotte accused her one day. "That's why Papa took us away."

"I didn't tell him to leave, Charlotte. Your father and I simply don't get along anymore and have to live apart. No one's to blame." It cost her something to say that, but Charlotte wasn't buying it.

"You sent him away," she insisted, "just like you send us to our room."

"No, my darling. It's not that way at all."

"I hate you," Charlotte said. "I hate you."

Aubrey was sobbing on the end of the sofa. When Charlotte stomped out of the living room, Imogen put her arm around him.

"Hurts, doesn't it," she said.

Aubrey managed a miserable nod.

"It hurts me too."

Aubrey sniffled and peered up at her. "Really?"

"Yes, of course, dear. It hurts me terribly."

He blinked at her, upper lip glossy with mucus, pale brow creased with suspicion: mothers feel pain? It was clearly the first he'd heard of it, and he looked far from persuaded.

The Saturday morning shopping was grim. To the twins, the trip to the market without their father was not just a pale imitation but an outright abomination. They screamed and fought and wept and in general made it impossible to get anything done. After the first two weeks Carl agreed to take them on Saturday mornings, and the weekly shopping became peaceful but lonely. She saw with hyper clarity that modern civilization was built around couples. The first Saturday she went to the market alone there was not one woman of her age who was not accompanied by either a child or a husband. Not one. The second time she did see one—a blond woman with mousy features, even younger than Imogen—but she was dressed in mourning. Imogen knew it was peculiar, but for the rest of that day, for the rest of that entire weekend, she envied that young widow the simplicity of her situation. She envied there being no one to blame, no questioning looks. Then again, she told herself, I probably just wish Carl was dead.

"What a bundle of negative emotions you're becoming," Laura said to her on the streetcar home.

"Not without some cause, wouldn't you say?"

"Plenty of cause. But you don't want to become bitter. Such a horrible feeling and decidedly unattractive."

"Oh, don't *you* turn against me too."

"I'll never turn against you, my darling. I shall love you always. And I'll always be here when you need me."

A woman took the seat next to Imogen, an older woman who did her marketing on the same schedule and had spoken to her and Carl a few times over the years.

"No little ones today?"

"Not today. It gets so tiring for them."

"It does, poor things. Husband away?"

"Yes. Yes, he's away."

"You must miss him. I've always been struck by how good he is with your twins."

"Yes," Imogen said. "He is."

One day, as she was leaving work for the evening, she was halfway down the stairs when she had an impulse to visit Carl in his lab and tell him to please stop telling the children she had sent him away. Not that she knew he had, but she felt the need to snarl at him.

His lab was deserted. Imogen called his name but no one answered. Perhaps they were out hunting rats, a pursuit that consumed an increasing portion of Carl's time. She went into the first research room. The swimming jars were lined up in a corner, empty of water, fogged with dust. In the second room a dog lay curled in a cage. Beyond this, stacks of smaller cages housed rats. Some slept, some watched her with pink-rimmed eyes of polished jet, whiskers twitching.

Imogen went out to the main lab again and into a third research room on the far side. Test tubes, microscopes, funnels, and slides. She returned to the main lab and called Carl's name. She could hear the coldness in her voice, any note of love silenced. She opened the hall door and checked both ways. Taking a deep breath, and moving with deliberation, she walked through the first research room and into the second and set about opening the rat cages. One by one the little doors clattered open. Thirteen, fourteen, she had opened all fifteen cages before the first rat scuttled onto the counter and made the leap for freedom, hitting the floor with a squeak. She was about to open the dog's cage—he was looking at her with mournful eyes—but she feared he might kill the rats.

As she went down the marble stairs, she experienced a tiny chime of triumph. She heard again Ganz's assurance that all was not darkness, and thought she heard, somewhere above and behind her on the third floor, a flurry of squeaks and a skittering of tiny paws.

# 21

Now that Imogen no longer had to travel back and forth to Trenton, she was able to resume her work with patients. She found a solace on the wards that was not available in her lab. Bingham's fixation on focal infection had soured her on the search for somatic causes of mental disease. Perhaps, too, her anger at Carl had destroyed her passion for lab work. And somehow her patients seemed more reachable than before, more amenable to treatment—in a word, less loony. She found herself enjoying the talk therapy sessions, could feel herself becoming more skilful. Patients would meet her gaze, and a spark of recognition would pass between them.

"You've lived more," Dr. Ganz said when she described it to him. "You are understanding your patients more quickly. They will be sensing your greater empathy and responding to it."

"I thought I had empathy before," Imogen said.

"Dynamic range," Ganz said, and fluttered his long fingers over an invisible keyboard. "You have greater dynamic range, emotionally."

"Well. I'd rather just be perceptive."

"Dear me, yes," Ganz said. "Wouldn't we all."

And there was Donna. Now that her friend was without a husband, she reappeared in Imogen's life like a pet that had gone missing only to turn up on the doorstep years later. Same elfin nose and chin, same combative posture. Faint crows' feet around her eyes only made her more attractive, adding a touch of wisdom to the spikiness. Donna called her at work one day and they made arrangements to go out to dinner. Imogen scrounged up a graduate student to babysit and the two of them went to dine at the Hotel Baltimore's café. She had never been to such an expensive place before and would not have gone now except that Donna insisted.

"No, we must," she said. "You've been through a lot and you look like hell, Imogen, you really do."

"Kind of you to notice."

"Oh, don't take on. I just mean you look like you've been through the wringer, which you have."

Donna herself looked trim and stylish and ready for fun.

"Now you mustn't stint," she added, when they were seated. "This is my treat and I feel like spending money."

Imogen remonstrated, but it was hopeless when Donna had her mind set on anything. They each ordered a seafood cocktail for an appetizer—lobster for Donna, crab meat for Imogen.

"You're stinting," Donna said. "Stop it at once."

"I like crab. And stop nagging."

Donna sighed. "You're such a little nun."

"And you're a termagant. So nothing's changed."

The Baltimore had recently modernized. In place of the usual waiters in black, the café was staffed by women in white aprons who served food from clanking trolleys.

"It's like being at work," Imogen said. "All the nurses."

"We've got to get you out of that place. Honestly, Im, you can't spend the rest of your life working for Jonas Ganz—what about that New York job?"

"It was kind of you to mention me, but I don't want to leave the Phipps. I want Carl to leave."

"That man should've been booted out immediately, given the stated policy."

Imogen had told her Ganz's reasoning on that score.

"Well, of course you didn't want him fired when you were still together. But surely Ganz can understand how things have changed."

"I think he does, but—"

"Ganz always sees five sides to every story, you notice?"

"Apparently Carl has become indispensable."

"Nonsense. Ganz is a fool."

"He's not. If he was a fool, it wouldn't hurt so much."

The waitress brought their soup, and Imogen tried a spoonful of her consommé Colbert.

"This is delicious. Thank you so much for prying me out. How is the turtle soup?"

"A touch over-turtled for my taste, but very tolerable."

Donna talked about her practice for a while. She had many female patients, almost more than she could handle. She was on her own now.

"Really? What happened to Snake Walcott? I'm sorry—I can't say his name without laughing."

"He's moved to California. He's breeding cats."

"No, really—what's he doing?"

"Breeding cats. That's *really* what he's doing. Abyssinians, apparently. Don't look at me like that."

"But it's hilarious. Surely you of all people see that."

"He's eccentric, all right? Lots of brilliant people are eccentric. You're eccentric, too, you know—giving up a man you loved to marry a man you didn't."

Imogen put down her spoon, more loudly than she'd intended. "In the first place, Quentin was a boy, not a man. And in the second place, I was not in love with him."

"No. You *loved* him. There's a difference."

"Let me finish. In the third place, I *did* love Carl. I was *mad* about Carl. I couldn't *wait* to marry him."

"And look where that got you." Donna reached across the table and touched Imogen's wrist. "I don't mean it harshly."

"How *do* you mean it?"

"Every time you would tell me about Quentin—and you talked about him a *lot*—you would get this, how do I put it, happy, *enthusiastic* look on your face. It's the way people look when they're telling you about a story they loved. A book. Except when you were busy blaming yourself for sending him off to war."

"I didn't send him off to war."

"No, you *didn't*. Exactly my point. And you were so shipwrecked when you heard that he'd been killed."

"Because he was my *friend*. I was terribly fond of him. And he *did* join up because of his feelings for me, and he *did* get killed. It's not a story, Donna, it's a person's life. And death. And it's my life too."

They went silent as the waitress cleared away their soup bowls and served Imogen her sage hen and Donna her venison.

"Goodness," Imogen said, hoping to change the subject. "This is the best thing I've eaten in years. A fancy dinner at home is boiled ham."

"Did it not occur to you," Donna pressed on, "that the intensity of your response to his death indicated something more than friendship?"

"Yes, it occurred to me, and no, that doesn't make it true. Why are you harping on this?"

Donna went on as if she hadn't spoken. "Whereas your attitude to Carl, in the early days anyway, struck me as less like love and more like obsession. You didn't *want* to be with him, you *had* to be with him."

"It's called being *in* love. It'll happen to you one day."

"Maybe. But I think you had to be with Carl because he looked like a good replacement for your father—yes, you of the absent Papa—handy with tools, take-charge manner, believer in progress."

"Really, Donna. You don't know what you're talking about. You weren't even around. I'm not going to deny I made a bad choice in Carl, but why don't we talk about *your* romantic life. Lack thereof."

"That's my girl," Donna cried. "Stick that knife in."

"You did ask for it."

"Of course I did. I always do."

So Donna told her about the breakup with Snake Walcott—yes, she admitted, they did have an affair, but only after she ceased to be patient or pupil. She then related a condensed version of a shorter affair with a Hopkins professor of endocrinology. And an even briefer version of an even briefer liaison with a female psychiatrist at the MacLean Institute in Boston.

"Don't look shocked," Donna said. "Don't look shocked or I'll stab you with this fork and you'll go through life with four adorable little holes in your cheekbone."

"I'm not shocked," Imogen said. "A little surprised. Or maybe not even that." She was remembering the time Donna had kissed her full on the mouth.

"Look, I'm not an invert. I don't lie awake at night fantasizing about women. It's just sometimes one feels the need of someone else's finger. Not to mention tongue."

"*Now* I'm shocked," Imogen said.

"Darling, I hope you don't blush like that with your patients."

"We're in a restaurant, not the consulting room—*darling*."

"Speaking of which, I had a very interesting visitor a while back—not a patient. But first I want to order dessert."

Imogen ordered steamed raisin pudding with fruit sauce; Donna chose Bavarian cream.

"My visitor," she said between spoonfuls, "was Jeremy West."

"Jeremy West, the novelist?"

"None other. And very charming he was, too. I think he fancied me."

"All men fancy you. How extraordinary, though, that you met him. You said he wasn't a patient?"

"He's researching a novel. Thinking of setting it at the Phipps, or somewhere very *like* the Phipps."

"That's a change. His books are usually set in some place that could be anywhere—another country, even—they're so dreamlike. So how was he?"

"I don't know." Donna shrugged. "Pleasant, polite, a bit goofy. Shy, I think. I got the impression that talking to strangers did not come easy. He's tall—masses of curly hair. Walks with a—not a limp, exactly—but carries himself carefully. I suspect a war injury but didn't ask, obviously."

"Weren't you excited? I love his books."

"I had read one of them—and quite enjoyed it. Can't see myself getting very worked up about the stuff, but I see what you mean about dreamlike."

"Which one did you read?"

"*Vanessa*—not a bad portrait of obsession."

"Did he have a lot of questions?"

"Not really. And they were quite prosaic—where did we eat, where did we sleep, what was it like working for Ganz. Nothing about treatment, Freud, medication. Not even much about patients. At first I thought he was trying a cagey way of exploring treatment for himself, but I dropped that idea when he started with his questions. They weren't the kinds of things a prospective patient would ask."

"I'd love to meet him someday."

"Maybe you will. I had the impression he'd have more questions."

They moved on to other topics. Over coffee, Imogen told Donna about Dr. Bingham and his treatments, and about her findings.

"And Ganz is making publication dependent on Bingham's signing off on your report?"

"I'm afraid so."

"Clearly that's never going to happen. Which means you won't be allowed to publish. Do you remember what happened to Daniel Mellon at MacLean? His research showed no difference between therapy with a psychiatrist and therapy with a nurse. His dean stood in his way and in frustration he sent his research to the *New York World*. They rewrote it, of course, which made his claims even more sensational and he was totally blackballed. He lost his position at Mellon and has not been able to secure another one, despite the fact that he's one of MacLean's brightest. It's a club, Imogen, and they set the rules."

"Ganz will let me publish. He knows Bingham's treatments are dangerous."

"Imogen, take my advice. Get yourself into a training analysis *now*.

In two years you'll be ready to take on patients yourself, and you won't have to work for idiots like Ganz or Bingham."

"That's not fair. Whatever you may think of Dr. Ganz he's not like Bingham. He wants only the best for his patients. He's not *harming* people."

"I have to tell you something." Donna reached across the table and took both of Imogen's hands in hers. "I'm not sure this is the right time, but there may not be a better."

"What is it?"

"I'm moving to New York to set up practice."

"Oh, please don't. Donna, you know how much I rely on you."

"And I on you. Which is why you should come with me. With your experience it's not going to take you long to get approval from the New York Psychoanalytic Society. You'll make a hell of a lot more money."

"Even if I wanted to go—which I don't—I'd have to find some other job while I was in training. Who knows how long that could take?"

Donna squeezed her hands.

"Come to New York."

The Bingham meeting was arranged for the second week of January. Far from the sedate, scholarly atmosphere that might have been preferable, and despite all the advance letter-writing, it had the frenetic, panicky feel typical of a last-minute arrangement.

"I invited Bingham and his wife to stay with us," Dr. Ganz told Imogen, "but they've parked themselves at the Emerson."

"He's probably only just now read the report," Imogen said. "I mean, really read it. And he realizes what it means."

"But you were keeping him up to date. No one could miss where your research was heading."

"Well, I told you what he was like when I was in Trenton. Except for the last few weeks, he seemed to think I was certifying his success."

Dr. Ganz frowned and stubbed out his cigar with some violence. "I fear we're in for an unpleasant time of it."

That was Tuesday. On Wednesday morning, Dr. Bingham went on rounds with Dr. Ganz, but Ganz could not get out of a series of appointments in the afternoon. The three of them finally assembled in Dr. Ganz's office on the Thursday.

Before Bingham had even sat down, he went on the offensive.

"Imagine my surprise, Dr. Ganz, to find myself, at the age of fifty-eight, attacked in the most vicious manner by a woman of thirty-two. And who is this woman? How many papers has she published? One. Which is neither about schizophrenia nor manic-depression nor paranoia but about syphilis. I, at the age of fifty-eight, have been director of a state asylum for over ten years. I have published dozens of papers, performed hundreds if not thousands of operations, yet I am called upon to defend myself to a junior member of your staff. A female."

Ganz tried to interrupt but Bingham was already red-faced and did not notice.

"Here I am dragged away from important work for this utterly trivial exercise. We cure people at Trenton, you know, we actually *cure* people—and I'm not talking about the society neurasthenics and adolescent suicide attempts you truckle with here at the Phipps. No. I'm talking about hard-core, chronic, full-blown schizophrenics—now able to go home, some even able to work—released from a living death on the back wards. And I am taken away from this work to answer the spurious objections of a *girl*."

"Dr. Bingham, please. Dr. Lang is hardly—"

"I don't see what my sex has to do with anything," Imogen put in.

Bingham talked right over her. "And a suffragette, no doubt. A professional complainer."

"Or my age. Or my politics—if I had any."

"You see how she speaks to me!"

Ganz raised his hands, palms out, for calm.

"Dr. Bingham. Please. Let us conduct ourselves in a spirit of inquiry. Dr. Lang is a highly respected member of my staff and an experienced researcher and clinician who was approved for this task by your medical board and by yourself."

"At *your* recommendation. Obviously we had nothing else to go on."

"Let us discuss the facts of the matter," Ganz said, "and see where we are. Dr. Lang, perhaps you could begin by outlining how you selected the cases and how you came up with the data in your report."

Imogen couldn't help noticing Dr. Ganz's hands were trembling as he spoke.

"The general plan," she began, "was to review older cases first, so that enough time had elapsed to judge longer-term results; then to review current cases to illuminate the immediate effects of treatment; and finally to study a group whose results were especially good—by which we hoped to reveal the possibilities of the treatment, the best course."

Bingham was glaring at her like some jungle creature about to pounce, and pounce he did.

"Right there," he said, jumping to his feet, "right there you have a major error. How can you have any meaningful findings if you don't first study the rates of discharge *before* I got to Trenton?"

"My brief was not to study the results of your hospital, but the effects of your treatment. I chose 1920 as the starting point because by then the surgical and dental procedures had been in use for two years and more—time enough to work out the kinks and improve procedures."

"What do you know about it?" Bingham said. Then, to Ganz, "What does she know about surgery and focal infection?" And back to Imogen. "Do you know the first thing about medicine? How many bones are there in the human body?"

"Really," Ganz protested mildly, "I don't see how this will—"

"Let her answer!"

Ganz, apparently cowed, made a note on one of his ubiquitous index cards.

"I don't remember the exact number," Imogen admitted.

"You see! Not the first thing! She doesn't know the first thing!"

"But I can name them. Starting from the cranium, there's the frontal, parietal, temporal, occipital, sphenoid, and ethmoid. In the face we have mandible, maxilla, palatine, zygomatic—"

Dr. Ganz cleared his throat noisily. "Thank you, Doctor. I think that will—"

"Nasal, lachrymal, vomer, the inferior nasal conchaie. In the ear, the malleus, incus, and stapes—"

"Dr. Lang, thank you. Please resist the urge to continue and let us move on."

"Rote memorization," Bingham grumbled. "Proves nothing."

"The hyoid, the clavicle, the shoulder blade—"

"Dr. Lang, please! The first group?"

Imogen adjusted her glasses and peered at her summary.

"The first hundred were purely consecutive. Of these, I found a 12 percent recovery rate."

"What absolute trash," Bingham said. "You can't expect me to listen to this."

"Dr. Bingham, please allow Dr. Lang to lay out her findings."

"Findings? These are pure invention, Ganz! She doesn't even say what she means by 'recovered.'"

"I do, actually, and the appendix with patient summaries shows clearly what it is not. It is not, for example, Frank Spica—now a vagabond given to tantrums. Nor is it Yolanda Watts—unable to work or even remember where she lives. Nor Miles Conklin, actively paranoid and a neighbourhood pest given to frightening fits of anger. Bessie Jones is catatonic."

"You spend most of your time in a lab. What do you know about diagnosis?"

"Now is not the time to question Dr. Lang's credentials," Dr. Ganz pointed out. "I repeat: she was approved by yourself and your medical board."

"Twenty-six of these patients are currently in hospital," Imogen noted, "either at Trenton or elsewhere."

"Which does not mean they are unimproved."

"One could not call them cured."

"They might be cured of functional paranoia and now be suffering from Korsakoff's."

"They aren't. Check the appendix."

"Twelve percent, Ganz. It's libellous."

"Dr. Bingham," Imogen pressed on, "fully thirty-five of these hundred patients are dead."

"Meaningless, unless you compare it to other hospitals."

"Indeed, it is not much out of line with expectations for the severely mentally ill. However, it renders impossible any claim of 85 percent recovery—unless you count death as a positive outcome."

"Are you being sarcastic with me?"

"I'm simply stating a fact."

So it continued for the next two hours. Every finding, every assessment, every atom of arithmetic only served to fuel Bingham's rage. Ganz for the most part remained silent, leaving Imogen to state her case and suffer the fury of Bingham's replies. She felt like a sapling facing a hurricane, and through it all Dr. Ganz, pale and agitated, made notes on his index cards. They adjourned at four o'clock, having made scant progress, and it was only after Ganz's repeated entreaties that Bingham agreed to meet the following day.

Imogen went home exhausted, almost stuporous, unable to give the twins the attention they needed. When she failed to stop Aubrey from once again abducting one of Charlotte's dolls, Charlotte thumped him on the head and cascades of tears, male and female, ensued.

She slept badly. She woke in a sweat from a dream in which a team of surgeons was dismembering a live pig. It had a cat's face, and turned pleading, human eyes to Imogen, who was unable to do anything but observe. Shaken, she climbed out of bed, heart pounding, and went to the window, pulling the curtains aside. The backyard mulberry tree, slick with rain, looked twiggy and disconsolate. It came to her with three-o'clock-in-the-morning certainty that Bingham was never going to sign her report. He had nothing to gain by doing so, and everything to lose. Her future was slipping from her grasp, and she thought how illusory her sense of control had been. Whether or not her Trenton study would be published, her status, her income, her romantic life (now over for good) were all shaped by forces entirely beyond her control. She curled up once more and prayed for sleep, quick and dreamless, to return.

The Friday meeting went no better. Bingham bridled at every number, took issue with every diagnosis, and insisted on revisiting the arithmetic behind every table. He accused Imogen of extreme bias and, repeatedly, of slander.

"Dr. Bingham," she said at one point, "you noted yesterday that I spend a good deal of my life in the lab. Why? Because I too believe it quite probable that underneath every psychosis some somatic cause lies hidden. Infection might yet turn out to be one of those causes, but the question before us is, 'Do your surgical and dental treatments help, harm, or have no effect on psychotic patients?' You say they help in 85 percent of cases. My findings say no—those changed for the better being so few that their improvement cannot be ascribed to your treatment."

"Rubbish," Bingham snarled. "You've adopted idiosyncratic selection methods and ignored standard practice, which is to go by admissions and discharges."

"Those cannot be reliable," Imogen countered for the third time, "because administrative changes may increase or decrease discharges where there is no change in mental condition."

"You've picked all the worst outcomes and hold them up as representative."

"That would be reprehensible, if true, but it isn't. One group was entirely selected by you personally. Sixty-two patients who, you thought, had shown the greatest improvement. Seven of them are now in other hospitals, fourteen are back in Trenton, and twenty-seven are dead."

"That's right, ignore the rest. Very fair."

Ganz looked up from his index cards but said nothing. What spell had transformed her formidable chief into this dormouse? Imogen fought an impulse to thump him on the head the way Charlotte had hit her brother and send him wailing to another room.

She took a deep breath. "Of the other cases, five are living at home but unimproved."

"According to whom?"

Imogen read from the summaries.

"Lisa Mark—no initiative, flat affect, deteriorated interests. Mel Perkins—actively hallucinating, delusional, paranoid. Marvin Poole—marked deterioration, memory loss, delusional. They're all in the appendix, Doctor."

"Yes, yes. I suppose no one has recovered, in your view. You see, Ganz? She sees nothing but failure."

"Five patients recovered," Imogen said. "Three of these, upon admission and according to records, are manic-depressive. Their symptoms display the usual periodicity."

"And you therefore don't count them!"

"I *do* count them, but I note that recovery in such cases is the expected outcome, regardless of treatment. The other two appear to have made excellent recoveries."

"Very generous of you. Thank you so much."

"Tabulations for this group are 15 percent recovered or improved, 40 percent unimproved, and 42.5 percent dead."

"Listen to her, Ganz. She's a one-woman lynch mob. Tell her she's got it all wrong. How can you sit there in silence while she tars me with these accusations?"

Ganz roused himself. "You mustn't see it in that light, Dr. Bingham. These are scientific findings. We are discussing facts, not accusations. We simply want you to—"

A look of horror contorted Bingham's features and he emitted a choked squeal. Imogen feared a heart attack but he pointed to the bookshelves where a white rat scurried back and forth.

"Oh, for God's sake," Ganz said, and called out, "Mr. Penn! Mr. Penn, we've got another one!"

Mr. Penn appeared at once, armed with whisk broom and tennis racket. He moved toward the shelves but the rat scuttled between his legs and out the door, Penn bobbing after him in pursuit.

"I must apologize, Dr. Bingham. Some miscreant let the rats out of our psychology lab. They've been turning up everywhere."

"Perhaps we should call Mr. Kromer," Imogen said. "He has a certain affinity with rats."

Bingham got up from his chair, red-faced and sweating, and left the office. Dr. Ganz rose and followed him as far as the door. Dr. Bingham was in the outer office fighting with the sleeves of his overcoat.

"We still have more ground to cover," Ganz said. "No doubt we can all use a break over the weekend, but let's finish up on Monday."

Bingham muttered something Imogen didn't hear and Ganz followed him out into the hall. Imogen packed up her papers.

"What did he say?" she asked when Ganz came back.

"Two-thirty, Monday afternoon."

"All right then," Imogen said with a cheeriness she did not feel. "I'll see you Monday."

"That went a bit better today, don't you think?"

"No. I can't say that I do."

"Bingham just needs time. It's hard for him to see things objectively."

"Till Monday then."

"Yes, yes. Till Monday. Enjoy your weekend, Doctor."


Imogen spent all her spare moments of the weekend thinking about the next meeting. She recognized that Bingham's arrogance and bluster hid a fragile man who truly wanted to help the victims of mental illness. She wanted to reach that man with her findings, with logic, with evidence. But that inner man was defended by a threatened ego that would use every available weapon to defeat that purpose. She empathized with his pain. She too hated to be shown she was wrong, hated to be corrected, and Bingham's torment was vivid. His agony suffused the room, the fiery flush of his cheeks screaming humiliation.

She examined her conscience to see if she had been disrespectful, or peremptory. She had not. The facts themselves tortured Bingham, no matter how gently she tried to present them. Dr. Bingham, the facts said, you have been a fool—worse, a kind of monster. You are maiming and sometimes killing people who have come to you for help. How could one soften such an indictment?

In the end her fretting was to no purpose. Bingham sent Dr. Ganz a message on Sunday evening saying that his wife was not well and he would be returning to Trenton forthwith.

"I've written to the Trenton board," Ganz informed her Monday morning, "and asked them how they want to proceed. One thing is certain—the report cannot be published until Bingham signs it."

"If that's truly the case then you are telling me the whole exercise was pointless—because he is never going to sign it."

Ganz must have heard something new in her tone. He squinted at her over his reading glasses. "I don't think we need be quite so pessimistic, Dr. Lang. Perhaps the board will help him see the—"

"And Carl is here to stay, is that the case?"

"I beg your pardon?" Ganz looked puzzled by the sudden change in topic.

"Carl Kromer," Imogen said. "My husband? You won't be dismissing him, despite his affair with a student and despite policy and precedent?" She heard, with some alarm, the flint in her tone.

"I told you, Dr. Lang, my hands are tied on that matter."

"I see. Then I'd best get back to the lab."

She left his office and walked out past Mr. Penn and into the corridor. She pressed the elevator button but then decided to take the stairs. She was halfway up the first flight when she paused, gripping the marble rail. A minute went by, perhaps two, before she reminded herself to keep calm, to take a deep breath and count to ten. Having done this, she turned and went back down the steps and back to Ganz's office. Mr. Penn stood up. "Did you forget something?"

Imogen went by him and into Dr. Ganz's office without knocking. He was standing with his back to her, staring out the window, wreathed in cigar smoke.

"It's wrong," she said. "It's wrong, Dr. Ganz, and you know it." Her heart was pounding high in her chest and she had to fight to keep her voice normal.

"I'm sorry," Mr. Penn said from behind her, "she walked right by me."

"It's all right, Mr. Penn. Thank you."

Mr. Penn withdrew and shut the door behind him.

Dr. Ganz puffed on his cigar. "Go on, Dr. Lang. You were saying?"

"It's wrong to let Bingham continue with his surgeries, knowing what we know. People's teeth are being torn out, leaving them unable to eat, unable to smile, and stigmatized for life."

"Many surgeries have unfortunate side effects. Obviously Dr. Bingham is going to weigh those beside the possible benefits of extraction."

"There are no benefits. You know it and I know it, and now the Trenton board should know it."

"The agreement with Dr. Bingham was—"

"Why are you hiding behind this ridiculous agreement? Who ever heard of requiring agreement from the subject of a study that finds him incompetent or dangerous? Did you have Donna's agreement when you fired her?"

"Dr. Lang, you are overstepping. Matters concerning other personnel are hardly—"

"We're not talking about Phipps personnel. We're talking about a man who is killing people."

"His mortality rates are no higher than any other abdominal surgeon's."

"Abdominal surgeons are attempting to treat *abdominal* problems, not mental problems. There are no indications *in favour* of his performing such surgeries. There is no evidence of benefit and ample evidence of harm. He is wounding and killing helpless people—my study proves it beyond a doubt, and yet you sat there and let him yell at me and call me unqualified the whole time. You let him brush it off as if it were nothing."

"You exaggerate, Doctor, and your tone is approaching insubordination." Ganz gave her a hard stare, and she remembered how his eyes had frightened her years ago. She was too angry to be frightened now.

"Bingham isn't curing *anyone*. He's *killing* people. You must allow me to publish."

"I have told you—our agreement with Trenton precludes it, under current circumstances."

"Those circumstances will not change. Dr. Bingham cannot accept the truth. He *will* not. Are you going to let him continue lying to himself, the world, and his victims? These are helpless people, Dr. Ganz. Utterly defenceless against him."

Ganz stubbed out his cigar, and looked her up and down. "You are highly excited, your complexion is florid, your voice is raised, and you keep pointing a finger at me. In short you are in the throes of rage and the reason is perfectly clear."

"The reason is injustice."

"It isn't me you're angry at, Imogen. You're finally venting your rage against your father. You think it's against me, but it's against your father who wronged you so long ago."

Imogen was momentarily stunned into silence. Then, "I cannot believe you just said that to me. Are you really trying to undermine scientific facts with this?"

"Clearly there's a good deal of transference going on in your relationship to me. You came here very young, away from your home, following a recent breakup, and I—speaking psychologically—took you in, gave you a home. You found a father figure who offered you respect and even affection, in contrast to your actual father, one who even cared for you when you were ill. It's only natural that you should transfer daughterly feelings toward me, given our therapeutic relationship, which comes on top of the teacher–student, and employer–employee relationships, which are already fraught with transference and always must be negotiated with care."

"Exactly. And as psychiatrist, teacher, and employer, you are in a prime position to exploit that transference. Which is perhaps why you kept me labelled an *intern*, for God's sake, after years on the job, and still grossly underpay me. There is your counter-transference—you can't bear to see one of your birds with broken wings do really well, develop her own therapeutic techniques, publish a book, or assert her independence. That's why Donna had to go. Can you really be so blind to your own counter-transference?"

Dr. Ganz walked to the door and held it open. "I bid you good day, Dr. Lang. You may come and apologize when you are ready."

Imogen didn't move. Dr. Ganz was at least partly right about her transference, and the old buried anger he had provoked would not be silenced.

"What would make you betray me and my work in this horrible way," she went on, "if not counter-transference? Why would you insist on keeping Carl—my tormentor—on staff, when policy clearly states he should be removed? You never wanted me to marry in the first place—perhaps you now want to make sure I never marry again. Why would *that* be, Dr. Ganz? And you talk to *me* about transference?"

"Mr. Penn," Ganz called to the outer room, "please see Dr. Lang out. We are quite finished here."

"Please, Dr. Ganz. My career and my happiness may be of no concern to you, but think of those poor patients. You *know* they deserve better, even if I don't. Suppose I were to publish on my own."

"You can't. You haven't the right. The Trenton contract was with the Phipps—a loan-out agreement for your services on a work-for-hire. You do not own the report and you cannot take it anywhere outside these walls—or Trenton's."

"Dr. Ganz—"

"Enough." Ganz raised a peremptory hand. "This conversation is concluded. I'll expect a written apology on my desk in the morning. Otherwise you can consider your employment terminated."

That night, after the children had gone to bed, Imogen composed two letters. The first was to the director of the juvenile court in Lower Manhattan, accepting the position of psychiatric consultant. The second was to Jonas Ganz, resigning from the Phipps, accompanied by her final report.

# 22

Less than a month later, Imogen moved to New York. Carl offered no strenuous objections to her taking the twins with her, provided he had ample access to them. Three days after her arrival, she began working as a consultant to the juvenile and family court system. Her job was to provide psychiatric assessments—sometimes of the little criminals, sometimes of their parents—which the judges used in determining appropriate punishments and occasionally to assess an inmate's likelihood of reoffending upon release.

Sometimes she was asked to assess children who were not charged with any crime but who were unmanageable at home or in school. It was strange work, because none of the parents or children were her patients. She would interview them for an hour and then type up her assessment. She had the use of a cramped little room on the second floor of the courthouse for the purpose. The interviews took place in a larger space that was made even more depressing by its efforts to look cheerful: amputee Teddy bears and one-eyed dolls. Most of the interviews could have been done by a competent social worker—the root problems being social rather than psychiatric.

Soon after her arrival, she followed Donna's advice and began training as a psychoanalyst under the auspices of the New York Psychoanalytic Society. The institute supplied a patient. Their beautifully produced syllabus assured the prospective analyst that much care went into matching patient to trainee. The case would be challenging, but not so challenging that a beginning analyst could not make progress.

Imogen's patient was a man who was exactly her father's age, and it was clearly no accident he'd been assigned to her. He was unethical in his business practices, unfaithful to his wife, and hypercritical of his daughters. If they had tried to find a patient most likely to stir up her own difficulties, they could hardly have done better.

He very quickly stopped paying. Sessions through the institute were not free but fees were adjusted according to what a patient could afford. It soon became apparent that this man was not the humble clerk he had claimed to be; he was in fact an officer of the firm and earning much more than Imogen. But he always had an excuse, always promised to pay next time.

He had a daughter the same age as Imogen and at whom he was constantly angry. This manifestation of his repressed desire was cartoonish in its extremity, and though he professed to seek help he was in fact seeking medical justification for his nasty behaviour. As the process of transference began to take hold—as Imogen came to stand in for the daughter he could not possess—their sessions became fraught in the extreme.

Imogen's training analyst was a Viennese Jew named Reinhardt—a smug, short-tempered bully who constantly belittled her efforts. He made much of the idea that you can't analyze anyone without first analyzing yourself, and that it is a painful process. Imogen knew that patients must come to their insights at their own pace, whereas Reinhardt would hurl them in her face. "Are you so bound up with your own absentee father that you can't see what this man is telling you? It's obvious to everyone else: he has been ejected from the bed of his wife and now he lusts after his daughter, who resembles whom? His *wife* at the age he married her! His mother at the age his father died! His lust is profoundly disturbing to him and is therefore masked by his attempts to control his daughter and his rage when he cannot. On top of this, he is being rejected by another cold female—you! The very analyst to whom he has turned for help. And you, not wishing to see it, allow it all to be buried under what you see as proper analytical decorum but is in fact your own desire for daddy!"

In addition to the four sessions a week with her patient, she had to endure two of her own with Reinhardt—two sessions in which he would endlessly berate her. "You're angry with this man because he is the father who abandoned you! You are withholding your empathy from him!" Imogen would deny it, saying she was allowing him to reach his own insights. "You are hostile to him. You think he cannot see this?"

She wondered if Reinhardt was trying to trick her into becoming supportive of this patient, but he was not there for support, he was there for analysis. Whenever she wavered, and said something commiserating, Reinhardt would say, "Tea and sympathy. You should open a tea shop. This is not what you are paid for." As if she was being paid.

The whole field of psychoanalysis seemed to be dominated by these Viennese characters, but Imogen told herself they couldn't all be bullies, and they weren't all men. Anna Freud, Frieda Fromm, and Karen Horney were becoming quite prominent, as was Donna Artemis, who had a thriving practice on the Upper West Side, and whose presence in the city made all else bearable.


Imogen's days were crowded, stuffed with people and appointments, assessments to make, reports to write and sometimes to defend in court, and yet real human contact was rare. Where her days had previously been filled with patients, students, nurses, and fellow psychiatrists, she now found herself surrounded by lawyers, judges, juvenile delinquents, and parents of breathtaking incompetence.

And Judge Hollis Wainwright, with whom she seemed fated to have more cases than anyone else, could have been a male avatar of Lila Quinn. He had no great respect for psychiatry and none whatsoever for Imogen. One depressing day, Imogen had just given a report favourable to the parents of a delinquent boy.

"The boy threatened his neighbour with a knife," he pointed out, "and you're telling me he is not by nature violent."

"I believe this was an isolated incident and a reaction to circumstance," Imogen responded, sounding to herself like a junior version of Jonas Ganz. "If his circumstances change—as his parents promise they will—his behaviour will very likely improve."

That got the boy a year in reform school.

Later that same day Judge Wainwright castigated her in front of another set of parents: "You never say anything useful. It's always 'maybe this' and 'maybe that.'"

"Yes, Your Honour. That often reflects the nature of the case."

"I suppose you think this young girl is suffering from penis envy."

"I can't know that, Your Honour. Even if I were a certified psychoanalyst, which I'm not—yet—I couldn't analyze her in a one-hour interview. No one could."

"Then what good are you, that's what I want to know."

And yet, when they passed each other in the halls of the courthouse, Judge Wainwright would nod to her as if their relations were perfectly civil.


She suffered bouts of guilt for having deprived her children of the father they so wildly adored. Two weekends a month, Carl would rent a suite in a cheap hotel on Eighty-Ninth Street so he and the children could visit. Nearly a year on, they still cried for him, especially when Imogen had transgressed against some statute in their junior sense of justice. Tears and tantrums followed any visit with Carl, the visits having gone so well that the twins could not bear them to end.

Despite all this, the family of three had developed a happy life. There was food on the table, a cheerful Irish nanny in the afternoons, and Washington Square to play in. Some of Imogen's happiest times were sitting on a bench with a book while the twins played under the trees. All the local mothers got to know each other, and they were friendly until they realized Imogen was the very succubus they most feared—an unattached woman. They still allowed their children to engage with Aubrey and Charlotte, but from Imogen herself they kept a cool distance.

She didn't even mind this, really; they had little enough in common. Besides, she had Donna Artemis to fill that need for female companionship. Donna adored the twins, enjoyed cooking, and even tended to enjoy the same books as Imogen. What more could you ask of a friend?

Although her departure from the Phipps was a sorrowful affair, Imogen was surprised—and gratified—to realize that she was not depressed in its aftermath, and there were times when she experienced something approaching peace. Of an evening in her tiny Tenth Street apartment, her work for that day completed, she could sit and read a novel, or the latest stories in the *Saturday Evening Post*, or sometimes listen to a humorous radio program. The children were asleep, the dishes were done, and the noise from Sixth Avenue had quieted to a rumble. Her miniature parlour was radiant with the heat of the gas fireplace.

Whether it was walking the twins to school in the morning—Charlotte chirpy and often singing, Aubrey either solemn and dozy or full of questions such as why do squirrels transport bits of bagel and newspaper everywhere—or giving them a bath in the evening—when Charlotte's eyes seemed to exert a magnetic power over shampoo, leading to whimpers and soggy hugs—or listening to them read from their textbooks, Imogen absorbed joy from their merely being near. Sometimes she believed she wanted for nothing, not a thing in the world other than to protect her children from harm and raise them to be kind and useful to others. If she could accomplish this, their natural gifts for happiness would ensure them lives that were full and satisfying. At such times she forgot her own desires for love and meaningful work. At such times, in other words, she knew herself to be happy.

Since splitting up with Carl, she had felt it important to reconnect with her family—as much as she could bear—and for the twins to get to know their grandmother, at least. She had made two trips with them to Chicago, during which her father managed to be absent. But her mother made an effort with Aubrey and Charlotte—finding colouring books and various games to amuse them—and she seemed to actually experience a modicum of joy in their uncritical company. It occurred to Imogen, watching the three of them, that her mother was above all a fearful person, and her first grandchildren—so eager to love and be loved—were the company she had always been meant to keep.

In her work for the court she saw children who were devastated by abuse, abandonment, and neglect. Children who had been starved and beaten and never bathed, whose scalps were heaving with lice; children whose merest request for a token of affection or sustenance was met with derision or blows. Such children filled Imogen with wonder, not at the violence or deceit they had adopted as weapons in their quest for survival, but at their still being alive at all. She stood amazed at the unstoppable power of the will to live, and that it should be banked like an unquenchable fire in the bruised and wounded bodies of creatures so vulnerable. Her heart swelled with shame that she, with so little provocation, had toyed with the idea of suicide when these children, all but overwhelmed with reasons to hate their existence, chose obstinately—sometimes quietly, sometimes in a rage—to live.

One Saturday in late October Imogen sat on her favourite bench—the one on the uptown side about halfway between the arch at the foot of Fifth Avenue and University Place. There was a large hollow tree there that provided homes to several families of squirrels, some grey and some black, the virtues of segregation apparently lost on these scuttling New Yorkers.

Imogen always purchased a bag of peanuts from the corner vending cart and she and the twins shared them with their furry, twitchy friends. Aubrey liked to place a peanut on his shoulder and allow a squirrel to scramble up his sleeve and snatch it away. A better mother, Imogen scolded herself, would never tolerate the risk of rabies, mange, and God knew what other rodent malady. But the delight on Aubrey's face was irresistible.

It was a fine autumn day, brisk enough for scarves and bright enough to make the eyes water. Smells of fallen leaves mingled with the aromas of roasting chestnuts and pretzels, and a crystalline quality to the atmosphere made the colours of the leaves and sky and brickwork seem to jump as you turned your head. Beneath the arch two men were plunking ukuleles and singing songs—their sweet voices disrupted by their bursts of laughter when they forgot lyrics.

Imogen had just started reading a new Jeremy West novel. The dust jacket showed a man at an upstairs window—a man in shadow, leaning against the window frame in a thoughtful posture, observing the city below. It could have been a New York apartment, it could have been a London terrace, it could even be what she finally realized it was—a hospital. The ambiguity continued even into the title, an unusual one for West, who usually chose proper names for his books: *Vanessa*, *Chloe*, *Mister Grimes*. The book in her hand was called *If True*.

The protagonist, whose name was Gwen, is in a fever of excitement over her upcoming marriage to a railroad executive named Bannock. Bannock is an attractive person of the man's man type. He likes hunting and boxing and drinking and running a damned sound railroad. But shortly after war is declared, he signs up and the wedding is put off until he should return. Gwen, aghast at the atrocities of the Germans, and understanding the nature of her man, encourages him to go, even though at night she trembles to think what fate he may meet.

Imogen was enjoying West's nimble prose, but by the end of chapter two, Bannock is shipped off to France and Gwen's life takes a turn that Imogen read with a thrill of recognition. For Gwen is not only a doctor, she is a psychiatrist about to take a job at the prestigious "Phelps" Clinic in Baltimore. That's *right*! she almost shouted aloud, remembering that West had visited Baltimore and had even spoken to Donna about the Phipps. And here he was writing about it.

To Imogen's mind, Gwen seemed too naive to be a psychiatrist, and she found the woman's enthusiasm for sending her fiancé off to war repugnant. West got much of the medical world right. He was somehow able to imply the setting while eschewing detailed description. And he managed to obscure his probable ignorance of psychiatry by focusing on a single patient named Hansen, a poet who dominates any room he happens to be in. Along the way, Jonas Ganz made a brief but recognizable appearance as a kindly eccentric whose ideas of staffing run to "hiring as many emotionally wounded women as possible." Aha, Imogen thought. Donna got a word or two in there, I see.

Hansen, an able-bodied soldier at Fort Meade, has been sent to the Phelps as a test case. The army medical corps, although unable to certify that Hansen is malingering, wants and expects him to be found sane and sent back to the base and eventually to the front.

"Mumma! Mumma, Aubrey spit on my foot!"

Charlotte kicked her brother and a flurry of swats and counter-swats ensued before Imogen could sort them out and turn everyone homeward. Tears were dried, apologies made, tempers soothed, and by the time the family trio had made their way back to Tenth Street the Battle of Washington Square was relegated to childhood history.

All through the rest of that Saturday, Imogen felt the tug of West's story, as if Gwen and Hansen and Bannock were waiting in another room to resume their conversation. But it was not until after the children had been tucked into bed and read to and kissed that she was able to change into her own nightgown and climb into bed with Jeremy West and his characters. Other than the cameo appearance of the director, none of his creations resembled anyone she knew. It was an aspect of West's writing she had noticed long ago: he never described his protagonists in any detail. Occasionally he might endow one with a single vivid trait—an earlier book involved a hero with flaming red hair—but this novel featured no one like that. Gwen notes in her first assessment of Hansen that he has "attractive eyes with a perpetual expression of eagerness," but other than that he was not physically described.

It was clear by the third or fourth chapter that the author had not embarked on a realistic depiction of mental illness. Hansen, whose madness takes the form of strange, lyrical monologues, is also subject to lucid periods that occur far more frequently, and conveniently, than would be observed in a real-world psychosis. Imogen was not so literal-minded as to allow this to impinge on her enjoyment. And she took great pleasure in the dialogue as Gwen tried to uncover what lay behind those poetic flights of speech.

The young psychiatrist is in no hurry to diagnose her patient, having been trained by her stern director that finding a category was the least interesting chore in psychiatric care. That'll be Donna again, Imogen thought; West must have taken good notes.

Sometimes Hansen exhibits a kind of reverse Capgras syndrome, "recognizing" all the other patients on the ward from previous admissions to other hospitals (hospitals to which he has never been admitted, in cities the other patients have never seen). He greets them warmly as if they are old friends, leaving them bewildered, bemused, and in several cases shaken. Other times he is euphoric, exhibiting signs that would be noted on his chart as ideas of reference and pressure of speech. At still other times, Hansen seems to believe that he is a ghost, that he in fact died some years ago in a train accident on the Canadian border.

"But you're breathing," Gwen points out. "You're able to talk."

This provokes from Hansen an elegant monologue on "all the dead can teach us," and the passage was so lovely that Imogen read it three times.

"Would you agree with me," Gwen says, "that dead men do not bleed?"

*Oh no*, Imogen thought. *Don't try logic on him.* Hansen thinks a moment before nodding an affirmative. "Yes. That is true."

"Here, then. Let me prick your finger and we'll see if you bleed." Hansen offers his hand, and she pricks his little finger, a scarlet bead welling at the tip.

"Obviously they do bleed," Hansen remarks, and refuses to speak for the rest of that day.

During one of Hansen's lucid periods, Gwen takes him for a walk in the Phelps's cloistered courtyard. As they are sitting on a bench by the fountain, a monarch butterfly alights on Gwen's sleeve, multicoloured wings flexing open and closed, open and closed. They watch it in silence for a moment, then Gwen observes, "He's probably tired. You know, they travel thousands of miles."

"Astounding," Hansen says. "So fragile a thing—hardly more than a bit of leaf—and yet such power."

Imogen smiled at the image, remembering a day long ago when she and Quentin saw a butterfly in—where was it?—Lincoln Park. The next passage made her catch her breath.

Gwen lifted her arm, so that the sunlight lit the beautiful wings like stained glass.

"Hinge," Hansen said, opening and closing his pale hand, four fingers flapping open and shut against his thumb. "Hinge," he said again. "Excellent word."

He held a forefinger up before her face, curling and uncurling it in an upright beckoning gesture.

"Hinge," he said gravely, as if about to read a monograph on the subject.

It was Imogen's own memory laid upon the page. She read the passage again. Any novel reader will occasionally come across a plot development or narrative situation that is remarkably similar to a moment in his or her own life. But Imogen was experiencing something quite different. This was the moment itself clipped from her life and pasted onto the page.

She leaned back against the pillows, her breathing rapid and shallow, trying to think what it could mean. She had never described this memory to anyone; it was the sort of fleeting thing that only has meaning to the rememberer. It was conceivable that Quentin had related it to someone, but Quentin had been dead for ten years. What sort of person would retain such a tiny, second-hand memory for so long a time—and vividly enough to reproduce it in a book? A novelist?

No, Imogen decided. I'm being silly. Far more likely it would just be a remarkable coincidence, in which an author had exactly described a moment from her own life. The only detail in which it differed was that Gwen, unlike Imogen on that day long ago, in a park in Chicago, does not burst into a fit of giggles. Remarkable, yes. But impossible?

Imogen shook her head and read on. Whereas before she had been absorbed in the entwined fates of Gwen and Hansen, she now noticed herself slipping out of the story and even skimming ahead for more similarities. I'm having ideas of reference, she thought, but the self-diagnosis did not stop her from plunging on.

Hansen writes obsessively, furiously, in a journal he refuses to show anyone, but one day a nurse finds a page he has thrown away and brings it to Gwen. It was a list of rhymes: Gwen, then, amen, again, wren, fen, pen, and so on, ending with Imogen. Her name in black and white. Imogen's earlier shock of recognition returned, though as a less happy shock this time, carrying with it a low-level sense of dread, as if someone had laid a cold hand on her shoulder. Hansen writes on graph paper, just as Quentin used to.

That question of probability again. The use of graph paper was not limited to Quentin, after all. Even if you allowed that he was a dead poet who wrote on graph paper and Hansen was a fictional poet who thought he was dead and used the same stationery. Nor was the name Imogen unique to Imogen Lang. Another coincidence, less striking than the first.

In the next chapter, however, Gwen is rooting through a cabinet looking for something, when she comes across an old photograph.

On the back, in her mother's hand: *Gwen, aged* 7. The image itself shows a little girl in a long dark dress, and around her neck, hanging from a white ribbon, is a tiny notebook and pencil in which "she printed the words she feared to speak." Like Imogen, the child Gwen is tongue-tied.

"This is too strange," Imogen said aloud. "Far too strange."

In her entire life, she had told only three people of her childhood affliction: Quentin, Jonas Ganz, and Donna Artemis. Donna had actually *met* Jeremy West, but Imogen could conceive of no reason why her friend would have told him such a personal confidence. She would not; she knew it was a tender spot in Imogen's childhood, and she had received the confidence with warmth and sympathy. So too had Quentin, along with writerly curiosity.

"You poor girl," he had said. "You must've felt completely bottled up, like a little grasshopper."

Dr. Ganz had seen it as an asset in her dealing with depressed patients.

None of them would have told anyone.

Obviously she had no copyright on being tongue-tied any more than on any other physical trait. But a coincidence on this level—a female psychiatrist at the "Phelps," who was tongue-tied until the age of seven?

There was nothing further for several chapters. Gwen finds it increasingly difficult to maintain her medical objectivity, and her relations with Hansen become more intense—more Jeremy West–like. It is on one of Hansen's lucid days, when Gwen has just commented gently on a painful memory her patient has related (and probably invented), that Hansen blurts out, "I wish you were my sister! How I wish you were!" Gwen lets that hang in the air a full minute before saying softly, "I wonder why you said *sister*?"

Hansen gave her a puzzled look.

"As opposed to what?"

"Why don't you tell me?"

"As opposed to fiancée? Daughter? Wife? Concubine? Queen?"

"Sometimes we choose one word when we fear—often unconsciously—we can't say another. Perhaps because it is too frightening."

"I said sister because I don't have a sister."

It was too much. Five pages later Hansen is saying "*certain* is my middle name," and a chapter after that he describes breaking up with the great love of his life "on a tiny island, in a tiny park, across a tiny bridge. No doubt it was a tiny event in the grand scheme of things, but that bridge, when we crossed it, felt to me like the Bridge of Sighs."

Quentin had kept a journal. That must be it. Quentin had kept a diary of some sort and somehow it had fallen into someone else's hands. Imogen got out of bed and threw on her dressing gown and went into the kitchen and dialed Donna's number.

"Donna? Donna, wake up, it's Imogen."

"Imogen. Darling, it's—it's three-fifteen in the—"

"I know. Sorry, but I need you to remember something."

"Remember something. Jesus. Give me a minute."

"What does Jeremy West look like?"

"*What?*"

"Jeremy West."

"Why could you possibly want to know what—"

"Just tell me, please. Whatever you remember."

"Imogen, this is so unlike you. Why are you so—"

"Donna, please."

A deep sigh on the line. Then: "He was tall. Over six feet, anyway. Lots of curly brown hair. Very pale. And he walked . . . carefully, as if he'd been injured. Like a war injury."

"And his face. What about his face?"

"Bony, I suppose you could say. Bony, pale, wide brow—and a cute little mouth. A girl's mouth, really."

"Dear God."

"Dear God what?"

"I thought you were going to describe a person I used to know—a man named Jack Wisdom. He was a friend of Quentin's."

"Quentin, your old suitor? The one who joined up?"

"They were very close."

"But you said I didn't describe him. This Jack person."

"No. You didn't. You described someone else entirely."

# 23

Quentin moved to New York City shortly after finishing his first draft of *If True* and took a lease on an apartment on West Sixty-Seventh Street. It was small, with only one bedroom and a galley kitchen, but it did offer a partial view of the Hudson. He had feared New York's noise and crowds would be inhibiting, but in fact his block between Columbus and Amsterdam was quite tranquil, and Central Park was practically next door.

Far from inhibiting, he found the streets of Manhattan with their stupendous variety of characters inspiring. He enjoyed the proximity to his publisher, and worked closely with Griffin Burke on a second, third, and even a fourth exhausting draft. Griffin invited him to lunches and dinners where he could talk endlessly about books with congenial colleagues. *If True* was published to good reviews and brisk, if not spectacular, sales. It was time to think of another story.

He spent many hours in the park, just thinking, and even more in the New York Public Library, flipping through the endless supply of periodicals and letting ideas drift in and out of his mind. He was much happier than he had been in Lake Placid. There was such a thing, he had come to realize, as too much solitude. New York with its busyness and plenitude offered more distractions than one could ever hope to indulge in. He developed an appreciation for Broadway and considered writing a play.

His happiness was shaken, however, when he found, quite by accident, that Imogen, too, was now living in New York. He was flipping through an issue of *Collier's*, and came across an article about the growing profession of psychoanalysis, which included a sidebar about the inroads women were making into the profession. "New York psychiatrist Imogen Lang" was quoted on the New York Psychoanalytic Society's training process (calling it "rigorous, thorough, and very rewarding").

To his dismay, it started him thinking once more about possibly seeing her. This was upsetting. After his brief haunting of her world in Baltimore he had managed to go home, write his novel, and clear his mind of her again. He didn't *want* to be thinking of her, he wanted his own life, thank you, and the peace of mind to write his books. But the knowledge that she was so close nagged at him. He looked her up in the city directory and found she was living on Tenth Street, but could find no entry for her husband. He thought about this for a moment, and considered that the most likely explanation was that Kromer's position at the Phipps required that he remain there until some later date.

In an effort to clarify matters, he wrote out his thoughts and feelings on a sheet of graph paper. Looking at these notes, he decided that the main reason she could still destabilize him like this was the knowledge that she thought he was dead. Donna Artemis, after all, had told him Imogen blamed herself. He wanted her to know he was alive, that he had not killed himself, that he had not only survived but was thriving.

That much was true, he decided. But he also knew himself well enough to know that this might simply be an attempt to insert himself into her life, which was going along perfectly well without him. Based on this assessment, he came up with a plan. He would indeed let her know he was alive, but he would also go away. A grand tour would be just the thing to clear his head once more and with any luck generate fresh ideas for his next novel. He began consulting guidebooks, and it was not many days before he found himself on Tenth Street, not twenty yards from Imogen's front door.

It was Saturday. She might be home, she might not. Of course it would be a shock for her to see him again, but nothing she wouldn't get over in the space of an hour or two.

He mounted the steps of her building. It was a typical New York brownstone, indistinguishable from the others on the block and divided into several apartments. He stepped into the vestibule with its six brass mailboxes. *I. Lang* was typed onto a tiny paper rectangle, the *a* out of alignment with the other letters. If her husband was travelling back and forth from Baltimore, surely they would put both names on the door. In any case, it was no proper concern of his.

No. He couldn't do it; he hadn't the right.

He shook his head and trotted back down the front steps and headed toward the hubbub of Sixth Avenue and when he got to the corner he turned downtown and ordered his feet to keep marching, carrying him away from Imogen. It felt right. It felt intrepid and robust, the decision of a competent, intelligent male, obviously the healthy course to take.

Two hours later, the Cunard ticket agent slid his papers under the grille of the wicket. He was British, with a wide moustache and perfectly round wire-frame spectacles that made him look more than a little like Rudyard Kipling.

"Progress, sir, we have made progress. My apologies for the wait."

"That's all right," Quentin said. "I've been reading your brochures."

"Yes. Make one want to survey the world from China to Peru, don't they?"

"I think for now I'll just stick with England and the Lake District."

The agent tapped the top sheet with a neatly manicured finger, pointing out the crucial items. "Second-class passage for one. Open-ended return. You're quite sure you wouldn't rather specify a date for your return journey?"

"Quite sure, thanks."

"Very good, sir. You're booked in a second-class cabin on the RMS *Sylvania*, departing from Pier 44, at 9:45 a.m. on 27 October, arriving Southampton, U.K., on 2 November. The *Sylvania* is a beautiful ship, recently refurbished. I've been on her myself. Splendid vessel."

"As long as she gets me there."

"Oh, a good deal more than that, I assure you."

The clerk shuffled the papers, pointing again. "I've also reserved a seat for you on the express train to London Waterloo, arriving just after lunch. You are booked for three nights at the Lombard Hotel and after that I understand you'll be fending for yourself."

"That's right."

As the agent worked his way through the remaining data, Quentin allowed his mind to drift—now to his British editor, whom he had actually met, now to his French publisher, whom he had not met but with whom he had exchanged several warm letters. Jeremy West's novels were more popular in France than in any other foreign-language territory—a prime reason for considering it as a later destination.

The clerk folded up the itinerary and Quentin wrote out a sizable cheque. The ticket was duly issued and enclosed in a handsome Cunard packet along with the other papers.

When he got back to Sixty-Seventh Street he took a small wooden box from the closet. It was a well-crafted thing of polished walnut with brass corners. He opened it and lifted out a slim bundle of letters and postcards. Several—the last ones Imogen had written to him—were painful. But he had also preserved playful notes written during holidays. They fanned out on the bed like a canasta hand, the loops and curls of Imogen's writing as evocative to him as the curls at the nape of her neck. He picked up a postcard, a picture of Chicago's Navy Pier, and ripped it in half, then into quarters. The next was a pale-blue envelope with her parents' address printed on the flap. Without opening it, he tore it once, twice, and dropped it on the bed.

"I could use a fireplace," he said aloud, as if the landlord were right beside him taking complaints. But the apartment, being steam-heated, offered no fireplace to feed with his scraps of memory, and so the pile of folds and corners, loops and curls, grew until he had destroyed every letter and every card.

All that remained was a single photograph of Imogen, much creased with handling, and missing one corner. She was sitting in a deck chair at some outdoor event, perhaps a concert. Whoever had held the camera must have said her name, because Imogen has turned around to face him over the back of the chair, a look of inquiry on her face. Although seventeen or eighteen at the time, her features had the openness, the guilelessness, of someone much younger. On the back of the deck chair were stencilled the words NOT TO BE TAKEN AWAY.

Quentin tore it in half and then quickly tore it again and again until the pieces could be reduced no further. Even as he engaged in this destruction he was aware that its very thoroughness contradicted its purpose—only a man still emotionally entangled would care enough to do it. He found a paper bag in a kitchen cupboard and brought it to the bed. Using both hands he scooped up the tattered pieces of his life and dropped them into the bag.

When he was sure he had them all he closed the bag and left the apartment. He was feeling good again, as if he had drained a wound. His old life, his burdened life, was in a paper bag about to be dumped into the garbage can out front. He even sensed the beginnings of joy building like a head of steam in his chest. He had got over Imogen before; he would get over her again. Confidence and optimism, the fire and fuel of creation, were burning inside him and he knew he would write many novels.

He went down the stairs two at a time, whistling under his breath, allowing himself a touch of pride—just a touch—that he was strong enough, had the emotional wherewithal, to choose a better life for himself. Perhaps in London he would meet a delightful English rose, or in France a dark-eyed angel who could envision no greater life than one shared with a neurotic and modestly successful novelist. Imogen had her life, and he wished her continued happiness; now he would have his.

He swung open the heavy inner door, went through the vestibule, and grappled with the outer door, which had a loose handle. He managed to get it open and stepped out into the dazzling October light.

"Hello, Quentin."

Quentin stopped at the top of the steps.

Imogen was looking up at him, a half smile on her face and in her eyes an expression that was to him utterly unreadable.

"My God," she breathed, "you really are alive."

Quentin stared at her the way a kitten stares at its first human, swaying with the impact. He raised the bag to his chest and squeezed it there.

Faced with his silence, she hurried on. "For so long—well, for two years, anyway, I just assumed you would not be killed. It just did not seem possible that someone like you—someone so alive to me, in my mind, in my heart, in my memory—that someone like that could be killed. Then, when Jack told me you were dead, I—"

"Jack told you."

"Yes."

"Jack Wisdom."

"Jack Wisdom. When he told me, it was as if the world had been torn. As if a great rip had opened up in it. I—egoist that I am, you see—I'd never realized how important you were to me. I was like a child who thinks that my Papa and Mama and lovely home always were and always will be; they are mine forever and ever, and I deserve them. But clearly I didn't deserve you."

"Imogen."

"And so I'm here to tell you that I'm just so glad you're alive—glad does not begin to cover it. I'm just . . . And now I can't stop talking because I'm afraid if I stop it'll all turn out to have never been. And I wanted to say how sorry I am, how stupid I was—how mean, and pompous, and just so—"

"Imogen."

"I was afraid I was going to hurt you—well, I was hurting you—and more than anything I wanted not to hurt you. And also I was excited about starting a new life." She hit her forehead with the heel of her hand. "Oh, I was such an idiot."

"You were young," Quentin finally managed. "Very young."

"You were so beautiful toward me, so generous and kind, and I don't believe you ever asked me for a single thing until—"

"No, don't blame yourself. I don't. I was pushing you too hard for something you didn't want. I was too . . . too everything."

"You must be cold," she said, gathering her scarf about her neck. "And I'm sure you want to get on with your life."

"No, no. Don't go anywhere. I'll just—wait right here and I'll get my coat. We'll go for a walk, shall we? Would you? Do you have time?"

"Yes, but I didn't mean to intrude, I—"

"Wait right there. Don't move."

He went back inside and placed the bag with its cargo of smithereens on the kitchen table; he had forgotten he was carrying it. He pulled his coat and scarf from the closet and ran back down the stairs, ignoring stabs of pain from femur and fibula.


"Were a lot of people misinformed about you?" Imogen asked when they were in Riverside Park. "Did your family get a black telegram? I know it happened to others."

"I believe, in my case, the black telegram was Jack himself."

"He went around telling everyone you'd been killed?"

"Just you, I believe."

Quentin walked more slowly than he used to, his left leg dragging a little without quite amounting to a limp. Imogen kept her own pace in check.

"Why would he do that?"

He told her about Jack's confession of love, and about his misery.

"He swore that he felt about me the same way I felt about you. I suppose his letter to you was a kind of wish fulfillment—that you would lose me forever and he would have me all to himself. Am I using the term correctly? Wish fulfillment?"

"Yes, indeed. Maybe you're right."

"I was harsh with him, I'm afraid. I was stupid. You should just accept a friend for what he is."

"You were worried he was asking you to reciprocate."

"He wasn't asking for that—at least he said he wasn't. He just wanted me to know his feelings. I see now that he felt the friendship was false as long as I wasn't aware. Now you'd think that I, if anyone, could understand this. But I didn't."

"Because of your feelings for me, you mean."

"Yes."

"But the situations were quite different. Jack had changed into something completely other all of a sudden. It was a shock."

"He killed himself not long after."

"Oh, dear. I'm sorry to hear that."

"Yes, it was quite a—quite horrible. I was a bad friend."

"How long after your letter was it that he killed himself?"

"Seven or eight months."

"So, hardly immediate. If he were still alive you'd probably be friends again. You were such great pals."

"It's kind of you to say."

"But it's true. It's the sort of person you are. He didn't live long enough to discover that about you. He deprived himself of you. Just as I did."

"No, God, I was so callow. I was too much for you. You did absolutely the right thing. Speaking of which—is it quite proper for us to be talking like this?"

"I no longer have a husband, if that's what you mean. Carl left me."

In the days leading up to this meeting Imogen had feared many things: that Quentin would slam the door in her face, or say a string of hateful things, or burst into tears. Or, if they should spend an hour together, that they would not know what to say, that they would find each other unrecognizable. Quentin looked much older—far more than ten years older—with streaks of grey in the hair that curled around his ears. And he now walked in this careful, hesitant way. But she felt him to be essentially unchanged and wanted nothing more at that moment than to open her heart to him.

She told him about Carl and their short, unhappy life together. Quentin listened, turning to her now and again with those hound dog eyes full of sympathy and concern. Even though he was a man, she sensed that he was understanding her better even than Donna did. Donna was a woman, and a psychiatrist, but she did not love in the way Imogen had and Quentin had. Indeed, that was part of her immense value as a friend. But Imogen found the tale of her misguided passion for Carl rolled easily off her tongue, and she could tell Quentin with neither exaggeration nor understatement exactly how it went wrong.

"I'm sorry you went through that," Quentin said. "I wish I—I want to reach back in time and save you from it, steer you away from him."

"So do I sometimes. Of course, that would steer me away from the twins, too."

"Ah, yes. Your twins."

"You know I have children?"

Quentin nodded. "I saw you. In Baltimore. Well, I didn't just *see* you. I followed you."

"No." She stopped on the path. "Quentin. You weren't—you aren't . . ."

He shook his head. "Don't worry. As soon as I saw you were happily married I resolved to stay away."

"Happily!"

"I know. I'm often wrong about people. It's a terrible failing in a novelist. I suppose psychiatrists aren't allowed to be wrong either."

"It doesn't bear thinking about, in my case. I think I'm pretty good in reading my patients, but I've been wrong about everyone else, it seems."

"Seeing you so, I don't know, *ensconced* in your life, I couldn't bring myself to interrupt. Couldn't bear the thought of history repeating itself. But every now and again, I admit, well, since I learned you were here in New York all this time . . ."

She searched his face. He was a character from one of his early novels—innocent, passionate, resolute. "I love your books," she couldn't help saying. "Even before I knew they were by you, I loved them."

"Oh. Well, writing my last book involved thinking about you a lot. Not the healthiest thing for me to do."

He looked away across the river. Imogen very much wanted to hear what he was going to say, but at the same time she was struck by his gentleness and honesty.

"Then, when I found you were here, I began to get excited again. And I knew that wasn't good—for anybody, not just me. And actually, the way I'm dealing with it, I'm planning to leave the country. I have my ticket."

He turned to look at her again. "So you see, you mustn't worry. I'm quite prepared to remain out of your life. Had you not shown up on my doorstep I would in fact be out of it."

"You're so certain you couldn't remain in it?"

"How do you mean? As a friend? No, I think we've proved that beyond all doubt."

"'Men and women are not friends.' That's what my mother says. She says everyone knows this except me—well, this was years ago."

"And what does Dr. Freud say?"

"Love objects. Sex objects. Friendship doesn't enter into it."

"How sad. I wish I could prove him wrong this minute, but I'm afraid we'll have to leave that to others."

"I really do like your books," she said again a little while later. They had passed the boat basin and Grant's tomb was not much farther. "More than *like* them," she added. "They stay with me long after I've read them. Your characters, and the passion of your protagonists. They're so like you that—"

"Easy, now—some of them are quite mad."

"No, they're not. I've worked with mad people and, believe me, your characters are not mad. Eccentric, yes. Volatile, certainly. But so loving, so generous, and so strong in the way they remain true to themselves and what they aim for. I should have realized long ago that Jeremy West was you, but it never occurred to me. One or two of the male characters reminded me of you, but—"

"I refuse to ask which ones."

Imogen smiled. "But it was only in reading the last one that I knew these characters had to come from you, even though I knew you were dead. I thought someone else must've got hold of your work or a diary or something. Frankly I suspected Jack Wisdom."

Quentin picked up a small stone and turned to face the Hudson, contemplating the grey swirl of the river. Then he hurled the stone into the water where it vanished with an inaudible splash.

"It's funny," he said. "Just as you're talking I'm realizing that I probably meant *If True* as a kind of message in a bottle. Not consciously, I swear. But I realize now I was hoping you'd read it. Obviously you'd have to realize it was me, if you did."

"Why don't you write under your own name? Quentin Goodchild—it's a marvellous name for a writer."

Quentin shrugged. It was the same gesture she remembered, a collection of spare parts hauled into the air by a magnet, then released. "I felt—as Goodchild, I mean—I felt I was obliged to write about the war. Stupid idea, no doubt, but I believed it. I still believe it."

"But you have the war in this one."

"Well, a little bit."

"It's powerful. This incredible mass violence offstage, so to speak, but affecting all the characters in these terrible ways."

Quentin winced as she spoke, clearly uncomfortable with praise. He pointed toward Grant's tomb. "You know, the Civil War was the crucial event of Henry James's lifetime. I've always found it hard to respect him since he never wrote a word about it."

"But it's hard to imagine a Henry James war novel. He probably sensed he'd be no good at it. I mean, isn't part of being an artist knowing your own strengths?"

Quentin looked doubtful. "Perhaps. Anyway, it certainly didn't harm his career, so what do I know?"

A mother and stroller passing by reminded Imogen she had better get home. Quentin insisted on walking her to the subway, and they turned toward Riverside Drive. Along the way Imogen told him about her work, her break with the Phipps, and her current frustrations with her supervision and her single, unpleasant patient.

"But this is what you want to do—be a psychoanalyst."

"Very much."

"I thought you'd always be in a lab, trying to find a cure for dementia praecox."

"So did I. But I don't see any cures on the horizon, and analysis offers a way to help people now."

"Not the same people."

"Just because you're not on a back ward doesn't mean you're not suffering."

"I wasn't being dismissive. Just trying to picture your new milieu."

The noise of the city seemed tremendous after the quiet of the park.

"When is your ticket for?"

"Two weeks from today."

"Oh, that's soon."

Quentin nodded and looked away.

Imogen put out her hand. "It was wonderful to see you again, Quentin. I only wish it had happened sooner."

Quentin shook her hand. His was intensely warm, as if he'd been resting it on a radiator.

"Maybe I'll just come down the subway with you—do you mind? I don't want to walk all the way back. Walking isn't what it used to be for me."

He moved slowly down the stairs, keeping his left arm close to his side as if clutching something under his coat.

"I hope someday you'll tell me about your war experience."

"First I want to know how you found me."

"In the city directory, of course. It's Jeremy West that's hard to find. Quentin Goodchild is right there for anyone to see."

The next two days were heavily occupied for Imogen. For reasons no one could fathom, the juvenile and family court systems came up with a surge of referrals for her, including five blond sisters ranging in age from five to fifteen. In addition, her training patient missed two appointments, both of which had to be rescheduled, forcing Imogen to shuffle everything else in her life. Meanwhile, her supervisor demanded she reread *The Interpretation of Dreams*, as he did not believe she had a firm grasp of its principles. It was just bullying, but Imogen's resentment burned inside her and made it difficult to concentrate. Charlotte came down with an earache, requiring a babysitter Imogen could ill afford, and copycat Aubrey developed his own imaginary earache that made her lose her temper.

Yet all the while this was going on, Imogen was very aware that her world had changed. She found herself thinking *when I see Quentin* or *I must tell Quentin*. Some part of her had evidently decided that they would be seeing a lot of each other; the matter was settled. While worrisome, it also felt as if she had been living in a house with slanted floors and crooked windows and now some alteration in the footings had canted everything back into its proper place.

On the third day she broke every rule she had ever learned about correct relations between men and women and telephoned Quentin. "I want to see you again," she said into the phone.

"Why?" Quentin said. "I don't mean that rudely, but I mean, I just really would need to know."

"Because you're alive. Because I need a friend. Because you make me happy."

Quentin laughed.

"Why are you laughing?"

"Why? Because it's wonderful to not be dead!"

She met up with Quentin often over the next few days. They had lunch in the Automat, a place that amused him highly. They met at the New York Public Library, where he was making notes toward a new novel. The courts didn't care where Imogen wrote up her reports, as long as they got written, so she wrote a few of them in the library, typing them out later at the court office. So here they were, face to face in a library again, what seemed a century after their student days.

They fell into their old pattern of camaraderie with frightening ease. Imogen marvelled that she could have ever let this person go from her life. How had she missed her own physical attraction to him? She had always loved his tallness, his angularity, his slouchiness, his asymmetrical face, his mouth, and those expressive hands. How, then, could she have fallen for the spurious manliness of a person like Carl? She had been studying the human psyche for many years, and it always filled her with wonder, but her own psyche left her, at this juncture, aghast. Imagine being so warped by your treacherous father that you reject the kind man who is utterly unlike him in favour of one who is all *too* like him. Perhaps this was one of the things that drew her to Freud, the way he gave you a thousand different ways to avoid calling yourself what you were: a fool.

Well, if she had been a fool, she also had the feeling she might soon be punished for it, sensing as she did that this time she was the one beginning to fall in love, while Quentin remained aloof. He wasn't giving himself over to this shared experience with the same abandon she was, but why would he? He'd been burned before—and he had a ticket to Europe in his pocket, just as she had had a ticket to Baltimore in hers.

Imogen and the twins met him at the Central Park Zoo where he delighted the children by doing imitations of the animals. That weekend they went to the roller rink, and afterwards over hot chocolate Quentin recited "Jabberwocky" from memory, the twins calling for encores. On Tuesday he asked Imogen to go and see *Steamboat Bill*. She scrambled to find a babysitter.

All of this rushed by as in a dream, Quentin and their friendship completely familiar and yet vastly different. Imogen felt the approaching date of his departure as a kind of doom. Neither of them mentioned it. Soon they would have to; there was only one weekend left. Quentin asked if she would like to see *An Enemy of the People* on Broadway. She said yes, but the next morning, just as she was leaving her building to walk the children to school, a Western Union messenger appeared on the stoop and said, "You wouldn't by any chance be Imogen Lang?"

"I would."

"Telegram for you."

Imogen opened it and read, FATHER DEAD STOP. FUNERAL SUNDAY MORNING 11:30 STOP. END MESSAGE.

# 24

As she was living through it, Imogen's sojourn in Chicago for her father's funeral was the slowest, most leaden passage in her entire life. Each event, each interaction, seemed so heavy and elongated that time itself turned mucilaginous. A storm of contradictory emotions seemed to wipe from memory everything that happened so that, later, in trying to recall that gloomy weekend in late October 1928, Imogen could bring to mind only glimpses—moody impressions interspersed with the occasional murky photograph.

There was the train trip, eighteen lonely hours (the children stayed with Donna) that dragged endlessly at the time but constituted a mere flash in the remembering. Although she had made the trip more often in the past few years, a ball of dread formed in her stomach as the taxi bore her home to Emerald Street. Then her mother, arrayed in black—pale, drawn, and looking ever so much older—rose from a chair to greet her and thank her for coming, as if Imogen were a business associate not often in these parts. And Alice—tall, manly Alice sombre in charcoal velvet—a serious woman of forty-four now and, in the model of the modern businesswoman, correct and closed-mouthed, giving nothing away, inviting nothing in return. And her younger sister Caroline, erotically prim in a purple dress, drop-waisted in the flapper style, hair bobbed and clinging to her skull like a dark helmet, the severity so out of character it made Imogen smile. Her other sister, Victoria, lived in California now, and had not made the trip.

Imogen had grown up in an agnostic family where Jewish tradition was rarely mentioned, let alone observed, but her mother, aged in sorrow like a sherry in oak, had drawn closer to her heritage over the years. "It's the tradition," she would say, when adjusting the black drapery covering a mirror, or ordering from the florist a single—and small—floral tribute for the casket. Imogen had arrived too late to assist in the selection of a casket, but overheard her mother informing someone that it was constructed of solid plank walnut with no metal parts, "in keeping with tradition."

When Imogen had unpacked, her mother rapped on the door and entered bearing a single black ribbon that she attached to Imogen's left sleeve—the correct sleeve for a daughter. "You're supposed to wear it for thirty days but I don't expect you will," she said. "It's symbolic of rending the garments, as in Scripture."

"You've become religious," Imogen commented.

"Observant, dear. Not religious. Not religious per se."

"Is it comforting?"

"Go ahead and make fun if you want. You're above it all, I'm sure."

"There's actually very little I consider myself above, Mother. And why would I make fun of anything that brings you comfort?"

"You were always a cold one."

This observation was so unjust that Imogen had no reply to it. Over the next few days she did not revise her view that the household had veered Godward, what with the rabbi coming and going and relatives she'd never heard of appearing at the door in wigs and yarmulkes. She found them alien and annoying, but was not pleased with herself for this reaction. Over her ten years in Baltimore, Imogen had all but forgotten her Jewishness, although lately she had sensed it would be no disadvantage in New York psychoanalytic circles.

In an effort to bridge the gulf between herself and Caroline she asked what she thought of all the tradition.

"I have no feelings about it whatsoever. And I don't want any."

"Personally, I find it alien."

"Well, you're an alienist, aren't you?"

Imogen laughed. "Yes, I suppose I am."

She felt a spark of kinship with her younger sister until she realized by the hard set of Caroline's features that she had not intended a joke.

Her uncle Mason came by. He was older, frailer, a widower now, but still—to Imogen—the perfect example of the upright businessman, even if he did have to use a cane.

"You know," Imogen said, "I think you may be the single kindest person I've ever met, but I'm very glad I don't owe you money anymore."

"I made money off ya," he said. "Perfectly sound little investment."

"Well, it meant the world to me."

He looked around to make sure no one could hear them.

"Listen, I know you had a difficult time with your pappy. I had a difficult time with my own—terrible man, in many ways—but then they die on you and you just crash face-first into the fact that they were human after all. Just human—as in prone to make mistakes."

"Well, yes, I—"

"Completely obvious, I know. But it tends to hit harder than you expect."

The funeral itself was mercifully short, the coffin mercifully closed. The Psalms and Scripture readings were moving, but the eulogy, given by a white-haired gnome who had apparently worked with her father, seemed written for a man who bore no resemblance to Josiah Lang. The gnome took as his opening "Blessed is the Judge of Truth," and went on to praise her father's devotion to family, to justice, and to telling a good story.

That her father was devoted to his work, yes, that was true but you could say the same of many professional men; it seemed a modest claim on admiration. Then again, what could she—what could anybody—claim? When her mother told her he had died at Chicago's Grace Hotel, Imogen had immediately thought it must have involved some illicit liaison but it was not so. Alice had also been staying at the hotel because negotiations for the teachers' federation had stretched later and later into the nights. In the end, the intensity proved too much for her father and he died of a heart attack at the age of sixty-three.

Imogen looked around at the gathering. Perhaps thirty people. Those who were not relatives all looked to be business people. There was one young woman off to one side, dressed in a black suit with a grey silk shirt. Not a lover, she hoped, dear God, not a lover. She glanced over at her mother, who appeared too lost in grief to notice. And then she realized who it was.

After the funeral, the long ride out to Oak Woods Cemetery. The rabbi said a few words, and then one by one the women who had loved Josiah Lang, and suffered because of him, used a small spade to toss a handful of earth into the grave, the noise of it hitting the wood rattling Imogen's nerves. When two cemetery employees had finished filling the grave, the rabbi said the Kaddish. Imogen discovered that her uncle Mason was right: anger at her father did not preclude tears. She cried copiously into her handkerchief, her mother weeping beside her.

Some confusion ensued as mourners formed a short gauntlet for the family to pass through. Imogen caught sight of the young woman again, standing diffidently at the edge of the crowd, evidently uncertain where she belonged. Yes, her expression was too sad for her to be a mere colleague, and Imogen recalled, with a cramp of sorrow and loss, the little girl who had come running out of a stranger's house so many years ago, arms wide open, crying, "Daddy!"

She looked again, a few moments later, but the woman was gone.

Imogen remained in Chicago for another two days as her mother sat shiva but she could not stay the whole seven.

"Of course not," her mother said. "You have more important things to do. You have your life."

"I just have to get back to the children."

"Perhaps you should quit your job, then. Being a mother is a full-time business."

"Quitting my job is the last thing I should do."

"Are you sure you gave your marriage the attention it was due? Was your husband getting everything from you that a husband needs?"

"It was never within my power to please Carl, no matter how much effort I devoted to it."

"How could that be, my dear, with you so infinitely clever? Yes, aren't you always telling us you are."

"Carl doesn't like me, that's the truth of it. And if someone simply doesn't like you . . ."

"If that person is a husband, you must adapt your personality until he does like you. Anything less is a vocation of misery."

"Is that what you did?"

"In my case, it was not required."

"You just naturally went along with Father's having a second wife and second family? You didn't have to adjust your personality so that it was free of, say, pride?"

"Pride is a useless emotion for a woman. I learned to put my own feelings aside. You can do it too, Imogen, I'm sure it's not too late. Do it for your children's sake. Children need a father."

"I saw her daughter at the cemetery."

Her mother's weary eyes looked her up and down. "Did you. And how would you recognize her?"

"I saw her once—many years ago—by accident. I was out riding my bike and saw Father."

"Did you."

"She called him Daddy."

"Did she."

"*Daddy*," Imogen repeated. "It made my blood run cold."

"She was actually his mistress's daughter by a previous marriage, not your father's biological child. Her mother died eight years ago. Josiah was inconsolable."

"That must have been painful for you."

"Not really. He turned to me for comfort, you see. I was needed."

"But to see him mourning the loss of another woman—that wasn't painful for you?"

"Well, dear, I never wanted to see Josiah upset about anything, did I?" Her mother let out a deep sigh, closing her eyes a moment. When she opened them again, she said, "I loved him and honoured him, you see. It's what one does. If you think about it in the cold light of day you'll see that's really all that's required."

"And now you have another ghost," Laura said on the train back to New York. "There was a time when I was the only one."

"That woman's daughter is not a ghost," Imogen said, "she's a living person. And I have no wish to keep her in my life the way I've always wanted to keep you. I don't even know her name."

"Olivia."

How could Laura, a figment of Imogen's imagination, know what she herself did not? Mother must have told me, she decided, or I must have overheard it. Either that, or it's a complete trick of my imagination. God knows, I've seen enough patients absolutely certain that I've told them something (*You can be discharged on Tuesday*; *Your sister is under the control of Thomas Edison*; *Yes, I see the angels too*) when in fact I have said nothing of the kind.

"Father is now ghost number two."

"He's been a ghost my whole life. I think perhaps he'll be less of one now. And you're forgetting something rather important aren't you?"

"Quentin, you mean?"

"He's no longer a ghost. He was never even dead."

"No, but he was banished."

"I have never forgotten Quentin," Imogen replied silently, "and never will."

"You'd better. The *Sylvania* departs New York in twenty minutes."

There hadn't been time to see him before she caught the train to Chicago. She had sent a note by messenger. It tore at her that she hadn't found the words to put on paper that would tell him she couldn't bear the thought of his vanishing again. Aside from imparting the news about her father, all she had said was that she wished him a wonderful time in Europe and that she hoped he would be back soon—and to please write.

"You'll be miserable if you don't forget him."

"I've told you, I never shall."

"So there you are—another ghost," Laura said. "Quite a collector, really: Quentin, me, Father . . ."

We're all ghost collectors, Imogen reflected. Friends, fathers, mothers, lovers—anyone dead, anyone lost to distance or a change of heart—those who affect us stay with us always, no matter where they are, and continue to nourish and frustrate us. Freud restricts himself to mothers and fathers, but really it's everyone.

She found she had no wish to remain angry at her father; his death had released her not just from her anger but from the need to keep that anger burning. Why, she wondered, would one want to stay angry in the first place? Anger is so uncomfortable—why would one cling to it? An attempt to keep the loved one close? To obliterate the abyss opened up by whatever injury, real or imagined, they had committed?

She allowed her mind to wander over the happy times she had enjoyed with her father as a child—the times she was rendered breathless and giddy by his tossing her up in the air and catching her, the times he tickled her into paroxysms of laughter, unbearable yet ecstatic; his solemn patience while teaching her long division; his evocative reading aloud of Dickens and Carroll—Carroll in particular having become a lifelong love. He was so adept at dramatic reading that for the longest time Imogen assumed her father was a colleague of the authors and that he must see them often. She recalled her shock and disbelief, followed by resignation, on the evening when he had disabused her of this notion.

"Papa, where does Mr. Dickens live?"

"What do you mean, Imogen?"

"Where does he live? You see him, don't you? You see him and Mr. Carroll sometimes—at night? When we're sleeping?"

"No, my dear. Mr. Dickens and Mr. Carroll are dead—long dead. No one sees them now. They live only in their books."

"Oh."

"Did you imagine they were alive?"

"I thought you knew them."

"I know their work pretty well. I admire them tremendously. I suppose that's like knowing them."

She recalled the tone of his voice, the bemused look on his face—the look, she recognized now, of a parent who knows he has disillusioned his child in some way he can do nothing about.

If only that had been the limit of her disappointment in him—but no, she refused to dwell on that now, with the hills of Pennsylvania soaking in a grey autumn rain. She chose to recall instead a day at the beach—one of many, since her father was fond of swimming—Papa in his striped bathers tossing Imogen and her younger sisters around in the chilly waves of Lake Michigan. She remembered his teeth gleaming white in the blackness of his beard, the dark curls gemmed with droplets. Perhaps if Imogen had never ridden her bicycle so far from home, if she had never learned what she learned, the good times might never have stopped.


When she got home again the Tenth Street apartment was dark and stale and horribly quiet. She opened some windows and put the radio on softly. Smells of autumn rain and leaves wafted into the front room as she sank into an armchair. She got up again and went to the kitchen where she dialed Donna Artemis.

"Oh, you answered. I was afraid you'd be with a patient."

"I will be in two minutes. How'd it go with the funeral?"

"It was all right. I really just wanted to thank you for looking after the kids."

"Oh, you're welcome. We had fun—but they are really, really looking forward to seeing Mummy again. They're expecting you to pick them up at school."

"I will—I missed them."

"And your famous friend—has he departed for England and—France did you say?"

"His ship put out this morning. I marked the occasion by staring out the train window at the rain."

"This is a hard one, darling. Two, I should say. Two major losses. You make sure you go easy on yourself over the next few weeks."

"I'll be all right."

"I know you will. I'm just saying prepare yourself for sudden onslaughts of emotion. And you might want to consider a bromide, or even chloral, if you have trouble sleeping."

"Mm-hmm."

"Listen, it's exactly smart people like you who underestimate what the death of a parent may stir up—especially a parent who caused them grief. Am I annoying you? I'm annoying you."

"Actually it's good to know someone cares."

"I have to go, sweetheart. Let's have tea one day this week."

"I'd like that."

School would not be out for another couple of hours. She went into her bedroom and unpacked and changed out of her travel clothes. She went into the bathroom and had a thorough wash to vanquish the smell and feel of the train. Through all these things she was thinking of Quentin. Imogen had no real sense of how fast an ocean liner might travel, never having been on one. She pictured him standing by the rail looking out at the sea, which, judging by New York weather, would be grey and choppy. Would he still have a view of North America? Halifax? St. John's? In her mind's eye she saw elegant young women eyeing him, sidling into his range of notice, even without knowing he was Jeremy West; he was just too adorable to ignore. "Ache" wasn't quite the word for the pain in her heart, and she recognized it for the kind of pain that doesn't fade, a pain entwined with thorns of anxiety and jealousy as well as loss.

"Quentin," she said, and sat down heavily on the bed. "Quentin." Feeling the onset of tears she stood up and said, "No."

It would have been easier if she were at work—interviewing juveniles, writing reports. But school would be out soon; there wasn't enough time to make a journey to the courthouse. She had completed her outstanding reports on the train; they only needed to be typed up. Her next appointment with her single, obnoxious patient wasn't until the next day. There was nothing to do.

She went to the front room and slid the window closed. Outside, she saw the mailman coming up the street with his enormous shoulder bag. Perhaps he was bringing her cheque from the court. She picked up her keys and went down to the first floor to meet him, but when she stepped out onto the stoop it was not the mailman coming up the walk, but Quentin. He came towards her with gangly, careful steps and his bright, wide smile.

"Quentin," she said, and took hold of the rail. A quiver ran through her voice, though whether with laughter or with tears she could not have said. "Quentin, you really must stop doing this. I can't take any more."

"Me either," he said. "I'd sooner go back to Vimy."

"You're not going anywhere," Imogen said. "Not if I have anything to say about it."

He was standing in front of her now, tall, smiling down at her. The mailman came up the stairs and Quentin stepped back to let him pass.

"Afternoon," the mailman said, and they returned his greeting as he vanished into the vestibule.

"I'm going to wait until he's done," Quentin said.

"And then what?"

"Then I'm going to light the blue paper."

"Blue paper?"

"It's an army expression. Light blue paper and retire to a safe distance."

The mailman emerged. They watched him hurry down the path and continue along the street. Quentin stepped closer.

"Miss Lang?" he said.

"Yes, Mr. Goodchild?"

"I'm sorry. *Doctor* Lang?"

"Yes, Mr. West?"

"I'm lighting the blue paper, and one of two things will happen. Either you will allow me to kiss you, or you will not. If you will not, then I shall immediately go mad and you'll have to make arrangements for the asylum. If you do allow me to kiss you—"

Imogen, who had been watching his lovely mouth form these words, leaned forward and kissed him on the lips. He took her in his arms and they held each other until Quentin asked if they could eat at the Automat again.


Three weeks later they were standing in the shadow of a brontosaurus at the Museum of Natural History when Quentin asked Imogen to marry him. She said yes, and they kissed again. Charlotte and Aubrey, who had been misbehaving by running circles around a dyspeptic-looking platypus, came to a stop and stared, silent and open-mouthed.

On a blustery afternoon in the last week of November Imogen made a solitary pilgrimage to Central Park, walking up the winding path from the zoo to the boat pond. The pond was lazily circled by a gyre of mothers and nannies bundled in scarves, pushing prams. A low sun sent honeyed light and long shadows across the pavement and the benches where old men in caps read newspapers or barked at each other about sports and politics. Imogen walked past the pavilion to the statue of Alice and the Mad Hatter and the Dormouse, but it was being loudly conquered and claimed by red-faced children. She needed quiet.

She walked back down the other side of the pond and sat on a bench near the statue of Hans Christian Andersen, his bronze book open on his bronze knee. It wasn't long before Laura appeared beside her.

"I must say, you've done very well for yourself," she said brightly. "With Quentin at your side that's one less ghost to deal with."

"Actually two less," Imogen said. "Father has definitely loosened his grip on me. I felt it the moment we left the cemetery. Funny that dying should make someone less of a ghost."

"Maybe it's *your* grip that has loosened on *him*."

They sat for a while in peaceful silence. Nothing but bird sounds and a slight wind that rustled the fallen leaves, and somewhere in the distance an angry motorist honking a horn. Imogen felt a twinge of sadness, but Laura saved her from having to dwell on it.

"We have to talk about something, Imogen."

"I know."

"We have to talk about me."

"Yes."

"I don't think you'll be seeing me anymore."

Imogen nodded. "It's making me a little sad."

"Come now, goose. You've every reason to be happy."

"I know. And that's the reason we must part. I don't want to hold anything back from Quentin and, somehow, having a ghostly confidante doesn't seem right."

"You're absolutely making the right choice, Imogen."

"As long as you don't hate me." Imogen turned to her.

Laura was looking less substantial, more ethereal, but the great brown eyes shone with affection. "My darling sister, I could never hate you. Furthermore, I don't think we should use the word *part*. I can't actually go anywhere, can I? I'm already gone."

"Long gone."

"And you haven't forgotten me."

"And I won't."

"So perhaps, if you'll just look away a moment—maybe at those children over there in the matching red coats—I'll just . . ."

Imogen watched the two children—twins like her and Laura, and like her own, a boy and a girl, wearing tiny red car coats with matching caps fastened under their chins. They were taking stealthy steps toward a starling who seemed unconcerned. One of the children—the boy, naturally—made a little jump and the starling flapped off with a rude remark. Imogen turned once more, and felt rather than saw the last of Laura fade to the echoes of their laughter.

Later, as she walked across the park toward the sheep meadow, the fallen leaves thick beneath her feet and a deep blue calm above the palisade of hotels, she thought how strange it was, and yet how fitting, that once again her life was beginning with goodbye.

# ACKNOWLEDGEMENTS

I had reason to consult the works of many authors in the course of writing this book. As is usual with the magpie nature of the novelist's curiosity, I plucked a fact here, an anecdote there, and a single character might have had his or her beginnings from three or four different sources. Acknowledgement in such cases would only serve to bewilder, but there are three sources that I have relied on quite heavily.

For a broad view of psychiatry in general, Edward Shorter's highly readable and informative *History of Psychiatry* (John Wiley & Sons, 1997) proved indispensable. More specifically, *Madhouse*, by Andrew Scull, paints a harrowing portrait of psychiatric treatment at the Trenton State Hospital from 1908 to 1933. And Susan D. Lamb's Ph.D. dissertation, "Pathologist of the Mind: Adolf Meyer, Psychobiology and the Phipps Psychiatric Clinic" (Johns Hopkins, 2010), offers a fascinating description and analysis of daily life and treatment at the real institution behind my fictional one. Ms. Lamb kindly provided various clarifications via e-mail for which I'm enormously grateful.

Despite my plundering of these three authors' historical accounts, they are in no way responsible for any errors of fact in *Into That Fire*.

MJC
TORONTO, 2018

**MJ Cates** was born in Canada, studied psychology and literature at the University of Toronto, and has lived at various times in South Kensington, North London, and Ottawa, writing many novels and winning several awards under another name.